CORREUS

Son of a brilliant Roman general and a
beautiful slave, he was born to lead
the greatest army in the ancient world.

FLAVIUS

Correus's half brother and their father's
rightful heir, he became a man only
after imprisonment and torture.

YGERNA

A tribal holy woman and princess, she was
her uncle's helpless pawn in his games
of war and death.

BENDIGEID

Awesome king of the powerful Silures, he
held the future of Britain in his hands
—until the power led to his own
destruction.

FREITA

Correus's woman but not his wife, she
sacrificed her life to an assassin's
knife.

D0752634

Also by Damion Hunter

Published by Ballantine Books:

THE CENTURIONS

THE CENTURIONS SERIES
BOOK II

BARBARIAN PRINCESS

DAMION HUNTER

BALLANTINE BOOKS • NEW YORK

Library of Congress Catalog Card Number: 82-1658

ISBN 0-345-29826-8

 Created by the producers of
The American Patriot, Wagons West,
and The Kent Family Chronicles Series.

Executive Producer: Lyle Kenyon Engel

Printed in Canada

First Edition: June 1982

For Jack and Irene

Contents

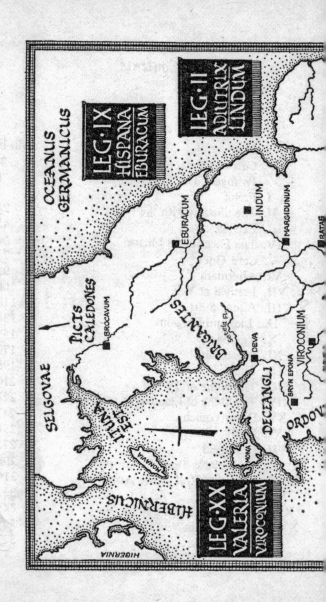

ROMAN·BRITAIN·75ᴬᴰ

LEG·II
AUGUSTA
ISCA

ICENI
TRINOVANTES
CAMULODUNUM
VERULAMIUM
LONDINIUM
RATAE
DOBUNNI
GLEVUM
LLANMELIN
VENTA SILURUM
COED-Y-CAERAU
CICUTIO
PEN-Y-DARREN
TY ISAF
DINAS TOMEN
PEN-Y-GAER
BURRIUM
GOBANNIUM
ABONA
AQUAE
SULIS
SILURES
VICES
ISCA
PORTH CERRIG
LLVENTIUM
RIVER WYE
CARN GOCH
MORIDUNUM
(DUN MORI)
CRAIG
GWRTHEYRN
DEMETAE
SABRINA EST.
DUMNONII
PORTUS ADURNI
VECTIS
BRITANNICUS
GALLIA
OCEANUS
OCEANUS

Cast of Characters

THE FAMILY OF APPIUS

Flavius Appius Julianus the elder, called Appius	A retired general
Antonia	His wife
Helva	His mistress
Correus Appius Julianus, called Correus	Son of Appius and Helva formally adopted by Appius
Freita	A German freedwoman
Julius	Body servant to Correus
Flavius Appius Julianus the younger, called Flavius	Son of Appius and Antonia
Aemelia	His wife
Bericus	Body servant to Flavius
Appia Julia, called Julia	Daughter of Appius and Antonia
Lucius Paulinus	Her husband
Martia	Maid to Julia
Tullius	Free servant to Paulinus
Forst	A German slave
Emer	A kitchen maid
Thais	Former nurse to Correus and Flavius
Tirza	A kitchen maid

ISCA SILURUM

Sextus Julius Frontinus	Military governor of Britain
Domitius Longinus	Legate of the Second Legion Augusta

Aulus Carus	Primus pilus of the Second Augusta
Octavius	Second in command to Correus
Silanus	Senior surgeon of the Second Augusta
Silvius Vindex	Commander of the Tenth Cohort, Second Augusta
Gaius Gratus	Legate of the Second Legion Adiutrix, at Lindum
Coventina	A woman of Isca
Catullus	A retired army surgeon
Publia Livilla	A kinswoman of Governor Frontinus
Julius Agricola	The next governor of Britain

MISENUM

Gaius Plinius Secundus	Naval commander at Misenum
Caritius	Captain of the flagship of the Misenum Fleet
Naamah	A Syrian dancer, in Pompeii

THE BRITONS

Rhys	A trader of no tribe
Cadal	King of the Ordovices
Bendigeid	King of the Silures
Ygerna	A princess of the Silures
Llywarch	A councillor of the Silures
Teyrnon	Chief Druid
Aedden Hywel Llamrei Llew Owen Rhodri	Captains of the Silure war band

Gruffyd	Chieftain of the Demetae
Maelgwn	Eldest son of Gruffyd
Gronwy	Youngest son of Gruffyd
Nighthawk	A man of the Dark People

Prologue: The Trader

"YOU MAY BE TELLING BENDIGEID YOUR KINSMAN THAT he will have our answer by Lughnasadh." The brawny fair man with the gold torque of a chieftain leaned comfortably in the next to the last gate of the great fortress of Bryn Epona. He had a fall of tawny hair like a lion, and the trader eyed him warily.

"Bendigeid is no kin to me," the trader said, pulling tight the packsaddle straps. "We're traders, not tribe folk." He kneed the pony sharply in the ribs, and it blew out its breath with a surprised look. "I'm away north to Brigante country," he added, as if to disclaim all connection with the subject of the conversation.

"You're dark enough for a Silure," the fair man said, studying the trader's brown eyes and cropped brown hair. "Or maybe it was a Roman lord who stepped in sideways." He grinned at the other man.

The trader finished with the pony and grinned back at him, laughing this time, his teeth white against the dark mustache. "Many men would be surprised if their mothers told the truth, Cadal the King. But my father was a dark man before me, and my mother not such a one as men take a risk for. Most likely you're right, and we were Silures' kin in the early days."

"It is only the possibility that you *aren't* that made me let you through the gates of Bryn Epona," Cadal said. It was a joke, but there was a sharp edge to it that was plain enough to the other man.

The trader raised a pair of sharp-angled brows in obvious skepticism. "And you hope to make alliance on a hatred like that?"

"Not alliance, no." Cadal, king of the Ordovices, looked down at the man with the pack ponies. Even lounging against the gatepost of his fortress, he could look

1

down on him, and the trader was not a short man. "Not alliance, only a war. A good war, to take gold and Roman heads. Afterward, the Silures may look to their own as usual."

Gold and Roman heads. Enough to bring Cadal and Bendigeid of the Silures together for one bloody season, the trader thought. A hunting party was coming down the chariot track from the top of Bryn Epona—three chariots with warriors and drivers, a pack of great gray hounds loping beside them, and a little dark man who wore an iron slave collar and ran like a hound among the rest. The trader stepped back out of their way and came face to face with the skull, sightless and grinning evilly, that was set into the gatepost. There was a second on the far post above Cadal's shoulder, and more set in and about every gate and doorway in Bryn Epona. A man's soul was in his head, and a strong man's soul made strong magic. *No way to end,* the trader thought, *guarding Cadal's doorpost.*

"Why are you so interested in this matter between me and Bendigeid of the Silures?" Cadal's voice cut sharply across the drumming hoofbeats as the chariots passed through and careened down the track to the lowest gateway in Bryn Epona's seven concentric walls. He raised a hand in salute, as one of his warriors turned and made some sign at the gate, and then fixed his eyes hard on the trader. Blue eyes, friendly enough, but with a touch of ice at the base.

"I'm *not* particularly interested," the trader said frankly, "but that is not always a wise admission to make to a king about to take a war trail."

Cadal's blue eyes looked amused, and he toyed with the heavy gold-and-red enamel bracelet that he wore high up on his arm, turning it round and round with one massive hand. "So it is all one to you, this making of wars?"

"Unless I happen to be caught in the middle when it starts," the trader said. "Whoever wins, they will still need to buy, and I will still have goods to sell. I told you, we are not tribe folk, my family. I would not like Rome to win, though," he added thoughtfully. "They buy readily enough but are less inclined toward the paying for it."

Cadal gave a sharp bark of amusement. "Then look you that you do not be selling the Roman kind anything you should not." The word "information" was unspoken but hung plainly in the air. The trader gave a visible shudder and a rueful smile to Cadal as he swung into the saddle of the lead pony. "Cadal the King may be assured that the arm of Cadal the King is far too long for anyone but a fool to do that. I am no fool. The god's greeting to you, Cadal of the Ordovices. May the sun and the moon shine always on your path, and the winds of change blow softly about your doors."

Cadal brushed a hand across his tawny mustache, hiding a smile. "Somehow I never thought you were a fool, Rhys. But if I were you, and not going back to Bendigeid, I should ride hard for Brigante country and stay there the season."

The trader nodded and lifted a hand in farewell. He brought it down hard on the pony's rump behind the bedding that was lashed to the saddle back, and the three animals moved out at a steady trot down the banked chariot track to the foot of Bryn Epona. At the gate he drew rein and looked back to see Cadal still leaning in the next to the last gateway, his red and blue woolen cloak making a bright splotch of color against the mud and timber wall, while the gate's guardian grinned bonily down from beside Cadal's left ear.

The trader passed out through the last gate, trailing the two pack ponies, and swung northeastward on the old trackway that led to the lowlands of the Seteia Estuary and then up across the heights of the spine of Britain, the Brigantian Hills. He would double back later, when he had put enough distance between himself and Bryn Epona.

The morning was getting warm, and the red and white pack pony behind him shook its head to drive away a cloud of midges. The trader loosed the pin that held his cloak of heavy, brown-and-black checkered woolen and turned in the saddle to tie it on the bedding behind him. It smelled warmly and steamily of horse, and he wrinkled his nose as he pushed its folds into a manageable roll. He had just pulled the last knot tight when his eye caught a flicker of movement—just the faintest shape, like a shadow—in the trees behind him, where the little river valley that the track's path followed sloped upward to a small wood that was strung along a rolling hillcrest. A hawk's wings flickered across his peripheral vision, and he turned his head to follow its lazy swoops above the hill-side, but it had not been a hawk he had seen. He swung his eyes back and it came again, the faintest hint of movement under the trees. He caught a flash of pale skin and a glint of light from something at chest height.

He narrowed his eyes, and the shape in the trees froze.

There was a rattle of pebbles and a furious voice, and a chariot came careening down the slope on the other side of the little stream-bed.

"Rhys!"

The trader swung around in the saddle and looked across the stream. Three of Cadal's warriors and their chariot drivers were splashing across the ford with their hounds beside them. He recognized the hunting party that had passed him in the gateway of Bryn Epona and slipped his left hand quietly onto the knife hilt that was stuck through his belt.

The lead man, a red-haired warrior with a gold torque and arm rings and the look of a man in a rising fury, scanned the valley and the dark-wooded hills that circled it, as his driver reined in the horses beside the trader's pack train.

"Good hunting to you, lord," the trader said politely.

"We're hunting that damned slinking ferret of a tracker, that's what we're hunting!" the red-haired man said angrily, and the trader realized that the little dark man with the iron collar was no longer among the hounds. The hounds themselves sat back on their haunches, tongues lolling, while the red-haired man cursed them.

"He shouldn't be hard to run down, not with dogs," the trader said, thinking with a certain amount of sympathy of the frozen shadow in the woods behind him.

"They won't take the scent," another warrior said.

"He's magicked them," said his driver, a blond boy of somewhere near fifteen. "Sidhe magic," he added, and made the Sign of Horns nervously. The gesture was repeated by the others.

"What's he done?" the trader asked. It must have been something grave to make a slave risk running.

"Nothing!" the red-haired man exploded. His name was Amren, the trader remembered. "Nothing to be beaten for, unless we haven't found it out yet. He just dived into a patch of scrub on a trail and never came out, and he'll be lucky to live through the beating I'm going to give him *now!*"

"Let him go, Amren," the warrior in the third chariot said lazily, "before you choke on your own bile. He'll be back when he's hungry, or else the wolves'll get him. What difference does it make, one more or less of the little dark ones?"

"He'll go to ground in some sidhe with his own kind," Amren spat, "and they'll begin to think they're lords in the land again, and we'll be too busy chasing runaway slaves to turn around twice. Besides, I want to beat some obedience into him. Rhys, have you seen that ferret?"

The trader shrugged. "If you cannot track him with dogs, lord, is it likely he'd let me catch wind of him?"

"I suppose not," Amren growled. His red hair was tied back with thongs for hunting, and a pair of light throwing spears and a heavy boar spear were lashed to the side of the wicker chariot. He was plainly a man who had been balked of both his property and his intended day's sport. He muttered something to the young driver beside him, a younger brother by the looks of him, and the three chariots swung around and fanned out down the riverbank in the direction of Bryn Epona, the hounds coursing back and forth along the reeds and gravel at the water's edge, their faces puzzled and unsure.

The dark-haired trader watched them go with a shiver of sympathy for the hunted thing in the woods behind him. If he wanted to stir up an unhealthy interest in himself among Cadal's warriors, he couldn't think of a better way than to hide one of Cadal's runaway slaves; but that iron collar hit closer to home than he liked to admit. He shrugged and put his heel to the pony's flank. The dark man would make his own way now—or not. But Rhys the trader would have no slave's death on his conscience to wake him in the night.

He moved on, leading the two pack ponies, still northeastward. Cadal's land was wild and ragged, a swift uprush of cliff or a sharp fall of rocky stream bed hurling itself away downhill to join yet another stream and then another larger one until, in the end, it emptied into the Deva or the Seteia, or the Sabrina far to the north. A land of rivers, this, and wild peaks, where a tribal lord could dig in and spit in Rome's eye. For a while, at least.

The dun pony he was riding threw up its head with a snort and stopped so suddenly that the trader nearly banged his jaw on the pony's head. He swore and looked to see what had startled it.

"Here now, where did you spring from?"

The little dark man regarded him solemnly. He had, so far as the trader could tell, come up from the ground like a mushroom. Certainly he had been all but invisible until he had popped up under the pony's nose.

"I came to tell the trader lord that I am grateful he did not speak of me to the red-haired one." The little man's voice was curiously accented and almost singsong, as if this might not be his native speech. "There is a life between me and the trader lord now."

"Yes, well, you'd better lie low or you won't live to enjoy it," the trader said. "I wasn't sure you knew I'd spotted you."

"Oh, yes, I knew. I have been too long among the Golden People. Otherwise you would not have found me. Unless you have the Sight. *They* did not see me," he added proudly.

The trader studied the little man's face. He was small, no more than up to the trader's chest, and naked except for a kilt of wolf skin and the heavy iron collar that ringed his throat. His eyes also were dark, and he had pulled his dark hair loose from its braids to hang down his back. He was marked on his arms and forehead with faint blue patterns, loops and spirals tattooed into the skin and faded to a soft color, wild and strangely beautiful. An odd, but not unpleasant, odor clung about him, and the trader suspected that it was the substance used to mask his scent.

"Where will you go now?"

"Back to my own kind," the little man said.

"Your own kind?"

There was the flash of a smile, like the flicker of a bird's wing. "We were here before the Golden People. We will be here when they and the Roman kind together have gone West-Over-Seas. I will find my folk easily enough."

"Find them—how long has it been?"

"Ten winters," the dark man said. "Maybe one more or less."

"Now look here, this is ridiculous. You would have

been a child ten winters ago. You won't even know where to look."

There was that flickering smile again, a little shiver of amusement. "I don't know *where* to look, but I know *how* to look; they'll find me. I will have to wait while they take this collar off anyway," he added. "Iron is a Wrong Thing. I couldn't go in a sidhe-house with it." He sighed resignedly. "I expect it will take a long magic to get clean."

"Are your own folk from these hills?" The trader seemed to be worried, despite the little man's assurances.

"Oh, no, mine are away to the south above Coed-y-Caerau, where the Romans are building their fort. But there are a sidhe-people in Cadal's hills, although they keep out of sight of Cadal's men."

"Why did you run, after all these years?"

"Why does the gray goose go south? I don't know why I ran, lord. Only that I woke this morning and this collar weighed more than yesterday, and I knew that tomorrow its weight would be greater still. It was time." He went down on one knee and put both palms to his forehead. "There is the price of a life between us." He looked up. "If you have need of me, any of my folk will find me for you. My name is Nighthawk in my own tongue. If Rhys the trader will ask for me by that, he will find me. Can you whistle?"

"Can I what?"

"Can you whistle?"

The trader looked amused. "Yes, I can whistle."

The little man made a short trilling sound that was almost a bird but not quite. He repeated it over several times and looked at the trader expectantly.

The trader mimicked him, and the dark man nodded.

"Whistle that call near an oak grove, and one of my folk will come for you."

The trader crossed his arms on the saddle horns and leaned down. "Are you so numerous in the land then? Or will I be waiting for a week or so until one passes by?"

"It may be that you will wait a while," Nighthawk said. "But they will come." He looked up at the trader. "Remember the call, lord. We are very few compared to the lords of the Golden People, but we are the adder in the grass, my people and I. You may want one by and by." He ducked under the pony's nose and trotted across the clearing, his bare feet soundless in the grass, and vanished entirely into the shadowed edge of the trees. Not even the iron collar winked back from the stillness.

In the morning the trader turned south, down the winding valley of the Sabrina to the fortress the Roman legions were raising on their hard-won toehold at the foot of Bendigeid's hills.

I

Freita

THE BUGLER OUTSIDE THE LEATHER WALLS OF THE TENT was putting his all into "Wake Up," and the man inside on the camp bed groaned and pulled the blankets over his ears. He had come back to camp only four hours before, and four hours is just long enough for the drugged sleep of exhaustion to make waking almost impossible.

As the last strident note died away in the cold air, he drifted up reluctantly from the depths of sleep to shrug back the covers and to feel on the foot of the bed for the tunic that should be there. His hand came up instead with a filthy shirt and breeches, and he sighed and put them down again, rising to rummage in the clothes chest for his tunic. As he pulled it over his head, he caught his reflection in the mirror propped against the tent wall on top of a second, higher, chest.

He stared balefully at the face in the mirror, leaning his hands on the chest, which rocked on the uneven dirt floor. When it rained, as it did at every opportunity in Britain, even in summer, little rivulets formed and flowed through the tent, bearing twigs and drowning insects on the tide. Isca Silurum was a half-built fort, and the half yet to come included the barracks rows.

A dark-eyed Briton with a sharp-angled face peered back at him from the mirror, behind the luxuriant growth of a brown mustache that got in his food and made him feel as if something had landed on his face. His brown hair was too long and had last been cut with a dagger blade. Somewhere in this Briton was Correus Appius Julianus, cohort centurion of the Ninth Cohort of the Second Legion Augusta, currently on the emperor's service in Britain, but he was hard to find. Hard enough that the gate sentries the night before had wanted to toss him into the guardhouse until the legionary legate should rise and deal with him in the morning. Only a grasp of Latin profanity that no Briton could have matched and the recognition of Centurion Vindex, whose cohort had sentry watch that night, had saved him from the fate.

Correus started to pull on his scarlet outer tunic and then changed his mind. No one knew he was back yet. Therefore no one would be looking for him to take parade this morning. His second-in-command could take parade. Correus was going to take a bath.

The Roman soldier regarded a bathhouse in his fort with somewhat the same attitude he accorded regular meals, and the baths outside the fortress walls had been the first buildings raised in Isca, after the commander's quarters.

Correus sank into the depths of the hot pool until only his nose and eyes showed, and lay there soaking himself into a civilized condition and a human frame of mind. He had thought longingly of baths—proper baths in bathhouses—more longingly even than he had of a safe conclusion of his mission, during the months he had plied a peddler's trade between the Silures and their sometime foes, the Ordovices to the north. Baths and a clean shave. He was lucky he didn't have a beard as well, he supposed, but it had grown in such an improbable ginger color that Governor Frontinus, inspecting it after two weeks' careful cultivation, had ordered it removed. "It looks like a damned actor's. People will be pulling it to see if they can unstick it."

A couple of off-duty officers strolled in and began to scrape themselves clean with a *strigil* before splashing into the pool. They recognized Correus, and being junior centurions, they saluted politely and refrained from comment. Last night at the gate, Vindex hadn't been so restrained, but Silvius Vindex and Correus Julianus went a long way back—back to their cadet days at the Centuriate training camp in Rome. The only people who hadn't been rude about Correus's appearance had been Governor Frontinus, whose idea it had been in the first place to use a cohort centurion as something between a frontier scout and a spy, and Freita. Freita. Correus's heart quickened at the mere thought of seeing her again. He dived under the water like a porpoise, scrubbing at his hair with his fingers until it began to feel clean again. He had a report to make, and then, please the gods, he was going to have a three-day leave to spend with Freita.

Mornings warmed quickly in the summer in southern Britain, and the solemn circle of men in the headquarters tent had draped their cloaks over their chair backs and rolled the tent flaps up on two sides to catch the light breeze that whispered through. There were six of them.

Sextus Julius Frontinus, governor of Britain, was a tall, angular man with heavy callused hands. Even when he was at rest his hands moved. Julius Frontinus was an engineer by love as well as by trade, and the heart and soul of the plans for Isca Fortress had been his. Beside him was Domitius Longinus, broad and muscular with bright black eyes under bushy, dark brows, legate of the Second Legion Augusta, with his second-in-command beside him —Aulus Carus, the primus pilus, commander of the First Cohort, a pale-haired, blue-eyed man, not quite thirty. Gaulish blood there, or a Briton's, Correus thought when he met him, and he felt a sort of kinship. Under Correus Julianus's Roman exterior was the heritage of a Gaulish mother. Next around the commander's desk were the cavalry commander of the two wings currently attached to the Second Augusta at Isca and the legionary legate of the Twentieth Valeria Victrix, stationed to the north at Viroconium. When the campaign got fully under way, Governor Frontinus would call in the Second Adiutrix from Lindum in the east to add its strength to his arguments as well. When that would be rested on what the last man in the circle had to tell him.

The last man was Correus, scrubbed and polished in scarlet tunic and gold-bordered scarlet cloak, his neck scarf precisely knotted under the edge of his iron lorica, his decorations and centurion's insigne strung across the front, helmet on his head, silvered greaves on his shins, and vine staff in his hand. Only the mustache stuck out

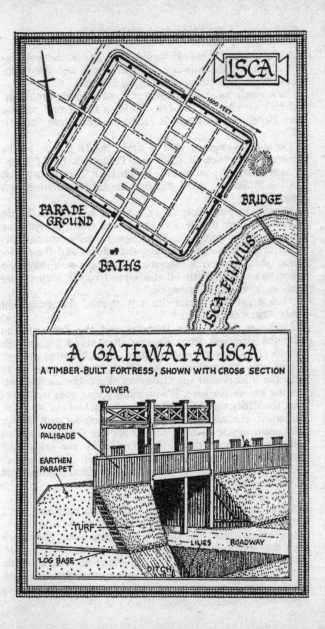

ISCA

1600 FEET

BRIDGE

PARADE GROUND

BATHS

ISCA FLUVIUS

A GATEWAY AT ISCA

A TIMBER-BUILT FORTRESS, SHOWN WITH CROSS SECTION

TOWER

WOODEN PALISADE

EARTHEN PARAPET

TURF

LOG BASE

LILIES   ROADWAY

DITCH

like a persistent weed. It would have struck the only familiar note to the chieftains of the Silures and the Ordovices who had talked so freely in his presence.

"It's much as you thought, sir," he said to Frontinus. "There's an alliance brewing, but it's a tricky one, and no one, Bendigeid included, is really sure they can bring it off."

Domitius Longinus shot a dark, beady glance at the governor and then at Correus. "Perhaps a bit of background first, if you would, Centurion? This is my first posting in Britain, and I still find the tribal relationships a tangle."

"Certainly, sir." Correus gave him a half smile. "So do I, and I've been out here almost a year *and* lived with the natives part of that time. There are two tribes worth worrying about in western Britain, the Silures and the Ordovices. And two—the Demetae in the south and the Deceangli in the north—that are pretty much sure to ally with us or whoever's strongest."

"I *had* got that far in the past month," Longinus said dryly. "Now tell me *why*."

"Yes, sir. Sorry. The Demetae and the Deceangli go with the strongest force because they aren't big enough not to. They haven't enough men, enough cattle, enough horses, enough anything to be a force on their own. As to why the Silures and the Ordovices don't like each other, no one knows for sure. It's an enmity that goes back further than they can remember. But from looking at them, I'd say it was racial. The Silures are smaller and darker than most of the Britons, and so are the Demetae, whose lands are next to theirs. The Ordovices are taller and fair-haired, like most of the other tribes. Tribal history seems to indicate two invasions of this island . . . uh, that is, before ours."

Longinus grinned. "Go on, Centurion."

"Well, this is all theory, sir, and I'm no historian, but I suspect that the Silures were the first invaders, who maybe intermarried with the native population—the little dark men that the Britons mostly keep for slaves. And the Ordovices are invasion number two—and kept their strain pure and maybe pushed the Silures out of some of their tribal lands. That ties in with local history so far as they know it."

"Then is an alliance between them possible?"

"Not a permanent one, sir; no, I don't think so. But a one-war treaty—that they may very well manage, given sufficient reason."

"Such as . . . the threat of renewed conquest in western Britain." Frontinus nodded. "Well, we suspected that much. I do trust you have something more concrete for us, Julianus?"

"Concrete enough, sir," Correus said. "Bendigeid of the Silures had Ordovician envoys in his hall at Porth Cerrig, and I traveled north with them when I left Bendigeid to peddle my wares in Ordovice lands." Correus stopped and chuckled softly. "In fact he gave me a message to carry privately to Cadal, the Ordovices' king, because he didn't much trust the envoys."

"Mithras god!" the legate of the Valeria Victrix said. "You could have got your head on a spear for that!"

"I could have got my head on a spear at any time in the last month," Correus said frankly. "Cadal of the Ordovices is a strong ruler, and Bendigeid is the most utterly ruthless man I've ever met. I don't think either had any particular suspicions of me—I learned the language from a man who was bred in these parts—but Bendigeid mistrusts on principle. He mistrusts the Ordovices, he mistrusts the Demetae, and he certainly mistrusts us."

"Whom does he trust?" Longinus asked.

"Himself. His . . . I'm not sure of the right word . . . his guardianship of his tribe. I don't think anything else really has the power to touch him."

"So he's pushing alliance with the Ordovices to fight the greater enemy."

"Yes, sir. And they're dancing about the issue sideways, but they'll most likely do it in the end. When I passed Bendigeid's message to their king, Cadal, he struck me as a lord with an eye to the main chance."

"The message, man!"

"Sorry, sir. Bendigeid wants a face-to-face meeting with Cadal at some neutral point. Cadal is to reply by another messenger of his own choosing. I was rather hoping the gods would put it in his head to use me, but he said Bendigeid would have his answer by Lughnasadh—that's the midsummer festival, and it's still a month off. I thought I'd better not wait."

"Yes, well, I think we can predict Cadal's answer now," Frontinus said. "And I want to catch the Silures before Bendigeid gets it. Now, Centurion, I want numbers. Horses, chariots, men."

Correus put his hand to his head for a moment, lining up the figures in his mind. "The Silures have perhaps six to seven thousand men warrior-trained," he said, looking up. "And as many foot fighters. The Demetae have less, but their horse herds are good."

"The Demetae have always been friendly," the legate of the Twentieth said.

"'Always' is not a very long time, counting from the Caesar Claudius's invasion," Governor Frontinus said. "And West Britain has been trouble since then, Demetae or no. Bendigeid's tribe has been raiding our outposts for the last ten years. If we're going to hold Britain, we've got to tie up these hills tight this time."

"Bendigeid is putting pressure on the Demetae," Correus said. "I doubt they know whom they're more afraid of, Bendigeid or us."

"Bendigeid, probably," Frontinus said dryly. "He's closer. Does he need their men that badly?"

"I don't think so, sir. It's their horse herds. The Silures lost some animals to disease last winter, and they'll need the chariot herds up to strength. The Demetaes' stock seem to have escaped the sickness."

"These Britons are a horse people," Frontinus said to the Second's legate, Longinus. "They count their true wealth in their herds."

"And the little hill folk?" Carus, the primus pilus, asked.

"I doubt they'll take a hand," Correus said. "Except for the ones who are enslaved by the tribes, our comings and goings don't really make much difference in their lives. And they would only be trading slavery to the Britons for slavery to us."

"Who or what are the hill folk?" Longinus asked.

"The original inhabitants," Correus said, "the ruling tribes before the Golden People. They keep to themselves and out of sight, mostly. One of them told me they would be here when we and the Britons had gone to Hades together. Some people don't believe they exist at all." He cocked an eye, warily respectful, at Governor Frontinus.

"In the Britons' slave houses I believe in them," Frontinus said, the brisk voice of the practical man. "As for underground cities below the mountains, I'll believe those aren't in a class with the beautiful princess and the two white dragons when I actually walk into one."

"That may be a local fairy tale," Correus said, "but they live somewhere. You've a few in your own backyard, Governor."

Frontinus picked up a sheaf of rolled plans from the desk and snorted. "There is nothing in these parts that I do not have surveyed, marked down, and duly noted, Centurion," he said. "And that includes hollow hillsides with hobgoblins in them."

"Yes, sir. But I met one, a slave on the run from Cadal's warriors, and he claimed his home clan was above Coed-y-Caerau to the east of here, where the sentry camp is."

"And how did you chance on this runaway, Centurion Julianus?"

"Pure chance, sir. I saw him duck into the trees just before Cadal's men came thundering down on the hunt for him."

"And you kept your mouth shut, I suppose?" Frontinus sighed. Centurion Julianus had an odd kick in his gallop when it came to the matter of slavery, generally the heritage of the slave-born themselves. "You're lucky you didn't put them on your own trail, damn it."

"I thought he might be useful," Correus said mildly.

"*This* is useful, Centurion." The governor laid a callused hand on Correus's sword hilt. "And when it comes to taking West Britain for the Emperor Vespasian, I'll leave my faith in a short sword and a pilum point with some muscles behind it." The asperity in his rough voice faded slightly. "Ah, well, you've had a long ride and not an overly safe one, and you'll be wanting to see that girl of yours."

"Yes, sir. Thank you. I'll be needing to send her to Aquae Sulis fairly soon."

"I don't doubt it. She's round as a barrel already." Frontinus snorted in exasperation. "Mithras send me back the days when officers weren't allowed to trail their household about with them on the army's denarius."

Correus stood up and saluted. He trailed his household

about with him at his own expense, as the governor knew very well. No one under the rank of legionary legate had ever pried a penny out of the army for that purpose. "Thank you, sir. I'm grateful for the three-day leave you promised me before I left."

"Three-day leave?" Frontinus looked mildly surprised, and Domitius Longinus chuckled.

"Indeed you did, Governor, although strictly speaking Centurion Julianus is my man, of course." His dark, beady eyes gave the ghost of a wink at Correus.

The governor laughed. "Oh, very well. Dismissed, Centurion. We'll send Bendigeid a request to stay laired in Porth Cerrig until your leave is up."

"Bide still!" The women scurried through the main chamber of the queen's court at Porth Cerrig, while the child stood on one foot at the center of the room and fidgeted. The old nurse who was combing her hair shook her by the shoulders. "Put your foot down."

"Why?" the child asked. She was barely thirteen, thin, and small enough to be lost in the great hall of the queen's court. This wing of the Silure stronghold above the cliffs had always been called that, but there was no queen in it now. There was only Ygerna, priestess and royal woman of her tribe, daughter of the king's sister, and the seal on his bargain with the Demetae.

"Because you are not a stork," the older woman said, "and because I cannot comb your hair with you swaying like a tree in a high wind." She gave the black hair a last swipe with the comb and set a gold fillet on the girl's head. She tugged the green-and-white checkered folds of her gown into place and gave her a quick look. "All right, put your cloak on. They are waiting."

Ygerna gave her a rebellious look from black eyes set under dark, slanting brows. "I am not ready."

"Yes, you are. It is a long ride to Dun Mori, and Llywarch will be angry if you keep him standing about."

And so would her uncle, Ygerna thought, which was more to the point. The other women bustled up and put her cloak around her shoulders, pushing a pin through its heavy folds and shouting for a slave to come and carry the baggage. Ygerna gave a resigned twitch of her shoulders. She hadn't really thought that she could delay their leaving, but she didn't like to be whistled for like a hound.

The women hustled her out the door and through the outer courts to the landward gates of Porth Cerrig, where Llywarch was waiting among the chariots. They boosted her up beside him into the red-and-gilt car, and Llywarch bent down to speak some last word to the king standing on the other side. Neither of them bothered to speak to her.

The boy who was Llywarch's driver shook out the black ponies' reins, and the other chariots swept into line behind them. Ygerna looked back past Llywarch's shoulder with time for no more than a swift, fierce prayer to the Mother-of-All that her uncle could drive the Romans out of their new fortress at Isca before he had to make good on the marriage he had promised to Gruffyd of the Demetae in exchange for his ponies.

At Isca Silurum, Correus picked his way through the piled stone and timber that was a legionary fortress in the making. A smile curved his mouth under the mustache. He had meant to ask the governor's gracious permission to shave, but it had totally slipped his mind and to go back now to ask did not seem propitious. Well, Freita wouldn't mind. He dodged around a legionary trundling a two-wheeled cart full of roof tiles, and a pair of surveyors whose outstretched lines crisscrossed the Via Praetoria to trip the unwary. The legionary with the cart full of tiles fell afoul of one, and the surveyors descended on him furiously, while a tripod and plumb line fell into the confusion. Correus sidestepped and began to whistle softly to himself, his mind full of Freita.

Freita was German, and she had laughed at him when the mustache first began to grow and told him he looked more like a German now and less like a snooty Roman. Correus had wondered once or twice since if the snooty Roman she'd had in mind was his father; but if so, it was the only remark of that sort she had ventured about the old general—remarkably tolerant of her, all things considered. He could still recall his father's last letter to him practically by heart:

My dear Son,

I presume you are counting on absence (and affection for the absent one) to alter my outlook on the subject which you broached yet again in your last letter. Your faith in my affection is touching (and justified), but I will not hesitate to tell you that it in no way affects my viewpoint on your throwing away a promising career.

Your concern for this girl and your desire to do right by her are admirable, but it is not only unnecessary that you marry her, but entirely necessary that you do not. For the slave-born (albeit adopted) son of Appius to marry a freed slave himself is to throw away everything your adoption was designed to achieve.

And in any case it is far too soon for you to be marrying anyone. Yours is not the case of your brother Flavius, who has the inheritance of an estate to think of and who was in a position to make an excellent match in his youth. Your career is all before you, my son, and the time for you to marry will be when you have achieved the name and position which, I am proud to see, you have already begun to make for yourself. In ten years, if I have judged you correctly, you will be able to have your pick from among the daughters of Rome's senatorial families and senator's rank for yourself if you want it. I never did, but times are changing. In the meantime, keep Freita with you if you wish. She is a good girl, genuinely fond of you, and she understands her position far better than I would have expected. But you are—and I regret to have to put it this way—absolutely forbidden to marry her. Your mother's views, I might add, are for once in complete agreement with mine on the subject.

My dear Son, this matter aside, I cannot tell you how pleased with you I am, and how proud at the name you are making for yourself in an ancient and honorable service that has been our family's tradition since the days of the Republic. . . .

The rest had been affectionate and congratulatory but had done nothing to alleviate the utter fury which his father's orders about Freita had roused in him. As for his mother, Appius's pampered slave and mistress, Correus knew perfectly well that Helva wanted only what would advance her son to a status that would ensure her contin-

ued ease after the old general's death. The thought of
Freita growing over the years to be the same woman as
his mother appalled Correus. When Freita had told him
she was pregnant, Correus, practically frothing, had gone
off to see the civil magistrate at Glevum about a marriage.

"No."

"What do you mean, no?" Correus, arrangements for
an unobtrusive civil ceremony in hand, returned to the
house he had taken outside the fortress at Glevum to find
Freita sitting placidly by the hearth with the cat on her
lap and an expression as stubborn as a pig's on her beautiful face.

Correus stomped the spring snow off his boots and
turned his backside to the fire—the house was too small
to boast a furnace and hypocaust. He stood, steaming
damply, while she shook her head at him.

"My heart, if you marry me, you will ruin your career.
I have learned enough of Rome in the last year to know
that. And you won't thank me for it ten years down the
road."

Correus took a deep breath and got a grip on himself.
Freita had an unsettling effect on him. She was a tall
woman, big-boned, with a crown of gold hair and sea-
green eyes like tide pools, and a white, milky skin touched
on throat and shoulder by the fading marks of an old
burn, the price of defending her chieftain's flaming hold
on the Rhenus border against Correus and his kind. How
they had come to love each other with such a beginning
was a mystery to them both but they accepted it gratefully. She was the other half of him now, he thought,
looking at her, and he was damned if their child was going to be born with the same mark on him that he himself
had had. It was a mark that was going to follow him for
the rest of his life. Freita knew it, but she wouldn't budge.

"You can adopt the child, you know. I don't think your
father would balk at that."

"It's not the same."

Freita sighed and pushed the cat off her lap and held
out her arms to him. The cat gave her an indignant glance
and curled up on the warm hearthstone, while Correus
regarded the pair of them in exasperation. She was as in-
furiating and single-minded as that damned cat, which he
had dragged all the way from Germany to his father's

house near Rome, to the new posting in Britain—howling all the way in a wicker basket. He didn't understand either of them.

"I thought that once we were clear of Germany, everything would be right," he said finally.

Freita took his hands and pulled him down beside her by the fire. "I've known since you took me to your family in Rome that you couldn't marry me. But we're together, aren't we? And we're going to have a child. I'm so pleased about that, you would think no one had ever done it before." She ran one hand through his hair and smiled at him and drew his head down on her breast. The fire spat and leapt up and died back again to a friendly glow; and Julius, the young slave who looked after the household when Correus was on duty, came in with an armload of logs, looked at the two of them, and left again forthwith. Correus sighed and gave up, abandoning himself to the feel of Freita in his arms. Tomorrow, he thought, kissing her, tomorrow he would insist.

But then tomorrow hadn't come for five months. In the morning the Second Legion was ordered out to dig a toehold on the southern plain above Sabrina Mouth to force the Silures into the Roman province of Britain once and for all. Freita and Julius followed as they could. When they reached the new campsite at Isca, Freita stoically pitched a tent and set about charming wood for a floor out of the Centurion of Engineers, while Correus was drafted by Governor Frontinus for his own form of reconnaissance. He hadn't seen her since the day he rode out of Isca—trailing two dejected-looking pack ponies and an assortment of copper kettles, amber beads, and knife blades—to locate Bendigeid and return to the governor without finding a spear in his back on the way as well.

Correus passed out through the lower gates of Isca Silurum, fully built now of timber and banked turf, with a sentry walkway along the top and deep V-shaped ditches outside, lined with "lilies"—sharpened stakes set slantwise into the dirt. He gave the sentries the password of the day and strode down the dirt track—past the parade ground and baths and cleared space where the amphitheater would be at such time as the legion had leisure to build one—to the cluster of huts and ramshackle structures that was the beginning of the civil settlement at Isca.

A boy of about fifteen was currying a gray horse outside one of those dwellings as Correus approached. There was an empty wooden bucket on the ground, and the horse's mane and tail were still damp.

"If you spent as much time on the household as you do on Aeshma, we might show a better face to the world," Correus said, glancing at the half tent, half wattle-and-daub structure behind him. The walls behind the tent leaned drunkenly to the left.

The boy looked up, his gray eyes lighting with pleasure. "Centurion! We didn't know you were back!" He bowed his head dutifully, but his eyes were dancing. "I'm that glad to see you! And if you think it's easier to wash this horse than build a house, you just haven't tried, sir."

Aeshma, whose name meant "demon," and who lived well up to his name with all but his cronies, whickered and butted his head against Correus's lorica. "No, I don't have anything for you, you fool. Back off." He rubbed the gray nose.

"And it hasn't been as easy as all that anyway, sir." Julius pushed a shock of mousy hair back from his eyes. "She's as crabby as an old sow, just like all women. You'd think no one had ever had a baby before." The boy glanced darkly at the tent. "She has a cold, too," he added.

Correus chuckled. "It comes of living with a cub with no respect for his elders, I daresay," he said mildly. He pushed back the double leather flap that formed the door and almost collided with a round figure wrapped in a cloak who came hurtling through it.

"Correus!" Freita flung her arms around him and hung on.

"Careful. You'll hurt yourself." He pushed her gently away and looked down at her. Her nose and eyes were red, and she was as round as a wine jug, but she was his beautiful Freita, and his heart turned over as he kissed her.

"No, no. You'll catch my cold." She smiled at him and tucked her arm through his. They turned through the doorway together, Julius forgotten, until Freita broke off coughing, a deep, racking sound that caught Correus up short.

"What are you about, to leave her in this condition in this damned, drafty hole?" He glared over his shoulder at Julius.

"Just *try* to make her leave before you came home!" Julius said indignantly.

"I'm all right," Freita gasped. "Julius did try. Correus, don't look like that. Now that you're here, I'll do well enough."

"Why in Mithras's name didn't you go to Aquae Sulis when you first got sick? And how am I going to send you there now in this condition?"

"I will be all right," Freita said firmly. The gray cat trotted across the plank floor and chirped at her inquiringly. She bent down to pick it up and began to cough again.

"You sure as Typhon will, because you aren't staying here!" Correus said. "Now sit down, put another cloak on, and put some more coals in the brazier. I'll be back in an hour."

"Is the governor free?"

The headquarters clerk looked up from his supply lists and blinked. The governor *sent* for his officers as a rule. Most didn't voluntarily come looking for him. "I will, uh, ascertain, sir." He poked his head through the dividing flap into the partitioned office quarters at the rear. In a moment he emerged and nodded to Correus. "The legate is with him, sir," he said, as if he thought the centurion might change his mind in the face of all this gilt and purple. "But you're to go in," he added as Correus stood his ground.

"Thank you."

He saluted Domitius Longinus and Governor Frontinus, who regarded him with curiosity.

"I would have expected you to be using that leave you pried out of me, Centurion," Frontinus said.

"That's just the problem, sir," Correus said. "I meant to use it to take Freita to Aquae Sulis, but she's too sick to travel. It's just a cold, but she doesn't look good. Not so near her term."

"I see," Frontinus said gravely. "And, uh, how may we help you?"

"I need a place for her to stay, sir," Correus said firmly. "Just until she's over her cold." It was not a request that even a senior officer would ordinarily have the nerve to put to the governor of Britain, but Correus didn't care. Not when it concerned Freita.

"I've seen that dump that passes for a civil settlement," Longinus put in, watching the exchange with sympathy.

"So have I," Frontinus said. "Best that you put her in my quarters for a few days."

Correus blinked. "I beg your pardon, sir?"

"Well, she certainly can't be expected to stay in that hovel, not with a chest cold, Centurion. The Praetorium's the only place that hasn't got mushrooms growing on the floor just now." He grinned at Longinus. "Though strictly speaking, that's yours, too, Domitius, although I happen to be occupying it at the moment."

"Far be it from me to deny what you see fit to give, sir," Longinus said, amused. "And, uh, where were you planning to sleep?"

"I'm not so grand that I can't sleep with the legion for a few nights," Frontinus said. "I've done it before now. *You're* doing it at the moment."

When Correus had saluted and left, still mildly stunned, Longinus turned to the governor with a questioning eye.

"I like that girl," Frontinus said. "I like her a lot, although I agree with young Julianus's father—with whom I have had some correspondence on the subject, which you will *not* mention to him—that he can't be allowed to marry her. But she's a good girl, and she's got more guts than most. Also"— he tapped the lengthy report which Correus had submitted along with his oral one—"Centurion Julianus has earned some peace of mind."

"Correus," Freita whispered, unwrapping the outer of her two cloaks and draping it over the carved back of a chair, "he *can't* have agreed to this."

"Well, he did," Correus said firmly, "and we're going to take advantage of it." The Praetorium, the commander's private quarters, was timber-built and stone-floored, with plastered walls upon which some legionary artist had begun a hunting scene of tigers and hippopotami and other unlikely prey, pursued by huntsmen mounted upon elephants. The artist was evidently a townsman who had taken his ideas of the chase largely from the Circus at Rome. The floor and walls were channeled for hot air from the hypocaust which would be built later, and in the meantime the room was heated with three iron braziers glowing warmly in the dusk.

Freita sank down on the bed, which was ornamented with carved claw feet and inlaid with thin rods of bronze around the frame. It boasted a pile of woolen covers that must have been the governor's personal property, and there was a small shale table beside it with a pottery lamp shaped like a duck. The lamp was lit and splashed a pleasant pool of light onto the blue and green blankets and the native rug that warmed the stone floor by the bed.

"Oh, Correus, this is paradise." Freita sneezed and bounced gently on the bed while Correus rummaged in the small clothes chest which Julius had deposited at the foot of the bed.

He pulled out a warm night shift. "Here, get into this, and get into that bed."

Freita got up and shucked off her mantle and gown near one of the braziers while Correus watched her appreciatively. Strange how beautiful a big-bellied woman could be. He had never noticed that before. She pulled the night shift over her head gratefully and wrapped the mantle around her again. "Oh, this is so warm. I don't think I've been warm since we left Glevum."

"The more fool you," Correus said. "*Why* didn't you go to Aquae Sulis when you got sick?"

Freita smiled and snuggled under the blankets. "I wanted to wait for you. And it's done no harm. I'll be fine now. The only trouble will be making myself leave this lovely room for Aquae Sulis." She giggled. "I mustn't stay too long. It wouldn't do to have a baby in the governor's bed."

Correus chuckled and kissed her. "No, that might be more than he's prepared to cope with. But you will stay until that cold is gone."

She put her hand on his wrist. "Correus, can't you stay with me?"

He hesitated. "I was going to send Julius to stay with

you, and I'll stay in the tent to keep an eye on Aeshma. He's jumpy as a tomcat. I think there's a mare in season somewhere."

"You ought to have that horse gelded."

"My father's horseman would have my head. You should have seen his eyes light up when he saw Aeshma. I should have left him in Rome, is what I should have done, and let him make himself useful with my father's mares. I only brought him because you like him, sweet. And I'm not sure Julius can manage him when you aren't around. If he kicks his stall down and goes looking for love in the cavalry barns, we will be in trouble."

"Julius will have to manage him when I've gone to Aquae Sulis," Freita said practically. "And Julius and I have had quite enough of each other's company lately. Stay with me, Correus." She grinned. "Then Julius can sleep in that cold tent instead of you."

"A telling argument." He sat down on the bed beside her, and she slipped her arms around him. "*Mmmm, you feel nice.*"

"So do you. Come to bed and hold me. It's been so long."

He nuzzled his face against her hair, breathing in the warm smell of her. "Too long. And before you go to Aquae Sulis, you're going to marry me."

"Hush. We'll talk about it later. Just get into bed, for now."

It was black-of-the-moon, a still, inky blackness that blotted out shadow and open space alike, when the shadow came over the wall in a cat-footed scramble and dropped to the ground in a hay rick behind the cavalry lines. The mailed sandals of the sentries clicked past on the catwalk above him, their lanterns cutting through the darkness where the shadow had been. He crouched, holding his breath, and when they had passed, he hurried silently into the darkness. Behind him a cavalry horse whickered and was quiet. The shadow froze and then moved on. He went silently through the night, and no man crossed his path. As the bulk of the place he sought loomed up, a blacker shape against the black night, he saw the faint gold glow of a lamp somewhere within, and his knife blade winked coldly in its light.

Inside, past the guttering lamp, he paused at an inner doorway and eased the oiled hinges open. The room was lit with the embers of a glowing brazier, almost as light as day to eyes that came in from the night. The man in the bed was deep in sleep and snoring softly, the sleep of a man who knows himself safe. Beside him there was a fall of pale hair on the pillow, but it made little difference to the shadow that his quarry had a woman with him. It was the man he wanted. The man whose death might mean the saving of his tribe.

The shadow shifted his grip on the knife hilt carefully and darted across the stone floor. His foot hit the rug by the bed and he stumbled, and the woman sat up, eyes open wide. The shadow hurled himself at the sleeping figure on the bed, and the woman screamed and threw herself at the man to waken him. The shadow's knife came down between her ribs.

II

The Shadow with the Knife

CORREUS WAS AWAKE AND ON THE MAN AS FREITA screamed. His sword and dagger lay forgotten on the governor's clothes chest, blotted out by blind rage and the picture of Freita's hunched body in the bed with blood coming up through her white shift. He caught the man by the throat and drove him down onto the stone floor, oblivious to the flailing knife blade. The knife came down and slashed along his forearm, and he let go of the throat long enough to catch the man's wrist and snap it with a sickening crunch. Sprawled on top of the attacker, he slammed his head into the stone floor, his long hands closing again about the throat. He had nearly killed him by the time the sentries came pounding through the door.

It took three of them to pull him off by main force.

"Let go now, sir! Grab his hands, Glaucus!"

"I'm trying! Typhon! No, sir! We're trying to help you!"

Correus lashed out in a fury as the sentry's hands pried at his fingers. He returned to the attack, this time driving his fist hard into the tribesman's face.

"Stop it, sir! Damn you, we're on your side!"

"Someone see to the woman—she's hurt!"

"Where's the governor?"

"Leave off now, sir, you'll kill him!"

"Centurion Julianus!" Governor Frontinus strode into the room, barefoot, with his purple cloak wrapped hastily around his undertunic, barely two steps behind another contingent of sentries.

"He got over the wall, sir!" one of them gasped. "We found where he came over."

Domitius Longinus was behind the governor, dark hair standing on end, a short sword in one hand and trying to push home the pin of his cloak with the other.

"Mithras god! *Julianus!*"

Their voices came dimly to Correus through the red haze in his head. Another sentry scrabbled at his hands, now tight about the tribesman's throat again, and slowly he began to loosen them.

"Grab him! Back off now, Julianus, that's an order! Someone get a surgeon!"

"Probus has already gone, sir," one of the sentries panted, pulling Correus away from the still form of the tribesman.

They tugged at his shoulders, and he rose slowly, shaking. There was blood in his mouth and a wet feeling on his arm where the knife had slashed him. "You won't help her by killing him," Frontinus said, and the words came a little clearer now through the mist in his head.

"Freita!"

She lay hunched on the bed, cradled carefully by a brawny sentry whose face was shocked and miserable. He was holding the bunched bedclothes to her ribs to stanch the bleeding, but there was a faint froth of blood on her lips and he knew from his own grim experience what that meant.

"Freita!" Correus knelt by the bed, ashen faced and panic-stricken.

"Careful, sir, don't bump her. The surgeon's coming."

Correus took her hands in his, and she opened pain-filled eyes and looked at him, recognition coming slowly. "The baby," she whispered.

He didn't care about the baby. He would have sacrificed the baby gladly, this one and all his hopes for the future, to keep Freita from slipping away from him. "Hush," he whispered. "The baby's all right."

The swell of her belly showed clearly under the nightshift and the shaken sentry watched it quiver as the child kicked; a trapped child now, he thought, his face twisting.

Freita's eyes clouded again. "Don't leave me!" Correus pleaded frantically, trying to drag her back, trying to hold her eyes with his. "Hang onto me. The surgeon's coming."

She said something he couldn't understand, and her hands tightened on his.

"All right, son, let me look at her." Silanus, senior surgeon of the legion, laid a hand on Correus's shoulder. He was also dressed in an undertunic and hastily caught-up cloak, but his face was alert and worried under a tousled shock of gray hair. "Move back, Centurion," he said again, and Correus drew away, his face gone white and haggard. Silanus set his medical kit on the floor and motioned an orderly forward to take the sentry's place. The orderly began slitting the white night shift down from the neck.

"Get those lamps lit," Silanus said curtly. "And everybody clear out. You too, Centurion."

Correus didn't move, and a cohort centurion in full uniform took him gently by the arm. "Leave her with Silanus, Correus." He drew him toward the door.

Correus looked at him numbly. Vindex. His cohort must have had sentry walk again tonight. His men who had let the shadow with the knife slip through. He shook himself. It wasn't Vindex's fault, but he could see by the look in his friend's dark eyes that Vindex thought it was. He let himself be led away, out into the commander's private office beyond the bedroom.

The sentries had thrown the attacker into a chair and none-too-gently tied his broken wrist to his good one behind him. The man's face was bloody and gray with pain, and he sat slumped in the chair, staring bleakly at the governor and Domitius Longinus the legate.

"What tribe is he, Centurion?" Frontinus said as Correus and Vindex came through the door.

Correus looked at the faded blue patterns tattooed on the man's face and forearms. His hair, tied back with a rough thong, was dark and so were his eyes, but he was too tall for one of the hill folk. "Not Silure," Correus said, looking at the patterns again. "Demetae, probably." Vindex eased him down into a chair, and he sat stiff and immobile as Frontinus turned back to the tribesman.

"Answer the governor or I'll twist that wrist again," one of the sentries suggested in rough British.

"Demetae," the man said. He licked his lips.

"Would you like some water?" Frontinus asked.

The man didn't speak.

Frontinus nodded at a sentry, and the man went out and reappeared with an earthenware jug and a cup. Frontinus set them on the desk. "Pain makes men thirsty," he said noncommittally. "There is water when you talk."

The man licked his lips again and looked at the circle of armored sentries and the angular gray-haired man in the gold and purple cloak, and once briefly at Correus. They would kill him, but water would make it more bearable. And there would be no second chance for his tribe now. He began to speak while the man he had been sent to kill watched impassively, heavy callused hands resting on his purple-cloaked knees.

He was a man of the Demetae, and it had been fear that had sent him over the Roman walls. Fear and the hope that a knife in the dark might do what the Demetae were not strong enough to do with men and chariots. Bendigeid of the Silures wanted the Demetae to make a hosting against the Roman Army of the Eagles which sat poised on the frontier of West Britain. The Demetae had a treaty with Rome, but that would be little salvation while Bendigeid's host lay between them and the Romans. By the time Rome avenged the Demetae, the Demetae would be gone. And if they made an alliance with Bendigeid, then they would die at Rome's hands instead—Bendigeid would use the Demetae warriors and horse herds as he saw fit to break Rome's advance, and the men who would be left when Bendigeid had won would not be Demetae.

The tribesman spoke dully, in a monotone, while Correus, equally lifeless, translated automatically when the tribesman's British went beyond the Romans' understanding. It was an interrogation within a nightmare, while his mind returned in agonizing fear to the blood-soaked bed-chamber beyond.

"And so you thought that if the Army of the Eagles had no general, there might be no war after all?" Frontinus said. "Why not put your knife in Bendigeid instead and keep your treaty? Did you think Rome would take no vengeance for a murdered governor?"

"The Roman kind are followers," the Demetae man said. "Without a strong one to follow, they sit and wait for orders. By the time a new governor could be sent, there might be trouble elsewhere to turn Rome's hand to, such as Boudicca made for us." The previous campaign for West Britain had been cut short by that vengeful queen's rebellion in the east. "But the Silures would have held King-making over Bendigeid's body. Like us, they are warriors." There was a touch of bitter pride in his voice at that. "And Rome could not have helped us in time against their new king. If Rome would. Also——" He looked at the knife that lay on the governor's desk, the blood slowly drying along the blade. "That is a Silure knife."

Frontinus almost laughed and then bit the sound back as he remembered Correus. "And so you would have killed me and put the blame on Bendigeid. Commendable foresight." His voice hardened. "Instead you have tried to murder a woman more than eight months with child. Your own folk would give you to the Dark Goddess for that. *I* may give you back to the woman's man."

The Demetae man looked at Correus. "It was not meant."

The governor looked at Correus also, searchingly. "Do you want him, Centurion?"

Correus shook his head. The fury and the red mist were gone. "In cold blood . . . no," he said thickly.

Frontinus nodded in satisfaction. "Good. That kind of thing puts a darkness on the soul that never quite washes out." He motioned to the sentries. "Take him out. If he has any prayers to make to his own gods, let him make them. Crucify him in the morning, but keep it out of sight of the Silures' hills."

They pulled him roughly from the chair.

"Take the water with you," Frontinus said.

Correus watched them go, his face still numb, as if he

sat in some other man's body. He felt Vindex lay a hand
on his shoulder in awkward friendliness.

In the stillness created after the sentries had trooped
out, the murmur of voices could be heard from the room
beyond, and a sharp expletive from Silanus that made
Correus's shoulders tense like a spring. Vindex shot a
glance at the two commanders and tightened his grip on
Correus's shoulder.

"Sit still, friend. You can't help."

They sat, the four of them—Correus, Vindex, Longinus, and the governor of Britain in his night tunic—
through what seemed like an aeon but was probably only
a few more minutes. Correus's hands clenched tightly into
fists in his lap, and he was seemingly uncaring that he was
shivering now with cold. Vindex took off his uniform cloak
and put it around him.

There was a short, wailing cry, which Correus seemed
not to hear, and the other three exchanged glances again.
The door swung open, and Silanus came out. There was
blood on his tunic, and his arms were red with it to the
elbow. His face was tired . . . and old.

He stood silently before Correus for a moment, then
shook his head. "She died, Centurion. I am sorry. The
wound was in the lung."

Correus sat unmoving, his face wiped clean of life. The
surgeon hesitated and went on. "The baby . . . it was
alive, and kicking, and I took it from her when she died.
It is early, but it will live, I think."

The orderly came in behind him, carefully holding a
small bundle wrapped in a purple cloak—Governor Frontinus's spare one, ransacked in haste from the clothes
chest. "You have a son, sir," the orderly said. He held the
bundle out to Correus, who seemed not even to see it.

"Do you want to see her?" the surgeon asked gently.

Correus stood up and went through the door. Freita lay
against the pillow, her golden hair fanned out about her
head. The bedclothes were pulled up above her breast,
but he could see that her swollen belly was flatter now under the blankets, and something had been wrapped tightly
around it. He did not look beneath them. Her hands were
arranged on top of the bedclothes . . . long-fingered white
hands, still warm. Her face was at rest, but a look of pain

and fright clung to it. He knelt down beside her, put his head against the hollow of her throat, and cried.

In the outer room the orderly stood uncertainly, holding the baby as a man would hold a strung catapult.

"It's only a baby," Vindex said mildly. He took off his helmet with the centurion's transverse crest of red, set it on the desk, and unbuckled his lorica. "They need to be cuddled. That's what my mother always said. Here, give him to me." Vindex had bright, dark eyes and a sleek, dark cap of hair like a seal, and he bent over the baby affectionately. The orderly relinquished it gratefully. "He's a fine one for an eight months' child," Vindex said with approval. "Gemellus in my cohort has a woman who just had a child. Go and roust him out of bed for me. Second tent, fifth century."

The orderly departed, and Vindex looked at the governor. "I'll, uh, return your cloak, sir, when Gemellus's woman has cleaned it."

Frontinus smiled. "Domitius, would you be kind enough to call one of your men to get these braziers lit. *My* mother always said that a nursery should be warm. Have Julianus keep the cloak for him, Centurion. It is not every soldier who can boast that he was born in a camp of the legions and swaddled in a military governor's cloak. Maybe it will be a sign."

Silanus looked dubious. "I hope I have done the right thing."

Frontinus hitched his chair forward to put his bare feet on the Persian carpet that graced the commander's study. "You had no choice. I am not aware that the Caesarean Law has been changed."

"There is always a choice in the end, Governor," Silanus said, "for a surgeon. Most of us have a choice or two on our consciences already when we get to my age. I am going back to my hospital. I don't think Centurion Julianus will be wanting to see me just now."

Frontinus looked after him. "Army surgeons unsettle me. I understand civilian physicians, and I wouldn't let most of them touch me with tongs. I understand soldiers and I understand aqueducts, both of which are highly predictable. But I have never met an army surgeon yet who didn't baffle me."

"It's the training," Longinus said as a pair of legionaries came in to light the braziers. "The civilian gives you a lot of large talk about the phases of the moon and the will of the gods, because there's no arguing with that and it's a nice excuse if you die. An army surgeon knows enough to know that it *doesn't* know, and it makes him odd. Ah, this must be your man, Centurion."

The orderly returned with a sleepy legionary in tow, hastily dressed and more than unnerved by a midnight summons to the commander's quarters. He wondered which of his illicit pursuits was dire enough for the governor to take notice of it. He blinked in surprise at the sight of his cohort commander with a baby in his arms.

"It's not mine, sir," Gemellus said jumpily.

"Of course it's not, you fool," Vindex said. "It's Centurion Julianus's, and the mother is dead. Has your woman enough milk for two, do you think?"

"Yes, sir, more than enough," Gemellus said, relieved.

"Good. Go and wake her up and tell her to get ready for us." Vindex filched a wax message tablet from the study desk with his free hand and scratched a note on it. "This will get you through the gate."

"Yes, sir." Gemellus looked thoughtful. "Uh, will the centurion be payin' her a bit, sir? She'll need extra food and the like to nurse two."

"Yes, he will be paying, you greedy oaf, and he will be grateful." Vindex fixed Gemellus with a steely eye. "But if you mention it to him before he's ready to talk about it, I'll see that you're cleaning latrines for a month."

Gemellus departed in haste, and Vindex looked sadly through the open doorway to the still figure by the bed. "I'd better go and get him. It won't do for him to grieve in that room all night." He hesitated and looked at the baby, which was sleeping peacefully now, muffled in the purple cloak.

"Give him to me," Frontinus said.

"Sir?"

"That poor woman is dead because she was in *my* bed. It's hardly an affront to my dignity to hold her baby."

"Yes, sir. Thank you." Vindex laid the baby in the governor's lap and approached Correus hesitantly. "Correus?"

The still figure looked up, and Vindex flinched. His

friend's face looked like a death mask. "It's time to go now."

Correus stood up. He gave a last look at Freita and brushed a hand across her cheek.

"Correus," Vindex said.

Correus turned and followed him out of the room, closing the door behind him. Vindex bent down to take the baby from the governor, but Correus suddenly put out his own arms.

"No, I'll take him."

Gemellus's woman was fat and none too clean, but her own baby looked healthy, and she cradled Freita's child capably against her breast when he woke and began to cry.

This house also was little more than a tent with two wattle-and-daub walls, but there was a banked fire still glowing warmly, and the floor was thickly laid with rushes. If the hut didn't catch fire, Vindex thought, the child would be well enough here. He put a coin in the woman's hand, and she nodded briskly.

"He'll be all right, sir," she said to Correus. "See, he's hungry already."

Correus took a deep breath and for the first time looked carefully at his son. The baby had a crown of pale fuzz and a red, wrinkled face. He could see nothing of himself or Freita in him. *Freita*, he thought miserably, his stomach clenching. His beautiful, beloved Freita, gone forever, irrevocably, leaving him nothing but a child he had no way of raising. A bastard child, like his bastard father. Correus made a choking sound and left the hut, Vindex trotting anxiously after him.

They buried Freita the next day in the little cemetery that had already begun to grow up along the road to Glevum across the Isca River.

DIS MANIBUS ...
TO THE GODS OF THE SHADES ...

Correus paid a legionary stonecutter to chisel the short inscription.

FREITA, LOVED WIFE
OF CORREUS APPIUS JULIANUS,
CENTURION OF THE NINTH COHORT,
LEGIO II AUGUSTA.

Governor Frontinus was in attendance, and he didn't
even raise an eyebrow at the word "wife." It was all very
illegal, and he didn't give a damn if it was.

Correus's cohort turned out unasked, in full parade kit
for their commander's lady, and a full century of Vindex's
Tenth Cohort was with them, on their commander's order. The legate and the governor himself made a prayer
for the lady's soul.

Julius watched from the edge of the crowd as Correus
laid a wreath of fern and summer wildflowers on the
grave. He had liked the lady, he thought miserably, even
when they quarreled. He wished he could have told her
so. Julius had never known a kind word or a gentle hand
until the centurion had brought him to look after the lady,
who had been a slave, too, in those days. Julius knew that
the centurion's will contained a clause that freed him,
also, and the centurion would do it before that—when he
was old enough to look after himself. Julius responded
with a devotion far greater than that which he gave the
gods. They had done little enough for him. If there was a
god in Julius's life, it was the centurion. It wasn't *fair* that
he had lost his lady, Julius thought angrily. Not when he
had loved her so much.

When the last prayers were made, Correus turned his
back on the grave and walked alone across Isca Bridge
back to the fortress. For the rest of his life he would never
fully remember the next two days. They were the leave
that was to have been spent with Freita, and the day he
buried her he passed up the leave and went back to his
cohort. He rode Aeshma, who was in such a state of
nerves, triggered by Correus's and Julius's moods, that
Julius couldn't handle him. He checked on the baby and
gave Gemellus's woman some money. He drilled his men
and called a weapons inspection under the sympathetic
eye of Octavius, his second-in-command. Correus didn't
remember doing any of it.

He looked like the walking dead, Octavius thought
nervously. If the commander cracked up, there would be

hell to pay when the legion marched, and that would be any day now. Before he hit the Silures, Governor Frontinus was going to show the Demetae what a mistake they had made. Correus told his cohort so at their first parade, but Octavius wasn't sure the commander really heard his own words. His face had the hunted look of a man who turns back to hide in his own mind. He might have slipped over the brink entirely if it hadn't been for the arrival of his brother-in-law and his half sister on one of their frequent travels.

Governor Frontinus was at his desk in the Principia tent when an optio poked his head in and announced that there were a couple of civilians waiting to see him.

"Have Trebonius deal with them." Trebonius was the camp prefect, in charge of all the matters that dealt with the fortress itself, rather than the troops that garrisoned it. Civil complaints were his problem. "I don't have time to cope with some farmer who's had his pig stolen by a trooper." On the frontier of West Britain, relations with the local folk were touchy at best.

"Not that sort of civilians, sir." The optio handed him a papyrus sheet sealed with numerous stamps, and the governor raised his eyebrows as he opened it. He had never met Lucius Paulinus, who was reputed to be writing a *Modern History* of the empire, but he was well acquainted with his reputation for getting under the army's feet while doing it. He was also acquainted with Paulinus's uncle Gentilius, author of the letter of introduction.

Frontinus growled and began to read it, but brightened as he read. He remembered hearing that young Paulinus had married recently, and it seemed that the lady of his choice was the half sister of Correus Julianus, who was making himself a problem at the moment. If the centurion's sister and brother-in-law could shake him out of the state he was in before the legion marched out of Isca, Governor Frontinus would be more than grateful.

"Send them in."

Frontinus studied them as they entered, and the optio presented them with chairs and found a cushion to add to the lady's. Lucius Paulinus was an unprepossessing young man, thin and sandy-haired with a pleasant, homely, freckled face, and ears that stuck out a bit. He looked young, but his gray eyes were shrewd and alert, and Frontinus placed his age at five years over his appearance.

Appia Julia was something else again. She had a handsome, classically Roman face, a tumble of dark ringlets piled high up on her head, and a curled fringe of hair across her forehead in grown-up fashion, but she couldn't have been more than seventeen. Her face was skillfully made up with what Frontinus supposed was as much paint as her conservative mother had considered suitable, but there was a mischievous faun's look about her dark eyes and the air of someone to whom the world is still very new and is proving most exciting. She was plainly the apple of her husband's eye, and from the affectionate way she tucked her small hand into his, the feeling was mutual.

"I'm pleased to see you both," Frontinus said genially. "I know your uncle, of course, Paulinus." He turned to Julia. "And I have some acquaintance with your father, my dear. You do him proud. You'll be wanting to see your brother, I expect."

Julia beamed at him under this avuncular treatment. "Yes. We'll be in Britain for several months, so I'm hoping to see them both. My brother Flavius is with the Second Adiutrix at Lindum."

"Oh? I didn't know that." Frontinus sighed. "I wish I had. It might have helped."

Paulinus made no comment. After having the misfortune to serve together in Germany, it was exasperating that Flavius and Correus should again be posted close enough to annoy each other. Whatever had gone wrong, Flavius was not the person to cure it.

Julia leaned forward, her face concerned. "What's happened?"

Frontinus noted Paulinus's reaction with curiosity. Bad blood, obviously, between the adopted son and the family's heir. But this pretty, cheerful sister might be the cure for what ailed Centurion Julianus. And it would keep her husband out of *his* hair. He explained, and Julia's face saddened.

"Oh, poor Correus. She meant so much to him. And there's a baby?"

Paulinus sat silent, his own face sad, remembering Freita as he had known her in Germany and her troubled, at times explosive transformation from vengeful, frightened

captive-of-war to Roman lady, and wife in all but name.
A transformation wrought by an unexpected love for the
man who had bought her initially from pity because there
was another, worse, man who wanted her. There had
been too much between them for Correus to shake off her
death lightly.

"I want to see him," Julia was saying. "But I want to
talk to my husband first. I think he knows my brother better than I do in some ways."

"Certainly," Frontinus said. "If you'll tell my optio here
when you are ready, he will send for him. Uh, as to ac-
commodations, I'm sadly afraid that there are none. The
Praetorium is only partly finished, and you will have seen
the civil settlement as you rode in."

Julia gave a shudder. "Freita was living in *that?*" She
wished Flavius's wife, Aemelia, could have seen it. It
would have cured her in a hurry of her notions about living on the frontier.

"I'm afraid so," Frontinus said. "But I'm sure you can
find good inns in Aquae Sulis or Glevum. Maybe even in
Venta, although it's a bit primitive." *Anywhere but in my
camp,* he thought.

"We have a tent of our own," Paulinus said. "And my
servant, Tullius, is with us. He's an ex-legionary himself
and sees to our needs admirably."

"My dear girl, do you actually let this man drag you
about the empire, sleeping in tents? I warn you, it rains in
West Britain at all times of day and with no regard for
season."

"It's a very palatial tent, I assure you," Julia said with
a giggle. "I made sure of that. And I have my maid with
me. I had to be firm, but she's getting used to it."

Frontinus retired, thwarted. "You're a very unusual
young lady."

"Do you know, I'm beginning to think so, too," Julia
said. "I led a very sheltered life before we were married,
so I never had a chance to find out."

"Unusual young lady indeed," Paulinus chuckled as they
strolled arm in arm past the neatly aligned tents of the
barracks rows. A cavalry troop trotting by drew rein politely until they had passed, more in deference to Julia
than himself, Paulinus suspected. In a green gown the

color of the hillsides and a cherry-colored mantle thrown
over it, she was a bright spot of color in the dirty half-
built fortress. Ruby drops bobbed in her ears, and there
were clusters of cherries embroidered on the hem of her
gown. "You routed him, cavalry and catapults, my dear."

"Do you know, Lucius," Julia said thoughtfully, "I
don't think he really wanted us here. Except to help poor
Correus, of course."

"No," Paulinus sighed. "They never do."

"Well," Julia returned practically to the matter at hand,
"what *are* we going to do about Correus?"

"I don't know," Paulinus said. "He will have to weather
this somehow. Be as sympathetic as you can, but for the
gods' sakes don't ask him what he's going to do about the
baby. If I know Correus, that's going to be a sore point
with him. It's all he has left of her."

"You don't suppose I'm going to suggest he expose it,
do you?" Julia asked indignantly.

"No, but your mother would, and so would that fool
Helva. So might your father, under the circumstances.
Fortunately they won't find out until it's too late for that
alternative."

"I'm not going to *ask* what he's going to do about the
baby," Julia said firmly, "I'm going to *tell* him. And you,
Lucius, are going to back me up."

Paulinus gave his wife a long look. "You're awfully
young."

"You didn't think so when you took me to Britain with
you. Or in Petra when that awful Arab offered you three
camels for me."

"You're just insulted because the price wasn't higher.
You said you wanted to see the world. It has a lot of un-
civilized places in it. And some that were already civilized when Romans were living in huts along the Tiber."

"So it does. You're getting off the track, Lucius."

"No, I'm not. I'm trying to give you time to make sure
you know what you're doing."

Correus, directed by a note handed to him by the headquarters optio, turned the cohort over to Octavius and
found his brother-in-law's tent pitched well upwind from
the ramshackle civilian camp.

Paulinus's hulking servant, Tullius, a time-expired legionary with arms like an ape and a friendly grin, was plucking a chicken outside the tent and explaining the fine points of the process to Julia's maid, a middle-aged woman with a long-suffering air verging at the moment on revulsion.

He stood and gave Correus a military salute, chicken still in hand. "It's fine to see you, sir. And I'm sorry to hear of your troubles." His broad face showed concern.

"Thank you, Tullius. Where are Paulinus and my sister?"

"Here, friend. Come in." Paulinus pushed aside the tent flap and beckoned Correus inside.

A bright red and green figure darted forward and flung her arms around him, yelping indignantly as his lorica scratched her face. Correus kissed her, trying to fight down the memory of Freita, who could never remember not to do that. They pushed him down into a pile of cushions, and Julia curled up next to him. Julia's description of her tent as palatial hardly did it justice. The floor was almost covered with thick cushions, and the walls were hung with rugs and tapestries enthusiastically collected by their owner on her first travels. Under the cushions was a plank floor pegged and slotted so that it could be taken apart and fitted back together without nails. The tent was curtained at the back to make two more rooms and lit by bronze lamps on weighted stands. It was replete with every conceivable luxury that could be packed on a mule or loaded in a cart. It had a distinctly Eastern air.

"I know," Correus said admiringly, "you bought it from Rhodope."

Since Rhodope ran the best traveling whorehouse on the Rhenus frontier, Paulinus choked.

"Lucius said that if I came to Britain with him, I would have to live in a tent sometimes," Julia replied, "and I said there were a few things I needed first."

Paulinus produced a flask of wine and three heavy pottery cups and pushed one of them into Correus's hand. "The governor told us what happened," he said.

"Correus, I am so sorry." Julia put her hands on his. "And you must let us help."

"Thank you, child, but I don't think there's anything that you can do," her brother said. He seemed calm enough, but his face had a fine-drawn, edge-of-the-abyss look about it, and his dark eyes were hooded, almost blank.

"Yes, there is," Julia said, "but we'll talk about that later. We were in Rome after we left the East, and everyone there is well. Papa is getting gray, but he still gets up every morning and works with Alan and Diulius and the horses. Alan must be almost as old as he is, although he has Forst to help him now, and Diulius had to have two teeth pulled by the tooth-drawer and made such a fuss about it that Mama threatened to have the field slaves hold him down if he didn't behave. Your mother is well, too," she added. "She claims she's getting old and had to have her apartments done over, although I don't see how a change of paint and bed hangings is going to keep her any warmer."

Since Helva was considerably younger than either Appius Julianus or his wife, the Lady Antonia, Correus didn't either, but he knew his mother well enough to know that any luxury added to her surroundings would *always* make her feel warmer. "How is Thais?" he asked after their old nurse.

"Well," Julia giggled, "she keeps asking me when I'm going to have babies. But *she* really *is* old, and she's not allowed to do much anymore. She sent you something." Julia rummaged in a chest and produced a neck scarf of thick scarlet wool in the standard military pattern. "I was to tell you to be sure you keep your throat warm when it rains," she said solemnly.

Correus smiled and took the scarf, his eyes lightening for a moment. "And Forst?"

"Oh, Thais has taken him over to mother. You'd never know him for a wild German now. He's fallen in love with Emer in the kitchen. You remember, Correus. The red-haired one you used to run after."

"Julia—" Paulinus said.

"Well, he did, and it's no use my pretending I didn't notice. Anyway, now that Forst has settled down, I think he'd like to marry her if Papa will permit it. Thais keeps consulting augers and making magics so it will turn out right. Let's see, who else. . . . Oh, yes, Cook had a temperament while we were there, but that's nothing new. He always has one when there's company."

"Inevitably," Correus said. "Part of any state occasion."

"And, uh, Aemelia is well, too," Julia said dubiously. Since Flavius's young wife had had the misfortune to fall in love with the wrong brother first, she was hesitant to mention her, but Correus had better be prepared. "She's coming out to join Flavius. Have you seen him yet?"

"No. I . . . there hasn't been time."

Well, that was a blessing, Paulinus thought. He remembered Correus's unhappy confession two years ago of the promise that their father had extracted from him and what that promise had cost Flavius and Correus already. Now Flavius was staff aide to the legate of the Second Adiutrix at Lindum, and Paulinus would like to get his hands on the fool who had posted the half brothers to the same province again.

"Will you be seeing him?"

"Oh, yes. We'll probably stay the winter in Britain, unless someone wants Lucius back in Rome."

"Still on the same road, Lucius?" Correus asked quietly.

"All roads are the emperor's roads," Paulinus said noncommittally. "You've gone that way yourself, by the look of it."

"Now I want you to listen to me," Julia said. Her voice had such a grown-up air to it and such a likeness to her mother's that Correus looked with surprise at his little sister.

"Your son, Correus. You are going to give him to me."

"I—"

"Have you really thought about it?" Julia went on. "No, I didn't think so. You're still much too unhappy, and I don't blame you, but you've *got* to think about it."

"He's with one of the soldiers' women," Correus said.

"Yes, I know he is. And you're going to leave him with her while you go off with the legion to the gods know where? What if you're killed? Do you really think that woman is going to go on feeding him when the money stops coming?"

"I didn't know what else to do." Correus closed his eyes and took a deep breath of relief. Everything Julia said was true, but he had tried to put it out of his mind because there were no other choices.

"Tullius!"

"My lady?" Tullius put his head through the tent flap.

"You are to find the hut of the woman of a soldier named Gemellus, and bring her and my brother's son and her own child back here to me. Take Martia with you."

"Yes, my lady!"

"She can come into my service until the child is old enough to be weaned," Julia said. "And if Gemellus doesn't like it, he can argue with Tullius."

"Julia, are you sure you know what you're doing?" Correus's face was concerned, but the protest was half-hearted. Julia was a godsend, and he needed her help desperately.

"I'm quite old enough to have a baby," Julia said firmly. "Thais keeps telling me so, so don't be a fool. That's your *son*, Correus. He's my nephew. He belongs with the family. And I'm the only one there is to take him, so you'll have to let me."

No one mentioned Aemelia, who would just as soon clasp an adder to her bosom, Julia thought, as Correus's bastard son by a German freedwoman.

"All right, dear, if you're sure," Correus said. "I'm grateful."

"She's sure," Paulinus said. "*I'm* sure. We're all sure. Now that's settled."

"What have you named him?" Julia asked.

"I haven't yet. It isn't time." Roman babies were named by their fathers on the eighth day after their birth. Named and held, the father's acknowledgment of paternity.

"Well, you must have thought what it's going to be," Paulinus said. "You've held him, of course. We'll take that as read, and I'll name him for you if the governor hauls you off to fight Silures in the next few days."

Correus thought about the purple cloak. "Frontinus," he said. "Frontinus . . . Appius Julianus," he added a bit defiantly. "Find a magistrate to draw up the adoption papers. I'll give you my proxy."

Julia hugged him, oblivious to the armor-plated lorica. "I'm so glad. He *is* your son, and Papa should have let you marry her."

No, he shouldn't, Paulinus thought sadly. He had liked Freita, but marrying her was the last thing his friend should have done. Not if his career in the army meant anything to him, and until he met Freita, it had meant everything.

Julia slipped her arm through her husband's as she watched her brother walk back toward the fortress. The baby lay swaddled in a clean blanket amid the Eastern opulence of Julia's tent, and the wet nurse was being sternly ordered to bathe under the firm eye of Julia's maid, Martia. She thought her brother's eyes had a lighter look as he left, but they were still haunted. Maybe the army would help, she thought, unconsciously echoing her husband's thoughts. It had always meant so much to him. Correus's beloved Eagles . . . maybe when the legion marched it would get better for him.

Correus paused where the road swung past the parade ground and looked beyond the marching men at drill who occupied it, to the distant form of his sister's tent with its wagon and pack mules behind it. Freita had left a hole in him that wouldn't heal, but he was not alone with it, no longer solitary in the tearing emptiness he had walked in for the last two days. He had Paulinus, and he had rediscovered Julia. He had his family. He would have liked to see his brother, Flavius, again, he thought. He might understand him better now.

In the meantime, that terrible blackness lifted at least enough to cope with the sad remnants of his own household in Isca's ragtag *vicus*. He had ridden Aeshma twice, carefully avoiding the hut itself, and it was plain that without Freita the big gray stallion had no place in Isca.

"I was wondering if you'd be back at all, sir," Julius said when Correus appeared at the hut door the next evening. "We've kept up the place like, me and the cat, but it's not much to come home to."

"I'm sorry, Julius. I didn't think I could face it any sooner." He looked about the little hut, as spotless as Freita had ever kept it, and the cat came up and twined around his ankles. "I've made arrangements to have Aeshma shipped back to Rome. Do you want to go with him?"

Rome. Julius's face lit up. "I think I'd better go, sir. They'll have to throw him for sure to get him on board if I don't, and he might hurt himself." *Rome*. "Would it be all right to take a day or two for holiday, like, on the way back?"

"Take a week if you like," Correus said. "But don't get into trouble. My father will be less inclined to get you out again than I would."

"Yes, sir! What about the cat, sir?"

"Take it to the quartermaster," Correus said. "He's been moaning about rats in the granary, so he'll be delighted." Correus didn't want to look at the cat. Aeshma was his horse, too, had been his horse first, but the cat was all Freita's.

He went and gave Aeshma's gray hide a final pat and told him what a fine time he would have terrorizing the rest of his father's stock. The gray stallion whickered and butted his head against Correus's chest, and for a moment Correus thought about keeping him here for no better reason than that Aeshma had been his and Freita's together, and he couldn't bear to sweep everything they had had out into the wind. But Aeshma was totally unfit for army work, and Correus didn't *need* two horses—he had Antaeus, who was properly trained, stabled in the cavalry barns already. "Behave yourself," he said into a gray ear, and Aeshma snorted at him.

Three days later Julius rode Aeshma out of Isca to catch a ship at Portus Adurni in the south, and the Second Legion sailed on its own errand westward.

III

Flavius

FLAVIUS APPIUS JULIANUS, NOTED ON THE ARMY ROLLS as "the younger" to distinguish him from his famous father, and known in the family as Flavius, sat cross-legged on the bed in his quarters in the Praetorium at Lindum. He was mending the red leather strap of a chariot bridle and whistling between his teeth. He had brought a new pair of ponies across with him when he had been given the

Lindum posting, and he still didn't like to think about the Channel crossing—they had worked themselves into hysteria and kicked down their stalls, and he had had to stay in the hold with them for the entire crossing. They were flighty creatures, all air and fire, but they had already won two local races, and Tribune Marcellinus had made him a fat offer for them. Flavius chuckled and inspected his handiwork. It was pleasant to have a flea to put in the tribune's ear.

He tossed the bridle onto the bronze and leather clothes chest at the foot of the bed and lay back, hands behind his head. Life was inordinately pleasant. Gaius Gratus, legate of the Second Legion Adiutrix, was a stiff-necked, birth-proud martinet, whose officers invariably put in for transfer within a month of their posting. In Flavius the army had found at last the buffer to keep life tranquil. Although the Julianus family could claim no more than knightly birth, they could trace their line back almost to the founding of the City. With Flavius's aquiline face and dark, immaculate curls, Gratus took to Centurion Julianus on sight, and Flavius responded with the ease and unselfconsciousness of one who knows his own birth and position to be above reproach. Since he was equally at ease with the legate's officers, they also took to the new staff aide, and Flavius became a sort of filter through which the legate's wishes were passed and rendered inoffensive. The cohort officers sympathized loudly with him, and Flavius responded in kind for form's sake, but in truth he didn't miss a field command. He had a talent for handling men but not in the role of a field officer. He admitted as much reluctantly, and some days not at all when the shadow of his brother and his famous father hung too heavily about him, but in truth he was well suited where he was. He was rapidly making himself indispensable to Gratus, a crony of the emperor's, and with his wife coming to join him, he couldn't think of much else to ask for.

Aemelia . . . Flavius whistled cheerily to himself as he thought of his wife. Aemelia's dark, flower-petal beauty would be as exotic in Lindum, where the native women were big-boned and fair, as a cultivated rose in a cornfield. Her father was a senator, and the legate would undoubtedly ask them to dine. There would be no protests at the Lady Aemelia's presence in Lindum, although Flavius would have to see to her housing himself, of course. Rules were rules. He had a house already rented, a pleasant one in the best part of the civil settlement, built in the Roman style, around a courtyard and heated by a furnace and hypocaust. A pleasant place to spend off-duty hours, and with Aemelia all to himself, her vision of him might improve somewhat. Flavius knew well enough that his wife had married him because she couldn't have his brother, and he had been glad enough to get her that way or any other. It had been an arranged marriage, looked on in kindly fashion by both Appius Julianus and Aemelia's father, who had summed up his opinion of a match with the wrong brother succinctly: "I'll cut your bastard's throat for him if he so much as looks sideways at my daughter."

He knew just when Aemelia had changed her mind about marrying him, Flavius thought. It had been when he had told her that he, Flavius, loved her—and that Correus didn't. He wasn't sure whether Aemelia believed that yet or not, but under that last uncertainty, her determination to defy her father and the world had crumbled. Her strength of will had been pushed far beyond its limits already.

Aemelia didn't love him, Flavius thought. And unaccountably, infuriatingly, he had fallen in love with her. But she had set herself to be a good wife, and with the action often came the desire. "Patience," he whispered to the empty air.

His reverie turned to a half-waking dream in which Aemelia was running to meet him along the canal bank outside Lindum Fort, her slaves struggling under a mountain of trunks behind her, and her dark eyes bright as a bird's at the sight of his own dear face.

A hand shook him from this pleasant vision, and he found himself blinking up not at Aemelia's parted lips and flushed cheeks, but at his optio's equine countenance.

Flavius groaned. "Oh, no."

"General's compliments, sir, and you're wanted right away," the optio said.

Flavius picked up a comb and ran it through his dark curls before a gilt-framed mirror. "What, uh, crisis is occurring at the moment?" He knotted his neck scarf carefully. "It all looked peaceful enough this morning. Oh, no, not marching orders! My wife's due to arrive any day now!"

The optio's long face was worried. "I don't think so, sir. There was a courier came in, but not from the west. He was on the Eburacum road. But the general's pacing like a wolf in a pen, and he looks mad enough to chew a sword in half."

"Oh, lord. Well, I'd better go and find out why." Flavius swirled his scarlet cloak around his shoulders, gave it a military twist, and stuck the pin home.

Nothing looked particularly unsettled as he crossed the narrow walk between the Praetorium and the Principia, the headquarters building. But Flavius recognized the harassed-looking man at the desk outside the legate's office as Gratus's personal optio, and his expression said plainly that he would rather be serving Hecate in hell.

"You're to go straight in, sir," he said.

"Thank you," Flavius said dubiously. The door swung open silently, and he poked his nose around it. "You sent for me, sir?"

The man at the desk looked up, and Flavius drew a quick, shocked breath.

"Yes, Centurion. Sit down, please." Gaius Gratus's face was pale under its normal olive tone, and his eyes were bright—the hard, sharp glitter of a man pushed one step past what he can live with. His hands were laid flat, palms down on his desk in a gesture like prayer.

"What has happened, sir?" Flavius took two fast steps into the office. "Can I get you anything? Some wine?"

"No, thank you, Julianus. I am not ill." He swallowed. "Sick at heart perhaps."

"Sir?"

"I've just had word of the one thing no commander wants to look in the face," Gratus said. "Mutiny."

"Not in the Adiutrix, sir!" Mutiny was a horror that happened more often than Rome liked to admit. But not in the Adiutrix. Flavius would have sworn for the Adiutrix.

"No," Gratus said. "No, it was the Ninth."

Flavius sat down slowly. The Ninth Legion Hispana had been unstable ever since it had been nearly destroyed in Queen Boudicca's rebellion some fifteen years ago. It had been reconstituted afterward, but a rebuilt legion was

thought to be unlucky. True enough now, it seemed.
"How bad?"

The legate of the Adiutrix took a deep breath and
spread the story out for his aide. It was bad enough. The
ringleaders of the mutiny had been caught and put to
death in the ancient, vengeful fashion decreed by the old
laws—death by stoning. And there had been two senior
officers among them.

"Mithras," Flavius whispered, and put his head in his
hands. Gratus went on relentlessly, but his voice was tired
and it shook. The Ninth Hispana was on the edge of col-
lapse, and its legate had sent him a desperate message to
say so. The strongest of the local tribes, the Brigantes,
were growing troublesome, and now there was nothing in
their way but a legion too demoralized to take the field.

"I've ordered three-fourths of our men north to Eburacum," Gratus said, "before the Brigantes start a war. We'll
march in the morning."

"Yes, sir. I'll see that everything's ready."

"No." Gratus put out a hand. "No, I want you to ride
to Governor Frontinus and tell him to keep an eye on the
southeast during our absence. There's no defense there
with us in Eburacum, and if his West Britons take it into
their heads to strike that way, we could have another
civilian slaughter on our hands." He handed Flavius a
tablet with a seal of purple wax. "That's your pass and
your orders to report to the governor. The rest you take in
your head. That's why I'm sending you and not a courier."

Flavius nodded. Courier-carried messages could be in-
tercepted, and couriers could be made to talk. It was urgent that the governor know what had happened in
Eburacum, and that he could expect no help in West
Britain from the Adiutrix. It was even more urgent that
some unruly tribe not learn that the civil settlements of
the southeast lay undefended. The rebellion in which
Boudicca of the Iceni had wrecked a legion and three
cities was not so long distant that most soldiers in Britain
didn't shudder when her name went by.

Flavius rose and tucked the wax tablet into his tunic.
"I'll start tonight, sir. I ought to make it as far as Margid-
unum. As I remember there's a decent inn there. I can
pick up a fresh horse tomorrow at Ratae."

"Just make sure you pick up an escort when you hit Silure lands," Gratus said with a grim smile.

Flavius saluted. He smiled back. He and the legate had always understood each other.

"And report to me at Eburacum as soon as the governor stops swearing and gives you the return message."

Flavius trotted back to his quarters, shouted for his body slave, and sat down to scratch a hasty message in wax to his wife. The slave, Bericus, came on the run.

"Pack my kit—no more than will go in the saddlebags. And saddle both horses."

"Yes, sir!" Bericus scented excitement in the wind. "Where are we going, sir?"

"*I'm* going to play courier for the legate," Flavius said. "*You're* going to Portus Adurni to catch my wife when her ship docks, to tell her so." He handed the boy the wax tablet. "Give her this, and take her to Aquae Sulis. I don't want her in Lindum till things settle down. There's trouble brewing, but you're to keep your mouth shut about that."

"Yes, sir. Uh, sir—why not Londinium?" Bericus's young face was wistful. "There's nothing in Aquae Sulis but fat old hens with gout."

"Londinium's awfully big, and she's awfully young," Flavius said. "And so are you. I think I'd feel safer with you in Aquae Sulis. If it's any comfort to you, you may take Nestor. I'm going to have to ride like Hades, and I'll change horses at Ratae. I'm damned if I'll leave Nestor there."

"Yes, sir." Bericus decided that more questions would be a mistake and scrambled into the bedchamber to shake out clean tunics from the clothes chest. His master's he folded carefully and rolled in a spare cloak, while his own were stuffed into the second pair of saddlebags with more regard for speed. He added to Flavius's a comb, razor, hand mirror, writing materials, and a flask of liniment advertised to cure sore muscles in man or beast.

As Bericus departed for the stables, Flavius sighed and began to buckle on the skirt of red leather strips that went under his lorica. One of the charms of being a staff officer was not having to wear armor except on parade. He buckled on the segmented plates of his lorica, strapped on greaves, and knotted the helmet strap under his chin, pausing first to affix the red transverse crest that advertised his centurion's rank. He tucked his vine staff under his arm and looked thoughtfully at the packed kit on his bed. He dragged a pair of soft boots from the clothes chest and managed to squeeze them in as well, in case it rained. It always rained in Britain.

The horses were saddled by the time Flavius reached the stables, and he gave Bericus a smile of encouragement when he found him already sitting, eyes proud, astride the bay Nestor.

"Give him his head, and don't push him. You have a few days to spare. More maybe, if they've had to wait out a storm at Grannona."

Bericus nodded, and Flavius checked the girth on the second horse, a chestnut of uncertain ancestry usually allotted to Bericus. He swung into the saddle. It was hot, and in the air there was the omnipresent smell of water from the canal, part of the system that drained the fenlands to the south and linked their rivers into a highway for the transport ships. The canals had been dug after Boudicca's rebellion, with the Corps of Engineers for architects and her sullen, beaten people for a labor force. They were a message cut across the fenlands: Rome does not forget.

They clattered across the wooden bridge as a barge poled by underneath, loaded with a farmer and his fat wife and a crate of clucking chickens. Market day in Lindum. Flavius wondered if this elderly and contented-seeming countryman had been among the baying horde that had sent three cities up in flames. They said that Boudicca had cursed the Ninth when she died. He thought with a shudder of the news out of Eburacum. It would seem the queen's curse ran true. Flavius put a heel to the chestnut's flank. He thought of Londinium burning. Londinium and Camulodunum and Verulamium—all rebuilt now, more populous than ever. They might burn again if he didn't get to Governor Frontinus before news of the troubles at Eburacum reached the restless tribes of West Britain.

"A transport *now*. Today. And an escort."

The camp commander at Glevum gave an implacable stare at the aquiline face confronting him from under a centurion's helmet and crossed his hands on his stomach, tipping back in his chair. "I've told you: I haven't *got* any transport and I haven't *got* any escort and the governor sailed three days ago from Isca. That's in a *boat,* you understand, and he's going right round the coast till he finds a nice place to stop. And it so happens I don't have a spare boat to send after him."

Flavius put both hands down on the camp commander's desk and leaned over him. "Let me explain. I have orders from Legate Gratus at Lindum to find Governor Frontinus and give him a message—*before* he engages the enemy." He produced his orders and held them under the camp commander's nose. "Now if I *don't* find the governor before that, the governor is going to be awfully unhappy, and the one he's going to be unhappy with is you. So you get me a courier ship and a courier's escort, because I expect we'll have to ride to catch up to him."

"Courier ships are for couriers," the camp commander said stubbornly. "I can't let anyone that comes along whistle one up for a free ride."

Flavius took a deep breath and pushed the wax tablet closer so that the camp commander's eyes crossed slightly as it approached. *"I* am a courier, and *these* are courier's orders. Now get me that ship."

The optio at the next desk had been watching this exchange thoughtfully and now came to his own conclusion. "He can't be a courier, sir. He's an officer."

Flavius exploded. "Which is more than you'll be if you don't get a troop of horse and a galley and a crew to row it out into that river in one hour! *Get me that ship* or you'll spend the rest of your tour cleaning latrines in an outpost in Numidia!"

The camp commander wavered. He was beginning to have the uncomfortable feeling that Flavius was going against regulations, but that he was also in the right. Since neither outranked the other, it was a stalemate until someone gave in, and apparently it wasn't going to be Flavius. The camp commander mulled it over. Glevum wasn't really his fort; it had been the home base of the Second Augusta until construction had begun at Isca. Far from holding the exalted rank of camp prefect, the commander was merely the man whose troops had been left behind as garrison. If he held up the governor's message, the governor might very well send him somewhere to rot for ten years or so. On the other hand, if the governor questioned the use of the courier ship, he had Flavius to blame it on. The camp commander put his fingertips together and thought until he could see Flavius practically hopping with fury.

"Well," he said slowly, "I suppose I can give you a galley, and there's a troop of Spanish cavalry eating their heads off with nowhere to go. You can have half of them. But the galley has to make turnaround and sail for Glevum on the next tide. Once you're landed, you're on your own."

Flavius started to protest, changed his mind, saluted, and waited patiently while the camp commander scratched his orders on a tablet. He presented them to Flavius, returned the salute, and folded his arms on his chest as Flavius took his departure. It had been a draw, he thought.

Outside the cavalry quarters, Flavius paused to extract a stylus and a smoothing tool from his saddlebags. When he presented his orders to the decurion in charge, they called for the full troop of thirty.

The galley nosed her way down Sabrina Mouth and into the channel, which divided Silure lands from the settled towns of the southeast. West of the Silures were the Demetae and Governor Frontinus had decided on a punitive strike against the latter as the first move of his campaign in West Britain. It would both show the Britons the error of assassination and give the governor another base from which to strike at Bendigeid's Silures. The galley that moved in his wake was sluggish (horse transport facilities did not make for a fast ship), but it was faster than a fleet, and by the time they rounded a jutting promontory into the bay of the Tuvius, they were not more than a day behind. Flavius was perfectly prepared to fix his orders once more and order the captain of the galley to wait there for him, but Frontinus's ships lay beached along the mouth of the Tuvius, and there was a sizable camp left guarding them. He would have little enough trouble getting back.

The troop horses clattered down the gangway into shallow water, and the sailors gave the lightened galley a shove back out into the river. The captain backed his oars and put her about—the tide was just on the turn.

"Good luck, sir!" he shouted, raising a hand as the oars dipped and pulled.

Flavius swung into the saddle with the cavalry troop behind him as the centurion of the beach camp came forward to investigate. He proved more astute than his fellow in Glevum, raised his eyebrows when he saw the orders, and gestured with his vine staff to a roadway that paralleled the river mouth northward and had obviously been under heavy traffic that day.

"They're only about a half-day's foot march ahead of you," he said, "and the Demetae have bolted for the high country so far as we can tell. You shouldn't have any trouble. Just as well to have a little insurance though," he added with a grin at the cavalry troopers.

Flavius cast a thoughtful look at the wide beach, spreading upward to low pastureland and woods, and the new road snaking through it. "Just so." He lifted his vine staff. "All right, ride!"

The road was really a native trackway leading northward from the natural harbor of the Tuvius, through a wide, flat valley of bog and water meadows yellow with flowers, to the high blue uplands where the native tribes would have their defensive holdings. The army had followed the trackway clear of the bog lands and then swung out cross-country when the way had moved into the trees. It was easy going through the gentle slopes, and leveling trees took time.

But their passing had stirred a current in the scattered woods that could still be felt. The wild things were only beginning to come blinking out of their burrows, and the birds were an unsettled hubbub that crossed and recrossed their usual territory, hesitant to land where the many-legged thing had passed.

Now as Flavius and his cavalry troop passed in the army's wake, the woods stirred gently once again. And another two-legged wild thing crouched at the forest's edge and peered out through a screen of wild grasses. *Romans!* He took a deep breath and wriggled deeper into the grass. He was only fourteen, with long, dark hair pulled into two braids and a thin, tanned body covered only with a brown tunic. A light throwing spear lay in the grass beside him, and there was a dagger in his belt.

These Romans were following the army's tracks, and as they branched off from the road (Flavius didn't fancy those trees, either) and swung wide around the green swell of a low hill, for a moment they were riding straight at him. The boy parted the long grass carefully and began to count. It was the first time he had seen Romans close up, and a ripple of fear went down his back. More than twenty horsemen in long, scale armor and red and yellow trappings, and another in their midst with different armor and the sideways red crest that he knew meant an officer of the legions. They halted briefly as one of the riders gestured with his crop away up the valley, and the man in the officer's helmet pulled it off for a moment and ran his hand through his dark hair. The boy narrowed his eyes and gave the officer's olive-skinned, aquiline face a long look until he pulled his helmet back on and the horsemen whirled and were gone away up the valley, riding hard. The boy hesitated when the Romans were out of sight. He was one of many sent to watch and keep still when the Roman ships were sighted off the coast, and the report of a handful of horsemen was not important enough to call him back to the war band. But there was something important about a man who rode at a gallop with a heavy escort behind the main army. The boy stood, picked up his spear, and trotted into the trees where a hidden deer trail ran upward, away from the river. They would fight soon, he thought, excitement beginning to outweigh fear, and he would become a man at the next Spring-Fire. A man's place was with other men when his tribe fought. If the chieftain believed him, it might be allowed, and then he would carry a spear with the war band while the other boys were still skulking in the trees.

The Second Legion was camped on the north bank of the river where it first widened to the sea, on rising ground above the water meadow. There had been a village there when the Romans marched in, locally known as Dun Mori, the sea hold, but it had been hastily abandoned and now its huts and two large halls were leveled, and what stone there had been in its walls was being rolled into the camp's fortifications. Scouts had fanned out to the north and east and were already beginning to come back.

"They're not as far away as we thought, sir. But they

won't have had time to gather in the whole tribe. Not unless they've been waiting for us."

Frontinus shook his head. "Not likely. They wouldn't have expected our arrival until they saw the galleys. No, I expect they'll try to hit us with what they've got while we're busy digging in, and hope for surprise."

The scout grinned. "We gonna give 'em one, sir?"

"Oh, I think so. I don't take kindly to being murdered in my bed." He turned to Domitius Longinus beside him. "I think two-thirds of our force, in that wood there, should do the trick. Your choice of troops and deployment, of course."

Longinus raised his legate's staff and touched it to his helmet rim. "As it happens, I had, uh, considered the matter already."

"Had you? I rather thought you would have."

It was hot, the sultry afternoon heat of summer, even in the trees, and the hidden cohorts could feel the sweat beginning to run down the backs of their necks and soak the padding in their helmets. They twitched with discomfort, but there was no sound other than a hissed order from a centurion to "put your helmet on, you fool!"

Above them the two generals sat side by side on their mounts in a vantage point screened by trees from the approaching Britons but with a clear view of the camp below, where the soldiers were apparently working unarmored on the ditch and walls, turning up unsavory debris from what had been the village rubbish heap. From the woods directly below the generals' aerie, they could catch the faint gleam of burnished iron and a quick flash of sunlight on the bronze standards of cohort and century.

Suddenly Longinus narrowed his eyes. "Look there, sir."

A cavalry troop was riding at full gallop up the track from the coast, and as they watched, the horsemen drew rein at the outer ditch, and a man in a centurion's crest slid from his mount as the centurion of the ditch crew heaved himself up out of the half-dug outer lines.

"Get that man up here!" Frontinus snapped. "And it had better be good."

His optio nodded and ran, half sliding down the steep hillside. He didn't suppose it was, though; nobody brought

good news at a dead gallop through hostile country. At
the foot of the hill he slithered to a halt and pulled off his
neck scarf, waving it over his head in the signal code
used on the watchtowers. He hoped to Jupiter someone
saw him. He didn't much want to be caught in the open
when the Britons got there. Yes, a man on the wall had
seen him. He waved back and then ran for the gate where
the cavalry troop was still standing. There was a brief
conference, and someone took up the cavalry pennon and
waved again. The troopers trotted through the open gateway and moved out of sight behind a line of tents while
the lone centurion kicked his horse into a gallop across
the open meadow.

The nearest cohort in the woods watched curiously, and
the commander raised his hand for silence. Then he, too,
narrowed his eyes at the oncoming horseman. There was
something about the way he rode. . . .

Flavius! Correus caught the word back before he called
his brother's name out loud. Flavius rode by without seeing him and dismounted to lead his horse up the steep
hillside after the optio.

"What is it, sir?" his own optio whispered.

"I don't know. That's—a Lindum officer. I . . . don't
know."

A sound cut sharply through the still, hot air, the distant bay of a war horn, and there was the tremor of hoofbeats on the ground.

The men in the trees sank back into shadow, and there
was utter stillness as the leading edge of the Demetae war
host came into view at the end of the long valley which
skirted the wooded hill to join the wide water meadow of
the Tuvius.

"Steady."

The chariots of the Britons thundered by, light, whippy,
wicker things sprung with leather that seemed to have a
life of their own. They were close enough for the hidden
soldiers to see the faces of their drivers, young men
mostly, each with a warrior beside him. The chariots were
brightly painted, and they and the ponies' harnesses were
strung with bronze and enameled bosses and, here and
there, the glint of gold. Knife blades were socketed in the
hubs of the spinning wheels, barely visible as they swept
past. The drivers and their warriors were painted like

fiends from hell, bright daubs of blue and ochre and red clay, and their long hair hung loose behind them, an invitation to each man's enemy to take his head if he could.

"Mithras god," the optio whispered.

Correus shook his head. "See, there aren't so many of them after all," he said as the last chariot swept by, followed by the foot fighters running hard at the ponies' heels. "They're chancing our not being ready."

As the chariots swept across the open meadow, the leisurely work of the ditch crews halted, and there was a scarlet ripple of movement as each man pulled off the outer tunic which had masked his armor. His helmet, shield, and pilum lay neatly stacked at his feet. Behind the line of tents Flavius's cavalry escort swung into formation.

"Might as well make ourselves useful," the decurion grinned.

Frontinus nodded to the trumpeter beside him, and the baying of the war horns was answered by the high sweet notes of the Advance.

"Now!" Each commander spoke to the standard-bearer beside him, and the bulk of the legion poured out from the trees at the war band's rear while the hidden cavalry drove hard out of their own concealment into the left flank.

"We've got 'em!" Correus shouted, excitement rising in his voice. Now he was back to what he knew, back to what he was good for, and the depression of the past days parted like a cloud. Afterward he would be sick, as he always was after a battle, but now was his chance for a fine red revenge on the tribe that had murdered his Freita. He ran with the rest of his legion, with the men of his cohort to either side of him, through what had once been the bean fields of Dun Mori, and the straggling rear of the British warriors stumbled and fell under a rain of flung pilums. In the front, the three cohorts of the ditch crew came out of the ground fully armed like the soldiers sown from dragon's teeth, and the leading edge of the Britons' advance went down in a tangle of screaming horses and broken chariots.

The Britons knew they were trapped, and after that it was only a matter of holding them to kill as many as possible before they could turn and flee.

Correus and his cohort moved in with the rest in relentless slaughter while the air grew heavy with the scent of blood and thick with dust from the furrowed ground. He stabbed with his short sword and moved forward as another man went down, stabbed and moved forward. It was merciless execution of a trapped enemy, but he didn't care. Every man who went down under his sword was the shadow with the knife in the camp at Isca.

The Britons were giving way, pulling back on their right flank where the Roman defenses were least, and Correus moved his men up to try to hold them. Out of the corner of his eye he saw a mounted officer flash by, riding hard for a point on the right. As the Britons spilled out through the only remaining gap, he saw a foot fighter, no more than a boy, shout something at two horsemen mounted on ponies cut loose from a broken chariot, and they wheeled into the Roman rider's path with two more behind them.

"*Flavius!*" This time he shouted it aloud. The Britons were on him, and the boy's knife sank into the horse's belly and the beast and its rider went down together.

Correus began to swing his first century out toward them, but the way was blocked first by a tangle of cavalry and loose horses caught up in their charge, and then by a detachment of Vindex's Tenth Cohort sent up to close the gap. The chance was gone. To move his men now would open up another escape hole for the Britons, and every man let go today could cost someone's life later in the taking. He had a cohort to command, and a position to hold, and for them he was losing his brother as he had lost his wife. The old rivalries didn't matter; Flavius was the other half of himself, a mirror image that was blood of his blood. And he had sworn to their father. . . .

Something in him snapped like an overtaut bow. The battle drew away like a tide going out, leaving a harsh light like a bright mist in its wake. He saw only Flavius's face—his own face, their father's face—lying in the hot grass with a spear through his throat. He didn't see the spear that sang past his right ear, taking the cheekguard of his helmet with it, or the jagged rock buried in the grass that rushed up to meet him as another spear thudded hard into his shield, and he fell.

IV

The Face in the Mirror

THEY FOUND HIM, WHEN THE LAST OF THE BRITONS HAD
fled or been slaughtered, with Octavius, his second-in-
command, still standing over him, dizzy and bleeding
from a wound of his own.

Octavius was hustled off to the hospital tent, and they
were left to puzzle over his commander. There was no visible wound, but he was out cold, so they carried him
back and left him with the walking wounded until the surgeons should have time to deal with him. By that time he
was partly awake and raving.

Silanus took a look at the bruise behind his ear and
snapped out an order to the nearest orderly.

"Get him inside, and don't bounce him around any
more than you can help. And for the gods' sakes get that
lorica off him!"

The orderlies stripped him of his armor and put him
into one of the camp beds set up on the dirt floor of the
hospital tent. The Roman losses had been slight, but there
were always some, and the atmosphere was ghastly with
the smell of blood and vomit and the vinegar and wine
used to wash out wounds or provide the wounded with
courage for what had to be done. Silanus, in a canvas
apron smeared with blood, bent over Correus's cot and
gently touched the bruise behind his ear. There were only
a few drops of blood where the jagged point of the rock
had abraded the skin, but beneath it was an ominous
swelling.

"Damn! I hate head wounds." Correus's eyes flicked
open and then closed again, and Silanus pulled the lids
back to look closely.

"Flavius . . ." It was barely a whisper. "Flavius . . .
Father, I promised . . ." His eyes came open again, and
he tried to sit up. "No! Hold, damn you! We have a line

60

to hold!" They wrestled him back to the cot, and his eyes looked frantically at Silanus. "Hold . . . He's my *brother* . . . steady now, and hold them . . . *Flavius* . . . I can't do both . . ."

Silanus knelt to catch the words which had sunk to a whisper again, and then turned to an orderly. "Get the governor."

"Governor Frontinus?"

"No, you ass, the governor of Egypt. *Move!*"

"I, uh . . . he'll be busy, sir. Won't he?" the orderly asked nervously.

"Yes, I expect he will be," Silanus said with elaborate patience. "Now go and get him."

The orderly departed in search of Frontinus, composing his message in his mind, so as to make it clear to that terrifying man that he was only the unwilling bearer of the request which had originated with the senior surgeon.

The governor, with Domitius Longinus, tracked down inspecting the fortifications that were already beginning to rise again, was predictably testy at the interruption, but when he heard that it was the senior surgeon who was asking, he nodded. "Silanus doesn't get hysterical," he said to Longinus. "I'll be back as quickly as I can. We're going to have to work fast, after what young Julianus told us."

His eyes met the legate's for a moment, and Longinus nodded. He made no comment, but the same thought was in both their minds. *Mutiny.* Each felt a brief wave of horror and compassion for the commanders of that cursed legion and the souls of its executed officers. And each felt a cold hand on his neck at the thought of the slaughter it could spark.

In the hospital tent, he found Silanus working over a cavalry man with a shattered knee. The man's face was white with pain, but his eyes were clouded with the opium Silanus had given him to dull both pain and knowledge. "He'll live," the surgeon said in a low voice, as he led the governor to the other side of the tent. "He may even keep his leg, but he'll never carry a spear in the cavalry again."

The governor sighed. That could be worse than death for a young soldier invalided out with the criminally small pension that the Senate allowed those deemed Unfit-for-Service. *I'm too old for a field command,* he thought sud-

denly. *When this is over I shall go and build waterways.*
Aloud he said, "What do you need, Silanus?"

The surgeon led him to Correus's cot. "I want you to
hear something."

"Good heavens! Julianus! Is he bad?"

"A blow to the head. There's no telling, but I think he'll
make it. But he's raving, and I think you should listen."

Correus had begun to mumble again, his hands pulling
feverishly at the light blanket that covered him. The
words came clearer now, the same ones as before. "Flavius . . . Father, I promised . . ." and then the words of
the Military Oath, the unswerving duty to men and legion that each centurion swore at his commission.

"I don't like this," Frontinus said. "I've been worried
about his stability since his woman died."

"So have I," Silanus said. "Especially since I may have
pushed him over the edge."

"You? You saved his child for him!"

"I weighed him down with one more responsibility—
and it looks to me as if he already had one more than he
could handle."

"Who is Flavius?"

"His brother."

Frontinus drew in a sharp breath, but he kept silent as
the surgeon went on.

"Apparently he saw him go down and couldn't get to
him because he had a line to hold. This might have happened some time back. I'm not sure."

"I am," Frontinus said grimly. "His brother was the
courier who rode in just before things broke loose. I
needed someone to get an order to the right flank, fast, so
I sent him. . . . He was handy. Old Gratus at Lindum
will be after my hide. I think the boy was rather a pet of
his."

"Well, I hope he wasn't carrying anything vital," Silanus said. He paused. "Because I've seen the Dead List,
and he wasn't on it."

"Are you sure?"

"My men have to certify every death, you know that.
This time there weren't many to do, Aesculapius be
thanked, and the Officers' Dead List had one name on it
—a junior from this legion. So if your courier isn't wan-

dering around somewhere on two feet, the Britons have got him."

They searched camp and battlefield foot by foot in the long summer twilight, checked and rechecked the walking wounded and the dead laid out for burial, and found nothing but a wounded Briton under a bush who drew a dagger and killed himself before they could question him. The courier's horse had been found—dead—but Flavius Julianus had come as close to vanishing into thin air as a man could do, and the governor's face went cold when they brought him the news.

When Correus awoke the next morning it was the first thing he saw—cold iron-gray eyes in a face that hadn't slept. Domitius Longinus was with him, his bright, black eyes also clouded with exhaustion, and Aulus Carus, the primus pilus, with a cut on his cheek where he had wrestled, too late, with the British prisoner for the knife. As Correus blinked and looked around him, he realized that he was in his own tent, having been carried from the hospital as he slept over Silanus's furious objections.

"Well, son, how are you?" Frontinus drew up a camp stool and sat.

"Well enough, I think." Correus raised a hand to his head. "It hurts like Hades, but I don't seem to be dreaming any more." He looked at the others. "This is, uh, quite a delegation."

Longinus gave him the ghost of a smile, but Carus's face was expressionless and ashen. He had only heard Flavius's message this morning, and it still had him by the throat. The primus pilus of the Ninth had been one of the two executed officers . . . stoned to death by his own men for the ultimate crime.

"What happened to your brother?" Frontinus asked abruptly.

"Flavius . . ." Correus closed his eyes. "I . . . I saw him go down, sir, not a hundred yards from me. They . . . killed his horse under him." He clenched his teeth for a moment. "I . . . I couldn't get to him."

"So I understand. I'm sorry, son. I sent him into that."

"He was a soldier," Correus whispered. *He was your brother*, his mind said.

"There may be some small comfort for you, but it's an

unpleasant one. I don't think your brother's dead. I'm afraid the Britons have him."

"The Demetae? But they don't take prisoners, sir, just . . . heads." Correus gritted his teeth and swallowed. "Have you . . ."

"Yes, and they didn't. They weren't trying to do anything yesterday but get out of a trap."

"But why? . . ." Correus's head was beginning to pound, and he struggled to focus on the governor's words. They came as if through a fog, the story of the horror at Eburacum, the message which could only be carried in a trusted man's head.

"We assume he was seen," Frontinus said, "and marked out as being important. If the Demetae find out *how* important, this whole province could go up like wildfire."

"Julianus," Domitius Longinus said gently, "would your brother talk?"

"Anyone will talk," Correus said sickly, ". . . eventually."

"There was no insult meant, Centurion, but some men will talk sooner than others. Which sort of a man is your brother?"

"I . . . don't know, sir. I honestly don't know. He's . . . my brother."

"Yes."

"The Demetae aren't strong enough to trouble us, not now . . . but . . . if they give him to Bendigeid . . . someone has to get him out . . . before . . ."

"Yes."

Correus pushed himself up on one elbow and sat on the edge of the cot. "Send me."

Frontinus glanced up at Carus. "Would you be kind enough to ask Silanus to come here?"

Carus nodded and left, and Longinus drew up another stool and sat down beside the governor. They gave him a long look in silence for a moment. "That depends on two things," Longinus said finally.

"Silanus's verdict? I'm all right."

"That wasn't one of them," Frontinus said. "Are you volunteering to save your brother's hide, or for your legion? Which loyalty?"

"Both, sir," Correus said.

"Well, you're going to have to straighten that out if

you're going to stay in the army," Frontinus said, "but I'll accept it as an honest answer."

Correus's head was beginning to clear, and he sat up straighter, shaking his crumpled tunic into place. "Sir, I stand the best chance of anyone. I know the country, and I think I know where the Demetae have gone to earth. And I can pass for one." He never had bothered to shave. There would be no suspicions from anyone who might remember Rhys the trader.

"Yes," the governor said quietly, "you may have to. And that is the other thing. If armed men can't get your brother out, then one man must go in. And I will send you only if you swear."

Odd, Correus thought, how quickly the governor's meaning came clear, as if it were all written out: Go over the Demetae's walls, and kill your brother. He must have known himself from the moment he learned that Flavius was taken and what he carried in his head.

"Well?" Frontinus's face was implacable but not unkind.

Father, I promised. . . . Correus clenched his fists together until the nails bit in and cleared that thought from his mind. The Demetae would kill Flavius . . . eventually. If it was all he could give him, he could give his brother a quicker death than they would. And his father would never forgive him. . . . He pushed that from his mind, also.

"I will swear."

Frontinus watched them ride out, with Silanus frothing at the mouth beside him because it was too soon, much too soon—Correus and two centuries of his Ninth Cohort, mounted and armed to the teeth but in dull brown tunics and with their armor carefully rusted to take out the shine. And their centurion in shirt and breeches and wolf-skin boots, bareheaded in the summer heat.

The camp was finished now to marching camp specifications and officially entered on the survey as Moridunum, a Latinization of Dun Mori, the native village it had erased—turf ramparts with an outer ring of ditch and wall and the sharp spikes of "lilies" blooming in the ditch. Here they would dig in and stay until Julianus and his men came back or until the fire came down from the highlands.

"Will there be anything else, sir?" the optio at his elbow asked.

"Yes," Frontinus said. "I want a courier sent out to Isca on the next tide, and I want Lucius Paulinus, the civilian, back here as fast as he can drag him."

"Will he still be there, sir?"

"Oh, I think so," Frontinus said.

"Governor, how good of you to let me tag along after all." Paulinus advanced with outstretched hand and wary eye. He couldn't imagine why Governor Frontinus had decided to allow him to nose about along his front lines, and he was suspicious by nature. On the other hand, perhaps the campaign was merely going extremely well. Every general liked to be immortalized for his successes.

"I thought you'd be willing to come," Frontinus said dryly. "You must have been perched on the dock at Isca."

Paulinus smiled. "Not exactly. But I must admit I was hoping to find transport, uh, independently."

"You try that," Frontinus said, "and I'll have you sent back with a gag to Rome. I'm well aware of the . . . opportunities Britain offers, and I'm flattered that the emperor trusts me enough to post me here, but I won't tolerate a watchdog yapping at my heels."

Paulinus made a vague soothing gesture. "Well . . . four legions, you know. But I assure you my *History* is quite genuine. Parts of it have been published already. First-hand accounts of major campaigns, written by someone who was *there*, not sitting on his padded backside in his garden at Rome, stealing from military dispatches for his facts."

"Yes, I understand you made a few people reasonably unhappy when your information failed to coincide with their dispatches. You're lucky I let you within a hundred miles of any fighting."

"Yes, sir." Paulinus eyed him curiously. "I'm grateful."

Frontinus glanced around him at the interior of the Principia tent. A flooring of rough planks had been installed, and the desks and records shelves and map tables of a command post were set up. A pair of optios were busy with supply lists, and a cavalry vet was complaining to one over some lack in his stores.

The governor hitched his cloak around his shoulders

and put his helmet with its stiff crest of eagle feathers on his head. "Come along, Paulinus. I'll show you around."

Paulinus followed him without comment, and they strolled out past the legionary standards with the golden Eagle of the legion and the bronze capricorn badge of the Second Augusta in their midst, along the Via Praetoria to the Porta Decumana, the gate opening southward toward the river. In the absence of baths, a group of legionaries was frolicking happily in the shallows, and the cavalry horses were being led to water downstream. Frontinus settled himself on a flat stone in the grass bank that overlooked the river.

Paulinus, still looking thoughtful, dropped down in the grass beside him with his back against the governor's rock. He stretched his thin legs out before him and pulled the rough brown wool of his traveling cloak about them. It was warm again today, but a sea breeze ruffled his sandy hair about his eyes and set the governor's helmet crest to quivering. He looked up over his shoulder at Frontinus.

"Now, sir, perhaps you'll tell me what I can do for you."

"Astute of you," Frontinus said. "I didn't fetch you out of Isca to further your literary career, but I'll trade you a pass to stay with the legion for two months—to be renewed if I see fit—for a piece of information."

"That would, uh, depend on the information, sir," Paulinus said warily. "With due respect."

"One of my most promising officers is showing every sign of beginning to crack. There's more to it than the loss of his wife."

Paulinus swiveled around.

"I want to know the reason," Frontinus finished.

"Correus?"

"What did young Julianus promise his father that concerns his half brother? I'm willing to bet you know."

Paulinus's gray eyes didn't blink. "And what would you do with it, sir, if I told you?" he asked carefully.

"Salvage a good officer, if I can," Frontinus said. "I need Julianus."

Paulinus was silent for a moment, listening to the splash and laughter below and the high thin cries of the shore birds fishing. He wondered if he would be selling Correus for a two-month pass. That promise had been a millstone to both of them from the start, and someone needed to poke his long nose in and tell Appius so. Governor Frontinus might be just the nose to do it. Paulinus decided he was betraying no trust.

"Correus is adopted, sir. I expect you know that. He's the natural son of the old general and a woman of his household. Appius adopted Correus to get him into the Centuriate when it became plain to everyone that that was where he belonged. He and Flavius went in on the same day. It's a bit of a burden to carry, being the great man's son. Rather a lot to live up to, you know."

"That doesn't seem to be young Julianus's problem," Frontinus said.

"No, but it's plagued his brother for most of his life. There's not a thing wrong with Flavius except that he's not the commander his father was or that his brother is, and he knows it. In some ways he's not as strong as Correus, but I suspect he's more resilient. But it's Correus who's the image of the old man."

"So must his brother be," Frontinus said. "The resemblance is striking."

"You've met him? Yes. Correus is a shade taller, and his hair is lighter—that's the Gaul in him. And he's left-handed. But they're still close enough to be twins, and I don't suppose that's helped much, either. Still, it's Correus who has his father's temperament, and as a result his father understands him better. And, I strongly suspect, feels guilty as hell because he loves him better. Old Appius has a terrifyingly strong sense of duty. Correus got his name and enough money to support himself like a gentleman, but Flavius is the heir, and Correus has never been encouraged to step an inch into his place. And the day they went into the Centuriate, my father-in-law took Correus aside, told him that he was the stronger of the two, and made him swear that he'd be there if his brother needed him."

"Damn fool," Frontinus said irritably.

"Yes."

The governor picked up a handful of small stones and began arranging them into a miniature bridge across a dip in the grass.

"I get the impression that you're fond of my brother-in-law," Paulinus said hesitantly.

The governor braced the end of his bridge with a rectangular stone and began to dig something out of the grass bank with his fingers. It was a flint chip, roughly worked to a point at one end. "You find these all over this country. Maybe they were made by the men who lifted the standing stones to the east of here. This is an old country." The governor turned his flint in his hand. "Yes, I am fond of him. Julianus has done some extremely tricky and dangerous work for me. He has an extraordinary talent for learning languages and blending into the landscape."

Paulinus nodded. "I didn't suppose he grew that thatch on his face for his beauty's sake."

"He's going to be everything his father wants him to be," the governor said. "If his father will kindly let him alone."

"Were you thinking of pointing that out?"

"I was."

"How did this come up?"

"His brother was riding courier from Lindum with a message that I am not going to tell you. He rode right into the first skirmish out here, and Julianus saw him go down and couldn't do anything about it. He took a knock on the head himself and went raving for a few hours. I listened."

"Flavius!" Paulinus's head jerked up. "Do you mean to tell me he's been killed?"

"No, but the Britons have got him. And I've sent his brother after him."

Paulinus ran his hands over his face and swallowed, thinking about going back to Isca to tell Julia that they were gone, both of them. . . . "Sir, what—"

The governor dusted his hands on the grass. "I am fairly certain that Correus will be back. But he may not be able to bring his brother with him. And that is why I wanted to know what he promised their father." He sat there for a long time on his stone on the grass verge while the curlews wheeled and cried overhead, and Paulinus walked slowly back to the tent that had been allotted him in Moridunum.

In the tent Paulinus sat on the camp bed and stared blankly at the leather walls, squares of smooth hide stitched together and dyed red. An officer's tent. There was a clothes chest and a folding camp desk that looked as if it had been hastily scrounged from elsewhere and he would, the governor had informed him, dine in the officers' mess. It was plain that the governor was not going to tell him what message Flavius had carried, but it was equally plain by the unhurried demeanor of the camp that here they would stay until Correus's men came back. Paulinus wrestled that around in his mind for a while and gave up. There were several possibilities, and matters would no doubt explain themselves in time. But he was glad he had left Tullius in Isca with Julia and Correus's baby. Tullius would have sense enough to hustle them onto a ship if all hell broke loose.

He reached into his baggage and dragged out the bound, blank sheets of his private journal. Conversing with himself on paper seemed preferable to staring at an empty tent and wondering if his friend were coming back.

. . . So Correus has gone off into wolf country with two centuries of men to fetch his brother out, and I didn't need to be told what his alternative is. May Mithras watch over them both. Not my god, Mithras, but those two seem to have found something in his worship to look to. Correus tried to persuade me to come to the ritual once, with talk of the path of truth and honor and the brotherhood of men; I replied that that left me wholly unsuited as a devotee on all counts and he laughed, but I wasn't entirely joking. This new god is too personal a deity for me, I think. I prefer to make my respects to the Thunderer in the time-honored fashion. One knows what to expect of the old gods of Rome—and what not to. This Persian god wants a place in the heart that I'm not sure I'm prepared to give. Still, may he put his hand over these two, who *have* given it.

This is my first visit to Britain, and I find it endlessly fascinating. Rome has been collecting tribute here since Julius Caesar's day, of course, albeit sporadically, but it wasn't until the emperor Claudius decided to bring it into the empire that we really had any knowledge of the land. The changes in the thirty years since then are astonishing. We are a nation of builders. When we come onto new ground, we raise a Roman city on it and thus say, "This is ours."

Londinium, destroyed in a tribal war and rebuilt only fifteen years ago, might be any city in Italy, except for the weather. The same can be said of Camulodunum and Verulamium, and all the Down Country of the south is beginning to take on a Roman look—Roman houses, Roman temples, and a native people growing Roman. And then to the north and west, suddenly the wild lands—high hill country with native fortifications guarding the passes, and tribe fighting tribe as often as not, but above all a wild feel in the air of being on the far edge of the world. And beyond that, who knows? The Pict lands, to start, the Painted People—all the Britons tattoo themselves, but the Picts do it from head to toe, which must be very strange and beautiful, although it is said that even the Britons of these parts consider the Pict a barbarian and not, perhaps, quite human. I don't know what the Picti worship, and suspect I wouldn't care to be introduced, but the southern Britons worship much the same gods as the Gauls, and, like the Gauls and Germans, they are a horse people. They worship Earth Mother in several of her infinite forms and a sun god whose festival marks the ripening of the crops at midsummer.

There is a Lady of the Horses called Epona, whose shrines may be found all over, and innumerable local deities, many of them Earth Mother or Lugh (their sun god) in tribal personification. The Underworld they see as a shining land of the perpetually young, somewhere in the west across the sea. Or alternatively as a realm beneath the earth to which entrance may be gained in certain spots. They make much of their dead and frequently lay them in graves with half their earthly riches, believing that at year's end they may come back through the gates of the sidhe—the hollow hills—and walk in their old haunts again. There are innumerable heroes and half gods, water sprites and prophesying heads, and a priestly class (outlawed by Rome in theory if not in fact) who claim descent from the legendary Old Ones who built the great stone rings with which the land is dotted.

It rains here. Even in summer it rains, especially in

the highlands of the west and north, and the water gets into our boots and bedding and supplies and drips down the backs of our necks; and in the winter, I am told, all foreigners have a perpetual cold.

It began to rain, even as he wrote, a warm summer rainfall that soaked quickly into the meadows—enough to wet the grasses, no more.

Enough to soak Correus's unhappy legionaries, grumblingly making their way into the hill country. They had been pleased enough at first to ride instead of walk, but they were foot soldiers, used to the steady twenty-mile-a-day pace of the legions, and they found speedily that while a horse gave more speed and was easier on the feet, for a man not used to the saddle it was no pleasure.

"If he wanted a damned cavalry, why didn't he take the damned cavalry?" a legionary grumbled, shifting his weight in the saddle. They had slowed to a trot as the way grew rougher, and he found it more painful than the cavalry canter they had maintained earlier.

"Commander took us cause we're his," the man beside him said. "It'll be tricky enough where we're going, I'm thinking, without the commander depending on some fool cavalry troop he's never seen before."

"Then they shoulda sent a friggin' cavalry *commander*," the first man said. "I joined up with the legions, not the friggin' auxiliaries."

"Aw, use your head. The commander practically turns into one o' them heathen Britons under your nose, and that's what's wanted where we're goin', I reckon. Or did you figure we'd just charge the Demetae straight on, all two centuries of us?"

"Tighten up there, if you please. And pipe down. This isn't a public meeting." The centurion of the third century went by at a canter and drew rein beside Correus just ahead.

"No sign of the enemy, sir." The junior centurion tapped his lorica lightly with his knuckles in salute. The rain dripped off his helmet rim, and he ignored it stoically.

"Very well, Centurion." Correus's face was muffled in the hood of a brown-and-blue cloak of native weave, and Centurion Aquila watched him curiously.

This was the first time he had served as second-in-command to Centurion Julianus, but Octavius was still in hospital with a healing cut in his sword arm, and so the commander, who wanted a reliable second, had elected to take the third century with the first, which came under his direct command. Aquila, a Neapolitan landowner's son who had done his Centuriate training only a year behind Correus, was gratified by the selection and prayed fervently that it might soon augur a cohort command of his own.

"There's just one thing, sir," he said hesitantly. "We'll have to rest them soon, or none of our apprentice cavalry will be able to walk in the morning."

Correus smiled, an expression halfway between amusement and—something. Although Aquila didn't know what mightily important piece of information the missing courier had been carrying in his head, he knew well enough why they were riding with rusted armor and dun-colored tunics into the Demetae's hills, and he wouldn't have stood in his commander's sandals just now for double his pay.

Correus squinted ahead through the falling rain and the gray green air and pointed to an outcrop of rock with a grove of trees below it that would give some shelter and readily available grass beyond. "Halt them there, and let them get out of the wet. I don't care if their backsides are sore or not, but I can't afford to have them hacking and coughing like a lung ward."

Aquila raised his vine staff to the horsemen behind him and pointed, and they quickened their pace gratefully. They would have only to tether their horses and pitch their tents, a welcome relief from routine. They would post double pickets that night, but there would be no Roman earthworks to mark where they'd slept.

At his desk, Governor Frontinus also sat listening to the rain tapping on the scarlet-dyed leathers of his tent. It would blur the Demetae's trail, he thought. He hoped Centurion Julianus really did know where they were laired. A fruitless speculation, since if Julianus didn't know, neither did anyone else. He also hoped Julianus didn't keel over halfway there from that head wound, as Silanus had grimly predicted. He sighed and began to read over the sheet of papyrus that lay drying on the desk before him:

To Flavius Appius Julianus, from Sextus Julius Frontinus, military governor, Province of Britain . . .

. . . It has come to my knowledge through no fault of your son's that he has bound himself with some sort of vow, always a dangerous thing for a senior officer who may find his vows at odds with his duty. . . . With respect, sir, a damn fool thing to do, and I can only warn you, you may lose *both* your sons by it. I can only suggest that you propitiate whatever gods are necessary, if any were invoked, and release your son from his debt at the earliest possible time. . . . Of course this is a private matter. This letter comes, through the hands of no secretary, from Sextus Julius Frontinus, etc. . . .

"That ought to stir up his temper," Frontinus said with satisfaction. "But I expect he'll listen." Appius Julianus had been a career soldier himself, and there were several points with respect to that profession that ought to fly home. The governor folded the papyrus sheet and put a stick of purple wax in the lamp flame. He rolled it carefully on the fold and pushed his seal into it.

Frontinus rose to call an optio and then sat back down again thoughtfully. He put the letter in a cubbyhole in the desk. Time enough to post it when Julianus and his brother both came back alive.

V

Carn Goch

THE SKY WAS FULL OF A WAXING MOON, AND IN TWO days it would be Lughnasadh, the night of the Midsummer Fires. A double line of horsemen trotted up the track like ghosts, silent under the moon. They rode by night now, bridle rings muffled with strips of rag. Correus wished for the thousandth time that he could have had his borrowed troop horses' shoes pulled, but it would likely only have

made their feet sore. Instead their hooves were wrapped in makeshift boots of cloth which had a maddening tendency to slip when the horses weren't trying to kick them off, but it helped to obscure their path. The Demetae as a rule didn't shoe their ponies.

They halted for a brief rest, and Correus studied the sky and the moonlit hills and tried to remember a way traveled months ago by daylight. The rain had washed out most of the trail they followed, and he was no more than a passable tracker. But he was almost sure now where the survivors of the fight at Moridunum had made for—Carn Goch, the Place of Red Stone, still northeastward by a day's ride.

He had passed that way in early summer and had seen it—a dry stone wall guarding what he had guessed to be some twenty-five acres along a ridge top lying between the Tuvius and the small lake that was the headwaters of the Isca River. It was built for warfare—not a village, but a place of refuge for the Demetae villages that lay along the edge of the Silures' western hunting runs and were most vulnerable to Silure raids. With the chieftain's hall at Dun Mori razed, it was to Carn Goch that the Demetae would go now for refuge from the Romans.

There was a scuffling and a spate of raised voices behind him, and Correus swung round in the saddle with fire in his eye to see who had broken silence.

"I ought to have you crucified," Centurion Aquila hissed, his hand clenched tightly on a legionary's collar.

"Sorry, sir, but you ought to see what's in those trees." The legionary gestured to a stand of oaks some fifty paces away. They had halted well into a wood for cover. "Well, look then," he said grudgingly as Aquila glared at him. "I was goin' to show you anyway." The legionary fished in his cloak and drew out a small, shallow bowl that shone gold in the moonlight. "Pure gold, that is. And more to be found, like as not." The men around him murmured and pushed close.

"Give me that!" Correus's voice snapped from beside and above him, and the legionary jumped.

"Aw, now, sir, I found it."

"Give me that or I'll leave you here for its owner to deal with." Correus held out his hand and felt the skin on the back of his neck prickle as he took the bowl. There was something dark and sticky at the bottom. "All right—" Correus peered at his face. "Porcus, is it? Now strip."

"What?"

"Down to your tunic. We may be watched, and you're going to make amends. That bowl is an offering. How long have you been in Britain, you fool, that you don't know better than to steal from an oak grove?"

"But strip, sir?" Porcus wailed, seeing both his prize and his dignity vanish as his fellows began to snicker.

"An oak grove is holy. You don't take iron into it."

"You don't believe in that heathen trash, sir?" another man said, as the unfortunate Porcus began to unbuckle his lorica.

"I believe in whoever put that bowl there, that this ass was fool enough to take," Correus said. "One more word out of anyone, and I'll leave him in that grove to test his theories."

Porcus's companion subsided under Aquila's raised hand as Correus dismounted and handed his sword belt and dagger to Aquila. "Hang onto that," he said. He ran his hands over his clothing quickly, thinking, but could remember no other iron. His cloak pin was bronze and amber, and the bracelets pushed high up on his arms were enamel and copper. "All right, you." He took Porcus by the collarbone, much as Aquila had held him, and marched him into the grove. The flat gold bowl felt hot to the touch, but it might have been imagination only.

The grove had a small clearing at the center where a single tree had been cut down and its stump left to form a rude altar. Correus knelt down before it, having no idea what ritual should be invoked, but he knew without question whose altar it was. Groves belonged to the Mother-of-All in her darker forms, whereas the hilltops and places of light were Lugh's.

He set the bowl on the altar and saw that it, too, was dark with old blood. "This is where you found it?"

Porcus nodded. "Sir—"

"Shut up!" There was another presence in the grove with them, and Correus knew without looking that it was Nighthawk's people. And that they would not be seen if he *did* look. Perhaps they would take the offering as it was meant and not waste their time telling the Demetae of the Romans in their wood. Nighthawk had implied that it was all one to them. He pulled his cloak pin free and jabbed the end of it hard into his thumb, gritting his teeth as it drew blood. It was not particularly sharp, and there was a bent place at the end where he had used it to punch a new hole in a packsaddle strap.

"Your turn." He handed the pin to Porcus who looked at it and winced.

"Draw blood, or I'll do it for you," Correus threatened. He held his own thumb above the bowl and squeezed a few drops out with the fingers of his other hand.

Porcus gave him a black look, but when Correus reached for the cloak pin, he obeyed. "*Ow!* Typhon, that hurts!" He started to suck his thumb, but Correus grabbed it and held it over the bowl, squeezing the dark blood into a little pool at the bottom.

"Be glad it's just your thumb," he hissed. His head was beginning to ache, and he ran his right hand over his forehead, still holding Porcus's wrist with his left.

"These gods are forbidden anyway," Porcus grumbled. "What's a gold pot more or less?"

"The Druid priests are forbidden because they stir up trouble," Correus said with as much patience as he could muster. "Rome has never forbidden anyone's gods. And it never pays to insult the Mother. But in this case I'm more concerned about her followers. If they decide you've committed a sacrilege, they may jump us, and then the rest of our men will have to come and get us out, and after that you might just as well send a message to the Demetae straight, saying, 'Look out, here we come.' Use your head. Damn! Mine aches like fire." He put his hand to his forehead again. More and more he felt something wrong in this place. He gave Porcus a shove. "Go on, get out of here. I'll be right behind you."

He turned back to lay a silver denarius on the altar. It would give him great pleasure to take that out of Porcus's pay. As he bent to place it beside the bowl, he could hardly bear to get his hand so close, and the prickling sensation on the back of his neck intensified. He had strayed into a grove of the Mother once before, in Germany, when Flavius had been hurt in a hunting accident, and he and Paulinus had been searching desperately for the shortest trail back to the camp. He had felt the same way then, with Flavius sitting bleeding in the saddle before him. He wasn't sure if it was the Dark Mother herself, or the unwanted bond that tied him to Flavius, or both, but with those unseen eyes on his back, it was all he could do not to run as he left the grove. When he reached his men, he mounted and put them onto the trail at a trot.

"There it is."

Carn Goch lay along the ridge top, its red stone walls silvered in the moonlight. A faint glow above them gave evidence of lit fires inside, and the sounds of human habitation came across the still air to where the Romans lay hidden in a screen of trees below the ridge—the murmur of voices and, once, the muffled whinny of a horse. The legionaries slapped their hands to their ponies' noses lest one of them whinny in answer. They listened in silence for a moment, broken only by the faint *hoo-hoo* of an owl (Correus hoped it was an owl) and the sound of a vixen calling to her mate across the hillside.

They had spent the day hidden in a thicket where they had forded the Tuvius, and then at nightfall had begun their cautious approach.

"If we sat out one more day, it would be Midsummer Night," Aquila whispered. "We might stand a better chance with a feast going on. And folk coming and going, I expect."

"I don't dare," Correus said. "One more day might be too late. Any man will talk sometime." His voice was deliberately cool, but Aquila could tell he spoke through gritted teeth, and he eyed his commander admiringly. By the time they had set out, rumor had already gone round the camp that the missing courier was half brother to their centurion.

"Do you think he's still there at all, sir?" Aquila whispered back. "Could they have sent him to Bendigeid?" There was no point in mincing words.

"They haven't had time. And I think they'll make Bendigeid come to them—they need his war band. That's one reason they're camped here. It's the closest holding to Bendigeid's lands. In fact, it's a defensive position, built to hold out against Silure cattle raids. But they'll open up the gates to them now fast enough. That's another reason I can't wait. I haven't the men to fight Bendigeid."

"Right." Aquila's hands were clenched tightly on the riding crop he carried in place of his vine staff. "Then let's get on with it, sir." He laid a hand lightly on the shoulder of the man behind him. "Send Cornelius up here to the commander."

There was a murmur in the silence, and then a third man slipped up beside them. He also wore native garb now, and there was a dagger in his hand. The moonlight slid bluely along the blade. "Ready when you are, sir."

Correus nodded, and the two of them slipped out of the trees into the low scrub that covered the slope below Carn Goch.

Aquila watched them without reaction, knowing that the men were watching him, but his stomach twisted suddenly into a knot. If the centurion were killed, Aquila would have his command, at least for as long as it took to do what the commander had been sent to do. He didn't want it. Not at that price.

*   *   *

Flavius awoke, for the seventh or eighth time—he had lost count—and shifted his weight to ease the screaming pain in his back. His hands were still tied behind him around the post, which seemed to be the central support of a round, mud-walled hut, and he could lie down only by arching his back around the base of the post. It bit into his lower spine until an hour's sleep in that position was enough to wake him screaming. He was dimly aware of lying in his own filth, but the shame of that had long since passed. He struggled to a sitting position. In another hour or so the pain of that also would become unbearable, and he would lie down again. If the Britons hadn't come back.

Flavius forced himself to open his eyes and look round the mud walls, tracing each crack from end to end and counting the stars that could be seen through the half circle that was all his view allowed of the smoke hole in the roof. It was an exercise he had devised to fight down fear and pain and the gnawing hunger in his belly. They had fed him only enough to keep him alive, and he had vomited up most of that when the questioning began. His face was streaked with blood, and there was blood on his undertunic, which was the only garment they had left him. They had not done anything to permanently disable him —perhaps they would trade him back to the governor in the end—but the memory of pain almost beyond bearing rose in his mind, and his stomach heaved. He knew that if he looked at his left hand, he would see only four fingers on it.

Almost beyond bearing, he thought dully. The Britons had given him that much—the measure of his own courage, and it had proved greater than he had thought. He would have liked to have told his father that. . . . The room began to blur, and Flavius tried to force the mists from his mind. The time for comfort found in oblivion had passed. *Almost beyond bearing* . . . the key was in those words. Every man had a brink beyond which he could not go, he thought. His had proved to be a greater distance than he had thought, but he would come to it eventually. Eventually he would go mad, and his mind would no longer control his tongue, and when the Britons came with their knives he would tell them what they asked.

They would be back soon. . . . He tried to think how

long it had been since they had gone but could remember only their faces, dark faces with wild patterns pricked into the skin and rubbed with some blue dye. . . . One with a wolf-skin cloak and a gold torque around his throat had stood silent, unmoving, leaning on a spear, while the others . . . It had been daylight then, he thought. They had made a fire and held his hand in it to cauterize the wound when they had cut his finger off. They didn't want him to bleed to death. The fire was still burning.

He wasn't even sure what tribe they were. Demetae, perhaps. There had been another man, outside the hut, loudly demanding entrance, and the chieftain had pulled the door flap down in his face. From something he had said, he might have been Silure. Flavius spoke some British, learned as his brother's had been, from his father's horse master, but he had never had Correus's easy tongue with a new language. In any case, it didn't matter now . . . not whether the man at the door had been Silure, or why the chieftain had shut it in his face. The enemy now was himself, and time, and there was only one weapon against that. He could stand anything one more time, if he knew it would be the last.

The door flap was pulled back, and the Britons stepped through, grinning like foxes. Flavius saw them only as dim outlines in the fire and smoke. It was the knife blade that glowed as clear and certain as an open doorway.

The man came out of the shadows almost at the tribesman's feet, and the Briton swung round with a leveled spear.

"Friend! Friend!" the other man said hastily. His hooded cloak was drawn around his face, and the man with the spear stepped closer.

"No one's allowed out after nightfall. Where did you spring from?"

"And no one drives a chariot with one damn horse," the hooded man said irritably. "I thought he'd come in with the rest, but he's gone missing again somehow."

"Then you had best know the watchword," the spearman said. "Give it quick."

"No one gave it to *me,*" said the man who was looking for his horse. "How was I to know? How many more of you are there out here, anyway? You're lucky I didn't knife *you*, springing up in the dark like that!" Where was Cornelius? The man in the hood forced himself not to look over the spearman's shoulder.

"Four," the spearman said, and then tried to bite back the word. His eyes narrowed. "I don't know you. Get that hood off quick!"

The other man raised his hands slowly to his face. The sentry would give the alarm in a moment, and his knife was still in his belt. "And why should you know me?" he inquired sarcastically. "Are you knowing every face in the—"

A shadow moved behind the sentry, and the man's eyes flew open wide. He sank to the grass with a moan, and the hooded man dived and drew his knife across his throat.

"Drag him under a bush." Correus let out a long breath and wiped his knife in the wet grass. "Where in Typhon were you? He was ready to yell and raise the whole hive of them."

Cornelius knelt and cleaned his own knife. "I met another of them."

"Mithras. Did you—"

"Yes, but he almost had me. He knew I was a wrong 'un right off. I told you I couldn't talk the language."

"I didn't expect you to have to," Correus said, getting his breath back. "It's your knife I need." There were rumors about Cornelius, including the unlikely one that held that he had been a professional assassin before he had signed on with the legion one jump ahead of a death sentence. But he was undeniably good with a knife.

"This 'un said four more, the poor fool." Cornelius gave a glance of vague pity at the body that he had rolled into the shadow of a hawthorn bush. "D'you suppose it was truth, sir?"

"I think so," Correus said. "We've been the whole length this side. Two for the main gate, and one each at the posterns. Plenty to raise the alarm if they spot a force moving in. They won't be expecting us, not this way." He gave Cornelius a twisted smile. "It isn't Roman."

"Fools, then," Cornelius said again. "Anything's Roman that wins a war."

"All right then. Bring them up." He squatted in the hawthorn's shadow until he heard a whisper of sound go by and saw moving shadows fan themselves out and drop down just below the ridge crest. Where the dry stone wall crossed flat ground at the top it was greatly thickened, and a strong timber gate was set between the stones. It would have to be unbarred somehow. He looked up to find Cornelius standing beside him again. Three legionaries in dulled armor with blackened legs and faces waited behind him. Two carried unlit torches in their hands, and the third, a shielded pot of coals.

Correus nodded, and they followed him wordlessly up the last sloping ground to the wall. The scrub here had been cleared, and they paused at its edge for a moment, then took the distance at a run, flinging themselves flat against the rough stone. *They ought to have ditched it,* he found himself thinking. *A single wall's no defense.* The gods be thanked they hadn't.

He stuck the torches through his belt and began to feel for a toehold in the stone as Cornelius tied the pot into a sling with his cloak and hung it across his chest. The wall was high but not as smooth-faced as it should have been, and Correus clung to the outer face at the top long enough to put his head up with caution. He had been right. One of the two rectangular buildings that Carn Goch enclosed was below him, with a few feet of empty space behind it. He pulled himself to the top and rolled quickly to the wall's edge and dropped. A moment later Cornelius came down beside him. He took the pot from his cloak and set it on the ground with relief.

"Bastard's hot."

Correus jerked with his hand for silence and stood with his ear to the timber wall beside him. The faint sound of shifting hooves and the snort of a pony came through it. The door would be on the other side. Beyond this building was a second, but judging by the number of open fires they had seen from the wall, most of the men in Carn Goch were sleeping in the open. It was not a settlement meant to live in, but a holding pen for cattle, women and children, and household goods, while their warriors met the enemy in the open. Between times, only a handful would live here, most likely in the third building that Carn Goch afforded—a circular hut, which was the usual form of dwelling in these hills. For now it would house the chieftain perhaps, or . . . There had been no sign of movement to be seen from the walls among the fires of Carn Goch, but Correus had seen the door flap of the hut swing open. He slipped to the end of the ponies' shed, with Cornelius padding silently behind him.

"How're you gonna find him in all o' this?" Cornelius whispered.

"I think I know," Correus said. "Sit tight, and keep that light under your cloak." He stepped from the shadow of the shed and strolled as if on some errand in the direction of the hut, while Cornelius watched him admiringly. He could generally tell a man who'd been drilled—it got into his walk and his backbone and stuck there like a signboard, but the commander seemed to be able to slip it off with his uniform. A talent, that.

Correus moved quickly with the hood across his face, all too aware that by torchlight he would be marked for a spy. The Demetae warriors would be tattooed as the assassin at Isca had been. Rhys the trader of course belonged to no tribe, and his bare face had not been questioned, but Rhys had no more business in Carn Goch by night than Centurion Julianus.

Most of the men were asleep by their fires, rolled in cloaks, but a few sat wakefully talking, and one was throwing knucklebones with himself, left hand against the right, by a fire that burned directly in Correus's path. Somewhere across the open ground another man was singing, and Correus shifted his path out of the way of the fire, as if making for that camp. There were always wakeful souls to gather when a harper began to sing, and the man with the knucklebones didn't bother to look up as he passed. There were no fires near the hut, and Correus was grateful for the darkness. There were clouds in the night sky, and if one would obligingly run itself across the moon, he could get closer.

And then, across the harper's lifted voice and the growing murmur of talk inside the hut, there was a scream: a harsh, tearing sound like an animal in a trap that went on and on. And no one moved. The man with the knucklebones looked up briefly and shrugged his shoulders, and even the harper didn't pause in his music. Only in the second building, beyond the pony shed, did someone flinch and try to shut out the sound, but she was a child and her terrors unimportant.

In the darkness outside the hut Correus, sick to his stomach, turned and moved blindly back the way he had come. At the pony shed he found Cornelius waiting for him, his face green in the moonlight.

"Was that—?"

Correus nodded. He picked up a torch and jammed it into the coals. It flared into sudden light, and he threw it viciously onto the thatched roof of the pony shed. "Come on!"

The hall beyond the pony shed was of the same open rectangular construction, meant to pen cattle or store goods or give temporary shelter in foul weather. Now it housed the chieftain of the Demetae and his three sons and the scarred, gray-haired man who was envoy from the Silures. The chieftain had gone to put the Roman to the question again, and his sons, finding the envoy in foul temper, had prudently withdrawn as well.

At one end the chieftain's ponies were penned, with his silver-mounted chariot and a haphazard stock of grain sacks and such goods as Llywarch had had time to snatch up from the guest hall at Dun Mori when the Romans came. Now he sat glaring at his surroundings at the other end, while the girl lay huddled in a cloak on a bed of straw beside him. She had begun to whimper in terror when the screams began again, but she was of little matter to anyone, save for her actual physical presence, and neither the chieftain's sons nor her kinsman had seen fit to offer comfort. Now she lay still, her mouth compressed tightly, and her cloak pulled about her ears.

The horrible screams went on and on, and Ygerna wriggled deeper into the cloak. It was no good asking Llywarch what it was; she knew that well enough: They were torturing the Roman they had caught, whom Gruffyd of the Demetae thought knew something important, and Llywarch was in a temper already because they wouldn't allow him entrance. Maybe he would be angry enough to take her away again. Ygerna had been promised to so many men before, beginning when she was not yet old enough to marry, that she was almost used to it. This time it was Gruffyd's eldest son, a boy some three years older than she was who accorded her less interest than he would a hound puppy. But this time she was thirteen, and it might actually happen.

The screaming stopped, and she raised her head a little. She was hungry, but no one had thought to bring her any food since that morning, with the confusion of trying to house a whole war band in a holding meant only to pen cattle, and Llywarch either quarreling with Gruffyd or prowling about Carn Goch on some quest of his own when Gruffyd's back was turned. The screams did not start again, and she sat up and brushed the straw from her hair. There was a low rumble of voices from outside. Maybe Gruffyd was coming back and would bring food. The rumble turned to shouts, and then a more terrifying sound—the faint crackle of fire.

"Llywarch!" She grabbed his arm and screamed. Above them the roof thatch was in flames.

The pony shed was blazing like a beacon, and the second building was halfway alight.

"The gate!" Correus shouted, and Cornelius threw down his torch and ran. Correus wrenched at the doors of the pony shed as the screams of horses rose from inside. The burning thatch was beginning to drop down onto the straw on the floor, and Correus pulled his knife and began to cut the ropes that penned the ponies in at one end. There were men beside him now, doing the same, and he hastily wiped a sooty hand across his face. How long, he wondered, until they realized the fire was torch-set?

A pony screamed and reared, and Correus brought his hand down hard on its rump so that it plunged past him into the men coming in behind. He flattened himself against the wall as more animals went by him, kicking and biting each other in their fear. A piece of burning thatch dropped down and set one pony's tail alight, and it reared in terror and trampled a man beneath it.

At the opposite end of the shed they were trying to drag the chariots free. Correus caught up a piece of blazing board and waved it above his head. The ponies poured through the doorway into the open, and Correus flung the board among the chariot wheels. Their wicker cars would burn like tinder once they caught.

Outside he could hear the sounds of chaos—the screams of men and horses and a sharp cry of warning as the roof began to come down. And beyond that the clear note of a bugle call.

The chariots were ablaze now, and the men in the pony shed began to fight their way through the smoke as the building went up around them. It burned like a bonfire, and the nightmare smell of singed flesh hung in the air. Correus flung another brand among the chariots for good measure, and someone caught him by the shoulder and spun him around. Correus drew his knife as he turned and drove it into the man's breast. He fell forward into the chariots, and the roofbeam came down on top of him. Correus dived through the inferno that masked the door and rolled as he hit the ground outside, smothering the flames in the dirt. To his left the second shed was going up.

"Romans!" someone shouted, and he pulled himself up and ran.

The main gates of Carn Goch stood open, and half the Roman soldiers were stampeding ponies through the gap, while the rest fought their way forward toward the fires. Cattle had broken loose from somewhere. They ran lowing and wild-eyed through the camps, and the soldiers began stampeding them, too. The Britons were trying to fight back, but most of them had been asleep when the fires broke out and didn't know who or what they were fighting.

Correus saw Aquila at the head of his men, looking like something out of the fire himself with his blackened face and armor, and plunged toward him screaming "Roma!" as he went.

Aquila saw him and a bugle call sang out, and the third century came up around him. He saw that Cornelius was with them, his cloak pulled well back from his face so he wouldn't get killed by his own side.

"The hut!" Correus screamed, and they turned and ran for it. The sky was aglow, and the Britons had given up trying to put out the fires in the sheds. There was no water source in Carn Goch, and what they stored in barrels wouldn't have bought so much as a break in the flames. They left it to burn itself out and turned on the invaders.

Aquila's men ringed the hut, and Correus dived through the door flap with Aquila behind him. Gruffyd and his warriors were gone, out somewhere fighting the Romans or the fire, and Flavius was alone, a contorted figure chained at the waist to the central post of the hut. There was a lit fire in the hearth, and by its light and the orange glow from the doorway Correus could see why they had not bothered to tie his hands again. The fourth finger was missing from each.

". . . oh gods," Aquila said sickly and made a retching sound.

Correus knelt beside Flavius and felt frantically for a heartbeat. His face was almost unrecognizable with blood and bruises, and his lips were cracked and bleeding. Above the stench in the hut Correus caught the faint smell of burned flesh again and then saw why; they had put the amputated stumps into the fire to seal it.

Flavius's eyes came halfway open as Correus touched him. "Knife . . ." he whispered. "Leave me . . . the knife." There was a warning shout outside, and Aquila spun toward the open doorway.

"Hurry, sir," Aquila said over his shoulder. The sounds of fighting outside had intensified as Gruffyd's warriors realized what was happening.

Correus wrenched at the chain that bound the prisoner to the post and saw that it was fastened with an iron lock. He took his knife and tried to pry the links apart, but the blade bent in his hand. He drew his sword and began to hack at them desperately.

The hut was growing hotter, and Flavius opened his eyes again. "Burn . . ." he whispered.

"Fire!" Aquila shouted, and Correus heard the crackle of flame. Someone had flung a torch over the Romans' heads and set the sloping thatch of the hut roof alight. Correus hacked at the iron links, and his sword snapped in his hand, halfway up the blade. Aquila and two others had torn their cloaks off and were trying to smother the flames, but the roof was too high, and in a moment it was blazing like the pony shed. Flavius lay still, watching it burn. "They wouldn't . . . kill me. I tried. . . . Burn . . . and do it . . . for them. . . ."

"Damn you!" Correus shouted. "You're not going to burn!" He dug frantically at the links with the broken hilt end of the blade and felt one give. A burning twist of straw dropped down onto Flavius's body, and Correus flung it away and wrenched at the chain. "Move! Damn you, help me!"

Flavius seemed to recognize him for the first time. As Correus screamed at him, he rolled to one side, and Correus wrapped the chain around the post and pulled. The weak link opened a little more.

"Get out, sir, it's coming down," Aquila shouted.

Correus jammed the thick hilt end of his sword in the open link and twisted it, prying the ends apart. He wrenched the next link through the opening and flung the two ends away from him.

"I've got it!" They pulled Flavius to his feet and through the doorway as the roof crashed in behind them.

Outside, his men had formed a wall between the hut and the avenging Britons. Correus could see their locked shields in the flames that gave the scene a red, unearthly glow, while the Britons howled and hammered at their flanks, striving to push them back against the fire. They held like a rock, and Correus's pride in them welled up even as he realized that the whole force of Carn Goch was turned on them now, and soon the wall would break.

"Fall back!" he shouted.

Cornelius came up from the chaos and took Aquila's place. "I'll help the commander!" he yelled above the tumult. "We need you to get us out o' here! That line's gonna go!"

Aquila lunged into the press of bodies, and soon the locked wall of shields began to fall back, splitting around the burning hut, enclosing Correus and Cornelius with their burden in their midst, while the Britons came after them. Slowly they drove the Roman lines back on the men behind them, but the first century had kept a corridor open to the gate, and they parted to let the retreating soldiers through, then closed ranks around them. The Roman soldiers had long since flung their pilums into the pursuing host of the Britons, which grew by the minute as the warriors in Carn Goch stumbled through the wreckage to converge on the Romans. The Romans were stabbing with short swords now at any warrior who ventured too close, and the front ranks of shields were splintered or weighed down with half-embedded spears. Spears were beginning to fly over their heads into the press of stumbling men, and someone moved up beside Correus and Cornelius and flung his shield above their heads.

"Get your shield up!" Flavius shouted. "I can walk!"

"I don't have a shield!" Correus shouted back. "Lean on me, damn it, or you'll fall!"

They were at the gateway now, and the retreat slowed and bottlenecked as the center stumbled through and the Britons pressed the flanks backward against the stone wall.

"Hold formation! Hold!" Correus heard Aquila's voice ring out above the noise, and slowly the flanks began to right themselves, fanning out in a semicircle of locked shields that fell backward like a funnel through the gates. They were clear of the gate now, and Flavius was stumbling beside him as they ran.

"Here, sir!" Someone pushed a bridle into his hands, and he turned to Flavius. "Can you ride?"

Flavius nodded. "Help me up." Correus put his hands around his brother's waist and lifted, and Flavius jumped and flung himself across the saddle. He slipped and cried out as he caught at the saddle with his mutilated hands, but in a moment he was upright in the saddle and reaching for the reins.

"Better let me lead him, sir."

Flavius shook his head. "Just . . . knot them for me."

The legionary hesitated, and Correus nodded. "Do as he says." Flavius could ride any horse Poseidon had ever put breath in, with or without his hands. The legionary knotted the reins and tossed them over the horse's neck, and Flavius put his heels to its flank.

Correus caught the horns of his own saddle and swung up as the last of his men poured through the gateway of Carn Goch. The rear guard had brought the horses up as soon as the gates had first opened and were waiting now, bridles in hand. The fleeing soldiers mounted and wheeled them in their tracks as the Britons raced after them and a fall of thrown spears rained down on their heels.

They set their horses' heads to the slopes below Carn Goch and, as they hit the level ground, kicked them into a gallop. The Demetae chariots were in flames, but their horses could be caught and ridden, and the Romans numbered only a hundred and sixty.

Less now, Correus thought, seeing a riderless horse with

Roman trappings running in their midst. He could see
Flavius ahead of him, unmistakable in a white tunic, and
watched fearfully as he swayed in the saddle. Prideful
fool. Correus put his horse into a flat run and began to
draw level with his brother. "Flavius! Draw in!"

Flavius slowed and turned to him, his eyes moonlight-
bright and fevered in his broken face. "I can . . . ride,"
he said.

"You aren't a centaur! Damn you, you've made your
point. Draw rein."

"To ride double and let you kill Antaeus? That is your
. . . best horse isn't it?" Flavius's eyes glittered with the
fever and the stubborn determination that fever can bring
with it to hold with a death grip to a single point.

Correus began to feel he was conversing with his own
nightmare. "So I can go back to the governor and tell him
I got you out of Carn Goch and lost you when you fell
off your horse?" He yanked furiously at Flavius's bridle.

Suddenly Flavius began to laugh, his head thrown back
to the moonlight and his mouth bleeding where it had split
open again. "He . . . wouldn't like it, would he? It would
be . . . such a . . . waste." He pulled back the reins, and
his mount slowed to a walk. "But just in case . . ." His
voice was thick, but there was a note of triumph in it.
"You can tell him . . . they don't know." He slumped forward onto the saddle horns.

Correus swung off his own horse and up behind the
saddle of Flavius's. He tied Antaeus's reins to the rear
horns and wrapped his arms around his brother's waist.
They moved out again through the moonlight, toward the
river and Moridunum.

VI

Aftermath

THE CHILD YGERNA HUDDLED INTO THE RED STONE WALLS of Carn Goch and made herself small. She still had one of Gruffyd's chariot ponies by the halter, and she reached up and rubbed its silky nose for comfort. The pony stamped and blew softly down its nose. The chieftain's sons had come running to pull the ponies out of the blazing hall almost as quickly as Llywarch had bundled her through the door, and seeing her, Maelgwn, the eldest, had thrust the halter ropes into her hand and bade her mind them. Now he would be angry, she thought, that one had panicked in the fire and pulled away.

Carn Goch was a shambles of blackened timber and overturned cookpots, the few animals that had not been driven off by the Romans milling aimlessly through the rubble. Gruffyd's silver-mounted chariot stood near the smouldering embers of the guest hall, listing over on a broken wheel, but it must be the only unburned chariot in Carn Goch.

The men had gone to gather in the straying ponies and cattle, and she supposed that Llywarch must have gone with them. There was no one else in Carn Goch but the dead and wounded and a Druid in a singed robe who was tending them. The hut where they had chained the Roman was gone, leaving only a circle of burned thatch with half the mud wall still standing, leaning in toward the burned-off stump of the center post. She had thought that the Roman had burned with it and been briefly glad that he had found that way out. But Llywarch, coming back in the first gray light, had told her that it had been the Roman that the other Romans had come for, and they had taken him with them. At least if that was what they had wanted, they wouldn't be back, she thought, crouching down against the wall. The Romans were the unknown

92

terror of her nightmares, inhuman marauders who stalked the land to prey on unruly children in her nurse's vivid warnings and had later been given a more real and no less frightening status as an implacable armor-plated army sent to destroy her home, her land, her gods—every safe and familiar thing. When the Roman ships had been sighted off the coast, she had been almost paralyzed with terror. And when the war band had gone back to fight for Dun Mori and come away with a captured Roman, curiosity had fought with fear for hours before she could summon the courage to steal a look at him.

It had been a surprise, almost a shock, to find the many-headed monster of her dreams was nothing but a man with an oddly angular face, smaller than most of her tribesmen, tied to his horse. His tunic was ragged, his shoes were only leather soles with straps to lace them to the ankles, and his hair had been cut short. She wondered if his captors had cut it to shame him, and then she remembered Llywarch telling her that all the Romans cropped their hair that way and thought it no disgrace. But still he was alien, frightening, and the horror she had felt later when the screams started had been only the involuntary sympathy of a child for something in a trap. She had backed her pony away to her proper place on the trail before Llywarch could miss her.

Where was Llywarch? It was midmorning now, and the men were beginning to come back with the strayed animals. There were no women. They and their children had been sent away into the safer holdings hidden in the hills, but Llywarch had refused to go with them, insisting instead that he and Ygerna stay with the war band until the alliance and the marriage agreements had been reached. Bendigeid was not the most patient of men, and he would be meeting now with Cadal of the Ordovices and would want Gruffyd's answer to bargain with.

Ygerna rose stiffly and tried to shake out the tattered cloth of her gown. Somewhere there must be water to wash in. She was barefoot, and her shoes were no doubt part of the smouldering wreckage of the guest hall, but she was still a royal woman of the Silures. Llywarch wouldn't like it if she presented herself filthy and smelling of the fire to Gruffyd and his sons. The men had dragged in a pile of cut saplings behind the ponies and were putting up a pen at one end of the hold. She could leave Gruffyd's pony there.

She led him to where the other ponies were tethered to a rope line and gave the white flank a pat of farewell. The pony had been her only company for most of the terrifying night, and she felt alone without him now.

"Here, child, have you been holding on to that beast all night?" one of the men said, sinking a sapling into one of the old postholes of the cattle pen.

"It's the chieftain's horse," Ygerna said. "I was afraid to let him go. The other one got away in the fire."

"Well, you can leave him with me," the man said. "And we picked up his mate with the rest of them, so you needn't worry." This must be the Silure maid Bendigeid was offering for young Maelgwn, he thought, taking in her scratched and sooty face and the tangle of black hair down her back. She didn't look old enough to leave her own mother, much less make babes for Maelgwn. And she was thin as a fence rail, but that might be just the hard days on the trail. "Here now, have you had anything to eat?"

"Not since yesterday noon."

"Well, there's a kettle and a fresh tub of water over there by the Druid's fire. Go and have some soup and a bit of a wash, and the world will look some brighter, I expect."

"Thank you. Have . . . have you seen Llywarch my kinsman?"

"He'll be with the chieftain, I'd reckon," the man said. "Maelgwn and some of the others have gone after the Romans, but they won't be catching them now. Better to have saved our breath. But the chieftain and your kinsman rode back in a bit ago, friendly enough, so maybe they've made agreement."

"Yes." Ygerna gave him an unhappy smile. "Yes, I expect they have by now." With his chariots in ashes and the Romans on his heels, Gruffyd needed Bendigeid's help too badly to argue.

"Well, go and eat while there's still some left," the man said kindly. "I'll tell them where to find you if you're wanted."

Ygerna found the soup kettle, and she ate quickly out of the iron ladle that was stuck in it and splashed her face and hands in the barrel of water that was one of the ones left full when they had given up trying to fight the fire. There was a boy her own age not far away, fitting a new shaft onto a throwing spear, and she went over to him.

"I need a comb."

The boy looked up briefly and returned to his spear. "Then go you and find one."

"Mine was burned," Ygerna said, remembering that she had been a woman for more than six months, and a royal woman at that, and he would not be a man for another year. "Give me yours, and mind your tongue better."

The boy gave her a long look, taking in the gold fillet in her tangled hair and the girdle of enameled links that belted her gown. It had been fine once, of soft red wool with a purple thread running through it. Ygerna stamped her bare foot impatiently, and he shrugged and reached into the pack beside him for a rough bone comb.

It was missing two teeth, but it served well enough. She sat down beside him and began pulling the tangles out. "I am Ygerna," she said after a moment, remembering her own manners.

"My name's Tegid," the boy said. "I am spear bearer to Lord Sgilti."

"You aren't old enough!"

"I will be a man at Beltane," the boy said indignantly. "I bet I'm older than you. And *I* saw the Roman's messenger and showed him to Sgilti and the chieftain."

"The Romans took him away again. Did you know?"

"Yes, but that wasn't *my* fault. And Sgilti says I may stay by him. His driver was killed in the fire. I was right —the Roman *was* important."

"Important enough to bring more Romans after him," Ygerna said. "Didn't it bother you when they . . . when they . . . We could hear the screams in the guest hall."

"When they put him to the question?" Tegid said. "Of course not. I told you, I am nearly a man." But she thought there was a whiteness at the corners of his mouth.

"It bothered me," Ygerna said in a low voice. "I tried to remember he was a Roman, but. . . ."

"Women always mind these things," Tegid said comfortingly. "Anyway, he's gone now. I expect we'll have to go, too, now that our chariots are burned. Is Bendigeid your uncle going to send us more?"

"I don't know," Ygerna said. "They don't tell me things like that." She put the gold fillet back in her hair. "Thank you for the comb."

Tegid put it in his pack and looked her over. "You look some better," he said. "Not much like the girl Maelgwn was tumbling at Dun Mori, though."

Ygerna sighed and stood up. "I'm a royal woman," she said bitterly. "It doesn't matter if I'm pretty." She turned away toward the main gate, her thin feet picking their way carefully through the cinders on the ground.

Tegid watched her go. "*I* think you're pretty!" he called after her suddenly, but he couldn't tell if she had heard him or not.

As she had been told, Llywarch was with Gruffyd, the chieftain, near the main gates, and she quickened her step when she saw him. He had his hand on a pony's bridle, and she recognized it as one of the black team they had ridden behind on the road to Dun Mori. As she approached, he swung into the saddle and then looked down at her as an afterthought.

"Llywarch!"

"I've been looking for you," he said, not altogether truthfully. "You are to bide here."

"Where are you going?"

"To the king your uncle. To bring up his war band," Llywarch added, looking at Gruffyd. "The terms are agreed to, so you will bide with Gruffyd's women now."

"But—". Ygerna bit back the words and nodded. With the chariots gone, the Demetae war band would be no match for an attacker. They would have to leave Carn Goch. Until Bendigeid's warriors could meet them, they would pull back into the hills where the women and babes were hidden. Ygerna watched bleakly as Llywarch kicked his horse down the slope and turned westward. Gruffyd's women wouldn't want her. Especially not the girl Maelgwn had been tumbling at Dun Mori. Ygerna remembered her —one of the queen's women, a year older than Maelgwn, with a round, pretty face and a bounce to her walk like a plump bird's. She had giggled with the other girls over "the Silure witch" the day Ygerna came to Dun Mori, and she would like it even less to have her wed to Maelgwn.

For the others, it was dislike born of fear; fear of the Silures with their lordly ways, who were stronger and more powerful than any tribe in West Britain.

"Go and make yourself useful then." Gruffyd laid a hand, not unkindly, on her shoulder and pointed to where the Druid was tending the wounded. "You can be a help there. And there's wood to be brought for the Midsummer Fires. The god won't wait for his due because it comes somewhat inconvenient."

Ygerna remembered that she also was a Silure. "As soon as I have seen to my own things. The ashes have cooled enough now to see if there is anything left unburnt." She turned away, her thin back very straight in the bedraggled gown, toward the remains of the guest hall.

"I have left the girl."

Bendigeid smiled, a not altogether comfortable expression on the king's face. "Then Gruffyd of the Demetae has seen the wisdom of my arguments."

"Gruffyd of the Demetae has a Roman legion on his tail," Llywarch said, "and a hold full of burned chariots. He had little enough choice."

"The Morrigan take him! He has waited too long!" Bendigeid slammed his hand down on the low wall beyond which the sheer cliffs of Porth Cerrig dropped down to the sea. His black eyes glowed with fury. "See, we saw the Romans' galleys go by, and they turned and made for Dumnonia. And then turned back as like as not and caught Gruffyd sitting on his tail in Dun Mori!"

"Something very like," Llywarch said. He bent his head a little against the breeze that blew in from the channel and crossed his arms on the wall. With Bendigeid it was as well to go carefully. "He took a Roman courier with a secret in his head at the fighting at Dun Mori and then went to ground with him in Carn Goch to try to beat it out of him. It must have been important, because the Romans came and took him away again, and burned what there was to burn in Carn Goch in doing it. He was happy enough to make alliance after that. He'll be away into the hills now, to lie low and wait for us to pull the Romans off his tail."

The king of the Silures spoke softly, but his was always a voice to remember. There was an edge to it, like a skinning knife. "You have never been a fool, Llywarch. Why in the Mother's name did you leave the girl? If Gruffyd has no chariots, I could make better use of her with Cadal of the Ordovices. We met at Lughnasadh and snarled like dog and wolf and exchanged guest gifts, and he went away again, thinking. But it is all still talk. The girl might have turned it."

"For a one-war peace?"

"I don't know," Bendigeid said, "but it might have turned Cadal to promise." Ygerna had been promised often enough before now.

"Gruffyd still has the horseflesh we need," Llywarch said.

"And no choice but to give it to us now, without a royal woman for payment."

"There was one other matter," Llywarch said. "Gruffyd was afraid. Afraid of the Romans, and afraid I might learn *why* the Romans sailed for Dun Mori when he hadn't yet broken peace with them."

"That is Romans," Bendigeid said. "Dun Mori gives them another foothold before they strike at us."

"Not entirely. Gruffyd sent a man into the new fortress at Isca to try to put a knife in the Roman governor. A Silure knife. If he thought I knew that, there would be a Demetae rider in Porth Cerrig now, telling you I died when the Romans fired Carn Goch. To take the girl out with me might have made him think."

Bendigeid didn't speak, and Llywarch gave him a cautious look. The king was neither a tall man nor more than passably good to look at, but he was the kind of man upon whom the kingship sat like a mantle that was felt and not seen. It had nothing to do with the gold fillet in his hair or the fine woven breeches and shirt or the gold at his arms and throat. It went deeper than the blue patterns tattooed on his face and breast, and it was brighter than the fire. It would still be there if he were stripped naked. It came from the god, and when the king died it would go back to the god. Llywarch had known the king since before the old king died, when Bendigeid was twelve, and he had been afraid of him then.

"I curse him." Bendigeid's voice came in a low murmur like the surf beneath Porth Cerrig. "I curse him by the Morrigan and by Lugh, by the Darkness and the Light,

by the land, the sky, the flame, and the water. May the
green earth open to swallow him, the sky come down to
crush him, the fires of his hearth burn no more, and the
sea come up to drown him." Bendigeid picked up a peb-
ble from the ground at his feet and dropped it over the
wall. It fell away in silence into the sea below.

Llywarch shivered. Not even a Chief Druid could undo
the king's curse. "How if Gruffyd goes to the Romans
now, instead?"

"Send word to Gruffyd that we have taken the war trail
and will join him north of Carn Goch," Bendigeid said.
"And may he still be waiting for us when the Romans
find him."

"Centurion, I am gladder than I can tell to have you
back among us."

Flavius opened his eyes in the hospital tent at Moridunum and found the governor looking down at him.

"Thank you, sir," he whispered. "I am . . . somewhat
relieved myself." He was still unutterably weary, but he
managed the ghost of a grin. "The last thing I remember
before this place is clinging like a limpet to a horse and
yelling 'I can ride!' I, uh, gather that I couldn't."

"No, your brother had you on a horse in front of him.
I might add that *he* lasted long enough to tell me that you
were alive and that you hadn't told the Demetae anything,
other than to go take a dip in the Styx. He then let go of
you, you fell off the horse, and he passed out and fell on
top of you. It was most impressive."

"Correus! Where is he?" It must have been a full two
days since they'd ridden in, he thought. He remembered
waking several times and being fed and drifting into sleep
again.

"Over there." The governor jerked his head toward the
next bed. Correus lay with his face to the wall, one arm
under his cheek and the other flung out across the blankets. He was perfectly still.

"Is he all right?"

The governor deferred to Silanus.

"Perfectly. The only thing that's wrong with him is
what's wrong with you. You both need a week's sleep."

"What about this man's hands?" Frontinus said. He
looked at Flavius hesitantly. "Do you remember?"

"Oh, yes." Flavius looked down at his hands. They were both bandaged to the first joint, and oddly long and narrow, like a bird's claws. "I remember." They hurt, now that his mind had cleared.

"I doped you up and took the stumps off even at the knuckle," Silanus said. "There will be less risk of infection that way, and you won't be catching them on things. I have thanked the gods, incidentally, for the Briton that stuck your hands in that fire. It is probably why you're still alive."

"Yes." Flavius lay looking at his bandaged hands, but said nothing more.

"Now see here, Centurion," Silanus gave him a hard look. "Not even Aesculapius can regrow a severed limb, but the human body is remarkably resilient. Unless you want to play the lyre, you should be able to get along very well. As far as I am concerned, you are not to be considered Unfit-for-Service. You will be able to ride and drive, write and eat, and swing a sword in the bargain. You may have more trouble with a pilum, so it's as well you're an officer. Does that set your mind at rest?"

"Yes," Flavius said. "Yes, thank you. But I was really thinking . . . It's odd to find out just where your limits are. . . . How far you'll . . . stretch, before something breaks . . . like looking in a new sort of mirror."

"Most people wouldn't care for that sort of knowledge," Frontinus said.

"I wouldn't have asked for it," Flavius said, his hands laid lightly on the blanket. "It . . . came." He looked up at the governor. "Thank you for getting me out of there, sir. Believe me, I'm grateful."

"So am I," Frontinus said. There was more to Julianus's brother than he had thought. He began to see some of the tangles in that relationship. "Gaius Gratus would have skinned me alive," he added, turning the conversation back on course. "I've sent a courier off to Eburacum to say 'Message received' and that you have been wounded, and I've given you leave to recuperate in Aquae Sulis—I believe your wife was to meet you there?"

"Yes, sir. Thank you. I'd just as soon she didn't hear about this from anyone else. She's very young."

"Whereas you are getting older by the minute," Fron-

tinus said dryly. "I expect you are, at that. I'm going to
send your brother with you. It will relieve his mind to
see you safely out of here, and Silanus tells me that he
shouldn't go into battle again just yet. Having ignored that
advice when I sent him after you, I feel I should listen
to him now."

"Thank you, sir. I'd like that. I was afraid he'd have to
go straight back on duty, and I don't think he should, either."

"Oh, I expect we can do without his services for a
month," the governor said. "Especially as he seems to
have set fire to most of the enemy's chariots already. And
I'd just as soon have him out of here for awhile. He looks
enough like you to be a twin, and he's the only other one
besides my legate here and his primus pilus who knows
why Gratus sent you to me in the first place. And since
some of the Britons also know *him*, and know him as a
Briton, I'd like both your faces gone out of here before
someone sees the light."

Flavius gave his brother a long look, and while he was
digesting this, the governor threw his parting shot. "Oh,
by the way, Centurion, you have been awarded the *corona aurea*, and your brother the *corona civica*."

At the door the governor paused and spoke quietly to
the optio who followed him. "You will find a letter ad-
dressed to Rome in my desk, on the right-hand side, I
want it posted, please."

Flavius and Correus sat in a pair of camp chairs in the
captain's cramped quarters aboard the supply ship *Capricorn*, returning empty from the coastal run to Moridunum.
They were still bone weary and sore in mind and body,
but they had the resiliency of youth. Each had awakened
gratefully to find the other alive and recuperating. And
carefully packed in his kit each carried the official promise of an award that most men could only dream about—
the *corona aurea*, the golden crown that signified bravery
above and beyond the standards already expected of a
Roman officer; and the *corona civica*, the golden wreath
of oak leaves given to one who had put his own life on
the line to save that of a fellow citizen. The crowns themselves would come later, a dress award to be worn proudly

on parade, in place of a helmet, but it was the papyrus sheets, written in the governor's own hand and packed reverently between clean tunics in their kits, that really mattered.

There was a letter from Paulinus, also, to be delivered to Julia in Aquae Sulis, where he had already written her to take the servants and the baby and wait for him in comfort. Paulinus had seen his wife's brothers off affectionately but had flatly refused to accompany them. He had pried a pass out of the governor somehow—he wouldn't say how—and had every intention of sticking to the army's heels until the governor revoked it.

"He's been drawing maps and writing descriptions of the weather for want of something else to do," Flavius chuckled, "and pestering the life out of your legate. I think Longinus would have chucked him out on his ear if he hadn't produced that magical pass. What Governor Frontinus was thinking of to let Lucius into camp, I can't imagine."

"Us, I think," Correus said. "I'm not sure why, but I smell a connection."

"I would have thought our dear nosy brother-in-law would have been the last person he'd want about."

"So would I, but there's something there. I've chewed it over until my head aches, and I still can't figure it out, but there's something there, all the same."

"The army moves in mysterious ways," Flavius said solemnly. He picked up the stoppered jar of wine they had been sharing and refilled their cups.

"Let me do that."

"No, I've got to learn." Flavius's hands were still bandaged, but Silanus had lightened the dressings so that his other fingers were fairly free. He raised his cup. "To Aquae Sulis, home, and family."

A shadow passed over his brother's face, and Flavius bit his lip. "Damn! Correus, I'm sorry. It must be unbearable, losing her that way."

"Not unbearable, no. I'm beginning to grow used to it, I think. But I feel as if something was . . . broken. As if it won't heal."

Flavius steadied his cup with both hands as the ship rolled on a swell. "Uncomfortable place to drink, Correus, I wish I had some words of comfort to offer. I don't think there are any."

Correus studied his brother's face curiously, trying to appear not to. It was the same face it had always been, his own face in fact, but there was a new look in it that Correus could not name.

Six months ago Flavius would have tried to find the words anyway and botched it, and they both would have been touchy—prickly and uncomfortable like a man forced to sit facing a mirror. Now . . . something was different.

"I told Father about the baby," Correus said at last. "Before Julia did. I sent Julius home with Aeshma and a letter. I . . . I'd been fighting with him over Freita, and I didn't feel like telling anyone before. . . . It was Paulinus who told you? I'm glad. I—I should have. I've adopted the child, or rather Lucius has done it by proxy. And I've put all the complications of having him granted a citizenship into the works, so I *had* to write to Father. It wasn't easy, getting started."

" 'Dear Father, you have a grandson, whom I am adopting. I will argue about it with you when I come home. Please tell Mother and Lady Antonia to keep their traps shut on the subject or I won't come home at all. Your loving son, Correus,' " Flavius suggested.

Correus began to laugh, and Flavius looked relieved. "Is that how you would have done it?" Correus asked.

"I wouldn't have had the nerve," Flavius said frankly. "But it might be the best approach all the same. Father will rule you all your life if you let him."

"It's not all that easy to go against someone you've worshiped since you were two," Correus said. "Do you remember the first time he came home on leave? He was a legate then, and I thought Mars himself had come down from the sky."

"Yes," Flavius said. "I used to think I was the sole owner of that burden. I'm sorry."

Correus was silent, listening to the splash of water and the cries of the gulls hunting garbage in the ship's wake. "I think I've needed someone to talk to since she died," he said at last. "I have never felt so alone. If it hadn't been for Lucius and Julia, I think I would have gone mad, literally. We had so short a time, especially here, where she was content. It was dreadful in Rome, and she had too many conflicting loyalties in Germany to be happy."

Flavius gave him a cautious look. "I wasn't sure you realized that."

Correus shook his head. "Freita wasn't the sort of woman to abandon a loyalty because she fell in love with a man. She was a . . . warrior. She wounded two of our men before they brought her in, did you know that? Even later, after that last fight with Nyall's army, there was never a time we were in Germany that I wasn't afraid for her."

"You *knew* about that?"

Correus gave his brother a startled look. "About what?"

"That it was Freita who warned Nyall about the legate's tame German and kept him out of our trap," Flavius said bluntly. "I didn't put it together until afterward when I remembered seeing her in that trader's camp the night you turned your German loose to run back to Nyall. She must have seen him, but at the time I thought she was just running away from you."

"You didn't say anything."

Flavius looked embarrassed. "No. At the time I thought it might be just as well if she did."

"But later? When you knew what she'd done?"

"It was done," Flavius said. "It was over, and we'd beaten Nyall anyway. And I'd begun to get a better idea of what was between you. I'm not such a beast as all that."

Correus let out a deep breath, blocking out a mental picture of what would have happened to Freita if *anyone* had known that. "I . . . I owe you a lot for that," he said shakily.

"Don't be an ass," Flavius said. "You've paid. . . ." His voice also began to shake. "Mithras god, you've paid in full. I'll remember that British hut as my view of hell for the rest of my days." He steadied himself and poured the rest of the wine. "I think," he said carefully, "that we should both get drunk. Because I'm going to voice a suspicion that may make you want to punch me."

Correus was beginning to feel as if he were drunk already. Flavius was an unknown quantity now, the man he had been was slipped sideways to show another man behind him.

"When you and I went into the Centuriate," Flavius went on relentlessly, "our father made you swear something, didn't he?"

"Swear what, for the gods' sakes?" Correus's voice wasn't quite level.

"Look me in the eye, Brother, and tell me he didn't," Flavius said. "Don't worry, I won't ask you what it was. I have a damned good idea. No one in his right mind would have posted us to the same legion in Germany unless you asked him to. I don't know why it took so long to dawn on me. And I'm willing to bet our father had something to do with our both getting shipped to Britain."

"No," Correus managed to say. "No, you're wrong there. You got the staff post because you're the only man in the whole army who isn't scared to death of Gaius Gratus. No, that wasn't Father."

"But the rest was," Flavius said grimly. "He had you nicely over a barrel, didn't he? He adopts you, gives you the family name, and your heart's desire—a post in the Centuriate. And then extracts a promise from you to play nursemaid to your brother."

"Flavius—"

"No, just listen. You're absolved. Officially. By me. And Father's going to get an earful."

"It wasn't that he didn't think you couldn't take care of yourself," Correus said helplessly.

"Yes, it was," Flavius said. "But I don't care now. But if we're ever going to be friends, you've got to let me mess up my own life. Will you swear *that* to *me?*"

Correus began to smile. "I wouldn't save you if you were drowning. How's that?"

Flavius smiled back. "A bit extreme, but it'll do." Then his face grew serious again. "Drink your wine. I want to ask you a question."

"Ask." Correus felt that nothing could surprise him now.

"Back . . . there," Flavius said. "In that hill fort. You knew what I was carrying. What would you have done . . . if you couldn't get me out?"

Correus took a deep breath and then a deep drink of the wine. Everything seemed very odd and clear-cut, as if only truth would serve. At last he looked Flavius in the eye and said in a low voice, "I would have killed you."

The answer came back clearly, and there was no uncertainty in Flavius's dark eyes.

"Thank you . . . Brother."

VII

Festival at Veii

JULIUS APPROACHED THE TOWN OF VEII CAUTIOUSLY AS Aeshma swerved and snorted at the traffic. He had purposely taken the gray stallion through Veii to avoid the congested streets of Rome, only to discover that it was festival day in Veii. Julius counted on his fingers, but he couldn't decide which festival. Some obscure local deity maybe—Veii was an old town.

Aeshma bucked in protest as a street vendor with a tray of clay horses dodged under his nose.

"Get your Veii race horse here! Bring you good luck all year!"

Aeshma tried to bite him, and Julius hauled the gray's head around and found himself looking up at a banner stretched over the street that proclaimed: VEII MID-SUMMER OPEN RACE, with the name of the sponsor prominently displayed. A troop of street dancers was performing in front of a wine stall a little farther along, and Julius regarded them wistfully. The centurion had given him some money to spend, and it began to burn a hole in his pouch while he eyed the festivities. It was intended to be spent in Rome on the return trip, but the centurion hadn't really said *not* to stop any place else. And there was going to be a race. Julius had never been able to resist a horse race in the same way that some men cannot pass a dice game. He kicked Aeshma into a trot, nearly bowling over a pair of farm wives, each with a brace of chickens slung by the feet around her neck. They shouted and waved their chickens at him indignantly as he turned

Aeshma down a side street. There must be a stable in Veii somewhere.

The Veii Midsummer Festival was in full swing when the servants of Appius Julianus made their appearance, dressed in their festival best, and with their own largesse to spend. Appius preferred that his slaves find their amusement in the bucolic celebrations of Veii and the smaller towns outside of Rome than in the City itself, where the opportunities for getting in trouble and being fleeced of their money were infinitely greater, and he decreed his holidays accordingly.

The German underhorseman Forst regarded the crowd with satisfaction and looked down with a gleam in his eye at the red-haired woman beside him. Festivals had a way of becoming even gayer as the day wore on, and one never knew quite what might happen during the celebration or after it, in the torchlit amusements of the evening.

"I will buy you a present," he declared. "What do you want?"

"I don't know yet," Emer said. She glanced at a stall of cheap red pottery ware with a likeness of the Veii Basilica stamped across it and shook her head. "I will tell you when I see it."

"If it's not too expensive," Forst said, and she grinned up at him. She had on a russet dress that blazed in the sunlight like her fox-colored hair and a straw hat to shade her face.

"I will be careful," she said, and he ducked his head under the hat and kissed her when none of the other servants was looking.

"Today would be a fine day to ask the master," he said experimentally, and Emer shook her head again and pushed him away.

"Don't, Forst. Don't spoil the day. I'm too happy to fight with you."

"One of these days you will have to think about it," he said.

His skin had tanned to a deep bronze in the Italian sun in the years since he had left Germany, but his blond hair was still long, worn twisted into an outlandish knot at the side of his head, and Emer thought for the thousandth time how wild he looked, how out of place in this crowd, in the household tunic and armband of a Roman house. Emer came of British stock, but she was native-born to Italy, slave-born. Forst's slavery was all on the surface, like the tunic and the armband. That difference had something to do with the argument that always came between them when Forst grew serious.

"Don't," she said again, and he shrugged, careful of the mood. He put his arm around her and talked of something else, and she leaned against him happily again.

The Perseus and Andromeda was a wine stall with a little open court cluttered with stone benches in front of the counter. Julius bought a cup of cheap, watered wine and settled down in front of the whitewashed wall, squeezing himself onto the end of a bench beside a fat farmer with straw on his boots and a hulking fair-haired youth who appeared to be his son. The talk was all on the horse race, the sort of free-for-all, open-to-anything-on-four-legs competition that often meant an open field where betting was concerned. Julius cocked his ears forward and settled in to listen.

"Hey, Polydorus!" the farmer shouted jovially at another man slouching gloomily on a bench opposite. "You comin' to the race?"

Polydorus did not appear enthusiastic. "Paid my entrance. I suppose I might as well. Too late to get it refunded now." He glared at the fat farmer. "*You* talked us into that rule, Marius."

Marius chuckled. "We all voted for it. Can't have entries comin' and goin' at the last minute—much too confusin'. Sorry to hear old Hector went lame, though."

Julius didn't think he sounded sorry at all. Neither did Polydorus, apparently. He had a round, red face under a fringe of dark curly hair, and it grew a little redder as he glowered at Marius.

"Open entry," Marius said happily. "Put in another horse."

Polydorus snorted, and Julius slipped off his bench and went back to the wine counter for another cup. "Why is the dark-haired man so angry at the fat one?" he asked the shopkeeper, putting his coin down on the counter.

"You're a foreigner, aren't you?" the shopkeeper said. A foreigner in Veii was anyone from outside the city limits, even one from Rome thirteen miles away. "Otherwise you'd be knowing. Marius got all the race committee to vote this spring that all entries were final a week before the race, and now Polydorus's beast has gone lame the *day* before, and he can't get his entry fee back."

"And Marius's horse will win?"

"I expect so. Unless somebody's got something I haven't heard of. Polydorus's Hector might have beat him—Polydorus thought so. That's the other reason he's looking so sour. He bet heavy, and now Marius won't give him *that* money back, either."

"But he could put another horse in for his entry?" Julius had begun to look thoughtful.

"Sure, if he could find anything in this town that could outrun my old granny that's not entered already."

Polydorus put his wine cup down and trudged gloomily down the street to the ironmonger's stall to see about the new kettle his wife had been pestering him for. Kettles! He should have been counting Marius's money in advance and planning his new barn; instead he was taking home a kettle to soften her up while he explained how he had happened to bet their barn savings on a horse that had just gone lame in its stall, and they weren't going to see one thin sesterce of it back again. Maybe he ought to take her something lighter, he thought. She'd probably hit him with the kettle.

"Master!"

Polydorus jumped as a barefoot boy appeared beside him out of nowhere, like a genie from a bottle.

"You are looking for a horse?" the boy said, like the voice of the genie.

"If you don't like horses," Forst said, "go and watch the pantomime. I will come and find you afterward." He waved a hand at the oddly assorted collection of entrants that made up the Veii Midsummer Open Race.

"Mostly those are not horses," Emer said, looking at the motley array of starters. "And I didn't say I didn't like them. I only said that if you are thinking to find any stock worth showing the master in *this* race, you are a bigger fool than the poor fools who own them now." There was one stand-out, a big black with a heavy head and long, powerful-looking legs, but the rest were an unprepossess-

ing bunch, pulled from their daily work at cart and plow.
It was one of the features of the Veii race that no pro-
fessionals, equine or human, were allowed. It was the
only rule.

"Maybe," Forst said. "You never know." He bought
them a sack of plums and some hot pastries from the ven-
dors who threaded their ways through the throng while
crying their wares, and they leaned on the track railing,
munching them companionably.

A trumpet, badly played, screeched into the chatter of
the crowd, and one of the horses reared and started to
buck. Someone ran out and dragged it to the starting line
by main force, and the trumpet screeched again. The man
on foot dived for the side of the track, and the race was
on.

At first it looked more like a dog fight than a race as
the entrants sorted themselves out in the first turn, the
riders fighting each other for position, aided by rocks,
riding crops, and anything else they had thought to keep
handy. The big black careened into a muddy gray animal
and cut across him to the inside, the rider turning in the
saddle to smack his crop down across the gray's nose.

That, as Forst said afterward, was when the race really
got going.

The gray screamed and sank its teeth into the black's
rump, and then into the black's rider's thigh. Forst narrowed his eyes. There was something familiar about the
way the gray's head shot out, teeth bared, and also about
the thin figure of the gray's rider, who seized the opportunity to pelt the black horse and its rider with rotten pears
that he pulled from a sack in his tunic. The black reared
as a pear smacked into his head just behind the eye, and
the gray shot past him, its rider kicking the gray flanks
valiantly as the gray seemed inclined to turn around and
fight instead of run. The rider aimed the gray at another
horse in the pack ahead, and the gray shot after that
quarry instead.

"That's Correus's gray!" Forst said suddenly.

Emer leaned forward intently. "Are you sure?"

"Watch him run. That isn't Correus on him," he added
gently.

Emer glared at him. Anything that had been between
her and the master's son had ended when he had brought

his German woman home with him, and if Emer had lain with Forst once or twice since, she had given him no right to make Correus his business. She started to say so, but Forst's attention was glued to the track again.

The gray squealed and bit at a sorrel ahead of him, and as the sorrel's rider turned a terrified face over his shoulder, the gray plunged past with no more than an inch to spare between the sorrel and a piebald mare on the other side. There was only one other horse ahead of them now, and its rider gave the gray a respectful distance as the gray went past. There was another commotion in its wake, and the black burst out of the pack, its rider waving his crop furiously at anyone foolish enough to get in the way. The gray's rider looked over his shoulder and took another pear from his tunic.

The black's rider responded with rocks, and the gray's rider gave a howl of rage as one thudded into his shoulder blade. He yanked on the gray's reins, and as the black came up beside him, he swung the gray's nose sideways so that the black's rider's other leg, the right one this time, presented itself. The gray obligingly sank his teeth into it, and the black swerved hysterically as another pear hit him in the nose.

"Now run, damn it!" the gray's rider yelled, and the gray abandoned its victim and streaked for the finish post.

The crowd spilled out onto the track, gathering around the winners, and Forst took Emer by the hand. "Come on!"

"Where?"

"To get the horse, of course, and save that fool's neck before someone kills him!" He craned his neck above the crowd, toward the finish post. "Damn, I've lost him! Maybe he's had enough brains to hide."

Marius sat moodily under a fig tree doling out money to the grinning cronies who had bet on Polydorus's Hector and never thought to see their silver again. Polydorus himself sat to one side counting a stack of coins into a big iron kettle. "You sure you don't want to sell that beast, young 'un?" he inquired of the dusty youth who stood waiting his turn to settle up with Marius.

"I couldn't, sir. He's a pet, like." There seemed to be no point in mentioning that the horse wasn't his, especially not in Marius's hearing. There might be some rule about that.

"A pet!" one of the bettors snorted and started to laugh, and another one said, "Sure, he keeps him for a watchdog! To bite the tax man!"

Marius swung around and saw Julius, and his face went purple. "You! You're the little bastard who came and wanted to bet on Polydorus's Hector!"

"No, I didn't," Julius said. "I just said Polydorus's entry. *You* never said Hector was scratched," he added, aggrieved. "Tried to cheat me."

"That's right!" someone shouted. "Serves you right, Marius!"

He probably would have got out of Veii with a whole hide if Polydorus hadn't called out to him as Julius departed jingling his winnings, "Mind, lad, if you ever want to sell that horse, you see me first! Him *or* his colts!"

"You swindling bastard," Marius growled as Polydorus's nonownership of the horse finally registered. "That's a professional horse! He's not even yours!"

"He was mine this afternoon," Polydorus said complacently, waving a bill of sale under Marius's nose. "I bought him before the race and sold him back afterward. All legal." He nodded proudly. "All the little lad's idea. He's a bright one, that young 'un."

Julius knotted the girths of Aeshma's saddle and brushed some of the mud from his hide. He'd have to bathe him before the old general saw him, but they'd decided, he and Polydorus, that a little mud would keep Aeshma from attracting too much attention in Veii before the race. Julius scratched at the mud and thought about the return trip. The centurion had given him some money to spend in the City, but now he had enough to make his holiday really interesting. Someone tapped him on the shoulder and he whirled around to find himself confronting Marius, with the tall bulk of the farmer's son looming behind him. Marius's thoughts were all too plain, and Julius made a dive for Aeshma's reins.

"Not so fast!" Marius made a grab for Julius and hauled him out of Aeshma's reach as the stallion lunged at him. Julius kicked frantically at his captors' shins, but there were two of them. They were going, they informed him, to sift him out until they found their money.

"It's *not* your money!" Julius said indignantly, and then suddenly a fist came out of nowhere and connected with Marius's ear. Marius dropped Julius, and Julius yelled and then a man he had never seen before hit Marius's son on the head with a board.

In coming to Julius's rescue, Forst hadn't allowed for the festival mood in Veii. Passersby, with a wine jar full of trouble under their skins already, joined in on both sides. One man was hitting everyone in reach with an old boot, and another punched first Forst and then Marius. Inevitably, it was only a minute before someone was yelling for help. As the heavy sound of mailed sandals approached, three figures heaved themselves up out of the fray. Forst pushed Julius and Emer up on Aeshma's back, grabbed the reins, and ran.

"You damned little fool!" Forst took Julius by the scruff of the neck and shook him like a terrier with a rat when they were well outside the city limits of Veii. "What in Wuotan's name were you doing?"

"Polydorus needed a horse," Julius protested. "I just sort of lent him Aeshma. The centurion didn't say *not* to," he added.

"The centurion also no doubt didn't say not to ride the horse off a cliff or swim him across the Tiber," Forst said. "What in the hell are you and the horse doing here anyway?"

"Taking him to the general," Julius said. His face sobered, and he reached a hand into Aeshma's saddlebag. "I—I have a letter for him, too."

Forst and Emer sat with their backs against a peach tree on the edge of an orchard by the dusty road that ran into Veii, and passed a wineskin back and forth. It was dusk, and the glow of torches shone in the distance. A faint wailing chant and the sound of pipes could be heard as a procession wound its way up the road.

"Whose worship?" Forst asked.

"The Horned One, I think," Emer said. "Whose else at Midsummer Eve?" The high, thin music of the pipes came closer, and they made the Sign of Horns because it wasn't healthy to speak without due respect of Pan on the edge of a wood at dusk.

They sat and watched as the procession wound past—a litter carried shoulder high, laden with grapes and summer fruit, with a kid bleating angrily in the middle of it. A half-dozen girls in gauzy dresses with flowers in their hair danced at the head of the line, while the boys capered behind them with goatskins tied around their shoulders, their torches whirling above their heads.

Forst had sent Julius straight home, Emer thought with relief, under threat of dreadful consequences if he so much as looked over his shoulder. There was no telling what trouble the little demon would get into if left to run loose on Midsummer Eve. She watched the procession disappear down the road with the wild music shining in the air around them.

The last time Correus had brought Julius home with him, his sins had been without number. "Cook will catch him stealing honeycakes again and have a temper," Emer said. Cook's tempers generally worked themselves out on his staff.

"Probably," Forst agreed. "Someone will always be in a temper with that one. I would beat him if he were mine."

"Well, Correus won't," Emer said. "I don't know why."

"Yes, you do," Forst said. "That one can't shake off his own birth any more than you can forget yours."

"Forst, don't."

"No," Forst agreed. "It's too fine a night." He took a deep breath. The air was warm and heavy-scented, and he thought he would as soon be himself as his master tonight, reading that letter alone in his study. Julius had told them what had happened when he had remembered the letter, but Forst didn't want to discuss Correus tonight, especially not with Emer, who had been Correus's lover before Correus brought the German woman home with him. And now she was dead, poor thing, and nothing was going to come of it but misery for both of them if Emer started looking in that direction again. Best not to talk of it, even, but to take the night and what was given them in it, if he could.

He passed Emer the wineskin, and she put the hat on the ground and tilted her head back and drank, laughing as some of the wine missed her mouth and ran down her chin. He wiped it with the back of his hand and kissed her, and her lips were warm as the night and tasted of wine.

After a moment he stood up and put his hand out, and they walked deeper into the orchard, into the dusk and shadows. The pipe music seemed to linger in the air, old and insistent, an older song than other gods'. He thought Emer felt its magic, too, and they started to run, laughing, caught in the music. They halted at the far edge of the orchard, where it spilled into open pasture, and there was a single tree, branches low-growing, that made a green cave beneath it. Forst dived into the cave and pulled Emer in with him, and she turned her face up to his under a tangle of fox-colored hair washed pale in the moonlight. She had lost her hat, and she smelled of the wild rosemary that grew by the roadside.

Forst put his hands in her hair and kissed her, and she sank into the grass under him. He put his hands on something hard in the grass and lifted up a reed pipe, delicate as a bird's bones.

"The Horned One's pipe," Emer whispered, her eyes glowing.

Forst tossed the pipe away. "No, only some shepherd boy's, I'm thinking." But there was something in the air, some wild music of their own or of the procession on the road.

"I won't change my mind," she whispered.

"You don't have to," he whispered back. The night and the music were enough. He pulled at the russet gown, and she gave a quick wriggle like a fish, and then she was naked in his arms, her skin pale as marble, but hot, not cold to the touch. He buried his face in the shadows of her throat, and she sighed and pulled him down to her under the cavern of the tree, while outside the old song ran goat-footed through the grass.

No such pleasures attended Julius. He had washed and stabled Aeshma, delivered that sad, accursed letter to the centurion's father, and been cornered and expertly questioned by the beautiful gold witch who was the centurion's mother. Julius didn't trust *her* at all, even without the centurion's telling him not to, which of course he couldn't do because the gold witch was his mother, and it wouldn't be respectful. But Julius distrusted Helva instinctively and gave her a wide berth when possible. Tonight it hadn't been possible.

She had fluttered out in a gold gown that made his head spin, put one scented white arm around his shoulders, and called him "dear boy." As always, Julius felt uncomfortably aware of his own body, and of being strung together all wrong, all legs and arms that knocked things over. And there had been no way for him to avoid telling the centurion's mother what would be common knowledge in the household tomorrow anyway, so he had. The centurion's mother hadn't liked the centurion's lady one bit, and now the whole time she was saying "how dreadful," Julius thought she was counting over senators' daughters in her head. As soon as she had let go of him, he had run as if the Sirens were after him, down the hill to the barn, and hidden among the horses.

It was just as well. Aeshma had kicked his stall down and was out looking for a fight, and Julius caught up with him just before he found one with the big bay who was the current lord of Appius's horse herd. He dragged Aeshma back, put him in another stall, and sat down gloomily outside it on a bucket, until Forst should come home and figure out what else to do. And Forst had had red-haired Emer on his arm and probably wouldn't be back till dawn, Julius thought disgustedly.

Julius had had his first tumble here on the old general's estate, with a field girl no older than he was, and it had eased a need, but it hadn't impressed him much. Now it was beginning to seem greatly overrated and more likely than not to just bring trouble, as he sat glaring at Aeshma and thinking about the centurion's lady and the centurion's mother and Forst, whose fault it was that he, Julius, was here sitting on a bucket all night. And if the centurion didn't watch it, that mother of his would have *him* hooked up again, to some "respectable" girl this time, with a good position, who wouldn't understand him and wouldn't like the army and like as not would make all his slaves wear fancy tunics and give them silly names. The centurion had better be careful.

Helva sat brushing out her gold hair by the light of a little silver lamp shaped like three-headed Cerberus. On the opposite side of her dressing table was Charon in his boat, and he was a lamp, too, and the combined glow gave a softness to the image in the mirror that smoothed out the few lines that marked her face by daylight. *I should try to stay in lamplight,* she thought. *I'll last better that way.* She laid the brush down and stared at it moodily. It had a gold back, set with coral, and Appius had given it to her years ago, when Correus was born. She wished she could have given him another child, the way his wife had done, but perhaps it was just as well. It would have ruined her figure, most likely, and at least she still had that, although Appius was growing less susceptible to it than he used to be.

In the end it would have to be Correus who would keep her from the one thing she dreaded—the lonesomeness of a life without the pleasures to which she was accustomed. Not as someone else's slave, and not in poverty —she knew Appius would never do that to her—but alone, no one's pampered darling, with only enough money to be comfortable. Helva didn't want to be comfortable. She had been more than that for too long. And the business of a great household—the great men who visited and the important affairs they dealt in—she didn't think she could do without those either, now.

She called to her maid to come and tie her hair up in rag curls for the night. Tomorrow would be time enough to talk to Appius. Tomorrow, when all the things she would have to say about a suitable marriage for Correus would have already occurred to him. You always got further, Helva had discovered, when a man thought something was his own idea.

In his study, Appius Julianus sat looking at his son's letter. So the woman they had fought so hard over was dead. And he had a grandson, his first. A half-German grandson, but Correus's blood nonetheless, and Correus was Roman to his fingertips. And the mother wouldn't be alive to hold him back. Appius sighed. He was sorry for that poor girl and sorry for Correus, but she had made her babe's future infinitely brighter with her dying. Appius pulled a sheet of papyrus from his desk and began to compose a letter to his son; a letter of comfort that would contain none of those harsh and practical thoughts. There were times when a lie could heal more wounds.

VIII

Aquae Sulis

It was dusk when the *Capricorn* reached Abona, on the eastern side of Sabrina Mouth, a primarily British settlement with, so the captain told Correus and Flavius, a passable inn. They were still fifteen miles by road from Aquae Sulis, so they hunted up the inn and bedded the horses in its stables for the night—Antaeus and the troop horse allotted to Flavius, which had taken exception even to the relatively calm voyage from Moridunum up the Sabrina Channel and was now wild-eyed with nerves and shying at the shore birds that swooped past to hunt in the ebbing tide.

"Bide still, you ass," Flavius said as the snorting horse executed a swivel and turn and fetched up legs braced wide apart as a curlew's shadow flitted by.

"Do you want to trade?" Correus asked.

Flavius shook his head. "He was well enough till we put him on the *Capricorn*. Funny, some horses just won't take a sea crossing no matter what. He just needs a night in stables. I could do with one myself. I felt like invulnerable Achilles this morning, but it seems to have worn off."

"It's as well to stop, then," Correus said. "And you need those dressings changed."

They found the inn and shouted up a stableboy, who appeared suitably awestruck by the appearance of two Roman officers and promised faithfully to see that the horses were fed and watered. Correus slung both their kits over his shoulder, and they headed gratefully for the large tile-roofed building of the inn, optimistically titled the Flower of Abona.

Yellow lamplight spilled through the windows onto the stone-paved courtyard, and three Britons in shirts and breeches were dicing in the lingering twilight with a middle-aged Roman who looked as if he might be a retired army man. It was pleasant country and good farm-land this side of Sabrina Mouth, and already the time-expired soldiers of Rome's legions were beginning to take up their grants of land here where they had served, encouraged by a government eager to consolidate its hold by breeding a civilian population with strong ties to Rome.

The inn was used to travelers, the waters at Aquae Sulis having been famous for their curative properties long before the Romans came, and it boasted a pleasant whitewashed dining room where bread and cheese and good stew could be washed down with native beer or a fair Gaulish wine. On the second floor were three bed-chambers built to house some six or seven travelers each, with as many more on the floor as could be fitted in dur-ing the busy season. Correus and Flavius said firmly that they would take the smallest of them, to *themselves*, please, and the innkeeper, having seen the color of their money, was pleased enough to comply. Who had been turned out to make shift in one of the other chambers they didn't ask, and Flavius, sinking gratefully onto a bed, said firmly that he didn't care, either.

"We ought to eat," he said sleepily, unbuckling his greaves and kicking them onto the floor where his lorica and helmet were piled. "But I don't know that I wouldn't rather just sleep. What are you doing?" He propped him-self up on one elbow to watch his brother.

"Shaving," Correus said, peering into a bronze hand mirror, which he had propped on a table against the wall. "I can't go about Aquae Sulis like this. I'll look a fool."

"I was beginning to wonder if you were permanently attached to that thing," Flavius said.

"I was beginning to be afraid I was." Correus's voice was slightly muffled as he carefully clipped the luxuriant growth to a quarter-inch length. "Julius thinks it's be-neath my dignity, and one of my men chalked up a pic-ture of a catfish with long curling whiskers and my face on the latrine wall. It was so good, I didn't have the heart to give him more than three days' punishment, but I un-derstand my second upped it to five after I'd gone." He put the scissors down and gingerly picked up a razor. "All the same, I'm thoroughly sick of it, and I think my use-fulness in that department is pretty much at an end anyway. Ow! Typhon! It itched like Hades growing in, but it's worse coming off."

"I could get you some fat from the kitchen," Flavius suggested helpfully, and Correus glared at him over the razor.

"I put a cream on it, you fool, but it's only meant for one day's growth."

"I know," Flavius said, "I've got a linimint in my kit. It's for sore muscles, actually, but it's the greasiest stuff I've ever encountered. I'm serious," he added hastily as Correus gave him a black look. "It ought to work." He rummaged in his kit and made an irritated sound. "No, I remember, I rolled it up in my cloak—I was afraid it would leak on the governor's scroll. It's still on the saddle. I'll fetch it."

"Don't bother," Correus mumbled, carefully scraping another half inch clean with the razor.

"I ought to get up anyway and eat something," Flavius said cheerfully. "And I can't bear to watch you wrestling with that thing. You'll cut your throat in a minute. Hold on, I'll be right back."

He departed with a clatter of hobnailed sandals on the stairway, and Correus resumed his shaving with relief. He had little faith in Flavius's linimint, but at least he could finish the job in peace and quiet while Flavius went to hunt for it.

He scraped the rest of the left side clean and stopped to sharpen the razor again before tackling the right side, the more difficult angle. There was undoubtedly a barber somewhere in Abona, but not at this hour, and no doubt the fewer explanations he had to make as to why a Roman cohort centurion was sporting a drooping mustache that would have done credit to a statue of Vercingetorix, the better.

He had just finished the right side and was trying to see in the inadequate mirror and failing light if it had left a pale streak across his upper lip, when it occurred to him that Flavius ought to be back by now. He wondered if he had forgotten the linimint entirely and had fallen into the dice game outside (in the carefree, almost lightheaded mood Flavius seemed to have developed lately, Correus wasn't sure *what* his brother was likely to do next) and opened the window to see. The dice players appeared to have gone, however, making for home, no doubt, before the late hour earned them some woman's scolding, and Correus paused in the window to try to catch the last twilight in the mirror. The oil lamp on the table had reflected in the bronze so brightly that it was worse than nothing.

The stable door was open, and the inn's boy was pushing a desultory broom across the flagstones. Correus leaned out to call to him. "Here, you, have a look in the stables, and see what's keeping my brother! Tell him I want my dinner, and I don't need his silly linimint."

The stableboy nodded and put his broom down with no reluctance. But in a moment he popped out from the stable again, his eyes wide and frightened.

"Here, sir, you'd better come down! He's had an accident!"

Correus dropped the mirror and took the stairs two at a time, wondering what could have happened. He couldn't have been kicked by a horse; horses didn't kick Flavius. He had what Freita had used to call the horse magic, the same understanding of the beasts that was Correus's, too. Robbers? Surely not, in the inn courtyard. But Flavius would be an easy target with his wounded hands.

Flavius was curled almost into a ball on the stable floor, in the straw of the loose box that housed the troop horse, and the horse was nuzzling him curiously. His face was drained nearly white, and he was plainly unconscious.

Correus dropped down on his knees beside him. "Help me get him out of here!"

The stableboy edged fearfully to the door. "Will he kick again, sir?"

"The horse didn't do it. I think he's just fainted. He— Oh my god!" Flavius's left hand was curled around his right one as if for protection, and the right was bleeding freely, the bandages torn and mired with dirt and manure. The mark of the horse's shoe could be seen across the knuckles and the flask of linimint was smashed in the straw beside it. "Get in here and hold the horse! He's put his hoof down on his hand and opened up an old wound!"

The stableboy edged around Flavius and took the troop horse gingerly by the bridle while Correus put his hands under his brother's arms and dragged him free.

"Now go fetch someone to help me carry him!"

The boy slammed the loose box door shut and scampered across the courtyard, returning in a moment with the innkeeper and a burly youth who might have been his son.

"Here, sir, what happened?" The innkeeper peered at Flavius as the younger man picked him up and started for the house with him, apparently requiring no help. "Not robbers, not in my own stables! Go on, you lazy bitch, and see where they've gone!" He aimed the toe of his boot at one of the hounds who had come trotting at his heel, and the dog gave him a puzzled look and sniffed at the stable door with disinterest.

"No, it was an accident," Correus said. "My brother has had a finger . . . amputated, from both hands." He ignored the innkeeper's curious look. "He came out to fetch some linimint. He must have dropped it, and the horse put a hoof down on him when he tried to pick it up. The beast's been skittish since we took him off the ship."

The innkeeper held the door open, and they carried Flavius in through the main dining chamber, past a curious crowd of travelers and late drinkers. They put him on the bed upstairs, and the innkeeper bustled back in with another pair of lamps while Correus unraveled the bandages from Flavius's right hand with a sharp, indrawn breath.

"He needs a physician. Is there—"

"Not in Abona," the innkeeper said. "The closest one is Catullus—he used to be a surgeon with the legions. He comes in now and again for a drink and the news and a game with the local lads, but he's gone away up the valley home a half hour ago, with a fair amount of drink in him. You won't get him back here tonight. You'd do best to take the centurion on to Aquae Sulis in the morning, I'm thinking."

"After his hands have a chance to rot with stable dung in them all night," Correus said grimly, Silanus's lecture on cleanliness and infection still fresh in his mind. "It's got to be done now. Get me two bowls of warm water, and a—and a bowl of vinegar." Wine would hurt less, he thought, shuddering, but vinegar was stronger. Correus had seen enough gangrenous wounds to have the soldier's terror of infection well instilled in him. It began with a reddening of the skin around the wound, then spread and blackened and the whole limb began to die. The presence of horse dung made lockjaw another terrifying possibility. One of their father's slaves had died in convulsions of that after cutting his hands on a hoof pick.

Flavius's eyes were still closed, but he began moving restlessly as Correus stripped off the last of the bandages. He must have passed out from sheer pain, Correus thought, looking at the mangled and bleeding hand.

The innkeeper and his son came back with the bowls, the innkeeper's plump wife hurrying behind them, her motherly face worried and her arms full of towels. They put the bowls of water by the bed and Correus, who had no idea in the world how to clean a wound, plunged Flavius's hand into one of them and moved it about under the surface as the bits of dung and dirt came loose and floated to the top.

Flavius's eyes came open, and he gritted his teeth. "Bastard stepped on me," he muttered. "Broke your liniment . . . sorry . . ."

"Hold on," Correus said. "We've got to get it clean." He pushed the bowl away and pulled the other one up, washing the hand again for good measure. "Hang on, this is going to hurt. It's vinegar."

"It already hurts," Flavius said. "It—*aaaaahhhh!*"

Flavius struggled to sit up as Correus ruthlessly plunged his hand into the third bowl and held it under.

"Hold him!" Correus snapped, and the innkeeper's son put his hands on Flavius's shoulders.

Flavius shook his head. "No! No, I'm all right now. Leave me be!" He forced himself to lie back, teeth clenched, while Correus counted to one hundred under his breath. He didn't know how long he was supposed to leave the vinegar on, but the longer the better, he supposed. When he took the hand out and dried it, Flavius was shaking, but he had made no sound. The stitches Silanus had used to close the skin over the amputated joint were torn, and the flesh was ragged with the bone showing through.

I'm no surgeon, Correus thought desperately. *I can't stitch this.* It would have to wait for Aquae Sulis. The bleeding seemed to be stopping. He wrapped the clean bandages from his kit around it, fervently hoping for the best, and said a quick prayer to the healer Aesculapius for good measure. He stood up stiffly and went around the bed to look at Flavius's other hand. There was no blood on the bandage, but it also was mired with dung, and when Correus pulled it off, he could see that it had soaked through to the healing wound inside. "Go and fill the bowls again," he told the innkeeper's wife. "We'll have to clean this one, too."

Flavius lay back on the bed and tried not to think about the vinegar. "I should have let you shave your face without my help," he said with a wry smile.

"I told you to, didn't I?" Correus said. "We'll get you to a proper physician in Aquae Sulis tomorrow."

The innkeeper's wife and son came back with the re-filled bowls, plus a dish of hot stew and wine. Correus cleaned the other hand as quickly as possible and salved it with the ointment Silanus had given him. When it was done, they propped Flavius up in the bed, and Correus fed him all of the stew he was willing to eat—about half —and held the wine cup for him.

He ate and drank obediently and then let them pull the covers up over him, but it took him a long time to sleep, and midway through the night he grew restless. By morning he was flushed and all too plainly in a fever.

Correus debated between trying to drag the retired army surgeon, of unknown skill, away from his sleep, or risking the ride into Aquae Sulis, where there would presumably be several physicians, as well as Flavius's wife and servants to help cope.

"Aquae Sulis," Flavius said firmly. "There's no telling how long it's been since this army fellow's done any surgery, and it'll take just as long to get him back here as it will to get me to Aquae Sulis. And I want to see my wife," he added. He sat up and held out his arms carefully, to let Correus slip his tunic over them.

Correus agreed, reluctantly, neither prospect seeming any better than the other. They paid their tab at the inn and were on the road to Aquae Sulis an hour after first light, Correus on the troop horse and Flavius, this time with only a token protest, astride Antaeus's broad golden back. Antaeus was renowned as the most unflappable horse in the empire and met all things which the Fates chose to send down his path with the unshakable dignity of a marble senator.

They arrived in Aquae Sulis in good time. Besides the speed of his half-Arab blood, Antaeus had the endurance of an ox, and Correus didn't care if he rode the troop horse into the ground. Bericus would have taken Lady Aemelia to the best inn available, and a wine merchant's boy, trundling a cargo of long-necked jars along in a handcart, said that that would be the Green Plover, near the sacred spring, and he would be glad to show the centurions since he was bound that way now. They followed the boy through the broad streets, fairly crowded now with strolling visitors bound for the baths or the cures promised by the priests of Sulis Minerva at the temple spring. Correus kept a worried eye on Flavius. His eyes were unnaturally bright, and his mouth had the flushed, dry look that comes with fever. If they didn't find Aemelia at the Green Plover, he decided, they would take a room anyway and find a physician first.

Fortunately, since there *was* no room, Aemelia proved to be in residence. Bericus appeared and, after a shocked look at Flavius, began seeing to baggage and horses, while an inn servant showed Correus and Flavius to his wife's rooms. Aemelia embraced him with wifely affection and Flavius caught her to him in a bear hug, unmindful of his bandaged hands. Over his shoulder she caught sight of Correus in the doorway. Her eyes opened wide, and her lovely face went stiff with shock.

"C-Correus?"

"I'm glad we found you," Correus said, pushing in past her and slipping his own arm around Flavius. "He should be in bed. And he needs a surgeon—someone who can clean a wound properly and stitch it."

"What?" Aemelia turned back to Flavius, her eyes now taking in the fading bruises on his face. "What happened to you?"

"A little . . . minor surgery," Flavius said, trying to smile. He was beginning to feel light in the head, and his right hand was throbbing. He leaned against Correus. "I think I'd better . . ." The room began to blur, and he couldn't seem to finish the sentence. Correus caught him as he started to fall.

"Where's the bed?"

Aemelia pointed through an arched doorway into a second room. Correus got Flavius up onto a bed covered with a light woolen quilt, and Aemelia was bending to pull his sandals off when she saw his hands. She put her own to her mouth with a gasp. "What is it?"

"He was captured," Correus said. He was unbuckling Flavius's belt and thanking the gods that they had had enough sense to tie his armor on the horse instead of on Flavius. "They wanted information," he went on, pulling the belt free and laying the back of one hand to Flavius's forehead. It was hot. "They cut two of his fingers off."

Aemelia gave a choked sound and sank into a chair. Correus continued without turning around. "He was sweating earlier. This tunic's damp clear through. There'll be clean ones in his kit. Where's Bericus?"

Aemelia stood up. "I'll find him," she said faintly. "Rusonia!" A fair girl in servant's clothes, some years older than her mistress, pattered in. "Go and find Bericus. He's probably still at the stables. Tell him we need a physician. *Now*. The best one. Tell him to ask the innkeeper. And then get the master's things, and bring them up here."

Rusonia gave a shocked look at Flavius and at the tall officer standing by the bed and hurried out. Aemelia turned to Correus and put out one hand to the arm of the chair to support herself. "I'm sorry," she said. "I think I have myself together now. What were they about to let him travel in this condition?"

"He was all right," Correus said. "It was healing. A horse put a hoof down on it in Abona last night, and now I think it's infected." He realized how pale she was. "Here, you look done in. I shouldn't have told you straight off like that. Go and sit down, and I'll find you some wine. I think the quieter he is for now, the better."

Aemelia nodded and trotted into the outer chamber—gratefully, Correus thought. Her eyes had kept returning to her husband's bandaged hands and were beginning to look panicky. He caught a passing inn servant, sent him to fetch her some wine, and then eyed his sister-in-law uncomfortably. He had assumed that Aemelia would take charge, in the way in which Lady Antonia or even Julia would have done, but she was sitting in her chair with her hands clenched tightly in her lap, all too plainly looking to him for directions. He had forgotten how young she was, he thought with sympathy, and then with a certain amount of irritation that Julia was only one year older, but Julia would have coped.

"Did you know that Julia's here? In Aquae Sulis, I mean?" he asked, seeking some soothing topic of conversation. The inn servant came with the wine, and Correus poured her a measure into the pewter cup on the tray and added water from the second jug.

"Thank you." Aemelia looked up at him uncertainly. "Yes, I bumped into her—quite literally—in the baths. I knew she was coming to Britain, of course, but I didn't expect to suddenly find her beside me in the swimming bath. She's staying at the Girl with the Jug, behind the Temple of Minerva. I was never so glad to see anyone."

"Poor kid, I'll bet you were. Flavius didn't like sending you off to wait for him in Aquae Sulis, but he thought it was better than Lindum right now." He didn't elaborate on why, and Aemelia didn't seem to wonder, fortunately. "When the physician has seen to Flavius, I'll get myself out of your way," he went on. "I thought I'd stay with Julia if she can find me a corner to curl up in."

"You . . . you could stay here," Aemelia said.

Correus shook his head. "I think Flavius has had quite enough of my company. It's you he'll be wanting to see —and without his family underfoot." *And I'm tired,* he thought. *Tired of being in charge and not knowing what the hell I'm doing.* He wished the physician would come.

Aemelia looked at him dubiously. She didn't know how to tell him that when she had met Julia, Julia had had a maidservant with her, carrying a baby whom Julia had presented to her, in a voice that brooked no comments, as her nephew. Julia had told her that the German woman had died, but she didn't know how to say anything about that, either. There was something dark in Correus's face that told her not to. He didn't even seem to be the same person anymore . . . not the one she remembered. What had been between them—he seemed to have forgotten that and talked to her as if she were Julia. Or he was hiding it, because she was his brother's wife now. Aemelia couldn't tell. *I can't tell anything about him anymore.*

She watched him, bewildered, over the edge of her wine cup. And what about Flavius? What if he, too, had undergone some mysterious change? What if *he* were a stranger when he woke up?

"I . . . don't know you," she said finally, frightened.

"I'm older," Correus said tiredly. *Older by two wars, and you never knew me anyway.* But he didn't say that, it would only have been cruel. He looked up gratefully as Bericus came in with a short, stout man in a carefully draped toga.

The physician put his bag down in the bedchamber and unwrapped the bandages, clucking as he went. "*Hmmm.* Yes, well it is most fortunate that you called me in, although of course at this stage—" He gave Correus and Aemelia a serious look. "There is inflammation, you see —redness, swelling, heat, and pain: the four cardinal signs. And the possibility of convulsion, of course, caused by the ill humors that have entered the blood. It will be necessary to bleed him to draw them out."

"He's already lost a lot of blood," Correus said.

The physician gave him a raised eyebrow and continued. "It is bad blood that is causing the trouble. An excess of blood attracted by the wound."

Flavius opened his eyes. "Let him do what he wants to, Correus. The man must know his business."

"It's up to you," Correus said. This man was supposed to be the best physician in Aquae Sulis, and Aquae was thick with physicians. "I don't know enough to argue."

Flavius nodded to the physician. "Go ahead."

"Give me that bowl." Bericus handed the physician the washbowl from a table in the corner, and the man took up a scalpel and tied a linen strip around Flavius's upper arm before opening a vein at the elbow.

Flavius leaned back against the pillows while the blood dripped into the bowl. At least it didn't hurt, he thought wearily. Everything else had hurt like Hades.

Correus watched dubiously. It seemed like a lot of blood. At last the physician seemed satisfied. He closed the incision and began to repair Silanus's torn sutures as well. Then he smeared both hands with a dressing and rebandaged them. Flavius gave a long sigh and settled into sleep. He did look less fevered.

The physician beckoned Aemelia and Correus into the outer room, leaving Bericus to sit anxiously at Flavius's bed.

"I will call tomorrow, my lady," the physician informed Aemelia. "To assure myself that the bleeding has indeed drawn the infection from the wound. These amputation cases can be very tricky, you understand. But I'm sure there's no need for us to worry just yet." He patted her hand in a fatherly fashion and was gone.

"Oh, dear . . ." Aemelia looked after him. "He seems . . . very competent. But I—what do I do when he wakes up?"

"Make him comfortable. Let him eat if he's hungry."

"What do I do if he has to—to—"

"Help him up so he can," Correus said, trying not to sound exasperated. "Or Bericus can help him." *If you're too delicate to watch your husband take a piss.* "I'll be at the Girl with the Jug, with Julia, if you need me," he added, retreating before his company manners deserted him entirely. He patted her hand, and then he too was gone.

The Girl with the Jug, embodied on its signboard by a dark woman with braided hair and a vaguely Egyptian face, proved to be an airy, comfortable inn, not quite so ornate as the Green Plover, but having, so Julia said, the advantage of catering more to army men and locals, and less to fat old hens with female complaints. It was plain from her speech that she much preferred the company of the former.

"A few more months with Paulinus and you won't be fit to be anybody's wife and mother," Correus said disapprovingly, and she gave him a hug and a cheeky smile.

"I'll be admirably suited to be *Lucius's* wife. And as to my maternal abilities, come and look at your son."

Julia had taken a suite of rooms on the top floor of the inn, with a wide, pleasant balcony that looked out over the inn's garden. Julia clapped her hands, and a large, capable-looking woman with a baby in the crook of each arm came in from the balcony. Correus recognized her after a moment as Gemellus's woman. She was considerably cleaner now and wore a servant's plain gown.

"You will remember Coventina," Julia said. "She has kindly agreed to stay with me until the child is weaned."

Correus didn't remember that Coventina had had any choice, but she seemed content enough, and certainly she was in the lap of Fortune here, as compared to the hut Gemellus had provided her with in Isca. It hadn't been much worse than the quarters Freita had endured, he thought, with the familiar twist in his stomach that her memory always brought him. Freita would have preferred a hut and his company to luxurious surroundings without him.

Julia took the smaller of the babies from her and cuddled him, nodding dismissal to Coventina, who bobbed a nervous bow at the pair of them and disappeared again. The baby was watching Julia's dangling earring, and she tickled his chin affectionately.

"She's scared to death of you," Correus said, eyeing Coventina's retreating form. He felt awkward and scared to death himself. This was his child, his and Freita's, and suddenly he was terrified of meeting it again.

Julia giggled. "It's not me. It's Martia who puts the fear of the gods in her. Martia has very definite standards on how a servant should behave, and she . . . uh, instills them ruthlessly. Coventina's being a free woman carries no weight with Martia, and she doesn't let it carry any with Coventina, either. Martia sees herself as the force of civilization, I think. Certainly the force of cleanliness. Coventina's not so badly off. She's getting the proper food and being made to stay washed, so her own baby's benefitting. Here, take your lorica off, and you can hold him."

Correus obeyed reluctantly, and Julia put the baby in his arms. He had a cap of thin, pale hair now, and bright inquisitive eyes beginning to turn from the dark blue of birth to some as yet indefinite shade. He burped suddenly and then looked in fascination at the shiny plates of Correus's helmet.

"Look how big he is for only a month old," Julia said proudly. "Now try and tell me I'm not a good mother. And he's as good as he can be. He never has colic or fusses. And don't think I leave him to Coventina, either. She feeds him, but I do everything else. He's already had a dip in Sulis Minerva's spring to make him strong, and the priest there read me his fortune and said he's going to be a soldier, so that's all right."

Correus sat down carefully with the baby in his lap. *You're so little*, he thought. *Do you look like me? Or Freita? You don't look like anybody yet.* "Is it so important he be a soldier?"

"Well, I thought it would be to you," Julia said. "He's your son."

Correus thought about that. "I want him to be what *he* damn well wants," he said finally. "I'm not going to do what Father did to Flavius."

"Flavius!" Julia looked conscience-stricken. "Oh, I didn't even ask! I get so wrapped up in the baby. Correus, how is he? Lucius wrote me what happened. Is he all right now?"

"Yes, I think so." He explained again about the horse. "But the physician looking after him is supposed to be the best man in Aquae, so I wouldn't worry. You can see him in a day or two, I expect. He'd like that." Correus pulled off his helmet carefully with his right hand, holding the baby with his left, and set the helmet on the floor beside him. The baby's eyes swiveled curiously toward the red horsehair crest. Correus ran his hand through his hair, a habit he had of smoothing the cowlick over his left brow. It stood straight up instead, as it always did. "Julia, I'm tired. I'm dead on my feet. I think you'd better take him before I drop him."

Julia scooped the baby up and settled back with him in her lap. "You need to sleep. Is Aemelia all right? I haven't seen her since I got Lucius's letter, and of course he said Flavius was all right, so I thought the rest of it was something Flavius ought to tell her himself. And Lucius wasn't very informative, anyway. Correus, what *did* happen?"

"Later," Correus said. "Julia, if I don't go to sleep, you'll be nursing *me*."

She showed him into a small bedchamber. "I'm afraid you'll have to share it with Tullius—"

"I don't give a damn." Correus kicked off his greaves and sandals and sank down on the bed. Feathers. They seemed to wrap themselves around him, and he was asleep before she could say another word.

He slept the day around, with Tullius tiptoeing in in the evening and out again the next morning without awakening him. It was late afternoon on the next day before he woke up.

Julia sent Martia to fetch whatever food the inn could provide at that hour and kept her questions to herself while he ate it.

He had taken a mouthful when there was a murmur of anxious voices at the door, and Martia came in with the fair-haired girl that Correus remembered as Aemelia's maid. She had a wax tablet in her hand.

Correus took it, peered at it, and said, "Damn!"

Julia squinted over his shoulder. "Is it Flavius?"

"I think so. I can't tell *what* she's talking about. Here you, is the master worse?"

"Yes, sir. My mistress, she—she doesn't know *what* to do with him. Please come, sir!"

The maid had spoken the truth. Flavius was burning hot and raving, and Aemelia was one step shy of a breakdown. Her face was terrified, and she caught at Correus's cloak as he came through the door. "He's worse! I—I don't know what to do. The physician came earlier and bled him again, and when he came back just now he said the *hand* would have to come off, and Flavius picked up a *knife,* and . . . and—" Aemelia put her hands up to her face.

"He tried to stab him, sir. I took it away from him." Bericus came in from the next room, his face frightened. "But he's in a bad way, and I've got to go for *some* surgeon!"

"Well, why haven't you?"

"Who would have stayed with Flavius?" Aemelia said.

"You, I would have thought," Correus said.

"Alone? I—I couldn't. Correus, he's out of his mind. I'm scared!"

"Have you looked at his hands?"

"No! I mean, yes, but they're—they're—I couldn't touch them!"

"Mithras god!" Correus snapped, his temper well off its tether by now. He turned on his heel and stalked into the next room. He took one look at Flavius's right hand under the half-removed bandages. The smell was overpowering—and unmistakable. "Bericus!"

"Yes, sir."

"That man is not to come near my brother or *I'll* stab him! Go and find a retired army man named Catullus. He has a farm somewhere around Abona. If no one between here and Abona knows him, the innkeeper at the Flower of Abona will. I don't care if you have to tie him up—get him back here!"

"Yes, sir!"

"That will take hours." Aemelia leaned in the doorway, her face tear-streaked.

"If the quack that did this is the best man in Aquae, would you trust Flavius to someone *worse?*"

"But this Catullus may be worse! Flavius said you didn't know anything about him, that was why you came here."

"My mistake," Correus said grimly. "At least an army man will know how to deal with an amputation—they see enough of them. Now come in here, and help me get these bandages off." The stench was sickening, and there was pus oozing from between the stitches. The skin around them had begun to blacken. Aemelia put her hand to her mouth. "Correus, no—oh, I *can't!*"

Flavius turned restlessly on the bed, and Correus saw that he had been pulling at the bandages on his left hand as well. "Then get your *maid* in here!" he shouted. "And go get some water! Make yourself some *use!*"

It was hours before Bericus got back with Catullus, the dark-haired Roman Correus remembered from the Flower of Abona. He proved to be neither the drunk nor the dotard they had envisioned and said tartly that the innkeeper in Abona had his head where most people kept their rear.

"I'd have ridden back the night he did this, and the damned fool ought to have known it. What does he think I am? Here, let me look at him."

By this time Correus had cleaned Flavius's hands as well as he could in warm water and then sat holding them so Flavius, in what was now a full-fledged delirium, wouldn't pick at the bandages. Aemelia had brought the water in, taken one sickened look, and then retreated to the outer room, where she had sat with her arms wrapped around her chest, weeping, until Correus thought he would go mad.

"Someone's been bleeding him," Catullus said.

"Yes. Then he wanted to take the *hand* off."

"Well, it may come to that," Catullus said grimly, "thanks to the previous *treatment*. They ought to stick to potting up skin cream for the magistrates' wives or go and learn surgery from a surgeon. Someone's done a decent job on this to start with, though," he added. "All right, I'm going to have to open this up again, cut away the dead skin, and cauterize it. And you're going to hold him so he doesn't try to stick a knife in *me*. You," he said over his shoulder to Aemelia, who had crept up to the doorway again, "come and help."

"*Nooo*—I can't. . . ."

"Forget it," Correus said under his breath. "Her maid's here, and the slave that brought you. Rusonia! Bericus!"

"*Hmmm!*" Catullus dismissed Aemelia and began working while Rusonia lit a fire and handed him what he asked for, and Correus and Bericus held Flavius's writhing body down on the bed. The surgeon cut away the blackened parts with a knife and laid a red hot iron along the live, bleeding flesh.

Correus remembered the next two days as if he had lived them through the dim curtain of some drug. He had been given opium a few times before to dull the pain of a wound that had to be probed or stitched, and it was that menacing but dreamlike quality that seemed to hang about him now.

Catullus came again the next day, and the next, to clean Flavius's hands, but they needed to be cleaned every two hours in between, and it was Correus who did it, carefully, as Catullus had taught him, washing the seared wounds and daubing them with copper salts and resin and then packing them over with a poultice of lint and honey, while Bericus stood endlessly waving the flies away.

Julia came the first night after Catullus had gone, took one look, and decided with her usual practicality that the most useful thing she could do for either of her brothers was to remove Aemelia. She took her off to another bedchamber, bullied the landlord out of a hot brick to put in the bed, and tucked Aemelia up in it with a cup of warmed wine.

Aemelia drank it obediently, hiccuping, and wiped her tear-stained face on the bedclothes. "I should never have come out here, should I?" she whispered.

"No, I expect not," Julia said. "Why did you? Aemelia, was it to see Correus?"

"No! Well, I did think . . . maybe we might see each other. But I wasn't . . . I was *trying* to be a good wife. Lady Antonia said I shouldn't follow the army," she sniffled. "But I thought she was wrong, I really did."

"She was right," Julia said, more gently now. She had heard enough frontier stories by this time to be sure of that. And she had seen where Freita had lived. "Aemelia, there's no point in trying to be something you aren't. Go back, and make a . . . a haven for Flavius to come back to. Don't try to stick it out here. It could get worse than this, you know."

"You came out here," Aemelia said.

"Lucius isn't in the army. And I think I'm more . . . adaptable than you are."

"That . . . that German woman came out here," Aemelia said.

"And look what happened to her," Julia said ruthlessly. "She was stabbed to death by a renegade tribesman who took her for someone else. They cut that baby from her dead body."

Aemelia made a choking noise and put her hand up. "No, don't—"

"Do you want Flavius to go in fear of that for you? It almost destroyed Correus."

"Correus," Aemelia whispered. "Julia, I don't know him anymore. It's like a . . . a different person with his face. I'm afraid of him."

"No, you just don't understand him." Julia stood up and smoothed Aemelia's hair back from her face. "Now sleep. I'll call you if there's any change in Flavius."

For three days they wrestled with the infection in Flavius's hands and the fever that left his whole body burning hot to the touch, but in the end they saved the hand. On the third day he woke rational and sweating as the fever left him and with his right hand beginning to heal. The left had been out of danger since the day before.

Catullus gave a grunt of satisfaction and wiped the back of his own hand across his forehead. "Well, son, you beat the odds," he said to Flavius. "Which of you here was the last to get any sleep?"

"I was, sir," Bericus said.

"Good. You're in charge. I'll look in every day for a while. I don't think there's anything more to worry about, but I don't want him to set foot outside these rooms until those hands are properly healed over. You—" He looked at Correus. "Go back where you belong, and go to sleep."

Correus went back to Julia at the Girl with the Jug, slept for another full day, ate, and slept again.

When he woke the second time, Julia thought he still looked like a fresh corpse and said so, but she didn't quarrel when he insisted on going to see Flavius. Correus still hadn't told her the details of what had happened to Flavius—or him, she thought—but there was no point in asking while he was in this restive mood.

Correus found Flavius still lucid and healing and, himself now greatly relieved, set out to make amends to Aemelia. The effort was more wearisome than otherwise, and when he returned to the Girl with the Jug to find Julia organizing a family outing to Aquae Sulis's famous baths, his sister's uncomplicated company was an agreeable relief.

The medicinal baths at Aquae were famous, but they also boasted a swimming bath and the usual cold, tepid, and hot rooms as well as a recently constructed steam bath. Tullius hung up his clothes in the changing room and went to work out in the courtyard with likeminded stalwart souls, while Martia, with Coventina and the babies in tow, enjoyed a sedate rubdown and a plunge for health's sake in the women's cold pool. Correus did a brisk three laps in the swimming bath and then went to soak in the superheated waters of the steam bath. Mixed bathing was less strictly regarded in the provinces, and Julia followed him. She poked a toe in gingerly and made a face but finally slithered down beside him. Her dark curls were carefully pulled into a knot on the top of her head, and she had tied a ribbon around her forehead. She eyed her brother's scarred, muscled body—as much of it as could be seen through the steam—with a thoughtful face. *The marks of old campaigns . . . He's beginning to look like Papa,* she thought. *He's too young to look like that.*

They were the only occupants at the moment. It was growing close to the dinner hour. Correus leaned back against the wall of the bath and let the steam soak loose the kinks in his neck and the groggy feeling of having slept too long.

Julia stood it as long as she could and then prodded him gently with a toe. "I'm melting like lamp fat. If I'm going to keep you company, this would be a good time to tell me what happened to you and Flavius out there."

So he told her, plainly and with no skirting around the horrors, and she listened solemnly until he was done. When he had finished, Julia leaned her own head back against the stones and closed her eyes, trying not to picture too vividly the things Correus had said. Mutilation. It was a horrible word. But it could have been worse, so much worse. Was that the way to put it to Aemelia? Probably not.

"How is Aemelia?" she asked him, hoping she wasn't pressing on a sore spot.

"Less hysterical," Correus said. He didn't seem to care, and Julia was beginning to have her suspicions about the depth of the tragic romance her friend had cherished so carefully.

"Were you ever really in love with her?" It was an offhand question, almost a murmur. The steam was making them both sleepy, and in this mood he seemed likely to answer.

"She was a . . . a picture." Correus waved a hand vaguely in the steam. "Everything people kept telling me I couldn't have, mustn't ask for. And *she* wanted *me*. That's a . . . strong attraction."

"That's lust," Julia said drowsily.

Correus opened one eye. "You've grown up," he murmured.

"Enough to know that, anyway," Julia said. "She's a kitten. With a bow on its neck. Pretty. Not like Freita. Freita was a mountain cat, Lucius said. I wish I'd known her better."

"Freita was me," Correus said.

Julia slid over on the bench beside him and slipped a hand through his arm.

IX

Lies and Bargains

THE COURTS OF BRYN EPONA WERE FULL TO OVERFLOW-
ing with the entourage necessary to support the dignity of
two kings. Inside the King's Hall, where the council table
had been set up, there was much politeness, while outside
in the second level where the guest chambers were, the
dark Silure warriors sulked in the sweltering September
heat. Cadal's fair-haired men glowered at them as they
passed from the lower courts to the upper where the
King's Hall was, sometimes on legitimate business, but as
often as not merely from suspicion—the master's hound
pack seeing that the interloper's dogs kept to their place.

"Agreement must be made by the winter," Bendigeid
said. "We will have that much time, but the Romans will
be out and hunting with the first thaw." His voice was
level, and he sat back in his chair, his hands flat on the
tabletop, the look of a man with much patience.

Across the table, Cadal, with his tawny hair loose down
his back under a twisted gold circlet, also lounged in his
seat, lids drooping with the air of one who has little need
to hurry. But the air between them snapped like the sultry
hours before a storm, and their household warriors, ranged
behind their lords' chairs, shuffled their feet and looked
warily at the others.

They flow away from each other like oil and water,
Llywarch thought, sitting between the two kings, with certain other of the council lords of both tribes. Dark men
and fair, older enemies than were the Roman kind, what
common ancestry they had was now buried so deep as to
make no bond. *We will be lucky if we can keep them together for one battle.*

Cadal tugged thoughtfully at the end of his mustache
and appeared to consider. "You are so sure that the Romans aren't hunting your hills already that you can sit in
Bryn Epona until winter?"

138

"The Romans are biting the Demetae at the moment," Bendigeid said with that half smile that showed the points of his teeth, like a wolf.

"Bendigeid, you broke faith with Gruffyd of the Demetae," a red-haired man snapped. "Why should we be trusting you to keep it with us then?"

The Silure men bristled, and Cadal chuckled. "A fair enough question, though not overtactfully put."

"Gruffyd broke faith with *me*," Bendigeid said. "He called the Romans onto his own trail when he tried to kill the commander of their Eagle Army with a Silure knife."

Cadal knew that well enough, but he was best pleased to put Bendigeid on the defensive. They had each employed that tactic all morning, setting out demands and concessions like pieces on a Wisdom board. Cadal nodded. He pushed back the sleeves of his red, gold-embroidered shirt and looked thoughtful. "And Gruffyd's horseflesh? I will count Gruffyd's men well enough used in taking the edge off the Romans' swords—and maybe holding them till winter—but two thousand of his ponies, chariot broken, for the common herd—that was the number promised, was it not?" He turned with a questioning look to the red-haired man, Amren.

Amren nodded.

Bendigeid looked at Amren, his blue-patterned face pale and dangerous under the fall of dark hair and the red-gold circlet that crowned it. Amren shifted in his chair in spite of himself. The king of the Silures had the Old Blood in him, and Amren didn't like the dark folk—particularly not when they could make him feel a cold hand on his neck by looking at him.

"The ponies are in Silure horse runs, well guarded," Bendigeid said. He dismissed Amren and turned his face to Cadal, pleasantly enough. "Gruffyd sent them before he realized I wasn't going to save his treacherous hide for him." He smiled, less pleasantly. "He had no particular use for them, since the Romans burned his chariots."

"Then they won't be taking long to burn his holdings as well," Cadal said. He had no particular sympathy for Gruffyd. The Demetae were too small and unimportant to play that game with Bendigeid. Gruffyd should have known better. "When the Roman Eagle Army has put Gruffyd's head on a pole," Cadal said, "they will be looking to the Silures next. Is the king of the Silures sure that he can wait till winter?"

"Surer than the king of the Ordovices should be," Bendigeid said, and his voice had grown a touch of menace to it. "I know the Roman kind. They will make sure of their hold in Demetae lands, and then they will go back to the fort they have built in the lowlands until the spring. They have tried to take Silure lands before, and always it has been harder than they bargained for. This commander is no fool. He won't take the war trail with only a month's good weather left."

"And why should that be a concern to me?" Cadal said.

"Because if the Romans strike and Cadal of the Ordovices has not made treaty, his tribe will stand alone when the Romans look to Ordovician lands. You were not thinking, were you, that the Romans will go no farther than *my* hills? If we go down, they will hunt you next. And if we win, they will pull back from us and hunt you *instead*."

Cadal took a deep breath and stretched his hands out in front of him. He turned to Amren. "It grows stifling in here, and it frays tempers. Send someone to fetch us beer. And open the doors."

Bendigeid stretched also and eyed Cadal with a certain respect. Theirs was an old hatred that went bone-deep, but Cadal was a master at this game.

Llywarch, watching them, dark head facing tawny one down the length of the table, thought how different they were. Not in body or in birth, but in the soul. Cadal was a dangerous man and a fine enough king, but he didn't possess the power that was in Bendigeid. Cadal had other men who were dear to him—companions among his warriors, lovers among the women. Bendigeid had only that dark power and the tribe. Not as individuals, but as a living thing itself. Cadal was a warrior. Bendigeid was a king in the old way. It would consume him, Llywarch thought. The god's gifts always did.

The beer was brought and the council lords and the kings' warriors drank thirstily, wiping their mouths with the backs of their hands. Cadal had sent enough, Llywarch noted, to take the edge off their ill humor, but not enough for any of them to get fighting drunk.

"In exchange for Gruffyd's two thousand ponies, I will give you a twentieth of the plunder, before any other division. Half of it will be given back again if the fighting reaches *my* lands." Cadal nudged the next piece out on the game board. There must be some price for trampled fields and corn stores used up. A war host on the march could eat a large holding bare in a week.

Bendigeid nodded. "And the amount to be doubled if we fight two seasons in mine."

Cadal nodded in return. It was not a promise he would have to pay on. Silure and Ordovice could ride together no more than one season before they turned on each other instead of the Romans. Cadal's war band would ride home with their plunder at the first fall-of-the-leaf.

Bendigeid knew it, as Cadal knew when Bendigeid lied. There would be no more than one battle anyway—a fine, red slaughter to take Roman heads and Roman gold and put the Morrigan's fear in the next Roman Eagle Army that looked their way. Then he could turn his war band and Gruffyd's ponies on the Ordovices and take back the gold.

"And what for a surety that neither of us lies?" Cadal said, knowing that they both lied.

"How long have we warred between each other, your folk and mine?" Bendigeid's dark eyes were masked and uninformative behind the spiral tattooing.

"Since first we came over-seas to Britain," Cadal said, suspicious.

"Have you a woman at your hearth, king of the Ordovices?"

"Several," Cadal said dryly. He was a fair man to look on, tall and well made, with a handsome face behind the blue stain that picked out the King's Mark of his own tribe. He had no need for a black-haired Silure girl in his bed.

"A woman taken to wife, before the Druids?"

"No. Not that." Cadal's expression said plainly that he had no need of that, either. He had sons already, one of them by a royal woman of the Ordovices. The council would choose the best among them to come after him.

"Then let you take Ygerna, who is royal woman of the Silures, born to a royal woman of the tribe and a man who was of the kindred of the king's house," Bendigeid said. "That there may be no more war between us, ever."

Llywarch gave him a thoughtful look but said nothing.

That the Demetae had Ygerna mattered little. She had never yet been wed where she was promised.

Cadal drank the last of his beer and laid the horn down carefully, thinking. A royal woman of the Silures would make a royal hostage if she were sent to Bryn Epona *before* the start of war. And wed after, if at all. He nodded slowly. "It is something I will think on, king of the Silures, if my council is in agreement. This is a matter they have the right to speak on. A wife's sons would be first to come after me."

And so Ygerna was bargained yet again. Providing, Llywarch thought, that she was still alive when the Romans had finished with the Demetae.

By the time Correus's leave in Aquae Sulis had expired, the recurring headaches were gone, and Flavius's hands had healed. The lifelong breach between them seemed miraculously to have healed itself as well, due more, Correus admitted, to Flavius than to any new wisdom on his own part. Aemelia had gone back to Rome, telling Flavius that his mother had been right—it was not in Aemelia to follow the army with him. And Flavius, sadly, had seen the truth in that.

Paulinus was also in Aquae Sulis now, having pushed the governor's tolerance slightly past its limits and having in any case learned what he had wanted to about the campaign for West Britain. No enlightenment had been given concerning Flavius's presence in Moridunum, and as both brothers closed up like a pair of clams at the mention of it, Paulinus let the matter drop. He was beginning to have a good idea anyway, and if his suspicions were correct, it was not a matter for his snooping but something best left alone.

Paulinus had arrived three days before Correus was due back at Moridunum, and Flavius to his duties with his own legion, and the three of them had gone tavern-crawling on their last night to the amusement of Julia, who had favored them with all the dignity of her eighteen years and read them a lecture for waking the baby when they came in, and then made them drink some horrid concoction of her own before they went to bed. Flavius had reeled off to his own quarters at the Green Plover, but Correus could hear his sister and Paulinus giggling in the next chamber and put the pillow over his ears to stop the sound. He and Freita used to play like that when they went to bed together, he thought miserably. The month's leave had healed a number of hurts and given him an adult sister who had grown into a friend, but the empty place where Freita had been was an active pain that didn't fade. He had learned only to put it at the back of his mind.

In the morning that pain was back in its hiding place again, and he kissed Julia good-bye with regret. He caught a transport back to Moridunum in an unfamiliar mood, reluctant for the first time to take up the life that had provided a home for three years, to pick up a shield and fight again, and leave Julia and the baby—his baby—behind him at Aquae.

It was just as well, he thought, rubbing Antaeus down in the transport's hold, as the ship wallowed out into the river and he caught the sharp scent of salt in the air. It would be too easy to get used to life with a family that wasn't his.

In the end, though, the army was deep enough in his blood that it slipped on like the accustomed weight of breastplate and helmet. Vindex was waiting for him, full of news, and took him off to his own tent, where he proudly produced a crock of native beer, hidden from the eyes of thirsty predators behind a jumble of saddle blankets and spare cloaks.

"This is good stuff," Vindex said. "As good as they brew on the Rhenus." Vindex had done his first tour with the Sixth Legion Victrix along the Lower German frontier.

Correus leaned back in his chair, helmet tipped down over his eyes, and wrapped his long hands around the red clay mug. "No wonder you learned to drink beer," he said lazily. "The Lower German legions didn't have anything else to do while *we* were clawing our way across the Agri Decumates."

" 'Crawling' is more like it, from what I heard," Vindex said with a laugh, relieved to see some of the tautness gone from his friend's face. It was an old and friendly argument with its base in the rivalry between the two provinces of Roman Germany.

"You may be right there," Correus said. "I built more

miles of road through bog land than I care to think about."

"Nobody told me when I joined the army that I'd end up building half the roads I marched on," Vindex said. "We'll all get a nice new set of calluses now, I expect. When the governor can't think of anything else for us to do, we build a road. Or an aqueduct." There was a splash of rain outside and then the steady drumming of water on the tent roof and the muddy street below. Vindex groaned. "I don't know why he doesn't just set out barrels to catch it. Damned sopping country. Well, at least it'll chase away the flies." He stuck a finger in his beer and flicked a small, winged creature across the tent.

"It doesn't sound as if I missed much," Correus said. "I expected to chase the legion down somewhere up in the Demetae's country, not find it sitting on its tail in Moridunum complaining about the weather."

Vindex shook his head, and his face was serious now. "No. It was over fast enough when we caught them. One good fight and a whole tribe—gone. The Silures left them to sit there like a hare in a trap, and with their chariots burned . . . well, they didn't stand much chance. I can't say I cared for it. I expect they were just expendable—to keep us off the Silures' tails for the rest of the season."

A whole tribe gone, just to buy time, Correus thought. He made a face at his beer. "Wasted. There's a good month of clear weather left."

"Well, yes and no," Vindex said. "They served their purpose in their way. The governor won't risk getting stuck in Silure lands with winter coming down and no adequate supplies in hand. We'll spend the next month digging in here and up around Carn Goch and Luentinum —deep enough that Bendigeid won't have a mind to try digging us out. Then we'll put the auxiliaries in, and the legion can loll about in the palatial surroundings at Isca all winter. The men'll hate that. Isca's a hole. And they're itching to fight somebody. We caught the Demetae at a place with a name I can't pronounce west of Luentinum, and I wouldn't have called it a battle. One of my juniors said if he wanted that kind of fun he'd have taken a job killing criminals in the arena." Vindex made a face and poured himself more beer. "Glad you weren't here," he said frankly. "Then we came back by way of the gold mines at Luentinum and left a garrison to see that the output falls into the right purse in the future. A tidy campaign, but I didn't like it," he said again.

"And the Demetae?" Correus asked. They had indeed been caught between a fire and a cliff. No wonder they had been afraid enough to try that desperate murder at Isca.

"Conscripted mostly, what's left of 'em." Fighting-age men would be sent to the auxiliaries for service elsewhere in the empire. Those who survived would be given Roman citizenship at the end of it, and if they chose to come back to Britain then, they would have had twenty-five years in the Roman Army to break tribal ties. "A few of the women and children will be sold, I expect," Vindex went on, "but mostly the governor's leaving the rest alone. We're here to pacify this province, not wipe it bare. Old Gruffyd, the Demetae's chieftain, and two of his sons were killed in the fighting, and we've made the one that was left, the youngest, the new chief. He's not old enough to make trouble, especially not with our advisers breathing down his neck, and it keeps the local folk happier to have one of their own. We're taking a hostage, too, for good measure, but I'm thinking the Styx'll freeze over before the Demetae'll fight for anything more than to keep food on the table again."

Correus nodded. A land denuded of its men and the strongest of its women was a land left to ruin. This year's crops would rot in the fields, most of them. And in the spring it would be all the survivors could do to clear a small part of the weed-choked fields.

"Do you suppose Bendigeid's enjoying his strategy?" Vindex asked.

"I expect he is," Correus said. Another tribe's death would leave no mark on the king of the Silures, so long as it bought life for his own. A strange, cold man with a bright, cold fire at the center. Correus had come closer to being afraid of Bendigeid than he was of most people. Not of the man himself, but of that cold fire at the heart that somehow wasn't human. Or maybe just wasn't Roman. The months that he had spent in a Briton's skin had somehow got under his own skin as well, Correus thought. The Gauls and the Britons were one stock, and it was the Gaul in him that reacted to Bendigeid.

"We took a Druid prisoner, too, after the fighting," Vindex was saying.

Correus brought himself back to practicalities. "Just one? There should have been more than that."

"If there were, we never saw them."

"They must have gone to the Silures," Correus said.

"Where, it is to be hoped, they give Bendigeid a pain in the mid-region," Vindex said.

The Druids were holy. Not even a king would dare deny one refuge. And they owed stronger ties to their priesthood than to the kings they served. The Chief Druid had the power to stop a war, although mostly they let the affairs of men sort themselves out as they would.

"What happened to the one you caught?" Correus asked. Druids were forbidden and bore a death mark when Rome could find them. The pantheistic Romans freely adopted other folks' gods, and left conquered nations' religions alone as long as their rituals contained no inhuman practices. But the Druids were trouble. Rebellion inevitably followed in their wake.

Vindex's face was puzzled and uneasy. "I never saw anything like it," he said slowly. "They brought him to the governor to be questioned. I happened to be in the Principia just then, fighting with the quartermaster, as usual—do you know they've sent us a whole load of pilum points and every damned one of them flawed halfway up the head? Anyway, this old Druid comes in under guard, in a ratty old gown that must have been made before Augustus was born and a hulking great collar like a sun disc that must have been two pounds of solid gold. Long hair like a wild man, and a beard down to his waist. He gives the governor one look—not afraid really, though he must have known what was going to happen. Just . . . thoughtful. Then he closes his eyes, says something no one can understand, and *dies*."

"What?"

"Right under our noses. Just crumples up and falls down. They thought he was faking, of course, and gave him a shove, but nothing happened, so they yelled for Silanus. And when Silanus gets there, he gets a queer look on his face and says, 'His heart stopped.' Just that, nothing more, and won't say another word." Vindex reached for the beer. "I tell you, Correus, it scared ten years off me."

The rain came down in a steady splash, leaving the ponies fetlock-deep in muddy water at every dip in the trail. A decurion of cavalry rode at the head, the hood of his foul-weather cloak pulled up over his helmet, and his thirty troopers squelched miserably along behind him. Beside him rode a thin figure in a heavy wool traveling cloak, with a bright blue-and-scarlet gown and blue calf-high boots showing under it. The cloak was a thick, oily wool, checkered gray and brown, and it shed the rain somewhat better than her escorts', she noticed.

"Have we much farther to go?" she asked carefully, in simple British. "Your men will be wet to the skin."

"Only to Moridunum," the decurion chuckled. His words were heavily accented but understandable. "They won't melt in a little water, miss, but my thanks for your caring." The cavalry troop was a military guard, sent to bring the Demetae's hostage to the governor, but she had plainly chosen to treat them as a guard of honor instead. Pretty nervy for a kid who didn't look more than twelve. She was a royal woman, whatever that meant, and some kin to the king of the Silures. The Demetae had bargained her to the governor to avoid sending a hostage of their own, and old Frontinus had seen the use in that fast enough. The Demetae couldn't fight off an attack by a troop of eunuchs just now, but a Silure hostage was a present sent down straight from Olympus. He took another look at the child's pale face and the dark smudges under her eyes. Scared to death under it all, he thought, and he didn't wonder. If the Demetae hadn't wanted her to sell to the governor, they'd likely have cut her throat for her after what Bendigeid had done—or not done was more like.

Ygerna knew better. To kill a royal woman was to bring the Black Goddess's curse on the man who had done it and on all his clan and tribe. They had merely shut her in a storeroom and fed her whatever was handy when anyone happened to think of it, until the Romans came to Craig Gwrtheyrn to get her.

Gruffyd's women had stripped off her torn gown—none too gently, with an accidental pinch here and there—and poured a bucket of water over her by way of a bath. Then they had put her in a new gown and given her the blue boots and given back some of her jewelry. She had the Demetae's harper to thank for that, Ygerna thought. He had shamed Gruffyd's women by telling them that they dishonored the Goddess by sending a royal woman to the Romans in that state. And because harpers were also Druids, at a minor level, they had obeyed him.

When the Romans had come, the women had led her out and put her up on her pony without a word while Gronwy, the new chieftain, who was not even a man yet, stood to one side with his mother and his council lords. Only the boy Tegid slipped up beside her pony while Gronwy was putting his mark to the papers the Roman carried with him. "Here." He pressed a little bead of amber on a ragged thong into her hand. "A Druid gave it to me, so maybe it's magic."

"Thank you," she whispered. She looked at the bead and closed her hand around it.

"I just wanted you to know *I* don't think it's your fault —what your uncle did. Amber's lucky. Maybe it will help. Though it didn't bring me any," he added bleakly. He leaned on a crutch, and his right leg was already healing with the foot twisted slightly outward. Now he would never be made a warrior when the other boys came to their manhood at the Spring Fires.

"Yes, it did," Ygerna said, with a grim twist to her mouth. He would never be a slave in a Roman mine, either.

The Roman officer was coming back, and Tegid turned and limped away quickly while Ygerna clenched her hands on the saddle and fought down her panic. The Demetae didn't want her; she was a hated outcast among them because she was Silure—but they were kin to her own people, and she understood them. It was the Romans who were the unknown, a monster out of a nightmare. They would kill her maybe, give her to their eagle god. *The Goddess will take them if they do*, she thought. *I will tell them that*. But maybe they wouldn't believe her. Or maybe the Goddess's magic didn't work on Romans. She didn't know. They might not even be human, not as her own kind were. She put her hand to her mouth to keep herself from screaming, calling out to Gronwy, pleading with him to take her back, not to let them have her. The Roman swung up into the saddle beside her, alien and arrogant under the scarlet and yellow plumes in his helmet. He raised a hand to the troopers behind him, and someone slapped a riding crop down on her pony's rump.

They rode out lordlywise through the broken defenses of Craig Gwrtheyrn, and a pair of boys quarreling over something in the road scrambled out of their way. Ygerna took satisfaction in that. *I am Silure,* she thought. *I am a royal woman and priestess to the Mother.* She studied the Roman's sharp, arrogant profile beside her and molded her own features into the same expression. *I will not be shamed before them.*

It was a long ride through the ruined country of the Demetae back to what had once been the sea fort of Dun Mori, and everywhere the hand of Rome lay over the countryside. The hill forts had their walls broken into rubble and their outer ditches filled in—broken and filled by the Demetae themselves while a Roman overseer looked on—and rebuilding was forbidden. The tribal capital at Dun Mori was to be built again in Roman style, and the new chieftain was forbidden to hold council or judge court cases any place but there, under the eyes of the Roman commander.

When they made the camp the first night, the Roman decurion proved to speak a little British with a heavy accent and to understand her if she spoke slowly to him.

"All right, pussycat," he said in Latin, swinging her down from the saddle. "Time for dinner. Here now! Stop that, I'm not going to hurt you, you little demon!" He repeated this last admonition in British as she continued her struggle. "Nobody's going to hurt you!"

"Then why did you take me?" Ygerna asked suspiciously, but she stopped fighting. She shook her black hair back from her face with as much dignity as she could muster.

"For a . . . a prisoner," the Roman searched for the right word. "To make Bendigeid talk peace."

"Then you are a fool," Ygerna said flatly. "But I expect you are not the chieftain. Maybe your chieftain will know better."

The Roman's face darkened, and then he laughed and

shrugged his shoulders and called to someone to bring the little hellcat her dinner.

Ygerna watched him thoughtfully. Maybe that was the way to behave then, lordlywise as if the Romans were no matter. At least he hadn't touched her again. She ate the bread and dried meat they brought her, making a face at the taste, then rolled herself up in her cloak under the tent they had pitched for her. A pair of sentries sat down outside and began playing some game with lines scratched in the dirt.

In the morning she greeted her escort loftily and with studious politeness, as if the cavalry troop were only the retinue due her rank. The decurion chuckled. He was going to enjoy watching the governor when he handed this one over to him.

"Thank you, Centurion Julianus. Please sit down."

Correus cocked a wary eye at the governor. The legion was making ready to pull out for the winter quarters at Isca, and Correus wondered uneasily if the governor had other plans for his own time over the snowbound months.

"Rest at ease, Centurion," Frontinus said, apparently reading his mind. "I have no intention of leaving you here to nose 'round Bendigeid's camps. Besides, you've lost your mustache."

"I can live without it, sir," Correus said frankly.

The governor chuckled. "You can always cultivate a new one if we need it. But I think it will be back to regular duty for you from now on. That will pacify your legate, and we've learned what we needed to. But I do have a chore for you at the moment. You collect strays, Julianus, don't you?"

"Sir?"

"That damned dangerous horse of yours—the one you had at Isca—and that insubordinate slave boy with the unsuitable name."

"Julius, sir? It *is* his name."

"I daresay," Frontinus said dryly. "And anyone else would have changed it. But the fact is, wild things come to your hand, Centurion, and I have another one for you: the hostage from the Demetae. She's not much more than a babe, and she's scared to death. The decurion that brought her in says she's got more guts than most of his men, and that's what worries me. She's immensely valuable, and I don't want her frightened into doing something foolish. You speak the language, Centurion, and you'll know how her mind works better than most. Mithras knows what she's likely to do, but she's strung tighter than a catapult, I could see that much. Go and tell her we don't eat babies for breakfast, will you?"

Nine. No more than nine. That was his first thought when he saw the thin figure hunched on the bed in the red leather officer's tent the governor had marked for her use. She sat up quickly when he came in and brushed a hand across her eyes, and he saw that he had been wrong. She was on the edge of being a woman, her breasts just beginning to show under her gown. But she was reed thin, with black eyes in a white face under black winging brows and a cloud of dark hair down her back with a gold fillet in it. There was gold and enamel jewelry at her wrist and arms. One hand was clenched about something knotted on a ragged thong around her neck, and she rubbed the other across her eyes again. She moved quickly, lightly, like a small, wild thing out of the woods.

Correus put a hand to his forehead and said in the Silures' dialect, "The lady is welcome, and the Mother is welcome at the hearth of Rome." It was the formal greeting to a priestess, and the child sat up straight in surprise, her dark eyes suspicious. Mostly, even her own folk didn't accord her that much.

"Who are you?" He wasn't a Silure. He was Roman to his fingertips, lordly and superior, as they all were, and iron-plated like a shellfish, which was a cowardly way to fight. But she had seen his face before somewhere. It might be better not to tell him that.

"May I sit down?"

Ygerna nodded warily. "Can I stop you?"

"No," Correus admitted, "since they sent me here to talk to you. My name is—Correus." He started to say "Centurion Julianus," but this was a baby after all. Surely his precious dignity could stand that she call him Correus.

"That's a British name."

"You're too smart for your own good, aren't you? It's a Gaulish name, but I expect it might be the same here at that. My mother was a Gaul of the Belgae."

"She is dead now?"

"No, I didn't mean that. Only that she isn't a Gaul any-more, not really. She's been a Roman in everything but blood since she was, oh, not much older than you."

"I am thirteen," Ygerna said with dignity. "I am a woman."

"I suppose you are," Correus said gravely. The tribes counted womanhood from the first flow of blood. But she was pathetically young. At one-and-twenty, Correus, with three years in the army behind him, felt immensely old by comparison.

Ygerna watched him thoughtfully. He looked like all the rest of them, strong-featured, with a face like one of their eagle gods, but he spoke like a Silure, a familiar, comforting sound among the voices of the rest that grated like the harsh, unintelligible cries of hawks in her ears. Her fear began to ebb just a little. And he didn't seem to be angry—or laughing at her as the cavalrymen had been, or terrifying as was the big granite-faced man with the eagle feathers on his head who was the chieftain of this place. He just sat quietly with his hands in his lap, fidgeting with the red leather strips that hung down below his breast-plate. His hands—Ygerna put her own hands to her mouth, as it came back suddenly to her mind, what Tegid had told her on Lughnasadh night before they left Carn Goch, standing in the glare of the Lughnasadh Fires while the Druids chanted out their prayers: "They cut off his fingers, and he screamed and screamed but he never told. He must have been a great warrior, that one." That was where she had seen his face—tied to a pony after the fight for Dun Mori!

"Your hands . . ." she whispered.

He looked down at them, puzzled. He wondered if she had the Sight, enough to see old blood on them. "My hands?"

"Not even the Druids can grow fingers back. What are you?"

Correus stood up, and she shrank back from him. "Not a demon, I promise you!" he said. "Do I look like one?"

"I don't know." Maybe the Romans were *all* demons. But this one was half a Gaul, or claimed to be.

"My brother," Correus said gently when he understood

her terror. "You saw my brother. Here, look." He held
out his hands. "Touch them. See—quite real."

She laid a small pale hand carefully on his. Her fingers were cool to the touch, clean, with neatly cut nails.
"Is that why you are here? Because of what Gruffyd did
to your brother?"

"To take vengeance on a little girl because Gruffyd had
my brother tortured?" Correus was indignant. "What do
you think I am?"

"I don't *know!*" Ygerna said. She looked ready to cry
again. "I don't *know* what you are! I never saw a Roman.
And *you* don't talk like one."

"If you never saw a Roman, how do you know what we
talk like?" Correus said. "I'm here because the governor
—that's the . . . the chief warrior of our army here—
thought that you were afraid, and it would help to talk to
someone in your own tongue."

"Why does he care?"

"Because, whatever you may think, we are not monsters. And because you are valuable to him. Too valuable
to let you work yourself into a terror and try to run away."
Or kill herself, but he wasn't going to put *that* idea in her
mind if it wasn't there already.

Ygerna lifted up her chin. "I am *not* afraid. If you kill
me the Goddess will curse you."

"I doubt that that would weigh with the governor," Correus said frankly. "But there's no point in running, because you wouldn't get past the tent door. Now listen,
what do I have to do to convince you that if we weren't
planning to take good care of your valuable hide, you'd
be manacled to a post in the stockade, not lolling about
here in a damned tribune's tent that's better than mine!"

Ygerna seemed to consider this. "Then if I am so valuable, let your soldiers go back to Craig Gwrtheyrn and
make Gruffyd's women give back the rest of my clothes
and the gold torque that Bendigeid sent to Gruffyd for
part of my dowry. Also, I will need a woman to wait on
me."

Correus threw his head back, thumbs hooked in his
sword belt and his face split wide in laughter. "That's better! The only other female in Moridunum at the moment
is the cook's cow, but I promise you when we get to Isca,
you shall have a dozen women if you like!"

* * *

"Here." Correus dumped an armload of clothes on her bed, brightly colored and sewn with gold thread and pearls and bits of amber. A princess's clothes plainly, with shoes of soft, dyed deerskin and a parcel wrapped in sheep's wool that spilled open in a little river of gold jewelry.

"You *did* get them!" Ygerna ran her hands through the pile of clothes—safe, familiar things with which to wrap herself in this alien place. "This isn't mine!" She held up an arm ring of red gold braided into an intricate pattern and clasped with an enameled flower.

"You made a conquest of that decurion of cavalry," Correus said. "I think he figured the Demetae ladies were holding back on him, and he, uh, picked up anything he thought you'd like, by way of evening the score, while he was in Craig Gwrtheyrn."

He could pronounce it, Ygerna noted. The cavalry man had just said "that place we took you from" when he talked of Gruffyd's holding. Gronwy's holding now, what the Romans had left to him. "There was a lot of score to even," she said, and smiled at him suddenly. "Thank him for me. And thank you."

The smile was gone as quickly as it had come, like a flash of light. But she *had* smiled at him, Correus thought proudly. She had never done that before. And it lit up the pale oval of her face like a torch.

"And now will you go outside, please. I want to dress."

"Certainly, Princess." Correus bowed solemnly and strolled outside the tent. Behind him he thought he heard Ygerna laugh. *I like that child,* he thought. The trouble he had taken to get a cavalry troop detached from duty to get her clothes back had been worth it. Robbed of his own child, he seemed to have adopted Bendigeid's, he thought ruefully. But she needed someone to pay some attention to her. Even with her worst fears allayed, she must be ready to die of sheer loneliness and boredom.

"Come back in and look at me!"

He poked his head through the tent flap. Ygerna spun around to show off the full effect. She had taken off the blue-and-scarlet gown that had grown trailworn even before she reached Moridunum, and was dressed now in a gown of white-and-green squares stitched over with russet embroidery and little bronze bells like tiny apples. It was an outlandish costume by Roman standards, but it suited her small, exotic face. Her black hair was tucked back from her face by a gold comb like a crescent moon, and she was wearing the stolen golden arm ring, much too big and pushed high up on her sleeve.

"You look as fine as Cleopatra," Correus said admiringly.

Ygerna whirled around once more and sat down crosslegged on the bed. She wiggled her toes inside a pair of russet shoes. "I feel clean again. Who was Cleopatra?"

"A queen of Egypt and a very dangerous lady. She took two Roman generals for her lovers and caused a very great war."

"What happened to her?"

"In the end she killed herself," Correus said. "But she's a legend now."

"Do your bards make songs about her? I should like to hear one."

"We don't have bards, not the kind the Gauls and Britons do. But she's in the history books, only you would have to be able to read Latin or Greek."

"I know a little Latin." Ygerna made a face. "More than your Eagle soldiers think."

"You must be learning very unsuitable words," Correus said. "Would you like to learn proper Latin? If you could read, it would give you something to do."

"Do you mean it is all written down? All your tribe's history? Among my people, writing is only for making magics. The bards memorize all the great stories and the generations of their chieftains' families back to the first gods. Can't yours?"

"No, but we have some great stories all the same."

"Why do you say 'we' when you're half a Gaul?"

Correus shook his head. "I'm not. I'm a Roman, Ygerna. Many of us are half-blood, generally with a Roman father and a mother from one of Rome's provinces. There are Roman citizens who have never seen Rome, but we all think of ourselves as Romans. Rome is the heart of things."

"Have you been to Rome?"

"Oh, yes, I was born there."

"It must be a very great holding for your king to send

his war band across the ocean. Or were your clans driven out?"

"No. No, you don't understand. We don't have tribes and clans, not the way you do. I don't think I could help you understand yet."

Ygerna thought that over. "Maybe not." She plainly had other questions to put in its place. "Why do your men marry foreign women? Are Roman women barren? I have heard that happens sometimes to a tribe."

"Our soldiers marry where they serve, a lot of them. To a soldier on the frontier, no woman looks foreign for very long."

The Romans would look foreign enough to the women, Ygerna thought, but she didn't say it because this one had been kind to her. "Is that what your father did?"

"Not exactly. My father is . . . higher up than a plain soldier. He was a great general, like Domitius Longinus who commands this legion. He married a Roman lady of the same kind of family—that's my brother's mother. My mother is a, well, like a concubine. When I was grown my father adopted me so the army would take me—there are standards for the Centuriate. . . . I don't know why I'm telling you this," he added lamely.

"I'll tell you about me if you like," Ygerna said.

"Go ahead."

"Well, it won't take very long. *My* mother was a king's daughter. In the old days, when our people made their first prayers to Earth Mother, *she* would have been queen, not Bendigeid."

"And your father?"

"He was of the royal house, too, in another line. I don't remember him very well. He was killed on a cattle raid, and Bendigeid never could make my mother marry again. She went to live with the holy women on Mona last year."

"The Goddess's women?" Correus had heard that there was some sort of sanctuary on Mona. Rome had burned it once, but holy places had a way of enduring.

"Yes. She is very strong in us, even though the kingship comes from the Sun Lord now. But we married with the little dark ones in the old days, and they are the children of the Goddess. Even now sometimes there are intermarriages—my grandmother was a sidhe woman.

That's why the Ordovices hate us. They are sun people almost entirely and leave the Mother's worship to their women. But they are afraid of the old magic. Maybe they think it will come back for them one day."

"Come back for them?" He looked at her carefully. It was the sidhe-blood, maybe, that gave Ygerna that small-wild-animal grace.

"The Mother is in everything," Ygerna said. "When the barley ripens in the summer or a woman suckles a babe at her breast, she is in that. And when a wolf catches a hare and kills it, or when it is war time and there is blood on the ground, she is in that, too."

"Yes, I know that much," Correus said, "though the Gauls are less the Mother's people than they used to be."

"Lugh Long-Spear has grown stronger," Ygerna said, "and the people count their kings in the male line now, but the Goddess is still there. She is everywhere. I am afraid of her, too, but she is part of me. Maybe she will go away from me now," she added sadly, "for coming into an unholy place." She looked suddenly older.

"Would that be such a tragedy?" he asked gently. "If she makes you afraid?"

"You don't understand," Ygerna said. "That I am afraid of her doesn't matter. Everyone is afraid of her. But I am her body on earth. It is through me that she shows herself. If she goes away from me, then what am I?"

"I don't know," Correus said. But he thought, *You will never be what you were before you came to us, no matter what.* He put his hands on her shoulders, feeling the brittle bones under the green-and-white gown. "You are still as thin as a bird. You had better eat your supper. We'll be gone at first light tomorrow, and it's a long way to Isca."

She was enough of a child still to be distracted. "Will we go in one of the Eagle ships that came to Dun Mori? Will you be there?" Somehow, beside the other Eagle men, this one had come to seem less terrifying.

Correus put an arm around her shoulders reassuringly. "Yes, I will be there. I will even hold you over the rail if you get sick."

"I shall not be sick," Ygerna said firmly.

X

Ygerna

THEY WENT BACK TO WINTER QUARTERS IN ISCA SILURUM by ship, a more practical mode of transport than a three-day march through presumably hostile territory. Correus wangled permission to sail in the flagship with the governor and his prize hostage. Domitius Longinus announced testily that he was going to put in for another cohort centurion since one of *his*—he favored Correus with a dark glare—seemed always to be detached for duty as either a spy or a nursemaid, but he gave permission all the same. Correus took it gratefully, knowing that Longinus had a point—he was going to have to spend the winter getting his cohort firmly back under his thumb. An absent commander was generally the equivalent of no commander in the eyes of a legionary, although Octavius, the second-in-command, seemed to have them well in hand. Still, it was hardly fair to Octavius to give him what amounted to a cohort of his own for six months and then step in and take it back again. That had happened to Correus once, and only the knowledge that his own command was due soon had made the position tenable.

The Silures were a coastal tribe, and most of them had been out at one time or another in the small open boats of the fishing fleets. Ygerna, once she had mastered her fear at the sheer size of the galley, had proved a good sailor and after only an hour or two of queasiness was asking Correus more questions than he could answer. He hunted up the ship's master, who proved to be an indulgent father with children of his own. He spoke enough British to get by, and Correus thankfully watched her trot away with him. Calmed by her growing easiness with Correus, she was gradually learning to banish her fear of the rest of them.

Governor Frontinus, ensconced under a canopy on the deck, saw him and waved him over. "Longinus tells me, with as much force as he dares put in it," Frontinus said, "that if I had wanted a staff aide I should have requested one. Do get back to your cohort and pacify him when we get to Isca, will you, Julianus?"

"Yes, sir," Correus said. "I expect he's right, you know." He gave the governor a careful look, and Frontinus folded his big hands across the gilded front of his cuirass.

"I never act on a whim, Centurion," Frontinus said placidly. "How are you getting on with that Silure child?"

"Fairly well. She's left off being scared of me—and most of the rest of us as a result, I think. To tell you the truth, sir, I like her. She reminds me of my sister when she was a young 'un."

"She's growing used to us?" Frontinus asked again.

"I think so, sir. Children are very adaptable, and I expect she's had more care from us than from her own people. She seems to have ranked high as a bargaining counter with Bendigeid, and not much else."

"Keep it up, Centurion. This is one bargain that's going to turn around and bite him, one way or another."

In Isca they made the happy discovery that the garrison cohort that the Second Legion had left behind had done a good deal of building. The commander's quarters and the hospital were finished, the heating system was ready to be fired up, and the smaller houses allotted to the tribunes of which they were, as Domitius Longinus said, mercifully one short at the moment, were ready for occupancy. Like a good many career officers, he was not overly impressed with two-year soldiers hopping their way up the political ladder with a short stint in the army. They installed Ygerna in the extra tribune's house and found a Dobunni woman from Glevum to wait on her.

The legion was at work on the half-finished barracks rows, but it wasn't an unpleasant task. There were good stands of timber to be had, and the men, given the choice of sweating on the barracks now or shivering in tents that winter, fell to with a minimum of complaint. The same could not be said of Ygerna, who was bored and still frightened and inclined to haughty dissatisfaction as a result. After the first week Correus had a thought, and he set out for the quartermaster's domain on an errand he mightn't have had the heart for earlier.

He repossessed the cat, which gave him a look of grave suspicion and then appeared to recognize him, and silenced the quartermaster's protests with the promise of any subsequent kittens. Correus looked at the cat and for a moment he saw Freita behind it, but he gritted his teeth, and the image faded out again. It was only a cat, and he had a better use for it than did the quartermaster. He turned back toward the barracks rows with the cat like a package under one arm. There was something vaguely comforting about the way it wound itself about his wrist.

He dumped the cat on the bed while he shucked off his lorica and helmet and began to unbuckle his greaves. It tucked one foot up and began to wash.

"Don't settle in," Correus said. He knotted a clean scarf around his neck and scooped up the cat again.

Ygerna was sitting on a rug on the plank floor of the house, trying to teach the Dobunni woman to play Wisdom. She waved her into the back room when she saw Correus. "She is very ignorant," Ygerna said, sweeping the pieces into a sack.

"No, she's not. She's a peasant. You're a king's daughter. You've been playing that game since you were five."

"I suppose so," Ygerna sighed. "But I am so lonesome, and there is nothing to do, and you're out with your Eagle men all day, marching them around in squares, which I don't see the use of anyway."

"I know," Correus said. "I brought you some company." He dumped the cat in her lap. It looked mildly surprised for a moment, made two experimental turns and settled down in a lump.

"Her name's Baucis," Correus said.

Ygerna ran a hand through the gray-and-white fur and snuggled her face down onto the cat's flank. "Where did you get her?"

"She was my wife's," Correus said.

Ygerna ran her fingers along the cat's back, making patterns in the fur. "You never said you had a wife."

"She's dead now. A Demetae tribesman tried to kill Governor Frontinus. He got my wife instead."

He had sat down beside her on the rug, and Ygerna

put a hand on his arm. "Truly I am sorry. You must miss her."

He remembered her, green eyes and gold hair and a cavalryman's sword scars on her legs, and the night they broke the bed in Rome and how she had insisted on dragging that cat two thousand miles with her.

"Yes. I miss her."

"Maybe you should keep the cat," Ygerna said hesitantly.

Correus smiled down at her. "No. The cat needs a lap. That's a German cat, did I tell you? She came all the way from beyond the Rhenus in a wicker basket."

"Was your wife a German?"

"Yes. She is buried here, just across Isca Bridge."

I shouldn't have asked that, Ygerna thought. The cat began to purr and knead, shredding the embroidery on her gown. Ygerna batted at its paws, and it yawned and looked at her through slitted eyes. "What does Baucis mean?"

"It's just a name from a legend. Philemon and Baucis were an old couple, very poor and very devoted to each other. When Zeus, who is the great god above all the others, was traveling in disguise, they were the only ones who would give him shelter. He made them priests in his temple afterward, and because their one wish was to die together, he changed them both to trees."

Ygerna shivered. "Like Gwydion turning Blodeuwedd into an owl. How awful to be a tree after you'd been a person."

"No, I don't think so. They only wanted to be together, you see. Baucis was a very good and faithful woman. I'm not sure it's a suitable name for that cat."

The cat yawned again and tapped at the gold balls on the end of Ygerna's belt. Ygerna scratched its ears. "No, she's just as she should be for a cat. I like her."

When he came back the next day Ygerna was curled up on the couch puzzling over the Latin letters he had set her to learning, with the cat droning like a hive of bees against her stomach.

"I came to tell you that the governor sent out an envoy to your uncle."

The stylus skidded across the wax tablet.

"Bendigeid had him killed," Correus said. "And sent him back across his horse."

Ygerna took a deep breath. "And what did the envoy say to . . . my uncle, first?"

"We can hardly know that can we?" Correus said grimly. He noticed the Dobunni woman for the first time. "Go somewhere else." She picked up the shift she had been mending and trudged into the back room. "He had *instructions* to say," Correus went on, "that the governor would offer a treaty that would leave Bendigeid the kingship of the tribe and return the royal woman to him."

"And for that?"

"Forts and roads to be built to link Isca with Moridunum, an end to raiding, and proper taxes paid."

"I could have told your governor that my uncle wouldn't buy me back," Ygerna said. "I didn't think he really thought he would."

"He may not have," Correus said harshly, "but I don't think he thought Bendigeid would murder a legionary tribune, either. He gave him back to his men, with his throat cut and somehow they had the sense not to fight and be slaughtered, too."

Bendigeid would have despised them for that "good sense," Ygerna thought. Briton warriors would have fought and been killed, because it would have been dishonorable to do otherwise.

"They went in there with a green branch in their hands," Correus went on, as if in answer to that.

Ygerna sat up shivering. To kill a man with a treaty branch in his hands—that was a great dishonor, a thing to make you accursed and unclean. Unless it was true that the Romans *weren't* human. Then maybe it would be all right. But they would pay Bendigeid back. She knew the Romans that well by now.

"And me?" she whispered. The safe feeling was gone, and the old terror of the unknown was in its place.

"It appears that the king of the Silures does not want the royal woman back," Correus said. "He told the decurion of the tribune's escort that the governor could kill you if he wanted to. And if you were really Goddess-on-Earth, then the Mother would save you. And if not, then you were no use to him."

Ygerna crumpled up on the couch while he stood glaring at her, the infamy of the murdered tribune still burning on his mind. She started to cry. "You can see how your tribe loves you," he said harshly.

"It's not that—it's the Goddess! She's gone away from me in this place, and she won't help me!" She was sobbing now, loud hiccuping gulps. "They'll kill me, and she won't help!"

I'm a beast, Correus thought. *She's just a little girl.* "Damn. Here." He sat down on the couch and pulled her onto his lap, cuddling her against his chest. "No one's going to kill you. I shouldn't have said that. I didn't know you'd think we really would."

"The k-king would," she said, "if it w-was him."

"Well, Bendigeid isn't the governor," Correus said. "I don't know what Bendigeid is. I think he's a monster." He took the gold fillet off and smoothed her hair.

"Why sh-shouldn't he kill me?" Ygerna said. She huddled against him, clinging, because she had thought for a moment that he, too, had gone away from her.

Because Rome makes use of what comes to her hand, Correus thought, *and you're too valuable to waste.* That was too brutal to tell a child. Maybe it wouldn't come to that. "He just won't," Correus said. "I promise." He put his cheek against her hair.

They spent the winter making ready for the spring campaign. Bales of pilum points and arrowheads and even dismantled catapults were sent in from the supply base at Glevum. The legionary armorer's shop mended dented gear and made replacements where needed. A shipment of cavalry remounts had been earmarked for Britain, and Governor Frontinus diverted the largest part of them for use in the western campaign.

"A bit nerve-racking having the governor of the province keeping his beady eye on you all the time," Vindex said, "but it does have its compensations. Some of those cavalry nags were on their last legs. The wing commander was so tickled, he was practically on the beach to meet 'em."

"Don't feel left out," Correus said. "The legate's ordered up a surprise for us, too. Ever put a catapult together?"

"Oh, no."

"Oh, absolutely. Two came in yesterday—one apiece; nice, isn't it? And being the most expendable, we get to do the honors."

Assembling a catapult was a task which most commanders would duck when they could, especially since the governor, who liked anything mechanical, had a habit of coming down in person to help tinker with the works. No one wanted to be the man who had accidentally blown a military governor's head off. Each cohort commander from the primus pilus on down had pointed at the man with less seniority and said, "Him", until the process had ended with the Ninth and Tenth Cohorts and their respective commanders, Correus and Vindex.

The catapults proved to be not two but three, an onager, the monstrous stone-thrower built for sieges, and a pair of bolt-throwing scorpions. Correus, who said he disliked them all equally, tossed a coin with Vindex and drew the bolt throwers. It took all day to set them up, calibrate the left and right torsion springs to an equal tension, and note the range and force of impact achieved for each trajectory. Since the torsion springs were made of animal tendon, the resulting differences in elasticity made the calibration a wearisome, fidgety process of trial and error. Unequal tension would throw the bolt off center, so they worked on cleared ground outside the fort, and anyone with any sense got out of the way. The maddening thing was that when all this had been done, they would have to be dismantled again to be moved, but the testing process would turn up any missing pieces, and Correus's careful pages of notes on the calibration would give the catapult crews a place to start when the machines were set up again in the field.

It was almost evening by the time they were finished, and the governor, who had indeed been helping and enjoying himself hugely, put up a prize of Falernian wine for a test of marksmanship with Vindex's onager crew. Correus went and got Ygerna and held her up on his shoulders to watch the scorpion crews as they wound the torsion springs back while the rest of the cohort made side bets with Vindex's men. It was cold and the sky was leaden, and Correus took his cloak off and made her wrap it around herself. She was still feather-light, pounds less than Julia had been at that age, but her face was no

longer so pinched and thin, and her cheeks were flushed
with the chill air.

"I'm too big to be carried," she said with as much dignity as she could summon with her chin in the scarlet
brush of his helmet crest.

"Then I'll put you down, and you'll miss the show."

"No. I want to watch anyway. Are you going to win?"

"I hope so."

"Sure we are, missy," the legionary beside her said.
"You just hold tight and watch now."

She's becoming a pet, Correus thought.

The crew completed their adjustments and nodded to
Correus for the signal. "Ready to fire, sir."

"Fire."

The crewman struck the trigger pin with a mallet, and
the bolt shot out. They cheered and made rude noises at
Vindex's crew when it struck within a foot of the white
chalk target.

Ygerna wrapped her fingers around the shoulder straps
of Correus's lorica for balance and watched the second
scorpion bolt fly upward in a low trajectory and then bury
itself in the ground by the chalked "X". It would go right
through a shield and the man behind it, or a wooden wall,
she thought in awe and looked down at the machine
again. It wasn't even magic—she had watched the pieces
being unloaded earlier. Just a thing—a monstrous thing
built out of bits of wood and cow's tendon. It was terrifying, but exhilarating, too, to watch the bolts shoot out of
its mouth.

"Correus, that thing scares me."

"It scares me, too." He had his hands around her ankles in case she slipped, and he loosened one carefully to
show her a blackened thumbnail. "The damned thing got
me once already, when we were stretching the skeins. I
hate catapults."

To her folk a machine like that would be a magical
thing, and the Druids would mutter over it and keep its
use to themselves, she thought. To Correus it was just a
tool, to be kicked when it didn't work and cursed when it
smashed his thumb. *I am beginning to understand Romans,* she thought.

Vindex's crew was lobbing stones at their own target,
and then the governor went out with one of the engineers,

averaging the scores and making allowances for the stone throwers' less accurate aim. He decided for the scorpion crews, and they cheered and went off to strong-arm their bets out of Vindex's men. Correus swung Ygerna down from his shoulders and took her back to the house.

"I'd better go see they don't drink themselves into a stupor."

Wishing he hadn't brought her back so soon, she gave him back his cloak, and he patted her head and trotted off, fastening it as he went. The cat nudged at her ankles and she scooped it up and sat down with it in her lap, trying not to think about those bolts punching through walls like a god's arrows.

Governor Frontinus spread a map out on his desk in the Isca Principia—the third map of the winter, twice updated from the reports of scouts, tribal defectors, and rumors in the wind. Domitius Longinus and the legate of the Twentieth Legion hitched their chairs forward. The air was still wet and cold, but in it there was the scent of something about to bloom. Spring—thaw and good sailing weather.

With rebellion being the common activity among the wild tribes of the north and east for so long, the grasp that former governors had gained on West Britain had slipped. Now the Iceni were no more, and the Brigantes were controlled so long as their garrison kept its sword hand plainly in view. There was the leisure—and the necessity—once more to attend to West Britain. Not a punitive strike, but a locking up, a settlement, of lands left wild for too long.

"It can't be done by land." Frontinus jabbed a finger at the map.

"We've a base at Moridunum," Longinus said. "And all winter we've had scouts and sympathizers in most of the coastal villages between."

Frontinus nodded. "There are places to beach a force here and here." He jabbed two fingers at river mouths opening to good harbor, between the Silure fortress at Porth Cerrig and the Roman base at Moridunum. "And good routes into the uplands. If we scattered the main war band, we could tie the country into a net through those river valleys."

"I've got two cohorts and most of my auxiliaries carrying Second Adiutrix standards, playing hide-and-seek with the Ordovices," the legate of the Twentieth Legion said. The rest of his men were crowded into Isca with the Second Augusta. "If they can keep Cadal thinking he's got the Adiutrix on his tail, he may think twice about moving south. I wish we *had* the Adiutrix, though. I take it they're still in Eburacum?"

"Yes, and I'm not going to budge them," Frontinus said. "They're needed there as much to put some backbone into the Ninth as to keep watch on the Brigantes." He drummed his fingers on the desk and shouted over his shoulder for the optio in the next room to bring them some wine. "Mutiny's a contagion," he said when the optio had gone. "I want it stamped into the ground before I let the Ninth loose on their own agáin. And I would be most displeased"—he looked at each commander in turn —"if the emperor got wind of it."

"Would he break the legion, do you think?" Longinus asked. Vespasian had cashiered four German legions for the same crime.

"He might," Frontinus said, "and I wouldn't give a damn, if I thought he'd replace it."

The legates nodded. The Ninth Legion was needed, rotten or not, because there wasn't another to put in its place. So now they were shy the Second Adiutrix into the bargain.

They sailed a week later. A detachment of the Second Augusta went north by land through the Isca Valley to make a pincer around the bulk of the Silure strongholds, with the troops based at Moridunum as the second arm. The rest of the Second plus the Twentieth went by water to drive northward up from the coastal plain.

The Silures watched the troop transports and the lean, menacing shapes of the war galleys that escorted them as the Roman fleet sailed under their noses past the cliffs of Porth Cerrig. And Cadal of the Ordovices sent a message by way of the Druids that the Romans were baying outside his own holds: He would come to their aid if he could.

Troops and horses, bag and baggage were unloaded at the river mouths, a spreading tide of gold and scarlet, spiked with the waving standards of cohort and century and the great, gilded Eagles of two legions. The coastal villages offered no resistance, the sympathizers in hopes of being left alone and the others because they had fled westward to Bendigeid or north into the craggy strongholds of the Black Mountains. In return, the Romans paid scant attention to the native settlements. They marched around or over them as their path chanced, striking quickly for the wide, open reaches of the uplands. Bendigeid's main war band had pulled back from Porth Cerrig before the Romans could trap it between themselves and the sea. Now it was lairing somewhere in the uplands.

"What are they doing now? Why won't they *tell* us anything?" Ygerna paced up and down beside the baggage wagons like a penned fox while the Dobunni woman sat on a camp stool placidly patching a shoe. She had been through enough wars, both before and after the Romans came, to know that no one ever explained anything. They just did it, and afterwards there was a new master.

"Hard to say, missy," a mule driver said. He was eating an apple. Probably stolen from some village they had passed through, Ygerna thought irritably. "But they'll tell us to move out fast enough if there's any trouble."

They were camped on a high plateau two days' march from the coast. Or at least she thought it was. They had doubled back so often, it was hard to be sure. But they had hunted down Bendigeid's war band—or maybe he had hunted *them* down. And now they were fighting, the king's warriors and the Romans she had watched marching in squares on the drill field.

She tried to picture them in her mind—her uncle's warriors, bright and fierce behind their paint, dark hair flying free, the chariots sweeping across the open ground in a glorious mass of color—fine, fresh paint and gold and silver trappings, the ponies freshly groomed and some of them with their hooves gilded. And the men behind them singing a battle music, the triumphant challenge of a thousand voices while the chariots' wheels set the ground to shaking. But their faces wouldn't come, they were gone away somewhere behind the paint, and she couldn't remember any of them. *I can't see them!* she thought, panicked. The king's, Llywarch's, even her mother's face was cloudy now. It was the Roman faces, kindly or cruel, that came easily to her now. They were out there, beyond the baggage wagons and the rear guard, where they wouldn't let her go, fighting her people with machines that shot bolts through walls.

It was like every battle he had ever fought—and like none before. They always were. The British chariots came in a wave across the high moor, their drivers howling like wolves on the hunt. The first time he saw a British chariot line, Correus had understood what Julius Caesar's men must have felt when they made their first foray into Britain more than a hundred years ago. Now they no longer brought his heart up in his throat, for he knew how easily that chariot line could break against a Roman shield wall. But there were thousands of them, far more than the Roman numbers. A legion at full strength numbered only five thousand, plus auxiliaries, and the governor had part of the Twentieth Legion off to the north, keeping Cadal pinned down.

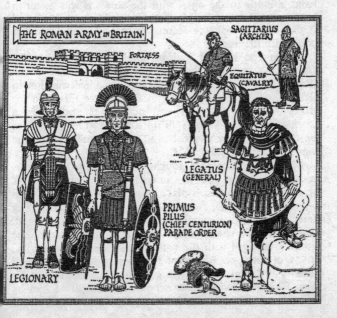

The chariots swept into the auxiliaries of the Romans' front line, and the auxiliaries countered with a rain of thrown pilums and then locked up behind their shields to be buffeted slowly backward until the momentum of the chariots was broken from its first wild rush to a massed tangle of wheels and horses where the scythes in the hub sockets were as deadly to the chariot ponies as to the enemy. The trumpets sang out, and the two legions moved in to pin the Britons before they could swing away again for another strike.

This was the point of "marching in squares," Correus thought as the Ninth Cohort of the Second Legion Augusta moved into place with oiled precision. This was the shield of Rome and the reason a Roman army could wipe the ground with an enemy twice its strength. The governor could detach and shift any segment of his army that he so chose with a single trumpet call, while the Britons, once the first charge was launched, were almost uncontrollable.

Bendigeid knew it, and knew that without Cadal's war band, a battle in the open with the Romans was going to be chancy. But they still had the strength of numbers, and if they could break the Roman governor's main army, it could turn the tide.

In the end he had had no choice. While he waited for Cadal's message, the Romans made a forced march through the uplands, and there was no other way but to fight. There were too many of them to take refuge in the Black Mountain holdings and not eat them bare in a week's time. And if they split up with the Romans so close on their heels, they would be too easily hunted down. The war band turned and fought.

Bendigeid's tribesmen fought as the Celts had always fought, fiercely, with a bravery often beyond their strength, and the hero's place went afterward to the man who led the charge, sword swinging and black hair flying free, a taunt to his enemies to take his head if they could. After the first charge they seemed to rise up from the ground, tattooed with the patterns of their clan and tribe, many of them naked except for short fighting kilts, their throats and arms ringed with gold. Correus saw one of his own men go down, and a Briton bent and lifted him by his helmet rim and cut his head off with a single sword stroke. The helmet strap came open, and the head fell out of the helmet at his feet.

There was a scream from the legionaries, and three of them broke forward. One caught the Briton from behind by his long hair while the others ran him through.

"You are Romans!" Correus shouted. "Get back in line!" Another trumpet sounded, and the whole cohort moved up, hacking their way forward. Two of the avenging legionaries pulled back among their mates, but the Britons caught the third, and a warrior with ochre paint in his hair lifted a bloody object and waved it above his head.

"Beasts!" The Ninth Cohort's standard bearer choked on the word. "They're animals!"

Correus swung his sword and a moment's space opened up between his line and the chaos of the battle. He turned around to face his own men in a fury. "I'll put a pilum through the next man who breaks ranks! Hit them, damn it, and keep your formation!"

The cohort surged forward behind him, driving slant-wise to the British advance, with Vindex's Tenth Cohort to their left and the Eighth behind and to their right.

Something was moving. The battle had a different feel to it, and the British chariots were beginning to untangle themselves and turn for the rear. Correus thought of the governor and the legate Domitius Longinus, who would be perched on respective vantage points from which the legions and their cohorts could be moved like the sections of a chorus on a stage. They would view the battle as a pattern, see each strength and weakness as the opposing lines hurled themselves against each other. But into the middle of it, a man could only see the men to left and right of him, and the enemy before, and over all he could smell a stench that would be nearly unbearable on a hot day.

The trumpets called again, insistently, and Correus pulled his men around him and drove them forward to make the point of a wedge, with the cohorts to either side forming the sloping sides. They hammered it into the British flank, and the Britons began to turn. Just for a moment he felt something wrong, a shift in the momentum, and he looked frantically for the trouble. To his right the Eighth Cohort's standard wavered and then righted itself, and the wedge moved on. But there was a lightness on the right side now, a feeling of something not in control. Correus swore. If the right didn't hold, the Britons would push back through it, out of the circle into which the Romans were gradually drawing them.

The Eighth Cohort standard-bearer would be shield to shield with the Eighth Cohort commander, Correus knew, just as his standard-bearer was at his own elbow. And the cohort wouldn't rock like that just for the loss of the standard-bearer. The Eighth Cohort's second-in-command was back with the baggage, Correus remembered, with a torn ligament. If the commander were down . . .

The right rocked again, still fighting tenaciously, but beginning to lose formation. He had maybe thirty seconds to make up his mind.

"Get Octavius up here!" Correus shouted at his optio.

He gave the cohort to Octavius, gritted his teeth, and plunged back through his own lines. If the commander were down . . . if the commander *weren't* down, the commander could, and probably would, try to get Correus bounced down the ranks to latrine orderly. But something had to shore up the right before the Britons found the hole and went through it. He fell over the twisted wreckage of a chariot with a catapult bolt embedded in it—the Romans had used them to deadly effect while the armies were still separated enough to be sure of their aim—and came up with the front line of the Eighth.

The gilded wreath-and-hand standard of the cohort was still upright, held aloft by its original bearer in his lionskin hood. The shield line was still together, but there were gaps in it, the men from the rear moving too slowly to fill the slot each time the Britons broke an opening in it. There was no sign of an officer—any officer—anywhere.

"Close up!" Correus shouted in his best parade-ground voice. "Close up and hit them! Put your *backs* in it!"

The standard-bearer jerked his head around. He gave a shout and waved the standard, and the cohort began to pull together.

"Where's your commander? Where's Centurion Albinus?"

"Dead, sir," the standard-bearer shouted back over the noise.

"And your third? There are four more centurions in his cohort, damn it, where are *they?*"

"How should I know? Was you wantin' me to go and look for them?"

There was a limit to what any man's nerves would take, and the standard-bearer was obviously already well past his, left alone in charge of four hundred and eighty men he couldn't control. Correus saved his speech regarding respect for officers for later.

"All right, let's go! Roll 'em up!" They couldn't hear him, most of them, but the men in the front could see him, a tall unmistakable figure in a cohort commander's crest, and it put new heart in them, and the ones behind picked it up. The cohort moved out, and suddenly it was easy as the Britons found the last hole stopped up. They were falling back quickly now, and ahead to the left his own cohort and Vindex's were driving the wedge clean through, splitting the war band in half. Octavius seemed to have a good hold on the Ninth, and it was too late to go back now. Correus took the Eighth Cohort through the broken ranks of the Britons at a trot and wheeled them around to keep the split halves from rejoining.

With slightly less than two legions, they had smashed a good half of Bendigeid's main war band and scattered the rest to the four winds. By the time the Silures could recover, the first strings in the net would be knotted.

When the dead had been buried and the cohort commanders, led by Aulus Carus, the primus pilus, had made their own prayers for Centurion Albinus, Domitius Longinus called Correus into the Principia tent and gave him the cohort.

"The Eighth, sir?"

Longinus gave him a look of elaborate patience. "The one you took it upon yourself to steal this afternoon. I've no replacement for Albinus, and I want some backbone knocked into his juniors. They should have taken over after their commander's death. There's no excuse for your even having to *think* about taking that cohort over in the middle of a battle. Kindly explain that to them and that it will be a long time before they are considered for promotion to anything higher than cavalry vet. In the meantime, I'm giving the Ninth to young Octavius. He did well enough with them last summer. You might tell him that if I'm sufficiently impressed, I'll make it permanent at the end of the season."

"Thank you, sir." Correus saluted and left in haste. Somehow a compliment from Domitius Longinus always left him with the underlying sensation of having been chewed out.

He passed the legate's words on to Octavius and, somewhat more gently, to the four juniors of the Eighth Cohort. He had talked briefly to the Eighth's second-in-command, who looked likely to be invalided out permanently, and had learned from him that the late Albinus had discouraged any responsibility or action whatsoever on the part of his subordinates. He'd break them of *that* in a hurry, Correus thought.

His tent was up, and Julius, now restored to his service from his errand in Rome, had scrounged a meal from somewhere and laid it out as appetizingly as possible, with a cup of wine beside it, on the camp desk. Correus shed his helmet and bolted the food, which was all it deserved, and looked wistfully at the bed, neatly arranged by Julius with a pillow and a clean blanket.

"Have you seen Ygerna?"

"Off orderin' someone around, I expect," Julius said sourly, "like she was Cleopatra." He had a low opinion of Ygerna's general usefulness in the scheme of things and an even lower opinion of her haughty attitude toward himself.

Correus chuckled. "I'd better go check up on her. You were no prize yourself at her age," he added. He gave Julius a speaking look, and Julius subsided. He had been such a chronic troublemaker and runaway that he had been publicly labeled as such in the slave market before he had come into the centurion's service.

"I had some cause," Julius ventured.

Correus nodded. "So does Ygerna."

Julius snorted and began to polish the centurion's helmet. It struck him that being a royal princess, even a hostage one, had it all over being a slave. He didn't expect anyone had ever beaten Ygerna.

Correus found her sitting cross-legged on top of her folded tent in a baggage wagon, eating her dinner and making a face at the dried meat and barley bannock that had been the rations for the past few days. They would stay here while the wounded rested and the scouts went out, and the legions were already half dug in, with the ditch and wall up and the rope corrals laid out for the cavalry mounts and the baggage mules. Ygerna sat chewing silently and watched the camp grow up around her. The cat, an old traveler, was asleep on a rolled-up rug, and the Dobunni woman was sweeping bare a patch of ground for a floor and grumbling because there was no one to help her set up the tent. Ygerna flicked an eye in Correus's direction and continued to eat.

He leaned his arms on the side of the wagon. "Are you even remotely glad to see I'm still alive?"

"I am not glad to be left sitting here in a mule cart with nothing but swill to eat and no one to tell me what is happening. Make one of your Eagle men put my tent up."

Correus reached up and lifted her down from the wagon, and she kicked him. "You have the temper of a fiend."

He shouted at a passing legionary—not his own—and browbeat him into setting up the tent.

"Why are you mad?" he inquired.

"I am not mad," Ygerna said with dignity. "I have sat here all day and no one will answer any questions. I don't know why your governor-chieftain has taken me here, because he hasn't even looked at me. He just told the mule-drivers to watch me. I am not a mule. Also, I wish to relieve myself."

Correus chuckled. He looked around. A small stream ran through a corner of the camp, the water peaty and sour, but usable. Upstream a clump of windblown scrub grew beside it. It was dusk. He took her outside the walls and solemnly stood guard while she went behind the scrub.

"Not in the water, mind."

There was no answer and he was just beginning to wonder if she was fool enough to run, when she came around the patch of scrub, straightening her belt and gown. "I know that." She gave him a look. "But I thought about it."

"Well, you'll have to use the water, too," Correus pointed out. "Why are you so mad at us, truly?"

Ygerna sighed and sat down on a rock. "I don't know.

I tried to remember things, my people's faces, and I couldn't. They are my kinfolk and they may all be dead now, and I couldn't see their faces. And it is your Eagle men who have done it. I hate you."

Correus crouched down beside her. "Truly?"

"No. But I don't know why not, either. Or why I can't remember my own folk, or why I was afraid you would be killed. It is wrong not to hate you."

"You didn't feel that way a month ago. Is it because of the battle? You knew that was coming."

"Yes, but I didn't know I wouldn't be able to remember them!" Ygerna said.

"Move over." Correus squeezed onto the rock beside her and put an arm around her shoulders. "You are young. Memory fades very fast when you're young. It's not your fault." It was his fault. He'd done everything he could to blur those memories. He pulled her closer. "It's not your fault."

She was oddly aware of him, even under the armor, and something she couldn't explain gave a little lurch inside of her and her face felt hot. "That hurts." She put the flat of her hand against the iron plates of his lorica and pushed him away a little. "Like a lobster. Why do you wear it? It is a cowardly way to fight."

"It's a highly intelligent way to fight," Correus said indignantly. "Killing is a great waste. The most successful battle is one in which the enemy surrenders with the fewest men lost on *both* sides."

"What is the point of fighting an enemy if you don't kill them?"

"We want to pacify West Britain, remove a threat to the rest of the province—not destroy it."

"What you want will destroy it anyway, I think," Ygerna said solemnly. "And if there is no blood, the Morrigan may look elsewhere to feed, and you will be sorry."

"I can easily believe your grandfather took his wife out of a sidhe," Correus said. "You sound like a witch. I thought the Goddess had left you."

"Maybe I will make a magic and find out," Ygerna said darkly.

"And shrivel me up like a winter apple?"

"Maybe."

Correus stood up. "In the meantime would Your Grace

allow me to escort you back to camp? It is getting dark, and I want my dinner."

Ygerna picked a trail of bramble from the laces of one shoe. When she straightened up he thought she looked a little embarrassed. "I was afraid you were going to be killed. I am sorry I said I hated you."

"I know."

She pulled something over her head and handed it to him. It was a drop of amber on a ragged thong. "Here. It is supposed to be lucky. Its luck comes somewhat sideways, I find, but I think it will keep you alive."

He put the amber around his neck, tucking the disreputable thong into his tunic front where the legate wouldn't see it. "Thank you, Princess."

He held out his hand, and she took it and let him lead her back to the camp.

"They have begun another fortress, at Pen-y-Darren. We caught one of their patrols and left the heads in the water upstream."

"Good." Bendigeid nodded. He was rewrapping a sword hilt with fine bronze wire, a delicate task more often left to the goldsmiths. "Send me Owen and Llew when they come in."

The Druid across from him looked up. He sat on piled deer hides on the floor, with a bowl between his knees, watching the patterns the torches made in the dark water. He was Teyrnon the Chief Druid, and most men had the sense to be afraid of him. Bendigeid's captain saw his look and backed out again.

"And how long will the king of the Silures trade no more than a few heads for another fort raised among us?"

"Until the Chief Druid can devise a better plan," Bendigeid said. "We have killed many of them by raiding in the past month. You saw what happened when we met in open battle."

"The Druids do not make war," Teyrnon said. "We deal with the gods only. It is for the king to hold the sword against the enemy."

"It would be more to the point if the Chief Druid would deal with his underlings in Cadal's hall!" Bendigeid snapped. "He has refused the alliance altogether now that we have lost men to the Romans. I do not think he is as afraid of the Romans in his own hills as he claims. If the Druids ordered it, he would come."

"Druids do not make war," Teyrnon said again, flatly. "It is not our place in the way of things. The king of the Silures would do well to remember his own place!"

Bendigeid stood up. "Teyrnon Chief-Druid may find *his* place somewhat uncomfortable if the Romans win!" He sheathed the half-wrapped sword, holding the roll of wire carefully. "I am going where the gods are less thick about my ears. I have need to talk to someone who has not put his head under his cloak!"

The Druid spread his long fingers out across the surface of the water. "There will be a burning. I can see no more than that. But it may be that the king of the Silures began it when he threw Gruffyd of the Demetae to the Roman kind and taught the king of the Ordovices the trick of it!"

Bendigeid went outside, where a clear, cold sky left the holding walls sharply etched in the moonlight. There was a fair amount of noise coming from a building across the courtyard where such of his captains and household warriors as were not raiding the Romans were getting noisily drunk in the respite. A woman's high-pitched laugh carried through the cold air, and someone shouted something and she shrieked again. The door slammed open, and Rhodri, the captain who had reported the new fort at Pen-y-Darren, stumbled out. He stuck his head in a rain vat to clear it, shook the water off him like a hound, and went back inside. The voices came closer and then dimmed again as the door swung closed.

The king leaned his back against the mud and withy wall of the house and thought about going inside. He recognized another woman's voice as Llamrei's, a woman almost as old as he and still unwed. He had lain with her sometimes; it might even be for him that she had stayed unwed. She would be glad to see him. So would his captains and spear brothers. It had been a long time since he had sprawled in the rushes on the floor and gotten drunk on mead and harpsong, with a woman in the crook of his arm. He put his hand on the door and then drew it away again. How long had it been, he wondered, since he had taken his pleasure without finding it barred with shadows like the ground under trees. How long since he had been the king?

XI

Moonshine

"MY DEAR BOY!" APPIUS JULIANUS HELD OUT BOTH
hands as Flavius swung down from the saddle in the outer
court of his father's house.

The greeting was effusive, but Flavius thought his father looked slightly embarrassed. *Didn't think I had it in
me, did you?* He put both arms around his father, kissed
his mother on the cheek, and caught Aemelia up in a hug
that lifted her off her feet.

He is changed, Antonia thought, watching him.
Changed enough so that even his father sees it. Flavius
stood in the full sun, and there was the first hint of lines
in his face that hadn't been there before. He was tanned
from the journey, and his dark curls hung over his forehead and needed cutting. He grinned at them all and
heaved an exaggerated sigh of relief when Philippos, his
father's steward, bustled out with a small slave in tow
carrying a silver cup of wine to welcome the young master
back.

A groom came up to take the horses, Bericus began to
sort out the baggage, and more slaves appeared from the
house to bear it off to the private apartments in the east
wing.

His mother tucked her arm through his. "We've put
you in the Egyptian room," she said, referring to an apart-
ment with a pleasant green and gold design of lotus flowers on its walls.

Flavius grinned to himself. The Egyptian room was actually a suite of rooms normally reserved for guests, with
a skylight and a little open courtyard on the upper level,
where visiting senators could sun themselves and think
important thoughts in privacy. A far cry from the Spartan
quarters considered suitable for his boyhood, but fitting
enough for the newly appointed staff aide to the Praeto-

rian Prefect Titus, son and presumed heir of the emperor.

The family passed through the atrium, the central room of the house, built around a skylight of its own and a small tiled pool, then drifted through the far doors into the rose garden, Lady Antonia chatting placidly of domestic arrangements and Aemelia just holding shyly to his other arm. Appius walked behind them, his eyes on his son's straight back in the purple of an imperial staff officer and on the curiously elongated shape of the hand that he put around his wife's shoulders.

The air was warm and full of bees. They settled themselves around the pool in the rose garden. It had an edge of rose-colored tiles and delicately floating water lilies, counterpoint to the squat shape of a carp the cook was keeping in it until dinner. Flavius pulled off his cloak and spread it on the stone bench for the ladies to sit on. Under it, he wore a light cuirass and a purple sash similar to a tribune's uniform. He had left off being self-conscious about his hands a year ago, but his mother drew in her breath in a sharp gasp when she saw them.

"I'm sorry, Mother. I forgot you hadn't seen me since—"

"I have," Aemelia said, "and it still makes me wince. It must have hurt so."

"So do a lot of other things," Flavius said cheerfully. "It doesn't hurt now."

"Neither does your promotion, I expect," Appius said. "I'm impressed myself." He was impressed with Flavius, too, but there didn't seem any way to say it without being pompous. "It is no bad thing to be serving the next man to wear the purple."

"I'm a good staff officer and an uninspired field commander," Flavius said frankly. "It's a relief to be put where I feel useful."

"You were useful enough on Gratus's staff," Appius said. "He'll be chewing on his helmet feathers without you, but I heard he was the one who recommended the appointment, with a second from the governor. Now he'll be running through staff aides at three a month again. He must love you like a brother."

"Rather more at some points, I should think," Flavius said. "Poor Correus fished me out of a British camp and then nursed me through the worst of this." He held up his hands. "It got him a *corona civica*, but I imagine it was a relief finally to see the back of me." Flavius gave his father a somewhat pointed look. He thought that Appius acknowledged it.

"How is your brother?" Antonia asked.

Flavius flicked an eye at Aemelia, but her rose-petal face registered only polite interest, and the hand which she had laid on his shoulder didn't move. Her hair smelled of oil of jasmine.

"He's all right now, I think, but he was close to the edge a year ago. That woman's death nearly killed him."

Appius studied him. "I suppose you are thinking I should have let him marry her."

"No, sir. Julia said that, but I think she's swayed by hindsight. I *don't* think you should have, not unless some oracle promised you ahead of time the woman would get killed."

"Flavius!" Antonia looked shocked.

"I think that's a fair statement," Flavius said mildly. "An adopted child is one thing now that the poor woman's dead. A live wife would have been quite another."

"Indelicately stated, but accurate," Appius said. "His letters sound better now, but still . . . sad. I wish I'd had an oracle."

"Awful, it was. Really." Tirza pummled the dough with plump hands, lifted it, and smacked it down the other way 'round on the marble board. "He came into the kitchen to see Cook, and I don't know when I've had such a shock—he hadn't got any fingers!"

"He's got eight fingers, you fool," Emer said. She was stirring cheese into a sauce with a whisk, and it was stifling standing so close to the stove. She brushed a stray tangle of red hair out of her eyes with the back of her hand.

"Did you see 'im?" The wine steward's boy was pouring an amphora of white cooking wine out into a bowl. "Was it awful?" He balanced the amphora on the floor, point down, and leaned on it, awaiting details.

"Dreadful," Tirza said, ghoulishly important. She slapped her hand into the dough for emphasis, and it came away with a horrid sucking sound. "It must have hurt something dreadful! How anyone could bear it!"

"Not as much as your backside will if you ruin that pastry," Emer said as the cook glared across the kitchen at them over the bird which he was carefully stuffing. "And I don't suppose he had much choice." She sprinkled a pinch of herbs into the sauce and tasted it gingerly.

Tirza shuddered but turned her attention back to the dough. The life of a slave in Appius's household was not particularly exciting. The return of the young master with a promotion and a tale of torture and mutilation on the frontier was more drama than had come their way all summer.

The kitchen was crowded, its usual staff augmented by labor recruited from the gardens and the other house slaves, in preparation for the young master's homecoming feast. A pair of field slaves stood uncertainly in the doorway, blocking what little breeze there was, until Emer told them crossly to put their cursed lettuces there on the table and get out. The cook's small daughters were peeling onions and sniffling in the corner, and Niarchos, the majordomo, stuck his head in at the inner door at intervals to argue with the cook. Thais, the elderly slave who had been nurse to Flavius and Correus both, was at a table ignoring the cook's baleful stare and brewing a concoction to which she claimed Flavius was partial. Emer privately decided that Flavius would pour it out the window, but Thais loved both her former charges with a lifelong devotion, and Emer certainly wasn't going to interfere.

"He has come through it all wonderfully," Thais said now, with a quelling look at Tirza. "*And* with a *corona aurea*. Both my boys are a credit to the house."

"Master Correus helped me climb the apple tree when he was here," Cook's smallest daughter volunteered. "Is he coming home, too?"

"Undoubtedly," her father said, beginning to baste his bird with a dish of thinned jelly, "and then I will be forced to construct yet another dinner with the assistance of field hands! No, you fool! Put the asparagus there, in the snow box. And close the lid! Do you know what snow costs at this time of year?"

The slave gave him a petrified look and obeyed, carrying the asparagus as if it might bite him. It was late in the season for asparagus, he had been given to understand by the merchant who had delivered it, and worth its weight in pearls.

"I expect he will soon," Thais told the cook's daughter. "He'll want to see his child if Mistress Julia will just light long enough to catch them in one place for a week at a time. And he ought to be with his family. It might be a comfort, now that his poor lady's dead." Thais thought of Correus's German girl and sighed. Poor boy, he had loved her so, and it was all so impossible.

"Pooh," the little girl said. "She was just a slave."

"So are you," Thais said gently. "Does that make you so unimportant?"

"*She's* not bedding the master's son," Tirza said. "Some people who do that get to thinking they're more important than they are." She shot Emer a look across the lump of dough.

"You're not to speak that way in front of the children, Tirza," Thais said.

"Oh, I know all about that," the older girl said.

"Well, you shouldn't," Thais said repressively. That was what came of having no mother. "You should marry again," she told the cook.

"You should get out of my kitchen," he said. "Get the oven open for me, and get out of my way."

Emer grabbed a potholder and pulled the clay door of the roasting oven open. She put a lid on her sauce and set it on the rack over the stove to keep warm. "What next? Oh, heavens, the dormice! Do you really think Master Correus will come home soon?" she asked Thais as she shifted the tray of dormice onto the table next to her and began to mix cream and honey into a sauce.

"You show too much interest," a deep voice behind her said. "You will make yourself a spectacle."

"Mind your own business," Emer said. She poured some sauce into a pan and began to arrange the dormice in neat rows.

Forst lounged on the table beside her. "That is disgusting." He poked a finger at the pan of dormice. They were immensely fat, fed on nuts until they could barely move and then skinned and cooked whole. Others, awaiting a similar fate, climbed obesely over each other in a perforated clay jar by the wall.

"You are not invited to eat them," Emer said. She

sprinkled the dormice with ground nuts and poured the rest of the sauce over them.

Forst leaned on the table, and she reached around him for the pepper grinder. He was barefoot and dressed in the plain brown tunic that all of Appius's slaves wore, but he looked as wildly out of place in the kitchen as a thistle in a bed of lettuces.

"What are you doing here?" Emer said. "Go back to your horses before Cook has a temperament and the dinner is spoiled."

"Tirza is right," Forst said, prodding her.

"Tirza has a face that would dry up a water clock!" Emer snapped.

"You look some better than she does," Forst admitted judicially. "And a roll in the hayfield with the master is your own business, but you'll break your heart if you look for more than that."

"Get out!" Emer hissed.

"You aren't getting younger, either," Forst said. Emer was six-and-twenty, which was not young anymore.

"Get *out!*" The other slaves were watching them with interest, ears pricked.

"I'll come walk with you tonight," Forst said, "if I haven't found a woman with a better temper by then."

Emer slammed the pepper grinder down on the table as he left, and the kitchen staff reluctantly returned its attention to its own affairs.

"He baits you like that because you won't have him," Thais said quietly.

"He has no right. And no business to talk to me of the master."

"Forst likes Master Correus," Thais said. "There's not a slave in this house who doesn't. But I think maybe you like him a little too much, and there's nothing for you but hurt in that if you pin your hopes too high."

"I'm not such a fool as that," Emer said.

Thais sighed. Emer was still pretty, with the flaming hair and pale freckled skin that so many of the Gauls and Britons had, but she was six-and-twenty, and she'd never had a child. The older you were when the first one came, the harder it was.

"Then why not have Forst, child? You don't hate him or you wouldn't walk with him. Or are you thinking that

now that Master Correus's woman is dead that he will
look for you again when he comes home?"

"No! I mean yes, I am sure he will look for me, but it
isn't that. And yes, Forst attracts me."

The cook was mincing herbs and waved his cleaver in
the air. "Are you thinking that talk cooks dormice?" he
snapped.

Emer put a lid on the dormice and went to set them in
the second oven. Thais stirred her brew until Emer came
back to the table with a knife and a basket of apples.

"Then take Forst, child, while you still can. You should
have a man of your own who can give you children. The
master will let him marry you if he asks him."

Emer jabbed a paring knife into an apple and began to
core it. "I don't doubt it! I was born a slave, of slaves who
were allowed to marry. It hasn't been so bad, I suppose—
I've never known anything else, not like Forst. But I will
not breed children who will be born that way, and I have
told Forst so."

Thais gave her a sharp look. "I wondered once if you
were not carrying Master Correus's child."

Emer put her apple in an earthenware tray and picked
up another. "No."

Thais looked at her closely.

"It was Forst's."

When the dinner was over, the last guest departed and
the last pot scrubbed, Emer hung her dishcloth up on a
hook and gave the kitchen a final look. The lamps were
almost guttered, and the moon was coming in through the
open door. The dormice rustled sleepily in their pot. The
kitchen cat gave them a perfunctory glance—she knew
there was a wire screen across the top—and trotted pur-
posefully into the garden. Emer closed the door behind
her and went out through the cabbage rows to the road
that led past the upper pasture to the stables.

Forst was leaning on a paddock fence, watching a pair
of young mares drowsing head to tail, whisking away the
bugs that droned and zoomed in the warm air. He turned
as she came up and put his hands on her, feeling her
move at his touch under the light tunic.

She didn't say anything, but wrapped her own arms
around his back and turned her mouth up to his. He

slipped his hands between them and cupped her breasts, hard, and she pushed against him, needing him now, wanting him.

He knew I would come tonight, she thought. *I always come. So does he.* One hand was between her legs now, pushing through the folds of her gown, while the other was spread across her backside, holding her against him. She pushed her own hands under his tunic and felt him harden as she touched him.

He took his mouth from hers and pushed the stable door open with one shoulder. She followed him, her breath coming faster now, and her gown rucked up and tangled in her belt above one hip; above one white leg and the soft copper-colored hair beside it. Forst pulled the gown up slowly and tucked it into her belt at the other side. He ran his fingers through the red hair, downward, and she gasped and sank back in the straw.

He pulled his own tunic up, tucking it into his belt, and she lay back in the straw, knees apart, and watched him —with a tight aching pain between her legs because she wanted him so. His body was hard and scarred with old wounds, and his manhood stood out in front of him like a rod. Emer moaned, and he leaned over her and took the pins from the shoulders of her gown, pulling it down over her breasts so that only her belly was covered. She licked her lips, and he put one hand between her legs and watched her face as he moved his fingers inside her.

She cried out and put her hands on him, trying to tease him into her, wondering if he felt anything or only did it to see her like this, hungry and without control.

He put his mouth over one breast, his hand still between her legs and his teeth biting hard into the nipple. She tilted her head back in the straw and clutched his hand into her with her thighs. Suddenly he pulled his mouth from her breast, gasping, and pulled her legs apart with both hands, and she felt him drive into her, long enough and thick enough that it hurt on the first stroke, but she didn't care. She swung her hips up, pulling her knees back toward her, feet above his back, knowing only that she wanted him, all of him, even if it pulled her apart. It didn't. It never did. After a few seconds her passage expanded to fit him, and then there was only the feel of him inside her, drawing out that other feeling that was like no other, that would come to her in dreams, when there had been no chance to get it this way, and wake her, shaking, in the night. She wrapped her arms around his back, pushing herself upward to take him deeper into her, and let herself go, abandoned to that feeling, until it exploded into climax.

A moment later Forst shuddered and groaned as he reached his own climax. He groaned again and buried his face in her hair, still inside her. She lay still, just liking the feel of him in her.

Finally he heaved himself up and rolled over in the straw beside her. "Why? Why like this in the barn like a whore?"

Emer sat up and slapped him. "Because I need a man the way you need a woman. And if that makes me a whore, what does it make you?"

"Then why not marriage?"

"I am a slave. I will not breed more slaves. I am not a cow."

Forst turned his back on her, exasperated. He had been a grown man before he had been a slave. To him it was only another condition in life. To Emer it was an unchangeable state of mind. She had never been anything else. It colored everything she did.

"If you do not like things as they are, then do not walk with me anymore," Emer said. Her gown was still rucked up and falling from her shoulders, but her face was icy. She looked for the pins in the straw. "I will find another man."

"No." Forst turned over and put his arm around her, pulling her down against him. "No. I will take you this way if it's all there is, and I am sorry I called you names. You won't find another man who makes you feel the way I do."

"You are very conceited," Emer said, her face against his chest.

"Could you?"

"No."

Forst chuckled and rubbed his face against her hair. "Maybe you love me."

"Maybe I do," Emer said sadly.

* * *

It was a moon-filled night, restive and wakeful. Appius Julianus leaned against the sundial in the garden and looked up at the statue of Athena for advice. As usual, none was forthcoming. Her pale marble face was immobile in the moonlight, and she plainly did not care what his problems might be. At the moment, he thought ruefully, they seemed all to be entwined, like a nest of snakes. A four-year-old mistake, compounded by another he had had with him for five-and-twenty, if Helva could ever really be considered a mistake. Appius sighed. Helva was forty now, although disinclined to admit it, and if her gold hair had lost a shade of its brightness, there was no more gray in it than she could deal with with a pair of tweezers, and her face and body had lost none of their bright, butterfly charm. She was a pet, cossetted, spoiled, and disciplined only occasionally, a joy just to watch, and an infernal nuisance when she set her mind on something. She could still stir his blood for him the way she had done when he had first clapped eyes on her in a slave market in Gallia Belgica and had yielded to an impulse alien to his practical nature—to have that bright extraordinary beauty to himself, his alone. But he was twenty years her senior, and in the way of passing time, the blood stirred less now than it had in those wild early days when Appius had been a legionary legate and Helva had followed the army with him, and sung to him at night and kept him awake in bed until dawn, and wheedled from him every gift and favor her acquisitive nature could desire. Then Correus had been born, the same day on which Appius's patrician wife, Antonia, had presented him with Flavius, and Helva's tactics had undergone a subtle shift.

She has an eye to the main chance, Appius thought without regret. Helva had never loved him, and he had never demanded that she should. The older Correus had grown, the more she had pinned her hopes on Appius's love for their son, against the day when his physical need for her should fade. It was the babies, Flavius and Correus, rather than Appius's visits to Helva's bed, which had brought Helva and Antonia into a diplomatic war that tonight had showed every sign of escalating into open arrow fire.

Antonia was a descendant of Marcus Antonius himself, and duty to husband, hearth, and class was etched on every bone in her body. She was not a particularly hot-blooded woman, and if Appius wished to disport himself with a slave, that was his right and no encroachment upon her own position. Appius suspected she had been just as glad to have his ardor transferred to other quarters occasionally. She had even been fond of Correus and had taken him under her maternal wing when it became plain that Helva's usefulness as a mother was minimal. But never—*never*—could anything be allowed to dislodge Flavius from his rightful place, or to let a slave-born son outshine her own. When Helva had turned her catapults in that direction, Antonia prepared to return fire, and Appius felt like ducking.

Hostilities had erupted this evening almost as soon as the dinner guests had gone. Flavius had taken Aemelia off to bed as soon as it was decently possible, and Helva, who had naturally not been included in the dinner party, had made her appearance in the atrium, trailing a piece of embroidery at which she had been sporadically at work for months.

"How nice to have Flavius home again," she said, beginning to set delicate stitches into her work. She was dressed in one of her best gowns, Antonia noted with irritation, and more than enough jewelry to open a shop. Just in case a strolling guest should happen to catch sight of her in the garden, she had said demurely when Antonia had informed her that her attire was unsuitable for a meal in the servants' hall. "It wouldn't do for the master's guests to see me looking all anyhow." Since the master's guests weren't supposed to see her at all, this was a debatable point, but beneath Antonia's dignity to pursue. Helva generally managed to drift through the gardens or past a doorway at the right moment. Tonight she had managed to insinuate herself into the predinner small talk in the gardens and prattle artlessly to a senator about her son in the Centuriate. There was something, Appius thought, watching the senator practically begin to salivate, to be said for the Eastern custom of keeping women swathed to the eyes in veils.

Now she settled herself on a couch in a flutter of pale draperies and smiled benignly at Antonia. "It must be wonderful to see him again." A sigh. "I do miss Correus." The implication that unlike Flavius, Correus was single-handedly holding the heathen back from the empire. "Such a shame that Flavius won't be able to hold a field command anymore, but not his fault, of course. I *do* think he's come through it all wonderfully. And lovely for you to have him home in Rome from now on."

"Flavius is perfectly capable of holding a field command or any other command," Antonia said. "There are very few things for which the little finger is a necessity. Flavius is on the staff of the praetorian prefect, which is so important that it is practically an appointment from the emperor, but of course you couldn't be expected to understand such matters."

Helva smiled. "No, I'm afraid politics are beyond me. I must content myself with understanding the active-service army well enough to follow my Correus's career." Appius had made his own name as a field commander. Helva would lose no chance to point out which son was following the paternal footsteps most closely.

"Yes, I've always thought it best to concentrate on matters within one's own sphere." Antonia's voice was placid, condescending. Legally, of course, she had every right to have Helva beaten within an inch of her life to teach her better conduct, but since she was the mother of an adopted son of the house of Julianus, that was unthinkable. Helva was a slave and not a slave. She owned enough jewelry and other property to have bought her freedom ten times over if she had wanted to, which she didn't. She was quite comfortable as she was, concerned only to see that Correus's career advanced sufficiently to maintain that comfort after Appius's death.

It was at this stage in the conversation that Appius had beat a retreat into the garden. He had had quite enough advice on Correus's career lately. A letter from Sextus Julius Frontinus, who had once served under Appius Julianus and now had the gall to tell him how to manage his children; another from his daughter, Julia, mostly about the baby, and advising him solemnly to make no protest over the adoption if he didn't wish to push Correus into "something desperate," whatever that meant; and a third from Flavius, written a year ago, and followed up tonight with a short, pointed interview.

I have misjudged him, Appius thought, remembering Flavius hissing in his ear while his mother and Aemelia's backs were turned, "Have you released Correus from that damned promise yet? And if not, why the hell haven't you?"

He should have given Flavius the chance to stand on his feet in his own way, Appius thought. And he had nearly taken that chance away from Flavius forever by making Correus his keeper. Flavius had the Demetae to thank that he hadn't, Appius suspected. Ironic, that. *But what do I do about Correus?*

Appius looked up at the statue of Athena. "You might share a thought, you know. Just this once." She stared across the rose garden.

Appius let himself out by the far gate, where the statue of Priapus stood, member jauntily erect, fertility personified, caretaker of all that grew. "Your help I don't need," Appius said, bowing respectfully as he walked by the little god. "You got me into this."

The night was warm and still, brightly moon-washed. The pasture fence and wooden bee boxes showed white against the grass. The only sounds were the myriad insects humming in the tall growth by the roadside and the crunch of his sandals in the gravel.

In the stables, the air was steamy and smelled of horse. Appius stopped and ran a hand down a bay stallion's nose. The bay whickered and danced about the stall expectantly.

Why not? Appius unwrapped his toga and draped it carefully on the loose box door, where the bay slobbered on it. Appius, in his undertunic, got a bridle from the tack room and swung up on the bay's bare back making as little noise about it as possible. The horsemaster, if he was about, would without doubt come bustling forward with offers of saddles, assistance, and advice on the danger of the master's breaking his neck. Appius turned the bay's nose south to where a wide dirt road skirted the lower pasture down to the chariot track. Beyond the banked oval track was a training ring with poles and barrels for practicing fast turns, and an assortment of banners, spears, and other distractions designed to unnerve a green horse. A series of jumps had been left standing in the grass verge beside the road, and Appius kicked the bay into a canter.

The bay bunched his muscles and flew over the first jump, landing almost noiselessly in the grass, and gathered himself for the second. It was like having wings. Appius gripped the horse's broad back with his knees and settled down to enjoy himself. An owl swooped across the skyline and dove into the grass of the lower pasture, coming up again with something in its talons. The world looked much simpler by moonlight, Appius thought, reining the bay in to a trot beyond the last jump. The bay was sweaty; he was going to have to rub him dry. And bathe himself, he thought, as his thighs started to itch from the salt. He could see the dim shapes of horses moving toward them across the pasture, and he pulled the bay's head around before he could quarrel with that gray devil Correus had sent, who was at home now with a harem in the lower pasture.

At the stables Appius slid off the bay's back and turned him into the loose box, looking for a rag with which to rub him down. There was one hanging on a hook by the stall gate and he set to work in the half light from the open doors.

Someone with a lantern came around the corner and halted abruptly as its light fell on the bay's stall. "I'll do that if you like, sir," Forst said.

Appius noted with some amusement that there was a cudgel in his other hand. "Thank you, I can manage. Were you looking for horse thieves?"

"Yes, sir." Forst hung the lantern on a hook and propped the cudgel against the wall.

"You're extremely alert."

"I was walking, sir. I felt restless."

Appius nodded. "So did I. There is something in the air tonight, I think." He gave Forst a long look over the bay's back. Except for the hair, he wouldn't have known him for the man he had bought four years ago to teach his sons to speak German and fight the way the Germans fought. The knowledge had served them both well on the Rhenus frontier, and since then Forst had been assistant to Alan, the time-expired cavalryman who was horsemaster for the remount herds. (The chariot ponies, which were the other half of the horse farm, were Diulius's province.) Forst could speak Latin now, and he no longer frightened the other slaves, but what was under that civilized exterior, Appius had no idea. "Did you find some solution to your . . . restlessness in the night?"

Forst shook his head. "No, sir." He stood against the wall, arms crossed on his chest. "Only to accept a thing, if it won't be changed."

Appius didn't prod him for details. They were not his business. "I, also. We seem to have reached a common understanding by moonlight. Sit down, man, I'm not the emperor."

Forst took a feed bucket from a hook on the wall and upended it.

"Odd," Appius went on, scrubbing at the bay's chest with a rag. "It has dawned on me tonight that my sons are grown men, and the time has come to back away. To stand on the sidelines and cheer, and to keep my hands off their business. And worse, that I should have known it four years ago."

"I don't have children, sir," Forst said thoughtfully, "but it occurs to me that that is a thought that's most likely always a mite slow in the coming."

Appius gave a snort of laughter. "Do you really think so, Forst, or are you just telling the master what you think he'd like hearing?"

"No, I've never told you a lie, sir."

"You haven't, have you. You close up like a clam instead."

"A man needs some refuge, sir," Forst said evenly.

"I expect he does at that." Appius hung the rag up on the hook. "Find me a hoof pick."

When Forst brought it, Appius held out his hand. It was plain that the master was in the mood to do his own work tonight, so Forst sat back on his bucket.

"What do you think of that beast that Correus has so kindly given us?" Appius asked.

"So far he's got top colts, sir," Forst said. "The stable-boys won't go near him, but he minds well enough with Alan and me. I wish we had another stud or so like him."

"He's too heavy. I think his colts are going to be."

"A few of them, sir. But the ones out of the Arab mares—Alan and I had the idea you might get a whole new beast out of those. The wiriness and temperament of the Arabs, and some of the bone and endurance of that gray."

"And the size? Cavalry has to be mobile."

"I never saw a half-Arab yet that couldn't spin around

on a flyspeck. And a bigger horse is none so bad if you're going to draft cavalry from the Gauls and the Rhenus folk." The Romans were a small race, but most of their auxiliaries came from the provinces. Forst, when he stood, was a good head above his master.

Appius chuckled. "We've tried for size before, but mostly they turn heavy and sluggish. I've a fair amount of faith in Alan, though. If he wants to try a new breeding plan, I'm willing to buy the stock he needs. Tell him to talk to me about it."

"Alan's old, sir," Forst said. "He doesn't think much of starting something that maybe someone else will finish."

"And maybe ruin? Alan doesn't trust anyone but himself to tell one end of a horse from the other."

Forst chuckled. "He trusts me a fair amount—when carefully watched."

I've never heard him laugh before, Appius thought. Did any man ever really know his slaves? Probably not. "Tell him to start the program," he said, on impulse. "If it looks worthwhile, I'll give the post to you when he retires. Can you write Latin yet? If you can't, learn it."

Forst's head came up fast, in surprise. "I'm a slave, sir."

"So is the steward of this estate," Appius said. "There are slaves in Rome with more power than most senators."

"I don't understand that, sir."

"We're complicated," Appius said. "Tell Alan to see me tomorrow."

Whatever it was that was abroad in the moonshine that night, Flavius felt it, too. The windows were propped open, and the moon turned the lotus flowers silver. Aemelia, in her night shift, was brushing her hair at a marble-topped table with fanciful crocodile legs. The flickering lamplight gave the crocodiles a jovial look.

"It will be nice to go to parties again," Flavius said lazily. "I should think you'll like that." He was stretched on the bed with his hands clasped behind his head, watching her. He would like it himself, he thought, spending his off-duty hours socializing in Rome instead of sitting in a Lindum wineshop drinking cheap wine and watching it rain.

"Yes." A vision of hitherto forbidden pleasures danced

in the mirror before her. Aemelia was not long out of the schoolroom, and the amusements considered suitable for a schoolgirl couldn't compare with those of a married lady. But it wasn't respectable to go to parties by herself, and without Flavius to escort her, she might as well have been still in the schoolroom. Her mother and Lady Antonia had definite ideas about the conduct suitable for a young bride.

Now, with Flavius on the praetorian prefect's staff, they would be invited everywhere. They could even have their own parties. . . . Flavius was going to build a house of their own. Holding court for envoys and foreign ambassadors and the leading men of Rome . . . Aemelia drew the brush through her hair dreamily, while Flavius watched her with amusement.

She's a nice girl, but there isn't much to her, he thought with sudden clarity. *She's relieved not to have to follow me about on some dreary frontier or feel guilty because she isn't. Not like Correus's Freita—but I couldn't have lived with Freita. Maybe that's why I love Aemelia; because she is less than I am.* What that said about himself, he wasn't sure, but he knew it for the truth in this odd, moonlit moment of knowledge. He shrugged his shoulders. It didn't matter. It simply was.

"We'll pick the site for the house tomorrow," he said, and smiled when her face lit up. He held his arms out, and she came and sat on the edge of the bed. He ran his hand down the front of her shift and she watched him solemnly. "It's not supposed to be a duty," he whispered. "It's supposed to be fun." He pulled her down on the bed beside him and kissed her. After a moment she slipped an arm around his neck.

The lotus flowers shimmered in the moonlight, and the cat-headed god on the far wall seemed to smile benignly at them. *You'll be happy with me,* Flavius thought. *You wouldn't have been with Correus.* He started to say it aloud, and stopped. Let her come to that knowledge herself. And if it suited her to keep Correus as a pleasant daydream somewhere in the back of her mind, it took nothing away from Flavius. The dried herbs in the mattress gave off a soft, sweet scent as they moved, and he cradled her in his arms, content with the night.

XII

Thaw

My dear Son,

This is a letter which should have been written four years ago—or better yet, not have to have been written at all. No man is infallible, but very few of us are willing to admit it, especially to our children.

Correus gave a snort of amusement. He thought he knew what was coming. It was a little late in the day for it, but he had to admire the old general for writing it.

Before you joined the Centuriate, I extracted a promise from you for which I never should have asked, and which I am well aware you had very little choice but to give. I release you now from that promise, utterly and irrevocably, with the hope that it has done no lasting harm—and the hope you will understand *why* I asked it.

The "why" wasn't something Appius could put in a letter, Correus thought, but he knew what it was. Appius had asked him to look after Flavius because he thought Correus was the stronger of the two—the spoken reason. And because Appius loved his bastard son better than his legitimate one and felt guilty about it—the unspoken one, never to be spoken. Sad, to give yourself a choice like that. Correus was sitting at his desk in the barracks at Isca, wrapped in trousers and leggings and two cloaks, with a brazier going a few feet away while the wind screeched around the door frame and the snow piled itself into drifts against the barracks walls. It was the first real storm of winter, and the supply wagons with the post must have just outrun it.

* * *

Flavius has been in Rome since the summer and told me in no uncertain terms to take my promise and put it in the Tiber. He is shrewder than I had thought. I am well aware that he did not learn about the promise from *you*.

The rest of the family are well. Lady Antonia and your mother send their love, when they can be distracted from bickering with each other. I have thought of settling an allowance on your mother and giving her a house in the country, but she dislikes the idea and so in some ways do I, so we go on much as we have been, fang and claw discreetly veiled, but generally at the ready.

Julia and Paulinus are with us at the moment, and as Julia is with child, they are looking for a suitable house and intend to stay put for a while. Your son is well, beginning to walk now, and seems to have taken no harm from the continual jaunting about to which Julia has subjected him. Her own child will no doubt receive the same treatment. He is rapidly becoming, as you were, the pet of every servant in the house and looks, to my grandfatherly eye, a great deal like you—and hence, of course, a great deal like me—but much fairer. His hair is a very fine gold now, almost what your mother's was when she was younger, and his eyes are a very remarkable shade of green—*his* mother's, I think, if you don't find it too painful for me to mention her. She was a good woman, and in spite of my objections to a marriage, I liked her. I am glad you have adopted him; you should have that at least. And since he is your firstborn, and you are as yet unmarried, any future wife will not be in a position to object. You will live to be glad of that, I can assure you.

Correus chuckled in spite of himself, putting the memory of Freita carefully into the back of his mind. Lady Antonia was fond of him, but she had made a number of pointed remarks on the subject of his own adoption.

Do you have any preference as to what name he shall be known by in the family? Your sister said, and I quote, that Frontinus is all very well to flatter the governor, but it doesn't suit a small child, and she has taken to calling the boy Felix. Since Flavius's firstborn will undoubtedly be known as Appius—he had better—I have no objections to Frontinus or Felix. I shall send this to you in a scroll case in order to include Paulinus's drawing of the child. It is an excellent likeness, I think. He has a way with faces that is sometimes *too* accurate. He did a sketch of his uncle Gentilius that comes close to being rude.

Correus reached for the scroll case and shook the second sheet from it. He had taken it for merely a continuation of his father's letter, and the scroll case for a protection against the civilian postal services, which stuffed their correspondence into canvas bags and jumped on them at regular intervals.

It was an ink drawing, quickly done but heart-stoppingly clear, as if the child had been caught in motion for a single frozen second. Over it, apparently at some later point, Paulinus had laid a faint wash of color, just enough to show the fairness of skin and hair.

Correus spread the drawing out flat and weighted it with an inkstand and a penknife from among the clutter on his desk. He put his chin in his hands and stared. There is very little to be said about a baby, even at several months, other than that it is one's own and, therefore, beloved. But this was a child of one year, a person in his own right, green eyes bright with curiosity and round baby face beginning to be overlaid with something of Correus's angular features.

He was still staring when the door opened and a small figure, muffled to the eyes like a mummy, darted in and pushed it closed again against the wind.

"Who is that?" She peered over his shoulder.

"That is my son. Ygerna, you are not supposed to be in barracks."

"Why not? You never said you had a son." She unwrapped the scarf from around her neck and shed the outermost of her cloaks.

"It wasn't any of your business," Correus said. "But you may look if you want to. My father thinks he looks like me, but I don't know. This is the first I have seen of him since he was a month old."

Ygerna looked from Correus's intent face to the drawing. "That is sad," she decided.

"Yes, I think so, too." Correus rolled up the drawing with his father's letter and slipped them into the scroll case.

You have leave due you, a voice in his head said, and as always, a second voice answered, *Why? To see a child you can't have?*

He is still mourning that woman, Ygerna thought. She was beginning to warm up, and she pulled off her inner cloak as well, spreading both out beside the brazier where they gave off the heavy smell of wet wool. She had finally outgrown the clothes with which she had come, and the Dobunni woman had made her new ones, salvaging what ornamentation she could from the old gowns. The top of her head still didn't reach his shoulder. "*Why* am I not allowed in barracks?" she prodded him to take that bleak look off his face—and the dead woman off his mind. "I am bored."

"Because you're a girl, and it isn't respectable," Correus said. "Though you're so young I suppose it really doesn't matter. But don't make habit of it. The governor won't like it."

"I am nearly fifteen!" Ygerna said indignantly, ignoring the governor. "So it does matter! But I wish to stay anyway," she added hastily.

Correus looked at her appraisingly. She was still as thin as she had been at thirteen and not so very much taller. But it was the sidhe blood that caused her diminutive stature, not her youth. He had trouble remembering how old she was because she was so small. But she was almost a woman now. She was going to have to stop running tame about the camp before some fool with a skin full of wine came to the same realization. He ruffled her hair. "Come along. I'll walk you back to the house before your woman comes looking for you. Behave yourself, and I'll play a game of Wisdom with you."

"Where did you learn to play this?" Ygerna moved a piece on the board and took one of Correus's men. She sat back to watch him deciding on his strategy.

"None of your business." He moved a piece carefully, baiting a trap.

Ygerna saw his intention and sidestepped, grinning. "You know too much," she said. "Too many things that Romans don't know, I mean. Why?"

"I can't tell you," Correus said patiently, thanking the gods that Rhys the trader had never spoken to the king's niece while he had peddled his wares in Silure holdings. "And I've told you *that* already. Be a good girl and stop prying."

"I am not a child!" Ygerna thumped her fist on the marble tabletop and made the game board jump. She glared at him.

"Then would the princess kindly cease to ask about things that I can't tell her?" Correus rephrased it.

Ygerna laughed. "That is better," she said with mock dignity. "All right, if you won't tell me that, then tell me something else."

"What, O Princess?"

"What is the governor going to do in the spring?" she said seriously. "Correus, I can't stand not knowing what is going to happen to me. I feel like something in a cage, and I don't know if they're going to set me free, or put a ribbon around my neck and keep me for a pet like the cat, or just have me for dinner."

"Not that, I promise you. As to the other two, I don't know, either." Correus's voice was serious now. "It depends on what Bendigeid does, and how the spring campaign goes, and where the governor thinks you'll be the most use."

Ygerna made a face. "The governor is no better than the king my uncle. I am tired of being of use to people. Does anyone care what happens to *me?*"

"I do."

Ygerna gave him a long look. "But you are not the king or the governor, are you?" she said finally.

"No." Correus sighed. "Look, I will tell you what our army will do in the spring. Truly, that is all I know."

Ygerna picked up the Wisdom board and set it on another table. "We can finish later." She sat back down across the marble table from him while the cat patted interestedly at the Wisdom men.

"Now. Tell me."

*   *   *

All summer long Governor Frontinus had laid down a gridwork, like the pattern on a loom, through the river valleys of West Britain. With every pass of the shuttle, a new road would begin its course, a new fort rise up to guard it. Perhaps a third of Bendigeid's total strength had been smashed in the first battle. The rest harried the Romans as they went. Sometimes two and three at a time would act as bait, drawing unwary patrols into ambush. Sometimes by night they would cut the tethered cavalry horses loose or burn what had been built the day before. They left Roman heads along the path of the new road, a day's work ahead for their mates to find, and they prowled like wolves around the outskirts of the camps. But slowly the grid moved on, tighter with each new fort and road. It was drawn almost closed by the start of winter. With the spring they would weave the last line, build the last fort, and Bendigeid would be trapped, able to shift his men only in small bands along secret tracks. Then there would be no movement possible on open land that would not cross the sweep of Roman patrols.

Bendigeid knew it. Already his forays were beginning to have the recklessness of desperation. In the spring the governor would slam the lid down and nail it shut with the two legions he had in winter quarters now and the long-awaited Second Adiutrix. The Ninth Hispana was as stable as it was ever going to be, and Gaius Gratus had taken his Second Legion back to winter at Lindum. Even the detachment of the Twentieth, which had harried Cadal's borders all summer, would move against Bendigeid in the spring. Cadal could preen himself on a victory and grow fat and lazy thinking he had driven Rome back. Or so it was hoped.

Ygerna listened gravely as Correus explained it to her, omitting only the matter of the Ninth Hispana and the governor's plans for Cadal. She leaned forward, arms crossed on the marble tabletop. Her face had left much of its childhood behind by the time he had finished. She spread out her hands and looked at them, as if they were someone else's, and then looked up at him suddenly, eye to eye.

"You told me you didn't want to destroy my tribe, only to make them . . . Romans."

"Yes."

"When Bendigeid my uncle is gone, your governor will be needing a new ruler for the Silures."

"Yes."

"So you were told to make me like you. To make me . . . Roman." She gestured toward the Latin scrolls and alphabet, the cat asleep next to the Wisdom board, the pictures of Rome he had brought to amuse her.

"Ygerna—"

She looked back at him, hurt. "I thought that someone liked me for myself. This time. You said you did."

He put his hands out, over hers. He could take both of them in one of his. "I was afraid you would think of that. But I didn't have to be told to like you. Truly. I will swear it if you like. On—" He stopped to think. Romans didn't regard an oath in the same light the Britons did. "On Mithras's name. Or on the legion's eagle. I wouldn't break either of those." He had never before noticed how dark her eyes were, like black water, with a light somewhere at the bottom.

"No, I believe you. It wasn't your fault, Correus." He was bareheaded, and she could see his face clearly. She gave it a long look, thoughtful. He still thought she was a child. And even if he didn't, it wouldn't matter, because what she wanted was not on the list of possibilities.

Outside, a trio of soldiers, just coming off sentry walk and muffled to the eyebrows against the storm, trudged by. One of them was singing.

Farewell for I must leave thee, I'm off to the army,
And I might not be back when it's over,
So come and hold me hand and watch the moon arisin'
And roll in me arms in the clover.

Ygerna went to the shuttered window and listened. "That is a new tune." She liked music, he had discovered, and could mimic any tune once heard, although the Latin words were still generally beyond her. She sang it over to herself wordlessly. "That is pretty."

"The words are very unsuitable," Correus said. "That's not a song for girls to sing, and you're far too young, if it were."

She looked at him over his shoulder. "Your governor

seems to think I am old enough to be queen of the Silures."

"Thaw. It is thaw." Rhodri pulled himself up out of the tangle of cloak and bedstraw in the house where the king's captains slept, as the first rays of winter sun came through the withy shutters. Outside was the steady drip, drip, drip of melting snow.

Across from him, two other bundles of straw and cloaks muttered and heaved themselves about, and Llew and Owen sat up, Owen as usual reaching out to see that his harp bag was where he had put it the night before. Owen would check for Fand, his harp, before he would look to see if last night's woman was still with him. He poked Llew with an elbow. "Listen."

"Water," Llew said. "Thaw's come. I hadn't thought to go to Tir-na-nOg so soon. I had other things to do yet." He made it a joke, but Owen gave him a black look.

"When *I* sail West-Over-Seas there will be a dozen Romans to row the boat and fetch my beer," Rhodri said, pulling on his boots. "I thought I'd kill them now, to be sure."

Every man went to Annwn, the otherworld, in the end, but it was ill luck to call it by name. They spoke instead of going West-Over-Seas, or of Tir-na-nOg, the Land of the Young, where no one was old, and there was drinking and fighting with companion-adversaries who would rise up again, whole, at nightfall, to drink and feast and tell cheerful lies of earthly prowess.

"You'll have a good season for them," Owen said to Rhodri. "They'll be up out of their holes in a week, and building again."

It was only a matter of time before there was a fort and a road on every passable stretch of Silure ground, before they were boxed in like cattle in a pen. No one knew it better than the king's captains.

Better to go to the Sun Lord on a spear-end, Llamrei thought. She sat up and began to dress. Like most of the Silures, she was small and dark, but her slimness was the wiry grace of a mountain pony. She had passed thirty on her last birthday and had never married. Whenever she felt the need, she found a man to ease it, and although Rhodri had complained afterward that he would as soon put the Morrigan on his staff, the next time Llamrei had looked at him, he had gone to her like a hound. It was Llamrei who did the choosing. Between times, any man who thought that a woman who rode with the war band was fair game generally found a dagger in her hand. There was only one man to whom Llamrei would go for his asking.

"I want to wash," she said now. "Is there any water?"

Rhodri nodded and pointed to a small barrel against the wall, freezing cold but with only a thin crust of ice on the top.

Llamrei shook the straw out of her cloak and stood up. She was dressed as they were, in trousers and wolf-skin boots, but her shirt was hung across her shoulders. They paid no attention to her nudity nor she to theirs. She was one of them, an old companion, warrior first, woman second. Across her breast was the same blue spiral pattern of the Spear Mark that the men bore. Llamrei had earned it. For five years now she had been one of the king's captains.

Llamrei tied her hair back with a thong and dipped water from the barrel, splashing it over her face and breasts and swearing at the cold. Llew came over and began to wash also, knocking the splintered ice free of the surface with the dipper. They rubbed themselves dry with their cloaks and pulled their shirts on, teeth chattering.

Rhodri and Owen and the rest were up, pulling on their boots, fumbling in the straw for belts and daggers, combing their hair, which most of them wore like Llamrei, at just past shoulder length, and tying it back out of the way.

"Food," Rhodri said hungrily. "I smell something cooking."

"There will be more cooking than just barley cake," Llamrei said. "The king will have to make the choice now, with the thaw."

Llew was fiddling with the small dagger he wore in his boot. He looked up sarcastically. "*Is* there a choice?"

"Don't be an ass," Owen said irritably. He slung Fand in the harp bag across his back. Llew and Owen were spear brothers, blood brothers, which was a sworn kinship deeper than any birth relation. It made them squabble with each other when there was a battle coming, from the cold fear of losing one another.

They kept it up as the captains crunched their way across the softening snow in the courtyard to the Great Hall of Dinas Tomen. There was barley cake cooking in the embers of last night's fire, and the ten captains picked pieces of it gingerly from the hot stones and dipped bowls of thin soup from the kettle that hung over the new fire. The vegetables were old and soft, and the meat scarce, but they had got by on much the same all winter. There would be better meat with dinner, but they knew that the barley stores were nearly gone. Although much of the livestock had been found by the Romans, they had been able to hunt. But the fields had gone untended all last season. What crops had not gone to ruin from neglect had been taken by the Romans or simply ridden over.

Rhodri dipped a horn of mead from the vat by the door and sat down between Owen and Llamrei. The mead was thin as well, watered to make it go further. Rhodri swallowed and made a face.

Llamrei dipped the barley cake in her soup and took a bite. They would have to hunt as soon as they could, she thought. Even the meat was running low now. There wasn't enough stock left to butcher without decimating the herds entirely, and a war band couldn't ride far on soup. She said so to Rhodri, and he nodded and gave her a quick grin.

"And raid a Roman grain house if we can."

"I am thinking we'll see little enough grain between now and the last hosting," another man, Hywel, said. He had lost his wife and two sons the last season, and he had lived through the winter in bleak endurance until he could carry a spear again. He was right, Llamrei knew, but she glared at him.

It was a bad way to end, caught like a wolf in a trap, but the other choice was not good, either. The rest had talked of it, of peace with the Romans, but Llamrei had stayed out of it. In the end it would be the king's choice, and then she would follow what Bendigeid decided. But thinking about it made her cold. She mopped up the last of her soup with the barley cake and wished for the hundredth time that it was not Bendigeid who was the king, but Owen or Aedden or any of the others who were of the family. But it was for Bendigeid that the god had spoken, the Druids said, pointing to the night sky and making magics with the fire, and in truth it had been plain enough to anyone who looked at him that he was the god's, in the same indefinable way that Llamrei was his.

"He's sleeping late," Llew said, and nobody asked who. It was the king for whom they had been waiting since they had first waked to the sound of dripping water.

"Teyrnon is with him, most like," Owen said. He drank the last of his soup and wiped the back of his hand across his mustache.

They will quarrel, Rhodri thought, remembering the night he had ridden in from Pen-y-Darren. *They have quarreled all winter*.

As if in answer, the inner door that led to the king's private chambers swung open, and the king came through, with the Chief Druid a half step ahead, as befitted his rank. The Chief Druid was greater than any tribe, greater than kings. It was to him that the sky spoke—and the great god who has no name, the self-created. In Teyrnon Chief-Druid was the sum of all knowledge and ultimately, if he wished it, all power. But his realm was beyond that of wars, and the Roman forts creeping up the Usk and Rhymney valleys were the king's matter, unless the Chief Druid wished to make them his. Plainly he did not. Equally plainly, unless Teyrnon put a Binding Law on him, the king would brook no meddling in his kingship.

Bendigeid sat down opposite the Chief Druid and looked from his captains to Llywarch and the other elders of his council who were filing in behind him. He glanced at the woman tending the fire, and she stuck the spoon back in the soup kettle and left. The king and his council got their own food, and Llew stood up and dipped a bowl of soup for Teyrnon. The Druid gave it a look of disgust and drank.

"It's what we've been livin' on all winter," Llew muttered and then made the Sign of Horns behind his back, because it was very bad luck to insult a Druid, especially a Chief Druid, especially if he heard.

When they had all settled in their places and the hounds, which followed their masters everywhere, had squabbled and snarled themselves into their own places under the tables, the king put his bowl down on the hearth, then rose and dipped himself a flagon of mead from the vat by the door. He wore a heavy torque of twisted, finely worked gold around his throat and a gold fillet in his hair, which hung loose over the shoulders of his cloak. His dark face was appraising, eyes lighting on each captain or council lord in turn, skimming over Teyrnon, and coming back finally to Rhodri and the rest.

"We have Lugh Long-Spear to thank for an early thaw," Bendigeid said at last, "but before we can harry the Roman kind again, there is another matter: the royal woman they are keeping in the fort east of Llanmelin." Llanmelin was an old stronghold, abandoned two years before when the Romans had built Isca Fortress too close for comfort.

Llamrei gave him a puzzled look. The king had refused to buy the royal woman back from the Romans two autumns since, and wisely so. The whole tribe knew that. "Why?" she asked.

"Because it is time we faced the fact that we may not win," Bendigeid said, and the council lords bristled. Llamrei closed her mouth tightly. They *would* not win, and the king and his captains knew it, but to say as much was unthinkable to the old men in the council. The tribe itself would survive, there would be something left, but it would not be the Silures as they had been. The king watched her, reading her thoughts as he always could, and Llamrei looked away.

"There will be no treaty with the Ordovices," Bendigeid said. "Cadal has sent word of that."

"May the Morrigan look hungrily at him," Rhodri murmured, and there was a small laugh down the captains' table.

"It is much to be wished," Bendigeid said dryly, "but without him we are on bad ground, and the royal woman becomes important. You know how the Romans dealt with the southern tribes."

Llywarch nodded. He had warned Bendigeid when the Demetae gave the child to the Romans, but it hadn't seemed important then, with Cadal ready to make alliance. Now it mattered.

"They leave a tribe to its own government, as long as it is done under their eyes," Llywarch said, "and as long as the tribe pays taxes that will keep it crippled. And to make sure of that, *Rome* chooses who rules."

"A ruler with some ties to Rome," Bendigeid said. "A royal woman, for instance, taught for nearly two years to eat from Rome's hand. If we leave her with the Romans, they will put her to their own use, and it may be that there will be no choice given to the tribe as to who comes after me. Also the Druids will be forbidden." He looked at Teyrnon. A king could hide the Druids from the Romans, hide them and lie for them, or he could stand by and let the Romans enforce their ban unhindered.

Teyrnon gave the king a grave nod. His mouth twitched into a faint smile, which made Bendigeid look back warily. "I am in agreement with the king on this," Teyrnon said. "It seems that all things have their seasons," he added dryly. "But it is for the king to tell me how a hostage may be taken from the fort by Llanmelin. I have seen it. It is a great fortress, and there is a Legion of the Eagles camped in it."

"Not from the fort by Llanmelin," Bendigeid said. "Thus far the Roman governor has taken her with him when he has marched. If he does so again, he will have her by him in a marching camp, and somewhat more easily come by. If not, there will be fewer soldiers left in the fort by Llanmelin to guard her. We will wait until the Romans have moved north again."

"It could be done, I think," Rhodri said. "It may be that the Dark Folk will help. They are kin to her, and to the king."

"They will not help if she dies," Llamrei said.

Owen looked at her. "Who said anything about dying?"

Llamrei shook her head. "It . . . might happen." Bendigeid's eyes were fixed on her. She could feel them. She made herself look back at him.

"You read my thoughts a little too well," he told her, and a murmur went down the table and through the council. "She must not stay with the Romans!" Bendigeid snapped. "If she cannot be got back alive, then we take the other way!"

"Kill a royal woman?" Owen looked frightened. A royal woman was the Goddess in her earthly guise and belonged to Earth Mother. To kill her was to be cursed, struck black and infertile in fields and herds and tribe; young men rendered impotent and strengthless, women left withered and barren. The breadth of her anger could pass across a land in a night, leaving nothing but blackened, twisted things in its wake.

Bendigeid sat quietly, waiting for them to master their horror. Then he said softly, "Before now a royal woman has made sacrifice that her tribe might live. It is the lot of those whom the gods touch to make that choice if necessary."

There was a small, uncomfortable silence. That was a holy thing, not to be talked of freely.

"Force the Romans to kill her," Hywel said. "The Goddess may curse *them* with our blessing."

There was a quick murmur of agreement, of relief, but Aedden spoke up reluctantly. He was the youngest of the king's captains and kin to him.

"N-no. If they didn't kill her when the king refused to bargain, then they have a better use for her, and I am thinking it is what we have talked of." His face was unhappy, but he turned to the two by the fire. "Teyrnon Chief-Druid, can it be done without danger?"

"Nothing that touches the Goddess can be done without danger," Teyrnon said slowly. "But it is possible, if every attempt is made to bring the girl out of the Roman camp alive *first*"—he shot a glance at Bendigeid, who sat impassively watching them argue among themselves—"that the Goddess will accept that we buy the life of the tribe with the life of the royal woman, if we must."

They talked in low, hurried tones, pushing the matter back and forth among them like a hurley ball until they could bear to touch it. It was not the death in itself they balked at, but what might follow it. The tribe was fighting for its life. One princess was a small price to pay when seen from that viewpoint.

Bendigeid waited until they had talked themselves out. "It is agreed. We will do anything short of leaving her to the Romans, before we take the other way."

"Whom will you send?" Aedden asked unhappily. Bendigeid had no sons. It was likely that it would be Aedden who would come after him in time. He wanted no part of killing a royal woman to ensure it.

Bendigeid shook his head, not unkindly. No one should have to face that burden before the god put it on him.

He looked the rest of them over. "Llamrei, because there should be a woman; Owen, because it is a matter for Druids." Bards were Druids also, on a lesser level. "Rhodri, because he is neither. If there is a decision to be made, it will be Rhodri's."

There was a murmur of assent, and Bendigeid stood up. Llamrei didn't protest. As one of the king's captains, she gave her first worship to the Sun Lord and not the Mother; but everyone honored the Mother, and there were some rites that could not be performed by a man.

Bendigeid looked at Rhodri. "We need the Dark Folk if we can get them. I will try."

They will read you, too, Llamrei thought. Bendigeid pushed open the outer door into the cold sunlight. The Dark Folk were left-hand kin to the king. His mother had been one of their own. They would see right through him. But the Dark Folk had a way of going at a thing sideways, so that forbidden things were skirted, but it was still accomplished. *He will make some bargain with them. And if we get that child back alive, he'll kill her himself.* It would look like an accident, she thought miserably, staring at the cold remains of her soup. The Goddess would know the truth, but her anger would fall on Bendigeid's head, and he was the king. It was the king's place to take the curse on himself and away from the tribe. *The Mother forgive me,* Llamrei thought. *I'm not going to stop him. She's been with the Romans too long.*

XIII

The Sidhe of Ty Isaf

DINAS TOMEN WAS WELL AWAKE NOW, AND NEW SMOKE was beginning to rise above the rooftops. The fortress had an odd, transitory feel to it—of too many people crowded into too small a space. Some were to the south in the fortress at Crug Hywel; some had stayed behind on their farms to try to wrest some harvest from the ruined ground and hope the Roman soldiers would pass them by, but most were crammed into Dinas Tomen, where the king was, where whatever was going to happen would happen first—the war band, which meant every man of fighting age, their wives, children, grandfathers, priests, and livestock—a mad encampment of huts, tents, wagons, and cattle pens.

The king of the Silures walked from the King's Hall to the pony shed in the lower court knowing that every eye he passed was fixed on him expectantly, dependently. He shook his head at the inquiring face of his driver, lounging by the shed door, and closed it behind him. Inside, he leaned his face against the cool upright stone that formed the door post and fought down desperation. *Do not think how, just do it.* A Druid had told him that once, when he was a child, a child's bow in his hand, looking in despair at a prey impossibly far away. Teyrnon, it had been, he thought, his beard darker then, only beginning to be speckled with white, and the gold sun disc on his breast catching the afternoon light that flowed along the upland moor. *Don't think how. If you think "how," the answer will be "you can't." Just shoot.* He had shot, and the hare had crumpled into the ground.

Bendigeid took the pony bridles of antler and russet leather from the wall, where they hung with the rest of the chariot gear, and whistled softly between his teeth. The black ponies in the far stall flung their heads up and whickered at him. The bridles were studded with silver bosses along the leather straps, and the antler cheek pieces were carved with the likeness of Epona among the horses. He bridled the ponies and led them outside. His driver had brought the king's chariot out, just in case, and Bendigeid stood waiting while he hitched the frisking blacks to it.

"Don't you want me to drive you, lord?"

Bendigeid shook his head again. "No. Go and pull the gate open for me."

The ponies danced through the gate. The way was slippery with half-melted snow, and he pulled them into a walk as the chariot track switchbacked downward to the long bulk of Ty Isaf at the hill's foot. Ty Isaf, the Lower House—the ancient grave mound that had been old when the Dark People were kings in the world. It was a holy place still, although no one could say what long-dead god lay sleeping there, and it was Ty Isaf which had given Dinas Tomen its name—the Fort Above the Mound. It was a bleak place, screened by stunted trees that grew up onto the top of the mound. The men of Dinas Tomen gave it a wide berth—the Dark Folk made their mysteries under the sod of Ty Isaf.

Bendigeid told the ponies to stand, then he knelt before the carved curbstone of the southern slope. There were two blocked entrances on either side and a false one in the north face, but it was the southern way, he knew, that led to the chambers within. The opening was narrow and no more than half a man's height. Even the Dark Folk would have to wriggle to get through. Bendigeid kept his distance from the darkness of that cleft in the ground and scratched with a stick in the dirt before the curbstone. When he finished, he stood and tossed the stick away with a jerk of his hand. He didn't like Ty Isaf. There was a feeling of old magic about the mound.

The glade was clammy with winter, but the ice was gone from the stream, and near the bank where the sun came through the screen of bare trees, the first green shoots were pushing up through the slush and wet ground. The king of the Silures sat on a flat rock by the stream and waited.

They would come, he thought idly. If they didn't, he could find them, but he didn't want to. Even with half-blood to the sidhe folk he didn't like going into one. Or maybe that was *why* he didn't like it—the fear that blood might call to blood, and he would never go out into the sun again. No, they would come to him. He had given them two days to find what was written by the curbstone of Ty Isaf and meet him there. They would come. Anything written in the Ogham script was magic and had to be obeyed.

"And a king's magic is greater than most," a voice said. The little man was standing ten feet away, just inside the trees.

"Do you read my mind so easily?" Bendigeid said.

"Maybe," the little man said noncommittally. "What does the king of the Silures want with the sidhe of Ty Isaf?"

"What are you called?" Bendigeid said. "I think I have seen you."

"Maybe. My mother was sister's daughter to your mother's mother. I am Fox," he added while Bendigeid worked the relationship out in his head.

"We used to play," Bendigeid said slowly. "My mother once took me back to her people for a summer. You have a scar on your foot where my puppy bit you."

"That was before you were Sun Lord to the Silures," Fox said. "Before you were a man, wearing iron."

Bendigeid nodded. The Dark Folk were forbidden to touch iron. Iron was the Sun Lord's creation, a conqueror's weapon. His father's kind had brought it to Britain and taken the land with it. To the Mother's children it was an unclean thing. The iron sword blade at his belt and the dagger in his boot were the mark of the gulf between himself and Fox.

Fox shrugged his shoulders. That was the way of things. "What does the king of the Silures want with the sidhe of Ty Isaf?" he asked again.

"There is a woman of my house in the Roman fort by Llanmelin." Bendigeid chose his words carefully.

"And the king wishes to get her back?" Fox looked dubious. "We cannot fight the Eagle men."

"Not in open warfare, no. But where the People of the Hills go, they go unseen." He used the old, polite name for them. "We cannot take the open ways without crossing the Romans' patrols."

"Why is it so important that the king find this woman?"

"The woman is royal woman of the Silures," Bendigeid said. "The Romans will profane her. And if they can, they will make her queen over the Silures. That will be an evil to the People of the Hills as well as to the Sun Lord's folk."

Fox squatted down on his heels and thought. What the Romans did made little difference in the lives of the sidhe folk. Most Romans never even saw one. But the Romans were a Wrong Thing, and it was wrong that they should have a royal woman, who was Goddess on Earth and belonged to the Mother. But the king of the Silures had never paid much homage to the Mother, for all that he was half-blood to her first children. "And what if we *cannot* get her back?"

"Then we will have to kill her," Bendigeid said steadily. "While the Romans keep her, she is death to my people. And maybe to yours also, if the Romans decide to go looking in the hollow hills for their sport."

"We were here before the Sun People," Fox said. "If *you* cannot find us, the Eagle men will not." Men who tried to reach a sidhe, one of the Dark Folk's secret steadings in the hills, often found that they had walked full circle back to where they started.

"*I* can find you," Bendigeid said levelly.

"You are half-blood," Fox said. "And even you are afraid."

"But I know how to find a sidhe—son of my mother's kinswoman."

It was a plain threat. Fox looked at him thoughtfully. The People of the Hills would have their revenge in the end—there were many ways, beginning with the milk sickness in cattle and ending with stillborn children and the black madness that grows hidden in grain. But none of that would bring back the dead of a burned sidhe. "The Silures have always been brothers to the People of the Hills," he said cautiously.

Bendigeid nodded.

"We would keep it that way, King of the Silures. But to kill a royal woman is a great evil."

"Not if it is her Call. Better she should go back to the Goddess with our help than be taught to betray her people."

"The Call is a matter of choice among the Sun People," Fox said. "Is it not?"

"There are times when the choice must be made by the people. Is that not the Goddess's way?"

Fox thought. "It is our way, and she is ours because she is the Goddess's. But I don't know. I think it may be a Wrong Thing anyway. I will have to ask."

He stood up and turned toward the trees, and in two steps he had faded between them into nothingness. Bendigeid sat on his rock and waited. He had never seen a sidhe man come or go, except once with the corner of his eye. They were simply there, and then they were not. If they didn't want to be seen, they weren't. This one would be back, when he had gone to his sidhe and spoken with whatever Old One ruled there now. It would be a woman, often immensely aged, but sometimes young enough to be fertile still. She was the Old One, whatever her age, and had no name but that from the time that the last Old One died, and she drank the holy drink and saw the visions. All the women drank it, but only one, the chosen one, would see the visions. Now Fox would tell her what the king of the Sun Men said, and she would make a magic in the fire, drink some of the holy drink, and decide.

Bendigeid got a crust of barley bread and some fresh cooked meat from this morning's breakfast from the pack in his chariot. They had slaughtered the last of the stock they could spare that morning. Any further reduction in the herds, and they could not be built back up again without the inbreeding that made weak bones and a too-small size. He sat back down on his rock to wait.

It was nearly nightfall before Fox came back. He looked almost misty in the twilight, but this time Bendigeid had been watching. He saw him when he was no more than two paces out of the trees.

"The Old One wishes to talk to the Sun Man," Fox said, and Bendigeid jumped. Beside the sidhe man another figure had walked unseen.

Bendigeid put his right hand to his forehead and bowed respectfully to the old woman. Her hair was a pale smoke color that melted into the twilight, but her face was oddly unlined, like a girl's. It was impossible to judge her age. Like Fox, her skin was marked with the blue woad patterns that had been old before the king's father's people had begun to use them. She was small, the top of her head level with the king's shoulder. The Silures were smaller than most of the Celtic tribes of Britain due to the mixture of the Dark People's blood in them, but Fox and the Old One were full-blooded sidhe folk, no bigger than an adolescent, even among the Silures. She wore a gown of rough woolen, checkered gray and green, and a belt of wildcat tails around her waist. Her boots were cat skin as well, and she wore a necklace of gold and coral that looked to be very old. Her eyes were dark. She stood looking unblinkingly at the king. He looked back, fixing his mind on a new set of horse trappings, gold and carnelian with enameled plates between the eyes. Let her read through that if she could.

The sidhe woman gave a snort of something that might have been amusement and squatted down in the grass, motioning to the king to do the same. "And why does the son of my mother's sister mask his thoughts so carefully?"

Bendigeid wondered if she really were kin to him, or if she merely spoke figuratively of a woman of her mother's generation. The sidhe folk counted their descent in the female line, but considered any child born in their own generation as a sibling. "My thoughts are my own. I am king of the Silures. Does the Old One tell to me things that are for the sidhe only?"

She made a motion with her hand, dismissing that. It was thin and long-fingered, with delicate bones like a bird's, and a bracelet of plover's feathers. "It is all the same to us, what the Sun Men do. But you have asked our help and have said to Fox that there may be a killing in it. *That* matters."

"There will be no killing unless there is no other way. I have also said this to Fox."

"But a killing all the same."

"A necessity," Bendigeid said, keeping his voice slow, patient.

"And for this 'necessity,' the king of the Silures comes in his fine chariot to beg *our* help."

She flicked her eyes at the beautifully painted chariot the king drove. He had left it tethered at a distance because of the iron wheel rims, knowing the sidhe folk would come no closer. It was indeed fine, a king's chariot, ornamented with gold and silver and enameled bosses on the sides. It was the mark of a man's station that he could make his possessions beautiful, and a man's horses often wore more jewelry than the man himself. But there was wealth enough in the sidhes, carefully hidden; old gold, fashioned into pots and jugs and necklaces made before the start of time. There would be very little use in offering gold as the payment for their help.

"I ask because we need you in this. And because the Goddess on Earth belongs to you as well as to us."

"Very well," the Old One said. She sat back on her heels and looked him in the eye. "We will take your people by our own trails as close to the Romans' camp as may be. We will make some happening for you outside the camp, if you wish it. And we will cast a shadow on the Romans' path if they follow you. We will do so much, and no more. We will not go inside the Eagle fort, and we will not put our hand to a knife in the dark. It may be necessary, but we will not do it. It is the Sun Lord who sold the royal woman away at the start." She stood up, plainly indicating that the interview was at an end.

The king of the Silures rarely felt the need to justify his actions to anyone, but the flat dismissal in the Old One's obsidian eyes provoked him. "The Iceni and the Trinovantes and the others—they were a great people once, kings in their own land, and you know the road *they* have taken! If my people do not end like those, it will be because of me!"

"It is all one to us, what the Sun Men do," the woman said, "but I am thinking you are right at that." She turned away to the trees, the cat skins swinging from her waist, and Fox trotting at her heel.

"I will sell away *any* one man or woman of my tribe if it buys life for the rest!" Bendigeid said.

The Old One turned her head back to him a little, the curtain of her gray hair blending with the deepening twilight. "Let the king of the Silures be remembering he said that."

The last of the snow vanished from the ground, and the smell of new grass was heady and almost cloying. Sextus Julius Frontinus began his season with an inspection of last summer's work, the warp and woof of the net he was pulling tight around the troublesome Silures. The Twentieth Legion went northward up Sabrina Mouth and then inland along the broad Wye Valley, while the Second Adiutrix finished the westward line that ended on the coast at Moridunum. The governor, with the Second Augusta in tow, took the southern section, pushed as far as Gobannium in the autumn, which would link with the Wye Valley forts at Cicutio. The meadows were yellow with flowers, and the high, thin call of the plover seemed to have left its winter loneliness behind. For a whole week it didn't rain, and the soldiers discarded their winter gear and pranced on the march like spring lambs.

Ygerna sat on the tailgate of her wagon, swinging her feet in the trampled grass while the Dobunni woman and Julius put up her tent. It was warm, even in the dusk, and she had pulled her dark hair back from her face with a bone comb. The cat was beside her, washing its toes. A hundred yards away a pair of legionaries was digging a latrine trench and loudly singing a rude song about a general and his horse.

She smiled as Correus came up, helmet under his arm and fresh grass caught in his lorica where he had wriggled along on his stomach with his second-in-command to sight the line of the north ditch.

"Hello, Princess. Standing the trip all right?" He kissed the top of her head.

"*Mmmm.* No one will tell me where we're going, as usual. And I don't like fish sauce on my dinner. And I am too hot." She lifted the heavy dark hair off her neck to let the light breeze blow against her skin.

"You're complaining," Correus said. "So you're fine. You only get sweet-tempered when you're sick."

Ygerna giggled.

There was a muffled oath, and Julius emerged, disheveled, from the folds of her tent. "Bastard's missing a peg," he announced.

"Then go and steal one from the quartermaster," Correus said.

"Yes, sir." Julius gave Ygerna a wary look and backed away.

"What have you been doing to him?" Correus asked. "I won't have you quarreling with Julius."

"I haven't done anything," Ygerna said indignantly. "Besides," she added, "you won't let me carry a knife."

"Just as well if you plan on using it on Julius. What happened?"

"He tried to kiss me. I hit him."

"Oh, lord!" Correus started to laugh. "What did you hit him with?"

"With my fist, of course. In the nose. I expect it hurt."

"I expect it did. Poor Julius. I should have thought of that. You're growing up to be awfully pretty, and Julius isn't much older than you are. I'll give him a talking-to, but you be nice to him. I won't have you two quarreling."

Ygerna gave him a thoughtful look. "You talk as if we were babies. How old are you?"

"Older than Julius," Correus said. *Older than the hills,*

he thought, looking at her. "Julius is lucky. Did I ever tell you, my wife tried to stick a knife in me, the first day I met her?"

"Did you try to kiss her?"

"No. No, not then." *Later, when I was mad. I still don't know why she forgave that.*

"Maybe she had the right idea," Ygerna said darkly.

Correus pushed the thought of Freita away from him, as he had learned to do. Julius came back with a new tent peg and a spare for emergencies. "I'm going to help get your tent up," Correus said. "And then I'll see if I can find Your Grace something to eat with no fish sauce."

He caught hold of one of the outer guy wires and slipped a peg through it. "So you got punched in the nose." He squatted down beside Julius, who was pounding the next peg into the dirt.

Julius maintained a dignified silence.

Correus pulled the cord taut and picked up a mallet. "Don't do it again. She's a princess. Even if she didn't hit you in the nose, you could easily get hung up on a cross by the governor."

"Don't worry," Julius said. His voice sounded tight.

"See here." Correus swung around and looked at him. "Were you just trying to catch a kiss, or is there more to it than that?"

"I wouldn't touch that little she-cat again if she was made out o' gold," Julius said. He smacked the mallet down on his thumb and swore.

Correus stood up. "Good. Then go and make friends with her. And try to remember she's a princess, and cut your manners accordingly."

"Yes, sir." Julius gave the girl in the wagon a wistful, unnoticed look. "I won't be forgettin' again."

Correus made his rounds carefully, lantern in hand, past the neat, straight rows of the Eighth Cohort's tents with the baggage mules in carefully pegged-out corrals between and the wagons lined up alongside. The governor could have taken a surveyor's kit and found not one corral or tent row an inch out of true. There was only the thin shred of a waning moon in the sky, and lantern and firelight blossomed about the camp, leaving the rest in blind darkness beyond the light's circle. In the shadows, the flags that marked the guy wires on the tent rows fluttered like pale birds.

A baggage mule snorted at him as he went by, and Antaeus, catching a familiar scent, stuck his gold head over the ropes and whickered.

"Here, you." Correus fished in a fold of his cloak where he had tucked a piece of barley cake, and held out his hand. Antaeus took it, leaving Correus's hand wet and sticky, and he wiped it on the horse's mane. A few of the mules ambled up expectantly, and Antaeus swung around and bared his teeth at them.

"Inelegant company you keep," Correus told him. He rubbed the horse's nose and went on. The lantern swung from side to side, sending shadows leaping across his path.

The Eighth Cohort's picket saluted. "Quiet tonight, sir."

"Yes, remarkably peaceful," Correus said. "Not even a dead horse in the water."

"I expect they'll be about it soon enough, sir," the picket said.

Correus nodded. He returned the salute and moved on, lantern swinging. He was ten paces away when a shout from the picket turned him back.

"What—"

"Dunno, sir, but there's a grandfather of a row going on over there!" The picket pointed toward the west gate.

Correus closed his lantern and tried to see. The camp was full of running feet, and figures silhouetted blackly against the dying campfires. His optio appeared at his elbow.

"Night raid, most likely," Correus said. "Put the men on alert," he told the optio, "but don't send them out unless you get the word. Remember last season." The whole camp had poured out the gates after the Britons then, while the ten men who had somehow slipped in through the darkness beforehand had set fire to the tents. No one had been killed, but the flames and stampeding livestock had wreaked havoc, and half the baggage and food stores had been ruined.

The optio nodded, and Correus set off at a trot for the commotion, opening his lantern as he ran.

The sounds of shouting came dimly across the camp, followed by nearby voices and confusion as the senior officers stumbled sleepily from their tents. Ygerna, in a tent

pitched near the tribunes', rolled over on her camp bed
at the noise and pinched the Dobunni slave awake.

"Go and find out what's happening."

"I can tell you what is happening. They are fighting
again," the Dobunni woman said sleepily. "If I go out
there, likely they will fight *me* in the dark."

"Go, I tell you!"

Feet ran past the tent, toward the noise. The Dobunni
woman sat up, grumbling, and pulled her shoes on.
"Someone will put a knife in me."

"I doubt it." The woman wore a white night shift and
pale braids hung down past her enormous bosom. She
stuck her head cautiously through the tent flap, then
slipped out. Ygerna sat up and pulled the light covers
around her.

There was a sudden scuffle outside the tent, and the
Dobunni woman's voice was cut off short. Ygerna threw
the bedclothes aside and reached for the leather case that
held her jewelry. There was a cloak pin in it with a
bronze point as long as her forefinger. The Romans
wouldn't let her have a knife. Shadowy figures stumbled
through the tent flap, and Ygerna turned to face them, the
pin in the palm of her hand.

"Princess—" A man stepped forward, and Ygerna sank
the pin into his shoulder.

Another one caught her as she turned to run and pried
the pin out of her fingers. The first man was swearing
and trying to see his shoulder in the darkness.

"It was a cloak pin," the second voice, a woman's, said.
She threw it into the corner of the tent. "Don't fight us,
you fool, we've come to take you back."

"No!" Ygerna began to struggle in the woman's grasp,
and a third figure and a fourth came up to hold her. The
cat jumped off the bed and crouched, spitting, beneath
it.

"We are friends, Princess!"

"No!" She fought on, panicked, biting and kicking.
"*Correus!*"

"We will have to put a knife in her," someone said.

"No, we take her home alive," the first man said.
"She's no more than a child, and she's afraid! Now see
here, Lady"—he gave her the grown-up title—"be still,

and no one will hurt you. We have come to take you home."

Ygerna fought down her panic. She was beginning to recognize voices from over the years. The first man was Rhodri. And Owen the Harper. Her uncle's captains. They would kill her if she fought them. She made herself be still. Maybe—just maybe—they weren't going to kill her otherwise.

"I can't tell what it is, sir," the sentry at the west gate said. "The legate sent Centurion Carus out with two cohorts, but they don't seem to be trying to get *in*. Maybe they're just makin' a noise, like, to keep things lively."

Correus sighed. That was likely enough. Heads on poles and fouled water, and an enemy that howled around the camp's walls and then melted into the night when they chased it—they were all common tactics to make the Romans jumpy.

An arrow sailed over the gate and hit the ground at their feet, and they jumped. "Ahriman take 'em!" The sentry bent to pick it up. "Must be a wild shot—it doesn't seem to be on fire." Fire arrows sent over the walls were another annoyance the Britons had adopted lately. " 'S a bit different from most." He held it out.

"Let me look." There were torches set in the gate on either side, and Correus held the arrow under one of them. "Here, hold this." He gave the lantern to the sentry, who held it up to add more light.

The arrow was small, shorter than a normal man's reach when he drew his bow back, and it had a bronze tip.

"Never saw one like that, sir," the sentry said. "Looks like a kid's."

"No," Correus said slowly. "I don't think so." But why? The little dark people kept out of the tribes' fights with each other or with Rome. It was all one to them, as Nighthawk had said. Most Romans didn't even believe there were enough of the Dark Folk left to have any power of their own—including the governor of the Province. Then why attack a Roman camp? They must have been given a very good reason.

There was a shout from somewhere behind them in the distance, and he spun around, a cold fear beginning to make a ball under his breastbone. He left the lantern and the arrow with the sentry and ran.

There was a fight of some kind going on and more running figures joined him as he sprinted for the eastern end of the camp. Someone stood in the roadway before the tribunes' tents, shouting and pointing. Correus recognized one of the tribunes' slaves. Outside Ygerna's tent he almost tripped over the Dobunni woman, cowering under the guy wires, her mouth bleeding and her eyes squinted almost closed in fear. One arm was thrown up over her head as if she thought he was going to hit her. He almost did. The tent was empty and a wreck inside, and it was plain what the Dark People's good reason had been.

He ran on toward the east gate, which stood open with more soldiers pouring through it. A pen full of baggage mules had been set free and were galloping about in the night, braying and falling over tent wires while the soldiers cursed and jostled past them. Under the torches by the gate was a sentry with his throat cut.

A rain of arrows came down around Correus, one bouncing off his lorica, and he was grateful not to have shed his armor before the uproar began. Ahead a group of mounted warriors made a block in their path, fighting with the still disorganized legionaries. And from the side, another flight of bronze-tipped arrows skimmed over their heads out of the dark.

The new grass was wet, but it felt sticky under his feet. The warriors began to pull back, and an arrow with a flaming tip came down in the front ranks of the legionaries. A sudden flame shot up from the ground, and Correus realized that the grass had pitch in it. Another arrow came in, and another. The burned men backed coughing out of the fire. Over the flames, Correus saw Ygerna's white face turned back toward the camp as someone brought the flat of his sword blade down on her horse's rump.

XIV

The Sidhe of Llanmelin

THEY STUMBLED BACK INTO THE CAMP AT DAYBREAK, singed, muddy, and snapping like a hound pack that has lost the scent.

Carus's two cohorts had come round from the western gate as soon as it became clear what was happening, and the legate had ordered out three troops of cavalry as well. But the Silure raiders vanished in the blackness as if a pool of ink had been poured across the valley. All sign of them stopped at the Isca River, close by the camp. Beyond that, the pursuers found no trace along any of the known trails, and two troop horses broke their legs on treacherous ground. Ygerna and her kinfolk might simply have sunk into the earth.

Correus trudged wearily back beside the primus pilus, Centurion Carus. The pair of them went reluctantly to report to their legate and the governor.

They found the latter disinclined to waste more time on the hunt when he had heard their tale. He nodded thoughtfully, eyeing their bramble-scratched legs and faces and the hem of Correus's tunic, singed from the pitch flame. " 'Never pursue a small force of the enemy on ground of his choosing.' A sensible enough maxim, so I think we won't go further. Nine-tenths of Silure land is under our jurisdiction now. In another two months it will all be. They'll have to surface somewhere then."

"And the child, sir?" the primus pilus asked.

"She's had nearly two years with us," Governor Frontinus said. "Two months of life on the run may well work in our favor. From what she's told Centurion Julianus here, there's little enough love between Ygerna and her uncle."

The primus pilus looked dubious, but he kept his peace. It *wouldn't* be easy to get her back before they forced Bendigeid to surrender. And weighing the chance against

224

more men lost . . . Carus was second-in-command of the legion; they were his men, all of them, and he wasn't willing to throw them away. But it was a pity, because Centurion Julianus was right—the girl wasn't going to live to see the king surrender, in all probability. Not after Carus had seen those little bronze-tipped arrows. The primus pilus's mother was an Iceni woman, and he was more inclined than the governor to put some importance on the Dark People's hand in the matter.

Correus thought he knew what the primus pilus was thinking, and he didn't blame him. But the primus pilus had not spent the last two years learning to love Ygerna, either. He had brought one of the bronze-tipped arrows with him. He set it on the edge of the governor's camp desk and braced himself. Cohort commanders did not argue with military governors if they wished to see another promotion in their lifetime.

"Yes, Centurion Julianus?" Governor Frontinus plainly knew he was about to be disputed with, but he seemed more amused than otherwise.

"That is one of the Dark People's arrows," Correus said.

"So Centurion Carus has just told us," Frontinus said dryly. "I will admit that there may be more to your talk of hill men than I had thought, but since this is the first we have seen of them, I can't think them much of a danger. Especially if, as you say, they don't use iron." He rested his hand comfortably on his sword hilt. "Iron has conquered bronze since man learned to forge it."

"I don't think the Dark People are a threat to *us*," Correus said. "Or even to Ygerna. But the fact that they helped Bendigeid at all—that's what worries me. They wouldn't have liked getting this close to us. They wouldn't have done it if Bendigeid hadn't forced them somehow. And that's not an overly safe step for him to take, so he must have had a strong reason."

"Is this all speculation, Julianus?" Domitius Longinus asked. He was perched on a camp stool on the other side of the governor's desk. His dark face was weary, and Correus thought that both commanders, like their men, had been up all night.

"Yes, sir. But I *am* sure of one thing—Bendigeid will kill her. He knows he's losing, and he knows what we want with her—" He looked from Longinus to the governor, but no denial to this theory was forthcoming from either. "That's why she's important to him now. If he'd won, it wouldn't have mattered."

"There's a curse on the man who kills her—or so the Silures think. The little witch told me in graphic detail what would happen if *I* killed her," Frontinus said. "Bendigeid won't do it."

"I've met Bendigeid," Correus said. "He'll do it."

Frontinus sighed. He was tired. They were all tired. He and Longinus had been up all night, chewing the problem over already, and the two centurions in front of him were practically weaving on their feet. He weighed the deterrent of the Goddess's curse against Julianus's assessment of Bendigeid. And for the hundredth time he weighed his later need of Ygerna against delay and lost men now. He turned to the legate. "*Your* opinion, Longinus?"

Domitius Longinus shifted on the camp stool and put his hands on his knees. His back ached. Frontinus had ordered Julianus to attach himself to the Silure child at a time when Julianus was bereft of his wife and vulnerable. Longinus didn't suppose that Frontinus was overly surprised that Julianus would fight for her now. But the practical worth of Ygerna against a break in the campaign now, against lost men—that was what counted, and, regrettably, there was only one answer to that. "I *do* think the attempt would cost us. I agree that we wait and hope that Bendigeid will be satisfied with taking the child out of *our* hands. And that if she isn't happy over that, she will have the wisdom not to say so."

"Centurion Carus?"

Carus flicked a glance at Correus, his face unhappy. But he said, "I'm afraid I agree with the commander, sir. And if they *are* going to kill her, they'd do it for sure if we even got close."

Correus tried to think of the words that would sway the governor, but there weren't any. No one had actually disagreed with him, they had merely weighed one value against the other, and Ygerna had lost. And they were right. As an officer of the legion, Correus could not make the balance come out otherwise. But he had held the child in his arms and said, "No one will hurt you," and she had believed him. The interview was beginning to take on an odd, dreamlike quality, like trying to run in water, and desperation was pushing at him. Did *Ygerna* know what Bendigeid wanted? If she didn't, it would be so easy. . . .

"Centurion Julianus!"

Correus jerked himself to attention.

"I am afraid that that settles it," Frontinus said, "I am not without sympathy, and I am aware of your feelings for the girl. Also that the responsibility for that rests with me," he added. "But I think that you are wrong in your suspicions. And even if you are not, I'm afraid the decision goes against you," he said, not unkindly. "And now I think we had all best get some sleep. We will break camp as soon as your men have rested. Dismissed, gentlemen."

Centurion Carus saluted, and Longinus rose from his stool tiredly.

"Wait, sir! Please." Correus pulled himself together and arranged his words in his mind.

Frontinus gave him an irritated look. He had been far gentler with Julianus than was his usual wont, and his patience was beginning to get holes in it.

"Sir, I have a long leave due," Correus said to Longinus. He hadn't taken any leave at all for nearly two years, since Aquae Sulis. There hadn't seemed much reason to. Or rather, a lot of reasons not to, and too many memories lying in wait. "Overdue, in fact, sir," he added, watching the governor warily out of the corner of his eye. "Permission to apply for it now, sir!"

Longinus gave him an exasperated look. It was his business and not the governor's, of course, to grant the damned fool his leave. But under the circumstances the governor was likely going to want his own wishes considered, and Longinus was not inclined to defer to the governor on a purely internal matter in front of his subordinates. He wouldn't put it past Julianus to be betting on that, either. The legate mulled it over. In truth, he thought Julianus had a right to go chasing off after the girl if he wanted to. It was his leave and his neck, and as for what he owed the army—not to get himself killed, for instance—well, the army had brought that on itself. The army had ordered Julianus to make friends with the little Silure girl. It could hardly complain because he had done so. Now he, Longinus, was probably going to lose a good cohort commander, and the governor could damned well write to his father when it happened. He gave a dark look to the governor and Correus both, then nodded. "Permission granted."

"Thank you, sir." Governor Frontinus said something in a low voice to the legate. Correus saluted and headed for the door before the governor could decide to countermand the order.

"A word in your ear, Julianus."

Correus halted.

Frontinus was regarding him grimly. "Your commander has seen fit to allow you to spend your leave chasing wild geese, and I can't say that I blame him. The fact that you asked in the first place inclines me to think that you are unfit for other duties at the moment."

"Yes, sir." There seemed very little other answer to make to that.

"Then kindly keep this in mind: Your leave due is two months. You have two months and not a day more. If you are not back by the end of it, you will be considered Unlawful Absent. Or dead."

"Yes, sir."

"More likely dead," the governor said.

Ygerna's tent was still a shambles. The Dobunni woman was creeping about at the back of it, picking things up and then putting them down again in no particular order. She was plainly too frightened to be any use. The cat was a pair of round gold eyes under the bed. Correus gave the Dobunni woman a black look and picked up Ygerna's jewel case. He tipped it out on the bed and found the red gold arm ring with the enameled flower on the clasp that the cavalry decurion had stolen for her out of Craig Gwrtheyrn. Her Silure kinsmen wouldn't recognize it, but Ygerna would. It might come in handy.

"They will send you back to Isca, I expect," he told the Dobunni woman. "See that the princess's things are there when she comes back for them." The cat looked out at him from the trailing bedclothes. "Take the cat with you."

*   *   *

Correus slung the saddle across Antaeus's back and rubbed the cold nose absently as the horse craned its head around to snuffle at his chest. Julius was packing the saddlebags and watching him dubiously.

"You should take me with you," he said.

"I shouldn't. You don't speak British, and you look more Roman than I do." There was nothing patrician about Julius's thin face and mousy hair, but he had the indefinable air of the city-bred.

Julius snorted and looked at his master. Correus hadn't shaved, and there was a day's worth of stubble across his upper lip.

"It will grow," Correus said, tightening the girth. If it didn't he'd shave it off again and tell some tale to account for it. It didn't matter.

"Then what am I supposed to do?" Julius inquired, returning to the subject of greatest importance to him. He was old enough now to resent being treated like a child.

"Go back to Isca with Ygerna's serving woman, and see that she doesn't steal everything in sight. Take care of the cat."

"I *am* sorry they took her," Julius muttered. "And I'm sorry I kissed her. Can you find her?"

"I had better," Correus said shortly.

Julius nodded and looked unhappy. "Do you know where they took her?"

"No, but I think I can find a . . . guide, near Isca."

"You're going back to Isca?"

"I don't have a choice. She's got to be in one of the pockets in the mountains we haven't nailed down yet, and I could wander around in those until I have a long, gray beard like a Druid and still not find her. Also, I need a horse that doesn't have 'officer's mount' stamped all over it. You can keep Antaeus exercised for me, too, when you get there."

Correus picked up the reins and swung himself into the saddle. Julius watched him, hands on hips. His expression was troubled and thoughtful. Correus looked back at him over his shoulder. "If you follow me, Julius, I will beat you. There is a first time for everything."

Julius set his mouth in a stubborn line. "Have I ever disobeyed you?"

"Not yet. If you do now, you aren't going to help her. Or me."

. . . so I have left the little devil in a camp above Gobannium with instructions to take Ygerna's slave back to Isca. By that time he won't be able to follow me if he's pigheaded enough to try.

Correus dipped the pen in the ink bottle and thought. He had given his brother-in-law and his sister his reasons for going, and they all seemed simpler to put down than his reason for writing to them in the first place.

If anything should happen to me—to put it bluntly, if I end up as a skull over Bendigeid's doorpost, which is entirely possible—I would be grateful if you would keep my son Felix for me. Even adopt him (with inheritance after your own children, of course) if you are willing. Since my own adoption of him has been formalized, there will be some pension for him, and I think that Julius Frontinus will be willing to give him a hand up in the world later on—he seemed to feel that the circumstances of his birth in themselves marked the child for a career in the Eagles. But unless *Felix* wants it, I do not wish him to be forced to it. I do not care for the idea of his learning to loathe my memory by being forced to live up to it.

I found Coventina here when I rode in this morning, and she told me that you had offered her service with you when Felix was weaned, and that she'd asked to come back to Britain instead. Unwise of her, I think, although she looked as if some of Martia's civilization has stuck. She is eagerly awaiting Gemellus's return to quarters at Isca. I would not regard Gemellus as sufficient inducement to return to Isca, although the fort has improved somewhat over the last two years, but then I am not Coventina. I gather that you gave her a very handsome sum when you sent her back, and I am grateful. You have been very kind to me and Felix, both of you. I have arranged to have a good part of my pay sent to you for Felix, but it can in no way cover what you have done for us. My love and gratitude both go with this letter.

I am going tomorrow to buy a horse and call in a favor. I will write to you again in a few months to let you know I got back with a whole hide. . . .

"Is this the best welcome the Silures can give to the royal woman?" Ygerna sat on her pony without budging and looked down her nose at the chaos that was the outer courtyards of Dinas Tomen.

Rhodri gave her an admiring grin. The little princess had learned something from the Romans—that lordly expression didn't belong to the child who had left Porth Cerrig two summers ago to be bargained away to Gruffyd of the Demetae. There were going to be a few sparks now, the next time she clashed with her uncle the king. "It is only that they were not knowing when to expect us, Princess," he said gravely. "See, here is the king now, and Teyrnon Chief-Druid, too."

Ygerna watched her uncle thoughtfully from narrowed eyes. The faces of Rhodri and Owen Harper and Llamrei had become familiar again on the wearisome ride on which the Dark Folk had led them. Now Bendigeid's face leapt up sharply from the rest—a dark face not overly handsome, but strong, unmistakable even over the years, marked with some power that set it apart. *If there is anyone who is not human,* she thought, *it is not the Romans, it is my uncle.*

They stepped forward to greet her. The Romans seemed suddenly very safe and normal, swearing at their catapults, compared with the king of the Silures and the chief of all the Druids. The Druids were wisdom and protection, but they were also mystery and never to be taken lightly. Ygerna had always been almost as afraid of Teyrnon as she was of her uncle. She was a royal woman, she reminded herself again. There was power in *that.* And she was grown now, whatever Correus might think. Ygerna made her expression haughtier. *Maybe I can make Teyrnon afraid of me.*

"May the sun shine on your path, lord. And on yours, Teyrnon Chief-Druid." She sat, plainly waiting for someone to help her down from her horse.

A curious crowd was beginning to mill about as the three captains and their warriors slid wearily from their mounts. Rhodri reached up to Ygerna. She swung her right leg over the pony's withers and let herself be lifted down. The king and the royal woman stood looking at each other.

"It is good that the royal woman comes to the tribe's hearth again," Teyrnon pronounced, and Bendigeid nodded.

"You are home now, Princess," the king said. "It would seem that you have grown since you left us. You have a look of your mother about you now, I think."

In truth, she had a look of the king about her, Rhodri thought, but he did not think she would care to be told so.

"Thank you," Ygerna said gravely, nodding to the king and then to Teyrnon. "I am glad to be home after so long. May the Goddess watch over you, for your care for her priestess."

Looking into the king's face, she was almost sure he was going to kill her. She hoped that the Goddess would see fit to resent it. Surely the Mother would come back to her now, away from the Roman kind. If she didn't, would Teyrnon know? "I wish to be alone now, for a day's passing," she said experimentally. "I am unclean."

Teyrnon nodded. "I will send what you need for the herb-fire."

One bridge crossed. "Set a guard on the door," she added firmly. "I want no man to blunder in and put his death on my hands." It was a rite forbidden to men. Not even the king could cross her threshold until tomorrow's sundown. She had that long, at least. And everyone who had touched her would be unclean, too. Ygerna turned her head to hide a quick, wicked grin as she saw Teyrnon bearing down on Rhodri, Llamrei, and Owen.

She came out of the guest chambers unsteadily and leaned on the edge of the rain barrel for a moment. A white, pinched face looked back at her under the fall of dark hair that spilled over her shoulders and floated on the surface of the water. Ygerna had used her uncleanliness to buy time, but she had also spoken the truth and had been careful to make the Cleansing properly. She had neither eaten nor drunk in two days, and it had been frightening alone in the guest chambers with only the herb-fire for light. When she slept, there had been visions, and the dark face of her uncle, and Correus calling her

name across the pitch-fired grass as the Dark Folk caught
at her pony's bridle, and someone shouting in her ear to
ride—if she didn't want a dagger in her. And there had
been another face, a woman's, golden as the corn and then
blood-red, and then black with eyes that had no pupils to
them. *I still belong to her,* she thought, shaken. *I don't
think she ever lets anyone go.*

There had been something of her own face in the
triple features of the Goddess. Ygerna plunged her hands
into the water, breaking the reflection into ripples. She
splashed the cool water over her face and dragged the
sleeve of her gown across it. She pulled her hair away and
squeezed the water from the ends. She could go rest in
whatever chambers had been allotted her now, with
women about her. Rest and eat, she thought hungrily.
After that, she had only to keep from being alone with
her uncle, until—until what? Until the Romans came and
put her in Bendigeid's place, and there was no one at
all of her tribe from whom she didn't have to fear an
"accident" in the dark?

Correus gave a wide berth to the sentry camp at Coed-
y-Caerau and turned the pony's head northeastward into
the woods beyond. Coed-y-Caerau was a watch-post for
Isca Fortress eight miles away on the valley floor, and the
name meant simply The Wood of the Fort Camps, but it
was an older name than the Roman barracks which domi-
nated it now. Just to the southwest of the sentry camp
were the old, slighted earthworks of a native holding. And
to the northeast, beyond an intervening spur of highlands,
was the abandoned fortress of Llanmelin, once a stronghold of the Silure kings. It had been abandoned when the
Romans began to build at Isca. And somewhere in between, if Cadal's runaway slave had told him the truth,
was a holding of the Dark People.

The air was warm, and bees swarmed in the hawthorn
flowers. At the wood's edge the light turned green and watery under the new leaf growth. There were trails crisscrossed everywhere through the woods of Coed-y-Caerau—
deer tracks mostly, some well worn by soldiers from the
camp on a day's hunt, some barely discernible among the
trees and damp undergrowth. Here and there a stream
bubbled by, or a spring flowed up from the ground and

splashed out a downward course for itself among the fern.

Correus took a faint trail that seemed to push its way
into the heart of the forest—the Dark People would be
leery of venturing too close to the sentry camp. Whistle
for his people in an oak grove, Nighthawk had said—if
he hadn't been lying, but there was very little reason why
he should have. Rhys the trader had saved his small hide
from Cadal's men, and by all accounts the People of the
Hills took such matters seriously.

Correus looked up at the green canopy. There were
oaks here and there, as there were in most woods, but so
far not a full stand of them such as made a holy grove
for worship. He wondered if he were allowed in such a
grove, then supposed he must be, or Nighthawk wouldn't
have said so. Nighthawk hadn't known he was talking to
a Roman.

Nor did the rider on the shaggy chestnut beast look
much like one now. He had retrieved his shirt and
breeches from the barracks at Isca, and the heavy brown
and black cloak was tied on the saddle behind him—a
native saddle, similar in style to the Roman ones but worn
with years of use and devoid of army markings. His feet,
which dangled nearly to the pony's belly, were shod in
wolf-skin riding boots, and his belt buckle was native
bronze-work with good enameling on it. The mustache was
half-grown in, and a healing cut, self-inflicted, across his
upper lip gave a useful reason for having shaved it.

It took him all day to find an oak grove, and part of
it he spent dodging a hunting party from Coed-y-Caerau.
He didn't want to have to justify himself to a troop of
Spanish auxiliaries who like as not didn't speak fluent
Latin and might be inclined to take him back to camp
first and ask the questions there. Coed-y-Caerau was on
the edge of the restricted zone and touchy about strangers.
He found a likely grove at dusk and tethered the pony
outside it, just in case, remembering the iron bridle bit.
A spear and native sword were slung behind the saddle
(no one with any sense went into a strange wood un-
armed), and he pulled the dagger from his belt and stuck
it through the thongs on top of his cloak. He settled down
with his back against a tree at the edge of the grove and
began to whistle the call that Nighthawk had taught him.
He hoped he had it right, after all this time—he had prac-

iced it off and on since then. The wood remained silent
xcept for the beginning hum of insects as dusk fell. Every
ew minutes he whistled again, and after a while he got
ip and lit a fire just outside the grove. Sometime after
hat he fell asleep.

He began again in the morning, with the cold suspi-
ion in his mind that Nighthawk might have found the
Dark People gone from Coed-y-Caerau because of the
Romans. He stretched stiffly, fished some food out of his
ack, and gave the pony a measure of grain. When he
irned back, the man was there.

He looked like the others of his kind that Correus had
een (he found it hard to tell them apart) among the
laves of the Celtic tribes—small, dark-haired and -eyed,
vildly beautiful with the tattooed patterns of his people.
Ie wore only a wolf skin around his waist and a necklace
f polished stones. Some of the tattooing on his breast
ooked newer than the rest, and Correus remembered that
ertain patterns were only given when a child reached
nanhood, and Nighthawk would have come to his in Ca-
al's slave house.

"Nighthawk?"

"The trader lord remembers."

"I'm surprised that *you* remember," Correus said. "How
id you know it would be me?"

"Two of my brothers went to see who it was in the
rove and came back to tell the Old One, so I knew it
iust be you."

"Then you found your people? I was afraid they might
e gone."

"It takes much to shift us," Nighthawk said with a
rin. He was leaning on a short hunting spear. "These
re our woods. The Silures went from Llanmelin when the
Romans came, but we—we just dug a little deeper in
ie hillside."

His voice still had the accent that Correus couldn't
lace. The People of the Hills would speak an older lan-
uage than the Silures, he supposed. The little man was
vatching him expectantly. "You told me when you were
unning from Cadal's warriors that you would help me if
needed it," Correus said. "I have come to ask help now,
rom you and your . . . your house." He wasn't sure how
he sidhe-folk grouped themselves.

"I am of the Sidhe of Llanmelin," Nighthawk sai—
Correus got the impression that it was a communal grou—
ing, perhaps of many houses. Or perhaps they didn't hav—
houses apart and were all one. "There is still a debt be—
tween me and Rhys the trader," Nighthawk said. "If ther—
is a forfeit on your life, it may be hard, but we will try
my people and I. Who is chasing you?"

"No one. There is a royal woman of the Silures who wa—
a prisoner of the Romans. Now she has been stolen awa—
again by her tribe and by some other house of your peo—
ple, I think. I want to find her again."

"Why? What is the royal woman to the trader lord—
She belongs to her tribe. The Goddess will be angry i—
she goes away from them again, now that she is safe."

"She isn't safe," Correus said. "Not from the king."

Nighthawk shifted his grip on his spear, so that h—
leaned on the other foot, and looked worried. "We hear—
that the king would have killed her if she could not b—
got away safe, which was an evil thing, but maybe neces—
sary. We heard from the Sidhe of Ty Isaf who helpe—
him," he explained when Correus looked puzzled. Night—
hawk grinned again. "There is nothing that one amon—
the People of the Hills knows that the rest do not." Hi—
face sobered again. "But we also heard that she *had* been—
taken safely. Do you wish to steal her again?"

"The king will kill her," Correus said. "He will kill he—
even now that she has been got safe away from the Ro—
mans, because he is afraid of her. He will kill her an—
dare the Goddess to curse him if she will. Is that not—
great sacrilege?"

Nighthawk nodded, and Correus thought he saw a flas—
of fear in the small, dark face.

"And might the Mother not curse the People of th—
Hills as well, for helping him to it?" he pursued.

"Yes," Nighthawk said slowly, some of his imperturba—
bility slipping away. "To kill her if they could not tak—
her from the Romans, *maybe* that would have been al—
right. To kill her now—" His eyes were frightened, an—
he moved so that he didn't stand inside the grove at all—
"The Sidhe of Ty Isaf didn't know of that."

"Will the Goddess be any gentler for their ignorance?—

"No. But why does Rhys the trader care? You are no—
a Silure or a sidhe-man."

Correus shook his head. "First, do you agree that you owe me a life?"

Nighthawk nodded warily.

"Then the life I want is the royal woman's, not my own. Will you help me find her before the king can arrange her death and maybe bring a curse on the sidhe-folk with it? Her life for yours, that I saved from Cadal."

Nighthawk nodded again. "It is agreed, because I owe you a debt and because the king must not do this thing. But you must tell me why you care. I will not take back my answer."

"Because I am a Roman," Correus said, and waited to see what the sidhe-man would do.

For a moment he thought Nighthawk would vanish into the forest the way he had come, but the little man didn't move. "I have never spoken to a Roman before," he said finally. "Are you human?"

Correus laughed, but he remained motionless, as a man does when a wild deer out of the forest begins to come near him. "Yes, I am human. And not so very evil either, only different."

Different was generally evil, Nighthawk thought, but it was too late to back out now. He had agreed. "I can't go back on a life-price," he said. "But I must tell the Old One, to see if she will let my brothers come with me." He looked dubiously at Correus, as if he didn't know what to do with him. "You had better come, too."

"You will have to leave the horse here," Nighthawk said. They had been moving for several hours, and the little man had finally ceased to look over his shoulder at Correus as if he expected the Roman behind him to have changed to some fearful shape. He kept a wary distance, though, even now.

Correus tethered the pony to a hawthorn tree and looked around him curiously. He could see nothing but empty hillside covered with a scrubby growth and a few hawthorn thickets. A slight movement caught his eye, and he spotted two thin cows grazing on the hilltop, but no sign of man. Nighthawk beckoned to him. He followed obediently, and then suddenly he saw a thin blue curl of peat smoke drift across the slope. Correus narrowed his eyes. The steading was dug into the hillside itself, with twisted

trees growing on the top and a screen of wild briars acros
the front. The entrance was low, no more than a tunne
through the briars. A Roman patrol could have ridde
within twenty feet and never have seen it.

Beyond the screen of briars, a wooden door frame wa
set into the hill, also low, so that even Nighthawk bent t
pass through. It was dark inside and smelled like a fox
den.

Correus hesitated in the doorway and suppressed th
urge to bolt. There were numerous tales of the hollo
hills and what happened to a man who strayed into one
The skin on the back of his neck prickled, but he fough
the feeling back down. If Nighthawk could conquer hi
fear of *him,* then Correus could master his own. But th
urge to take something of the sunlight with him into thi
dark place was strong. "Lord of Light go with me," h
whispered and ducked through the doorway.

Inside, he stood blinking in the dimness until he coul
make out the figures seated around the fire that was th
only illumination at the far end of the cavern. Nighthaw
had dropped to one knee before one of them and wa
speaking in some language Correus had never heard. H
looked over his shoulder once at the Roman and the
went on talking—explaining him, Correus expected—t
the seated figure, which Correus saw was a woman o
immense age and thin as a wisp of smoke.

When Nighthawk had finished, she looked up a
Correus and beckoned to him with a gnarled hand. H
came forward, trying not to choke on the thick smell i
the cavern and the smoke from the peat fire, and kne
as he had seen Nighthawk do. One of the others shifte
a little to make room for him, and Correus saw that the
were all women of varying ages, dressed like the olde
one in woolen gowns of some dimly patterned materia
They were at work—two of them grinding corn and tw
sewing on some heavy piece of cloth, one from each end
They didn't cease as the Old One looked at him thought
fully and then spoke in the same curious accent Night
hawk had.

"Why does an Eagle man come to the People of th
Hills for help?"

"Because there is no time to wait until our army take

the last of the king's strongholds," Correus said. "The royal woman will be dead by then."

The old woman nodded and tapped a finger against the bead she wore around her neck. It was the size of an apricot, and Correus thought that it was pure gold. "This was mined from the hills by our folk before the Golden People were ever a nation. What the Eagle men and the Sun's Children do to each other is all one to us. But the royal woman is the Mother's, so I must think. You will stay here, and my daughter will bring you food, and then I will tell you what we will do."

A younger woman slid forward and spooned something from a pot which sat on the edge of the peat fire, and the Old One watched Correus with something like amusement. To go into a sidhe was bad enough, thought Correus, but a man who ate of their food would wake in the morning to find a hundred years gone by and all his companions dust in the earth. Or so they said.

The woman handed him the bowl, and the Old One chuckled. "Are you afraid there is something in the stew, Eagle man?"

"Yes," Correus said frankly. "But I will eat it anyway." He didn't think he had any choice if he wanted them to help. He lifted the bowl and drank some of the broth. It had an odd taste, but it could have been only the peat fire's smoke or some unfamiliar game. It wasn't bad, only odd, and suddenly he was ravenous.

He finished and sat back on his heels, waiting. The Old One seemed to have gone into some sort of trance, and the other women had stopped their work and were sitting in a circle around her. Nighthawk had moved away to a respectful distance and squatted on his heels, also, waiting. Correus had heard that the People of the Hills were a matriarchy, and apparently it was true. He wondered what the men thought of it, and then decided that they probably had as little choice in the matter as had the women in a male-ruled world.

He wasn't sure how long it was, but he was content to sit and wait, and nothing seemed very troubling now— maybe there had been something in the stew after all. The Old One opened her eyes and pushed the gray hair back from her face and removed the two heron's feathers she had stuck in it. She fixed a bright, dark eye on Correus, and for a moment he thought of a crow with gray feathers.

"Tell me, Eagle man, why is it that you want the royal woman of the Silures." She pointed to a place by the hearth in front of her, and the other women scooted back again to make room for him.

Correus shook that peaceful, lethargic feeling away from him and slid forward. "Because the king of the Silures will kill her otherwise," he said again.

"And what is that to the Eagle men?"

"Because she is useful to us, and we need her," Correus said. He had the feeling that there was not much use in lying to this creature. "But with us, she will live and be well treated."

"She is Goddess on Earth," the Old One said. "How if the Romans profane her? The Mother will not like that, either."

"Would you really mind if the Mother cursed us?" Correus asked.

"I would not mind if the Mother lifted all your Eagle forts and dropped them in the sea!" the Old One snapped. "But it is not something to take lightly, and a curse has a way of spreading. Still, she will live, and maybe that is the most important. But I do not like it, either way. The Eagle men and the king of the Silures have made a great trouble with this. And you, Eagle man, is that all that is in your mind—the woman's usefulness?"

"No. She was given into my care when she first came to us, and I care for her. She is a child, and now she will be frightened."

"Not so much a child by now." She stared at him. "What are you called?"

"Correus."

"That is a Sun Man's name."

"Yes. My mother was a Gaul."

"Are you afraid of me, Roman with a Sun Man's name?"

"A little."

The old woman chuckled. "Good. Maybe there is enough Gaul in you."

"I'm a Roman."

"No one is ever only one thing. And the royal woman

has been with Romans too long. Maybe she should not have gone back after all."

"Then your people may help me?"

The old woman tightened her lips into a thin line. "The Goddess has spoken to me, and you have given me the right answers, so there is no question of what I allow or not. It is."

As she spoke, Nighthawk rose and slipped out of the cavern.

"Nighthawk and his brothers will go with you," she said, but her voice seemed to have lost some of its assurance. "This is a new thing, and I do not like it. Many new things have happened since my people were queens here, and very few of them have brought anything but evil. You are a new thing, Eagle man. A harsh wind and a bright light. It may be that you are fated, but I am not required to rejoice in it."

"I am sorry, Old Mother. But my thanks for your help." Correus rose, almost bumping his head on the ceiling, and left. He felt too large, too clumsy, in the sidhe-house. An intruder, a breaker of small objects. He took a deep breath of clean air as he came out of the briars onto the hillside. He saw, without surprise now, that his pony was still tethered to the hawthorn, not a pile of crumbling bones beneath it. *It is I who am a danger to them,* he thought. *I who take away their world.*

Nighthawk was standing by the pony, and five other sidhe-men had materialized from somewhere. They were barefoot and tattooed as Nighthawk was, with wolf or cat skins wrapped around their waists. They looked curiously at Correus, wary as wild deer but not afraid.

"I have told them that you are an Eagle man, but that the Old One has said it is all right," Nighthawk informed him. Correus had the impression that Nighthawk had gained some in reputation from having talked with the Eagle man *before* he had been judged "all right."

"Then you are not afraid of me anymore?" he said.

"I have thought about it," Nighthawk said. "I do not like Romans. I am afraid of Romans, and I do not understand them. And if you save a royal woman from a wrongful death, then my people will owe the Romans a debt, and I do not like that. But you do not look like a Roman or act like one, so maybe you aren't one."

"I assure you, I am." Correus was beginning to wish he could have said otherwise.

"Sometimes people don't know what they are," Nighthawk said. "And the Old One has said that this is your Fate, so it must be mine also, and if that is the case, I am not meant to understand."

He turned away down the trail they had come on, with his brothers behind him, and Correus swung up on the pony and followed. He felt like a giant that walks across some very small land, leaving destruction behind it, because it cannot see what it tramples.

XV

Dinas Tomen

"THERE IT IS, AS THE SIDHE OF TY ISAF HAS SAID," Nighthawk said in a low voice. Correus tilted his head to look upward at the walls of Dinas Tomen cresting a long spur that jutted from the central mass of the Black Mountains. The trail they were on joined a banked chariot track that switchbacked up the steep hillside to a gate in the southwest wall. The governor would have his work cut out for him when it came to taking Dinas Tomen at the last, Correus thought.

Below, where their trail joined the chariot way, was the long green mound of Ty Isaf, forbidding even in the sunlight. Someone had left a handful of pale flowers on the curbstone. The local sidhe-folk, he had gathered from Nighthawk, didn't actually live in the ancient long barrow, but took their name from it as being the place of most significance within their territory. The sidhe-houses seemed to have no place names of their own. Or perhaps they were secret ones and unspoken.

"The king's court has wintered in Dinas Tomen," Nighthawk said. "And it is still there, although the war band is likely fighting Romans elsewhere. It may be the king is with them," he added.

"That would be pleasant," Correus said. *And too much good luck to hope for,* he thought. They kept their voices low. Correus trailed two pack ponies behind his mount and would no doubt be recognized by some from his time in the Silure hills two summers ago. But it was a certainty that they had been watched since before they had crossed out of the Roman zone.

"Will you come with me?"

Nighthawk shook his head. "No, I will go to my own kind. If I sleep in a Sun Man's dun, I will be unclean again, and I didn't like the cure for that the last time."

"How will you know when I need you?" Correus looked up at Dinas Tomen again. He could think of no way to communicate with the sidhe-folk from inside it. Or from outside it, for that matter. As a rule, one didn't go to the People of the Hills. They would come to him. If they felt like it.

"My brothers will be watching," Nighthawk said. "They'll know." They had decided that Nighthawk's kinfolk should keep low out of sight, leaving only Nighthawk to travel openly with the trader. He was the only one for whose presence there was a plausible explanation.

Correus looked dubious, but he had little choice in the matter. If Nighthawk's five brothers, or whatever relationship they really were (he had discovered that "brother" might mean merely "man of my generation" or even "man of the same sidhe") could get to Dinas Tomen unseen by the Silures, he expected they could spy on them with equal ease. Certainly they seemed to know everything that went on. If Correus had wished to wait, they could have told him whether the king was indeed in Dinas Tomen with his court. But it didn't matter—Correus had to go in anyway. And if the king *was* gone, he thought—and felt cold—it probably meant that he had managed some death for Ygerna already.

He rode slowly up the chariot way, feeling watched, with the pack ponies trailing behind him. Halfway past the third turn he was stopped and challenged by two men who appeared to be sentries. One of them knew him and gave him a friendly grin.

"We heard you were coming. You'll get a feasting welcome, I expect. We've seen little enough of the fancy things this season. The women will be glad to see your face again." Another grin, and a leer. "They'll be thinking how to lower prices a little, so look you that you don't wear it out."

"I never lower prices," Correus assured him solemnly. "no matter what else gets raised. This is a business, mind you."

The sentry chuckled. "Well, you'll be welcome. And the Shining One knows there's gold enough to pay you. What we've been needing can't be bought with it. I wish you could have put the corn harvest on those ponies."

Correus shook his head. "And if I could have, the Romans would only take it off again."

"They let you through their lines?"

"Oh, aye, watched all the time, and knowing just what we carried. They don't mind if the king of the Silures buys himself a new arm ring, but no corn, mind, and no knives or spearheads, either, I'm afraid."

The sentry shrugged. That was logical, and the Romans were always logical, at least by their own lights. "Where's your little shadow?" He made the Sign of Horns as he said it. Sidhe-men made him nervous.

"Gone to roost with his kin somewhere," Correus said.

The sentry gave him a curious look. "Where'd you pick him up? They don't generally pop out in daylight like that."

Correus chuckled. "He was running like a hare with a pair of King Cadal's warriors baying on his trail. Dived behind a tree practically under my nose. I don't like Cadal's folk much anyway, so I looked blank and said 'What sidhe-man?' and they went off cursing. He owes me a life now, or so he says. I expect he'll stick with me till he thinks he's paid it back."

"Well, don't bring him in here if you can help it," the sentry said. "We've all got a touch of the sidhe in us, a ways back, but the pure-bloods make for trouble, and we don't need things stirred up any more than they already are." He was deliberately cheerful, but behind the smile Correus could see the strain of a man in a losing war.

"He wouldn't come anyway," he said. "It's been a long trail, and I'm hungry. So if you aren't wanting to look in my packs for Romans or more sidhe-men, I'll be taking them up yonder to see who'll buy."

The sentry waved him on with a friendly hand, then called out after, "What'd you do to your face?"

"Hit a Roman in the fist with it," Correus said over his shoulder. "He had a ring on. A slight difference of opinion over prices," he added. He clucked to the ponies, and they trotted up the chariot way, eager for the trail's end. They could smell their own kind, and a barn meant food.

The next set of guards passed him through with less chat, and he came at last into the outer courtyard of Dinas Tomen where the sheep and cattle pens were. By the time he reached the main level, a crowd had begun to gather around him, some recognizing him from two years since, others merely welcoming the trader as a diversion. Any break in the bitter confinement of Dinas Tomen was a diversion. It was no easy thing to feed several children on one person's barley ration, while the men fought a losing war and the fields went to ruin out of reach. Now there would be a feast, in spirit if not in food, and dancing and music, and new things to look at. The women clustered around him, their babies on their hips or clinging like limpets to their skirts, staring from behind the folds at the stranger and his packs. They were mostly women, Correus saw, with a handful of warriors, no more than enough to hold the gates of Dinas Tomen if they had to —it wouldn't take many to hold Dinas Tomen against anything less than siege engines. The warriors were boys or graying men. The few in between had healing wounds. The talkative sentry had walked with a limp, he remembered now.

Correus spread his packs out in a stone courtyard on the next to the highest level, and warriors and women both crowded around as he unrolled them. He had jewelry to sell, and glass pitchers and cups of Roman make, copper cooking pots, gold and antler and enameled pony trappings, charms to bring love or long life or merely good teeth, combs and polished metal mirrors, flasks of scent and eye ointment, and powdered, hardened sticks of medicine, also Roman made, and lengths of cloth, many of them silk—the Silures were a wealthy folk and had bought lavishly of such trade goods in better days.

In an hour he had sold almost all of it, except for one pack, set to the side. These were his best wares, reserved for the king and the king's house to buy from first. Such as were not sold would then be offered to the lesser folk.

When the crowd had begun to thin, a stout woman in a gown of good cloth came down from the top court and stood waiting until a gray-haired man had paid for a pot of eye ointment.

"The king sends to say that you are welcome in his hall, Rhys," she said.

Correus nodded and began to roll up his packs. Much of his business was in kind, bartered for goods a trader could sell elsewhere, and he packed away an assortment of unworked gold and finely carved bone and cured skins with a purse full of coins.

In the Great Hall, Bendigeid was lounging by the remains of the morning cooking fire. His shirt and breeches were elegant enough for a king with not much on his mind but a new arm ring, but there were thin lines around the corners of his eyes and dark smudges on the skin that hadn't been there two years ago. There was a Druid with him whom Correus recognized and saluted warily—Teyrnon, high priest of that outlawed priesthood—and another gray-bearded man who was probably a council lord.

Correus bowed to Bendigeid and gave the councillor a polite nod. "I had hoped to find the king in Dinas Tomen," he said. "I am remembering you had a liking for Tyrian dyes, and so I have bought some from a trader out of there."

Bendigeid raised an eyebrow. "I have little leisure to peacock about in a purple shirt these days, Rhys. But I shall buy anyway—to impress the gods. They have a liking for that sort of gesture."

Teyrnon snorted, and Correus unrolled his last pack. Why *was* the king in Dinas Tomen, he wondered, as he rummaged the little silk packet out of the folds. He hoped violently that it was because Bendigeid wouldn't chance being killed while he left Ygerna alive behind him, maybe to rule after him. If so, the king would mastermind his war band's raids from Dinas Tomen and wait his chance. *Mithras god, let me be right about that.* Correus had seen no sign of Ygerna anywhere, and fear was beginning to make him sick to his stomach.

"I must charge dear for the dye," Correus said, producing it. "It was none too easy to come by." Tyrian purple, the deep shade that came from shellfish, was the most costly dye in the world. "But this is a hearth gift," He laid out a silver brooch of ancient and beautiful work, almost as valuable as the dye. A hearth gift for a chieftain was customary; for a king, practically imperative.

Bendigeid examined the brooch admiringly. "You have an eye for beauty, Rhys. My thanks, and I will pay your price for the dye. What else have you brought?"

The formalities over, Correus spread out his goods before the king—the best of the silks and jewelry and a few fine pieces of Gaulish silver. There was a small statue in gold of a leaping stag with a sun disc caught in his antlers, and a glass pitcher shaped like a cluster of grapes, with the vine tendrils for the handle. The last pack had cost nine-tenths of the money Correus had spent acquiring a stock from the merchants who docked along Sabrina Mouth bound for Aquae Sulis. He lifted the arm ring with the flower clasp, hoping that his face was not as green as he felt.

"I have heard that the royal woman has come back to her tribe. If she would take this for a good wish, I would be honored."

Bendigeid nodded and flicked an eye at the stout woman who was poking at the fire, banking the coals for the evening. Correus clenched his hands under the folds of the pack until he was sure that they weren't going to shake. The woman took the arm ring and went off with it.

The king smiled. "A pleasant gesture, Rhys. Are you hoping to sell your silks?"

Correus was sitting cross-legged beside his goods. He laughed. "Of course, King. Being that you've never thought to take a wife . . ."

"You will get the attention of the women of my house in some fashion," the king said. "You will be a rich man before you are an old one, I'm thinking. You should take a wife yourself."

"*When* I am a rich man, I expect I will. It improves the choices some."

"How did you know the royal woman had come back to us?" Bendigeid said.

"Oh, from a Roman before I came here. They were in a fine temper over it."

"You run tame in the Roman camps, do you, Rhys?"

"They let me go where I will, mostly," Correus said carefully. "My kind stays out of wars. It spoils the business."

"You took my message to Cadal," Bendigeid said thoughtfully.

"I was going that way. And I spent the next season in Brigante country, as I said I would. But I didn't say I'd stay away forever. *That* would not be business."

"You were in the Roman zone this spring?"

"Aye. My goods come from the coastal merchants mostly."

"And what are the Romans doing?"

"Building forts. Building roads. Building Lugh-knows-what. Building, King. They are building."

"Rhys—"

"Look, you, King—I am not a tribesman, but this is my land, too. The Romans are not fools, and they do not tell me secrets. They build. That is all I know. They build very close to your doorstep," he added.

"Llywarch, I need your map."

The old councillor had been staring at Correus with thoughtful eyes. Now he rose and strode away, presumably to his own chambers. Correus watched him go, trying to think why the name touched a bell in his mind. Llywarch . . . the envoy who had taken Ygerna to marry Gruffyd's son. That was it. Ygerna had mentioned the name. And now for some reason Llywarch seemed to find Correus's face a puzzlement to him. Correus couldn't think why—Llywarch and Ygerna had both been in Moridunum the last time Rhys the trader had come through Silure lands. Could Ygerna have described him to Llywarch? Surely Ygerna wasn't such a fool. And surely Correus's face was not so remarkable that Llywarch would know it from a description. He abandoned the puzzle as Llywarch came back with a softened piece of deer's hide that had a rough map inked on it.

Llywarch spread it out on the hearth, and Bendigeid got out of his chair and knelt beside it. Teyrnon Chief-Druid sat and looked stately behind his beard, but his eyes were on the map, too.

"We have marked all the Roman roads and camps we know of," Bendigeid said. He looked at Correus. "Are there more?"

Correus scooted forward and looked. They had most of them. He took a cold cinder from the edge of the fire and made two more marks along the Wye, and another stretch of road beside the Isca—two halves of a circle north and south of Dinas Tomen. He might as well be truthful, he thought. If Bendigeid would give the battle up as hopeless, there were men on both sides who would be alive by fall. "There may be more." He put the cinder down and dusted his hands. "But those I have seen."

Bendigeid sat for a long time looking silently at the map. He had sent one more plea to Cadal now that Ygerna, who had been part of the bargain, was again his to give. But he didn't really expect an answer. And it hadn't changed his intentions toward Ygerna. If Ygerna died, the Goddess would go to another woman and make *her* the royal woman, and then Cadal could have *her*. But Cadal wouldn't answer. That was plain now. Bendigeid watched as the ink and cinder marks seemed to move of their own accord, ringing closer about Dinas Tomen.

Correus, in turn, watched the fire and not the king, in case his thoughts were too plain on his face. There was a light patter of footsteps, and he caught his breath and made a face of polite interest before he looked up.

"My thanks to the trader for the good wish," Ygerna said.

Correus touched his palm to his forehead, formal recognition of the Goddess on Earth. "If the Lady is pleased, then I am pleased." He looked her in the eye and gave a shallow sigh of relief when no sign of recognition crossed her face. "Perhaps I might have other things to interest the princess?" he suggested.

The stout woman drew up a chair to the hearth for her, and Ygerna sat. "I will look," she decided. The king was talking in a low voice now to Teyrnon and Llywarch, and other people were beginning to drift into the hall. Correus spread his goods out for Ygerna's inspection while the stout woman went back to poking at the fire. Ygerna ran her hands over the silk and held a few folds up to see how the light fell on it. If she were going to betray him and scream "Roman!" to her uncle, she would have done it by now, Correus decided and relaxed a little more.

She was dressed like a princess and a woman now, with a heavy gold torque around her slim neck and fine green shoes on her feet. Her hair was still unbound and there was a fillet around her forehead with the silver crescent of the moon on the front. Silver and gold and purple threads made a pattern like waves along the green hem of her gown. It was hot in the hall, and the short sleeves of the linen gown were pinned up at the shoulders to shorten them further. The arm ring he had sent was clasped about one white arm above the elbow. She was extraordinarily beautiful, Correus thought, and really not a child any more. Or maybe it was only the performance she was giving. It would have done credit to an actor.

She inspected everything twice, haggled determinedly with him about the price, and went away with the stout woman trailing behind her, and a length of blue silk under one arm.

He saw her again that evening, her face still cool and remote as the crescent moon on her head. The Great Hall of Dinas Tomen was decked with all the trappings of a feast, and if the food was scarce and the feasters mainly women, it was a bright evening all the same. Owen Harper had ridden in that afternoon from wherever it was that his warriors were harassing the Romans, with Fand across his back, and as soon as he had eaten, he unstrapped the harp bag and began to tune her. The bronze strings caught the torchlight like little wires of fire, and the music, to Correus, possessed an unearthly quality that could make a man forget hunger and thirst.

Owen sang first of the beautiful silver witch Arianrhod, maker of trouble and mother of gods; and then of Rhiannon the Good, for whom the magic birds sang, and who gave up immortality for love of a human king. The harp notes became a bird song as Owen spun out the tale of Rhiannon. It was one of the three hundred tales that any bard had to learn by heart at his training, but Owen was a master at it. His voice rose higher with the harp notes, and he seemed to waver in the firelight until Correus could almost have sworn that it was a golden goddess with a bright-feathered songbird on her arm who sat by the hearth, and not at all a black-haired man with a harp.

He looked down the table from his seat, where the king had given him the guest's place, to Ygerna at the other end. She was sitting with her elbow beside her empty bowl and her chin in her hand, lost in the harp song. The black hair stood out around her face like smoke. Under the silver moon she had a wild beauty that hadn't seemed to touch her in the Roman camps. *They are her kind*, he thought. *She was born to them*. And she was old enough now to stand up to her uncle, as much as any human could ever stand up to the king of the Silures. He wondered sadly if he had come on a fool's errand, to take her away from something she wished to keep, if the only reason she hadn't named him for a spy was a lingering fondness for him, and not a wish to go back with him. She must know why he was there, but what if she didn't want it? Correus took a drink of the watery beer that was almost the last of the king's stores and dismissed that thought from his mind. It didn't matter what Ygerna wanted. She was coming with him anyway. Correus's eyes slid around to the king's dark, masked, unreadable face. There was something of Bendigeid in Ygerna, he thought, but not enough to win. Not in the long run.

Owen put down his harp, and the hall woke and shouted and cheered and called out to him for more, but he shook his head. He took a long drink from his beer horn and began to make a dance music. The women got up from the benches and began to whirl across the rushes on the floor, arms linked and long braids flying. The un-wed girls wore their hair loose, and it spun out behind them like a curtain. After a moment Ygerna slipped from her seat and joined them. They circled the hall once more, weaving between the tables. Like bright birds, he thought, fluttering in the rushes. And then he saw that they had knives in their hands, point uppermost, that caught the torchlight on the blades. It was a war dance, a Spear Dance of the Women, and he knew that they, too, would fight to the death if it came to it, and then there would be nothing left of the Silures at all.

They gave him a place to sleep in the guest chambers; piled rushes with a deer hide that was almost as soft as his woolen cloak on the top. It was a matter of pride to give a guest the best. There was a fire laid on the hearth, and the ashes under it smelled interestingly of burned herbs.

Correus wrapped himself in his cloak and lay down on the deer hide with his packs for a pillow. He could see the bright, fine points of stars through the smoke hole above him, and he watched them while he tried first to think of a way to talk to Ygerna alone, and then to go to sleep. Neither proved very successful and when he finally did sleep, the problem of Ygerna chased itself around and around in his dream; the kind of dream that has no beginning and no end, and the dreamer does the same task over and over and never finishes and wakes exhausted; and the few solutions which present themselves in dreaming are always strange and unmanageable by morning light.

He woke with a crick in his neck from sleeping on a pack with a copper pot in it, and a vile taste in his mouth from having been too preoccupied to brush his teeth at night. It was hardly light, no more than the faint graying of predawn, and he felt as if he had only just begun to sleep soundly after the dreams had gone away. He blinked, trying to decide why he was awake at all when he realized that there was someone in the room with him. He sat up fast with his hand on his knife, and Ygerna's voice hissed at him to be still.

She was kneeling beside him, and her face was barely visible in the pale gray light that came down through the smoke hole.

"How did you get away?" he whispered. A royal woman was always hemmed in by other women, and slaves, and protocol.

"I told them I was going to pee," she said frankly. "They don't insist on watching me do *that*." She put out a hand to his face, and in another second she was in his arms, shivering against his shoulder. "Correus, get me out of here! Take me home!"

"That's what I'm here for." He stroked her hair. "Home? Are you sure? I was afraid *I* was going to have to kidnap you, too."

"No. *This* isn't home, not any more. I tried, but it isn't, and I don't belong any more, and I'm scared to death." Her teeth were chattering. She sat back and wrapped her cloak around her and tried to speak clearly. "He's going to kill me. He's afraid your governor will make me the queen. There will be poison in my food one day, if nothing else."

"Thank the gods. I was afraid you wouldn't know that, and not be careful."

"I am not a fool," Ygerna whispered. "But why did they send you alone? You can't have brought any men with you, not into these hills. Not without my uncle spotting them."

"I brought . . . something," Correus said. "And they didn't send me, I came. You may not be a fool, and neither is the governor, but he doesn't think your uncle will risk a curse to get rid of you."

Ygerna sighed. "Or I'm just not worth it to him. The governor is almost as practical as my uncle."

Correus looked uncomfortable, but he didn't bother denying it. "A little of both maybe. So it will be just you and me."

"But *you* came." She took his hand in both of hers, and held it tight for a moment.

"And we will have some help on the trail," he said, "but we're going to need a head start. Can you get free of your servants at night?"

Ygerna thought. "I will manage. I haven't tried to before, because having them around makes it harder for my uncle. But I will manage something." She smiled, a faint little wolf-smile that he could barely see. "They are beginning to be a little afraid of me."

When it was fully light, Correus took his ponies down the chariot track to the low ground around Ty Isaf on the pretext of cutting fresh grass for them. Most of the grass had already been cut to feed what was left of the herd animals in Dinas Tomen, and he turned them out to graze on the short new growth instead, and sat down on a rock to watch them. His rock was on the edge of a low clump of trees, and he wasn't overly surprised when Nighthawk curled himself up on the ground beside him, on the far side of the rock, out of the line of sight of anyone in Dinas Tomen.

"Tonight," Correus said. "There's a gate in the north

wall that's less conspicuous. It's not meant for horses, and there's only one guard."

Nighthawk nodded. "You cannot take the horses anyway."

"Will your people—the Ty Isaf people—help?"

"I have told them," Nighthawk said. "It is their doing, so they must undo it. The Old One didn't like it, but she drank the holy drink and talked to my Old One, and they will do it. Does the woman come freely?"

"Yes."

Nighthawk looked relieved. "Good. Otherwise it would be her Fate, the Old One says, and then they wouldn't help."

"Two hours after midnight," Correus said, watching the ponies instead of Nighthawk in case anyone was watching *him*. He felt as if he were dealing with some unmanageable cloud of spirits and not with humans at all. Maybe he was. When he turned around again as naturally as he could manage, the sidhe-man was gone.

When the ponies had grazed their fill, Correus took them back to Dinas Tomen. Llywarch was standing in the gateway as he passed. He gave Correus a greeting and another curious look, until Correus wondered if his face looked as guilty as it felt. There was a skull in the wall over his head.

Correus fidgeted around Dinas Tomen until nightfall, and then fidgeted his way through the evening meal. Owen Harper had made his report to the king and gone back to his men, and the evening had a tight, strained feel to it —merriment made for the sake of a stranger, with other, greater concerns, not to be talked of, lying just beneath the laughter. Ygerna paid him very little attention, and even Llywarch seemed to have given up on his puzzle and turned his mind to his dinner. Without Owen's harp song, it was only soup and bread and withered apples, undisguised.

Correus excused himself early, pleading his intent to be on the road at first light, and went to sit in the guest chamber before he acquired such a case of the jumps as would make itself plain to the king. He took all the coins from his packs and stuffed most of them into the purse at his belt, and the rest into his boot with the little sheathed dagger that was already there. There was another at his belt. The jewelry, he put on—arm rings and a silver torque with carnelian in the ends under his shirt, and two pairs of gold eardrops in his purse. The hides and cook pots would have to stay. He repacked them carefully and made a lump under his spare cloak with them on the deerskin bed, in case anyone should decide to look for his company later. And then, because there was very little else to do until two hours after midnight, he sat down and counted stones in the hearth and cracks in the wooden floor.

In an hour or so traffic in the courtyard outside ceased as the king's house took itself away to bed, and the chieftains' ladies and their warriors made their way to their camps in the lower courts. Gradually all murmuring died away as the lesser folk lay down to sleep among the wagons.

Correus got up and moved the withy shutter of a window just enough to see the sky. He sat back down and went over in his mind again the way from the guest chambers to the narrow gate in the north wall—past the Great Hall and the house where the king's captains slept, which tonight by mercy had only a handful of boys and walking wounded in it; past the well and the gate into the second court where the greatest of the chieftains' ladies had their camps. There would be a guard at that gate. And then there was only a narrow open stretch between the king's court and the outer wall. And the outer gate had only one guard—the terrain was bad for horses there, and the gate too narrow to take a chariot. Correus thought wistfully of the ponies penned in the king's stables on the south side of the hold. But he had known as soon as he had seen Dinas Tomen that he couldn't get them out again. He and Ygerna would go back to the Roman zone on foot or not at all.

When the moon was down and Dinas Tomen was as dark as the waters of the Styx he finally slipped the guest chamber door closed behind him and glided like a shadow across the upper court. Packs and ponies were abandoned. He had a sword and a dagger and precious little else— the hidden gold would buy him no favors from Bendigeid's men.

There was a narrow passage, darker than the night,

between the warriors' house and a small stone smoke-house, and Correus slipped into it, praying that no sleeper in the upper court had allowed his hound to roam loose in the night. In a moment there was a whisper like a soft murmur of the wind, and something brushed against his arm.

"Ready?" he whispered back. "Good girl."

She was bundled in a dark cloak, and he could barely see her, only a black shape beside his. He took her hand. "Was there trouble?"

"No, I put something in the beer. My women only. I couldn't get at the others." She had never made that po-tion before. If she hadn't added too much, it wouldn't kill them, she thought.

"Then come on."

They went quickly around the side of the smokehouse, and he jerked her back. There was someone coming by the well. Her hand tightened on his. They flattened them-selves against the smokehouse wall. The man had a torch in his hand, and he was almost running.

"Keep still," Correus hissed, and then he caught his breath. It was Llywarch, and his face was the face of a man who has solved a puzzle. Correus heard Ygerna's voice, two years past, asking him if he were a demon, that not even Druids could grow fingers back, and suddenly he knew where Llywarch had seen his face before. He had seen it on Flavius in Gruffyd's camp, and now he had remembered. The thought was across his mind and gone in a second, but he knew it for truth as he saw Llywarch running, running from wherever he had gone to think things out, to warn the king that Rhys the trader had a Roman's face.

There was no time to think about it. Correus caught him with his fist in the pit of the stomach as Llywarch came even with the smokehouse. Llywarch doubled over, and his torch hit the ground. As they grappled with each other, the light went out. Ygerna had rolled it in the dirt and the end of her cloak.

Correus fought frantically, trying to get his knife from its sheath. It would be only seconds before Llywarch got his breath back; even if Correus could kill him a second later, one scream would be all that was needed to bring the whole of Dinas Tomen down on them. There was a guard in the gate to the lower court not fifty feet past the well, and another in the north wall a hundred yards beyond it the other way. He got his hands around Llywarch's throat, but the older man's hands were on his wrists and he was strong. Correus couldn't take his hands away long enough to reach for his knife. He wondered if Ygerna had one, and if she had, if she would use it on Llywarch. It was terrifying—fighting in the dark to kill a man with his bare hands, a man who had only to scream to win. Llywarch wrenched almost away from him, and then suddenly went limp under his hands. Correus could hear Ygerna moving about behind him, and he looked around, dazed, for the unseen hand that had helped him. A soft birdcall whistled from the darkness ahead of them, and his hand felt blood on Llywarch's back. He probed carefully and touched the shaft of an arrow. Something out there had the night-sight.

He took Llywarch by the shoulders and pulled him into the passage between the warriors' house and the smokehouse, bumping into Ygerna as he stumbled out again over the body.

"Correus? Are you all right? I couldn't tell which of you was which in the dark," she whispered.

"Yes. Run!"

She tossed the doused torch next to Llywarch between the buildings and followed Correus across the last open space to the shadow of the well. He had his knife out now.

"All right. Go!"

Ygerna slipped up to the gate to make some talk with the guard until Correus could come around behind him. She had barely had time to reach the gate when there was another whistle and a frantic whisper. "Correus!"

When he got to the gate she was standing over the body, and Correus, whose own night-sight was growing better, looked for the whistler. A small form crouched on the rampart top.

"He's dead!" Ygerna's whisper was frightened now as Correus unbarred the narrow gate and pushed her through it. Even more terrifying than killing a man with her own hands was having something out of the blackness do it instead.

"Run," a new voice said in her ear. "Run, Lady."

XVI
Idyll

YGERNA RAN. STUMBLING, WITH CORREUS'S HAND IN hers, they followed the little dark man who could see in the night. They had three hours at the most before the hunt would be on for them. Less, if anyone found either of the bodies before dawn. Then the Silures would be baying like wolves on their trail.

As soon as they were out of plain sight of Dinas Tomen, they slackened their pace a little. The mountainside was treacherous, steep and rocky and worn with the runoff of many snows. A good place to break an ankle—and then they could just sit down and wait for her uncle to find them.

The shadow ahead gave a faint owl hoot, and another answered from the darkness. They must be the "something" Correus had brought with him, Ygerna decided.

"Did you bring the cloth?" he whispered.

She reached inside her shirt and pulled out a torn piece of wool. "I wore it under my gown all day."

"Good." He pulled another piece of cloth from his own shirt and gave them to the dark shape that popped up beside them. The sidhe-man put them to one side carefully and rubbed something that smelled vile on their hands and the soles of their boots, making them lift one foot and then the other.

"Likely the king will hunt you on four feet," the dark man said. "We will give his hounds something to worry them." He picked up the pieces of cloth, and the owl hooted again ahead of them. "Go now."

They followed the sound, and another small dark shape flitted along the ground before them, leading them back on their own tracks for a way and then turning sharply north. Ygerna didn't stop to wonder why north, when the governor's army lay to the south, or what hold Correus had on the People of the Hills. She just ran where they led her until her breath was ragged and her leg muscles ached. They slowed to a complete walk at last, on an uphill track into a wood, and she caught a gasping breath and staggered on. She could hear Correus's heavy, labored breath beside her. He was probably stronger than she was, used to twenty-mile marches in full gear; but the jaunty, swinging pace of the legions was different from headlong flight into a night full of terrors. She thought wistfully of horses, but the People of the Hills were not a horse people. And horses were hard to move silently when the countryside itself was alive and hunting them.

There were two shadows ahead of them now, and the sky was beginning to lighten a little. One of the shadows drifted away, and in a while another joined them. How much longer, she wondered, until they would have to stop, but she didn't ask; she just walked achingly, one blistered foot in front of the other, while the sky paled around them.

Their path brightened suddenly as the sun lifted a blazing head above the mountain crests to their right. The hazel wood around them was the greenish gold of sunlight in new leaves. The wood rose up the hillside before them, while a stream bubbled away past it. One of the sidhe-men spoke softly to the other and turned back the way they had come, a silent figure in a wolf-skin kilt padding softly through last year's leaves, until she lost sight of him in the dawn haze.

The other pointed to the hill ahead. "Beyond the scrub there, there is a cave. There will be food. Go to earth in that until we come back."

Correus nodded wearily. "How long?"

"Until we have wrecked the trail," the sidhe-man said, "and have seen what the king is doing." He shrugged. "How long is long?"

"We will wait," Correus said. He felt Ygerna sway a little on her feet and put a steadying arm around her.

She shook her head and forced herself to stand straight. "May the Goddess guard your path, Man of the Hills and kinsman of my grandmother. I will remember the debt."

The sidhe-man touched his palm to his forehead to her and was gone. She took Correus's hand again, and they pushed their way through the scrub at the base of the hill.

The cave smelled of foxes and was littered with bones, but someone had taken a young tree branch and swept the refuse into a corner. The air was dank, probably with seepage from whatever source fed the stream outside. It would be very close to its source, this high in the mountains. But the damp made the air cool and was not unwelcome. The day would be hot.

There was a cloth bundle just inside the door. They looked wearily at each other for a moment, weaving on their feet, and sat down with their backs to the cave wall and unwrapped the bundle. There was bread inside, flat barley cake, and some strips of dried meat, and they tore at it ravenously.

"I don't think I've *ever* been so hungry," Ygerna said, wiping the crumbs from her mouth. She began to yawn. "Or so sleepy. Correus, can we sleep now?"

"We'll have to," Correus said heavily. His arms and legs felt like lead. If they didn't sleep, they'd never make it.

Ygerna put her cloak under her head and curled up on the cool dirt. "Where . . ." she said, but she was asleep before she could say more. She was wearing a man's shirt and breeches, and she had pulled her hair back into one braid, the way the men did when they wanted it out of their way. There was a knife in her belt. With her face buried in the cloak she looked like the young warriors, just over the edge of their manhood, who were the fighting garrison left in Dinas Tomen. *So young,* Correus thought, unsure whether he meant Ygerna or the boys who would be out with the king's hounds and hunting for them even now. Old enough to kill, though. He lay down beside Ygerna, with his head on his cloak, feeling as the fox must have felt, lying low in this den with a hunt on its trail.

He woke after noon and sat up to shake the sleep and muscle cramps away. Ygerna was still curled around the pillow of her cloak, and he moved quietly to let her sleep. She had two gold torques around her neck, he saw now, and gold in her ears. There were ridges under her sleeves that were probably jewelry, also. The scabbard at her belt was leather with a pierced silver casing over the tip. Like Correus, she had taken all the wealth she could wear—it had been *all* they could take.

He went outside to the stream and got a drink of water—carefully. The woods were still, but he wasn't sure where they were or, more importantly, where the king's men were. When he came back, Ygerna was awake, and he pointed the way to the stream.

"Go quickly."

She came back, wiping her mouth on the back of her hand.

"Feel better?"

"I feel like a horse that's been ridden." She sat down stiffly.

"Me, too. That will wear off, though. Are your feet all right?"

"I've got blisters, I think." She began to pull her boots off.

"Damn." If her feet got infected, she'd be nearly crippled until they healed. Correus felt in the pouch at his belt. There was a small clay pot of salve among the coins, worth more than the money now. He pulled his shirt free of his belt and began to tear a strip off the hem. "Give me your foot." She put it out obediently, and he smeared salve on the heel where the blisters were broken open and the skin was rubbed raw. Her feet were little and narrow, like her hands, but the soles felt tough. She might be better off barefoot, he thought, if the ground wasn't rocky. "Leave your boots off until we have to move again," he told her, "and let the air dry those blisters. We'll put some bandages around them before you put the boots on again."

"That feels better. I would never have thought to bring salve." She stretched her feet out on her cloak to keep the dirt out of the salve. "Correus, where are we going?"

He put the salve away. "Back to Isca, but the long way. Nighthawk's people tell me most of Bendigeid's war band is between us and the Roman zone. By tonight they'll all be looking for us, too. We can't just run for it."

"How did you get the sidhe-folk to help? They helped the king."

"The king lied to them, and they don't like it. Also, the Sidhe of Llanmelin owes me a life-price."

"Why? Correus, who is Rhys, and why does my uncle let him run tame in his camp?"

He owed her that much, he thought. His spying days were over, and he was doubly marked now—for himself and for Flavius's kinsman. "Rhys only exists when Centurion Julianus doesn't," he said slowly.

Ygerna looked at him. "Rhys is a spy."

"Yes."

"Well, I always thought you were," Ygerna said. "Though I can see why you couldn't say so."

He waited for her to turn away from him. But Ygerna sat watching him thoughtfully.

"You are thinking I will hate you for that," she said.

"Yes."

There was a curious feel to this talk, lying low like foxes in the cave. They were bound to each other now, until they got back to Isca or were killed. It made them honest.

"Your spy saved me from poison in my food some night. I put a fair amount of value on my hide," she said wryly. "Do you think me so ungrateful?"

"I think you're a Silure."

"Am I? After two years in your Eagle camps, Correus? Am I really? I have thought a lot about it, especially in Dinas Tomen." She looked sad. "I don't know *what* I am, but I don't think it's a Silure anymore."

Neither fish nor fowl. How often had he felt the same way? Slave-born, patrician-adopted, fitting comfortably in neither place, at home only in the army. They sat looking at each other, the royal woman in boy's clothes, dark hair braided back from a dirt-streaked face; the centurion of the Eagles in checkered trousers and a dirty shirt. *Two sheep in wolves' clothing,* he thought suddenly, and felt like laughing. He held out both hands to her, and she came to him and leaned against his shoulder.

Nighthawk came back for them at dusk. He squatted down in the dirt and began to draw out a trail.

"The king is looking mainly in the south," he said to Correus, "but the hunt is up this way as well. They passed by you not far from here."

"We know," Ygerna said. "We heard them." Baying hounds and distant voices, moving to the north, she thought. Moving between them and the Roman lines along the Wye.

"We can get to here before sunup." The sidhe-man made a mark in the dirt and then drew in the sun's course to show them the direction. "It's only a cave, like this, but best not to lair in the same hole twice."

"Why not the houses of Ty Isaf?" Ygerna said. The sidhes were secret places; a fugitive could lie hidden there for weeks and not be found, if he wasn't afraid of the Dark Folk.

"The Sidhe of Ty Isaf is empty," Nighthawk said. "The king has found our arrows in Dinas Tomen, and he is hunting the People of the Hills as well as you. And he is half-blood to us. He will find what he hunts. The children of Ty Isaf are gone away because of it." He gave Ygerna a long look. "That was for you, Lady."

"I know," Ygerna said. "I am sorry. We will go where you tell us."

They followed him out into the twilight.

Nighthawk and his brothers led them in relays, and they followed unquestioningly now, sometimes by daylight but more often by darkness, doubling back so often that on cloudy nights they lost all sense of where they went. Sometimes their guides would give them landmarks to go by and then vanish for hours or even days. Then they would reappear to show them a new trail or a place to hide while the hunt swept by. The king pursued them with a tenacity born of desperation, and Nighthawk told them that Bendigeid had even called in his war band from its fighting to track them.

"I knew he would chase us," Correus said, "but not like this." He felt like a man pursued by Furies.

"He is losing," Ygerna said with a shiver. "Everything he has tried to hold is slipping from him, and he is afraid. The Mother pity him; I think it's the first time."

"Mithras god, and it's you he's afraid of," Correus said. They had stopped for the night in a hiding place that was no more than a cleft in the ground caused by some old upheaval, but it was overhung with hawthorn scrub and tall grasses; a safe enough place to light a fire.

They dropped in their tracks with the weariness of

bodies pushed to the limit, and kindled enough of a blaze to keep the wolves away. The wolves had other things to hunt now that the lean winter was past, Correus thought thankfully; they couldn't afford much of a fire. They ate the last of the barley bread—Nighthawk or his brothers would bring them more, he assumed; he was too tired to care. They spread Ygerna's cloak on the ground and lay down together on it, pulling his over them. They had been on the run for a week now and had learned—a memory that would never leave either of them—what it was to be hunted. It was only the presence of the other, he thought, that gave each the strength and comfort to go on. He put his arms around her and she nestled against him, as they had grown accustomed to doing, and slept.

In the morning they were on the run again.

Two days later they found the pool. They came upon it just after dawn, a small, deep hollow in the rock, fringed by alder trees. The stream that fed it at the top deepened and spread into silent water before falling away over a rocky lip twenty feet beyond.

Ygerna bent down to drink, and the waters of the pool lapped at her hands in the morning stillness, and Correus felt that he hadn't been clean in a year. On the far side, high rock jutted out of a screen of undergrowth—another hole to hide in if they had to. There was no sound but the water and a low bird song from the alders. Ygerna looked up at him wistfully. To bathe or go on? To run or to be clean again?

The lure of the water was too strong. They ran like goats over the top of the little waterfall to leave their clothes in the scrub under the rocks. Ygerna was barefoot already, leaving her blistered feet to heal, and she stripped off her shirt and breeches with a quick wriggle, like an otter, and looked back at him, laughing.

"Come on!"

Correus pulled his own shirt off over his head. Mithras god, how he wanted to wash. He shucked his boots off and then his breeches. They had lived in each other's pockets for a week now, and there was no modesty left in them. It was only when Ygerna turned back to face him at the edge of the pool that a shock like a sudden sword thrust went through him. Unclothed, her slim body belonged to no child. Her waist was a thin curve he could have put his hands around, but the line of her hips below it and the smoky triangle of dark hair were a woman's. Her breasts were small like the rest of her, but large enough in proportion, and tilted upward in the dappled shade of the alder trees in a curve that was made to fit a man's hand. A shape like flower petals was drawn between them and rubbed in with blue woad in the tribal pattern of a priestess. She had pulled her hair loose from its braid, and it fell in dark waves behind her. Balanced on one foot, she stood on the edge of the pool and waited for him.

Correus wrenched his eyes away. Horribly aware of his own nakedness, he ran for the pool and dived.

When they were clean, they put on their dirty clothes again, afraid to wash them and take too much time to let them dry. Correus, watching the thin form that might have been a boy's walking ahead of him up the stream bank, tried not to think about the woman's body that was under it. Ygerna was fifteen now, old enough to marry, by Roman standards and by those of her own kind. She had been telling him indignantly for years that she was not a child, he thought ruefully, but Julius had seen the truth more quickly than he had. Then he shrugged and caught up with her. Her womanhood didn't matter. The thing that mattered now was to run and keep running.

Nighthawk had told them that the king's men were still all around them, encircling the fugitives as they began slowly to work their way southwestward. Ygerna was beginning to toughen on the long march, Correus thought proudly. She could probably outwalk him now—she had youth on her side. They pushed on, and if anything could have forged a bond between them that would never break, it was this journey through the Silure hills. Tired, hungry, frightened, and alone, they had no one but each other and the brief glimpse of a small, dark shadow that showed them a new trail or a place in which to hide and then was gone. And all around them were the sounds of the hunt, real or only imagined, clamoring for their blood.

Nighthawk appeared again at dusk, his small face worried. "I had thought to go to the new road by the river where the soldiers are cutting turf," he said, "but the king's men are there. Laying traps for the Romans maybe, but I think mostly looking for you. They know you will try to get to the Eagle forts as soon as you can."

"Damn. We may have to go clear to Isca." Where the Roman zone was the oldest and strongest, Correus knew, it would be easiest to cross the lines.

"It is a long walk, Lady." Nighthawk looked at Ygerna, but she shook her head.

"It's a longer walk into Annwn," she said bluntly, "and my uncle won't send us there by any easy road."

The sidhe-man had begun to speak mostly to Ygerna, Correus noted. Even if she belonged to the Goddess, and as such was to be feared, she was of his own world after all, and a person of authority in it. And the more Nighthawk thought of Correus being a Roman, the less he understood him. All in all, it was less unnerving to talk to the Goddess on Earth and let *her* talk to the Roman. And if what Nighthawk had begun to think about the Roman and the Goddess on Earth were true, the less he had to do with *that* the better, lest the Goddess Above think to lay it at his door.

"What of the people of Ty Isaf?" Ygerna asked.

"They hide, Lady." Nighthawk shivered. "The king caught one, and the Old One has cursed him for it, but the king still lives and the man of Ty Isaf does not."

"Oh," Ygerna said softly, thinking of a hillside torn open and ruined. The Silures would have been afraid to do it, but Bendigeid would have made them. Something foul would come of it, she thought. So much blood and dark magic.

And Correus thought, *Whose fault? Bendigeid's? Rome's? The governor's? Mine?* At whose door should they lay the destruction of Ty Isaf? "I am sorry," he said helplessly. "Tell the people of Ty Isaf that Rome will give them what help they can."

"No, Eagle man. My kind will be here when the Romans have gone again. Especially if we do not have your 'help,'" Nighthawk added.

Correus nodded. The offer was kindly meant, but Nighthawk was right. The instinct to hide unnoticed was very old and very deep in the Dark Folk, and it was probably the reason why they were still here.

All the same he found his sleep somewhat long in coming, with Ygerna in the crook of his arm and Ty Isaf's blood on his hands.

There was almost half a moon in the sky now, and the hollow where they slept in tall grass was silvered with it. Correus, sleeping fitfully, woke again when the fire went out.

He started to get up and Ygerna whispered, "No, it's all right. I'm awake. It won't be long till light. I'll watch."

"Couldn't you sleep, either?" He could see the moon in her eyes.

"No. It's restless tonight."

"I know." He wrapped her in his arms for comfort, but something in the night began to whisper to him; ghosts or the moon or his own restless spirit. Ygerna looked up at him with those moon-washed eyes, and he knew that she felt it, too.

He was never sure afterward what mad instinct prompted him—maybe the image of Ygerna by the pool was closer under the surface than he thought—but he bent his head down and kissed her. Not a child's kiss, dropped lightly on the hair or cheek for comfort, but the kiss of man to woman; and she made a low sound in her throat and put her arms around his neck. After that it was too late.

Wolves or the Dark Folk or the ghosts of Troy could have come upon him and he would not have known it. Not with Ygerna in his arms. Her face was milky in the moonlight, her body shadowed where he leaned above her on his elbows, trying to catch his breath. Her hair was a pool of dark water around her head. A sidhe-creature of blackness and silver who might love him one minute and vanish the next, leaving him with only empty air in his arms. He was too far gone in the night madness to think clearly. He hadn't lain with a woman since Freita died, not even with whores. He hadn't had the heart for it. And Ygerna had taken him wholly, utterly, and left him bemused.

He put a hand gently on her breast, and she moved beneath him and pulled him down to her. He had tried to go carefully with her, but a body long denied forgets its good intentions, and he thought he had hurt her anyway. She hadn't seemed to care. The hands that fluttered along his back were urgent, questioning, and he felt her spread her thighs apart again and pull him down between them. He began to make love to her again, slowly this time, with hands and mouth, making himself wait.

She sighed and pressed her face against his chest. She had driven the German woman from his mind at last, or the night had done it for her. And the thing that had been impossible was hers now in this strange otherworld that was neither his land nor her own. Hers to hold onto while she could. She hadn't even minded that it had hurt at first. For tonight, for until Isca, he was hers.

Until Isca. For Correus also their flight became an enchantment now, a sidhe-dream from which he would wake at Isca. By day on the trail, with Ygerna in boy's clothes trotting beside him, Correus cursed himself for a fool. By night, with the heady smell of meadow grass around them, he lay with her in his arms and grew drunk.

Until Isca. They said it once aloud and then put the words away from them. Isca was another country, and they would cross into it when they crossed into the Roman zone.

Correus, with one last grasp at sanity, pushed Ygerna away from him and held her by the shoulders, his hands tangling in her hair. "It's not right," he whispered. "It isn't fair. Not to you."

Ygerna shook her head. "No. We have until Isca. Someone has given us that. It wouldn't be fair not to use it." The blue flower petals between her breasts swayed as she moved forward. Her slim feet twined themselves about his own. She put her hands on him, and he was lost.

I will be grateful, she thought as she felt him enter her, not painfully now, but welcome and familiar. *I will be grateful, and I will not ask for more.* Neither the governor nor Rome nor her own people would ever let her keep him, but until Isca, none of them mattered. She didn't even ask that he say he loved her. It would make no difference in the end.

The next night the Dark Folk woke them at midnight, their faces pinched and frightened, their small hands shaking them into consciousness.

The king was riding by night, they said, and he was on the right trail. Their voices were urgent as Correus and Ygerna scrambled into their boots and let themselves be pushed onto some path they couldn't see.

"Run!" Nighthawk said, and the fear in his voice put a cold hand to Correus's neck. If Nighthawk was afraid . . .

They ran, stumbling blindly over tree roots, the low-growing vines and briars scratching at their faces, and in the distance Correus thought he could hear . . . something, something that was not quite the baying of hounds, but an indistinguishable sound that might have been the voice of fear itself. The forest seemed to close around him, and he felt his breath come painfully as if something were clamped around his chest. Ygerna, in front of him, made no sound but her own labored breathing, but he knew that she felt it, too. Whatever was loose in the forest was death.

And then suddenly it was gone—the terrible hand that had gripped his lungs and the almost-sound that had pursued them. Nighthawk dropped to a walk. "They have turned them," he said, and Correus saw that the sidheman's brothers were no longer with them. And that it was daylight.

They trudged on, panic gone and bone-weariness in its place, until Ygerna began to stagger on the trail, and Correus thought that neither of them could go farther. Nighthawk stopped suddenly ahead of them, where the ground rose up sharply in a tumble of rock and wild berries. Correus gave him a puzzled look and then narrowed his eyes where the little man was pointing.

It was a sidhe-dwelling, differing from the Sidhe of Llanmelin in that it was adapted to a different terrain, but alike in its concealment, its blending into the earth around it.

"This is the first place the king will hunt," Ygerna said wearily. "You told us that."

Nighthawk shook his head. "This is the Sidhe of the Dancers, and it has been empty since before the Golden People came. No one knows why. Maybe they died. Or maybe it was only that the well went bad, and they moved on. The Old One of Ty Isaf didn't say. But unless the king comes this way by chance, you'll be safe enough here."

"Won't he track us?"

"My brothers have turned him onto their own trail," Nighthawk said. "Or he would have been here by now. Wait two days and if I am not here, go southeast."

The cave smelled old and, Ygerna thought, of some dark magic that hung about it still. She was almost too tired to be afraid, but there was the feeling of a presence that she couldn't shake, and she kindled a small fire and made a torch of a branch of dry leaves in it. As she lifted it, figures leapt up in the light, and she gasped.

Correus jerked his head up, his hand on his knife, and it was only after a moment that they realized what they had seen. Across the back wall of the cave they leapt and curvetted, antlered heads swaying to their step, bare arms and legs seeming to move in the flickering light—six antlered human forms painted in red ochre on the stone.

"What are they?" Correus whispered.

"The dancers of the Horned One," Ygerna said. "They are older than—anything. I wish now I hadn't seen them."

"They are only paintings."

"That's the Roman in you," Ygerna said. "They are old magic. Your mother's folk would know them." She put the light out. "I don't think we should look at them."

"They are only paintings," he said again, and pulled her onto his cloak beside him. "Sleep, and don't think of them."

"Do I have a choice?" Ygerna said wryly. "I can sleep here with the Horned One or outside with the king, my uncle."

"Of the two," Correus said firmly, "I will take the Horned One." But his back itched as if he could feel them, too, behind him, and when he slept there was something that came and danced at the edge of his dreams —not menacing as the king's presence had been, but old and full of power . . . and not to be denied.

When they woke, it was dark; even the faint glow that had come from the cave mouth was gone. They found each other and their food by touch, and when they had eaten, they lay down again and told stories to chase away the dark, tales of the high and far-off days when the kings and gods of the Dark Folk had warred with those of the Golden People, and their heroes had had the height of mountains. And stories of the gods who lived on

Olympus, and the Fall of Troy, and the Twelve Labors of Hercules.

And then slowly as the heroes of flesh and legend faded into the dark, they sat up and stripped their clothes off and put out their hands to each other. And in the cave of the Horned One, she was not fifteen and he was not a Roman; they were woman and man, and their coupling was a magic and a dance in itself.

On the second day, Nighthawk was waiting for them as they came blinking out into the light, and they realized that in that ancient magic, they had not even feared the king. The fear came back on the trail, but the magic lingered somehow, deep in the bone, where it would stay.

Correus lost track of time now, feeling more and more like a man who has slept in the otherworld. They worked their way slowly south, parallel to the line of the Wye Valley forts, but always with the king's men between them and safety. Nighthawk and his brothers brought them food and pointed to a landmark or a star and were gone again, to keep their watch on Bendigeid's movements. The Dark Folk could move across the hills unseen in ways that not even such a trailwise spy as Centurion Julianus could go. Nighthawk kept his distance now when he could, his old wariness of the Roman seeming to have tripled. Nighthawk knew what had happened. Correus was almost sure of that. The sidhe-man's small face registered such open horror that he apparently expected the Roman to turn to stone or the offending member to drop off at any moment. Finally Ygerna said something furiously to him that Correus couldn't hear, and he backed away with his hand to his forehead.

"What did you tell him?"

Ygerna looked slightly amused. "I threatened him. He thinks I make a sacrilege with you because I am the Goddess on Earth and you are a Roman. I told him that the things between a man and woman are the Goddess's business, and he is not meant to understand. And that if he said one more word, I would send something to him that would give him other worries."

Correus wondered if Ygerna could really curse the little man. He expected she could, especially since Nighthawk was so plainly receptive. The curse that Correus was worried about was a more tangible sort, and he kept enough grip on reality that night to talk about it.

"I would know if I were with child," Ygerna said. "I am not a priestess for nothing." She did not tell him that she would not know this early. If it happened later, then she would decide what to do. This would be all she would ever have of Correus for years, maybe forever. She would be sad for that later. Be sad for the child she couldn't have later. Tonight she would take what was given her.

She felt his hands on her and she shivered as they moved down across her belly and she felt his fingers slip inside her. She could read the want in his eyes so plainly.

"Ygerna . . ." He gasped as she touched him.

And then he was in her, his weight pinning her to the cave floor while the night mist rolled by outside. And the tie that bound them grew one knot stronger.

"There is only a little way to go now, and I think they have given up." Nighthawk stood leaning on his spear in the cave mouth. "You could make the fortress at Burrium, most like. Or two more days on this trail will take you into Coed-y-Caerau."

"And the king's men?"

"They have lost the scent. It was cold by the time they lost the false one. If you are careless, they will find you, but they have no trail to follow, and you could have gone away westward by Carn Goch for all they know. And they have their own hides to look to this close to the Romans."

Correus thought. They could drop out of the sky into Burrium, which had mostly an auxiliary garrison, and explain things and explain things and then explain them again. Or they could go by Coed-y-Caerau to Isca where the garrison command would know him. He felt too tired to explain anything to anyone. And it was only a day's difference. And if they went to Burrium, they would still have to get from there to Isca, but they wouldn't go without escort.

"We'll go by Coed-y-Caerau." One more day in the otherworld.

And then Llew and a troop of his warriors found them, above the valley of Burrium, found them by accident while they were laying man traps in the long summer dusk for the garrison at Burrium.

It was only a stirring in the hawthorn scrub, but Correus and Ygerna saw it at the same time and froze, and then suddenly the hawthorn erupted around them as Llew realized what had fallen into his hand out of the dusk.

They had barely time to pull their weapons when the Britons were on them, and they were fighting two against ten. It wouldn't take long, Ygerna thought, panicked, as a hand shot out toward her. She stabbed with her knife, and the man yelped and fell back, and she realized then that they wanted her alive. Even now, with the king's orders to spur them, no one wished to be the man who had killed a Goddess on Earth. They would have no such compunctions about Correus. A brown-haired man with a cloak wrapped around his left arm for a shield feinted at her and then lunged at Correus, and she screamed in terror as the blade came down.

It was the sound of pure fear, knife-sharp and paralyzing, and the Briton wavered just long enough for Correus to jerk back and block the blow left-handed with his sword, while the knife in his right hand shot out and sank in under the arm. The warrior stumbled back and caught his heel in the edge of a man trap on the trail. The steel jaws snapped, and he went down in a heap, but the rest closed in. Correus was back-to-back with Ygerna now, fighting desperately, but under the desperation was the sheer sick feeling that it had all been for nothing.

"Mother of gods, what was that?" the Gaulish auxiliary on the point of the patrol slued around and stared at his commander. The sound was still dying away over the twilit slopes.

"An animal maybe," an auxiliaryman said.

"*Nothin'* makes a noise like that!"

"Something does, but I'm not sure I want to see it!"

The decurion looked across the rolling hillside, the eldritch shriek still ringing in his ears. "Well, we're goin' to find out."

What it proved to be, as they rounded a hawthorn-covered slope in the direction of the sound, was a troop of Britons fighting with itself. At least eight or nine of them were fighting with two others. They seemed to be handicapped by the fact that they were trying to take one of them alive, while their intended captives had no such restrictions. As the auxiliaries came into sight, someone shouted, "Look out, man traps on the trail!"

Thank you very much, the decurion thought, taking no time from the business at hand to be surprised. Grab them first, and sort them out later. He waded into the fray with his shield up.

It didn't take very long. There was half a century of auxiliaries, and the two Britons who had been fighting the rest were plainly on their side. There were only two dead men by the time the auxiliaries had pulled the rest off and had them lined up at pilum point. They glared across the auxiliaries at their quarry.

The decurion turned to inspect the other two. One of them was a woman, he saw, his mouth dropping open in surprise. He closed it again with a snap. The other had a ragged mustache and dirty hair that fell into one eye. There was a sword of no particular pattern in his left hand and a knife in his right. He dropped them when the auxiliarymen waved theirs at him.

Ygerna was weaving on her feet, and Correus felt sick. He had come close to trading away both their lives for one more night with Ygerna, and it had brought him back to reality in a hurry. If Ygerna hadn't alerted the evening patrol from Burrium when she screamed . . .

Ygerna sagged against him. She had screamed in fear for him, but there seemed no point in saying so. It was over now, ended as surely by that chance-met patrol as it would have been by Llew's warriors. And the magic was fading in the twilight. . . .

"All right now." The decurion of auxiliaries advanced on them. "Will you please tell me what this is all about?" He spoke carefully in British.

"He is ours!" one of Llew's men shouted, and subsided as the decurion swung around and glared at him and an auxiliaryman poked him with his pilum.

The decurion turned back to the other Briton and the woman. "Can you understand me?"

The man gave him a weary salute. "Cohort Commander Centurion Julianus of the Second Legion Augusta," he said in Latin.

XVII
Bendigeid

AT BURRIUM, CORREUS EMERGED SICKLY FROM THE EN-
chantment of the past weeks, as a man comes from under
a drug. Once he had proved his bona fides to the decurion
of auxiliaries, the auxiliaries put Correus and Ygerna on
Llew's horses and walked Llew and his men behind under
guard.

With the panic of that brief, desperate fight fading into
a bone-deep weariness, Correus began to feel a little sorry
for Llew. If no one had seen fit to inform the garrison at
Burrium that the governor's hostage had been stolen, Llew
might well have concocted a tale for the decurion's benefit
that would have let him keep his catch. The Romans generally didn't interfere in the tribes' internal squabbles.
To have the fugitive Rhys turn out to be a Roman himself
was almost unfair.

Correus remembered Llew from two years before—the
brown-haired man with the serious face who was blood
brother to Owen Harper. He wondered what would happen to Llew now. They would send him to the governor
most likely, and the governor would try to convince him
to make Bendigeid see the light. When that didn't work,
he would go to the mines, Correus supposed, and Bendigeid
would have one less captain and that wouldn't change
his mind, either. It was all such a waste, he thought, and
felt even worse when he discovered that he didn't give
a damn.

The plain fact that he had kept under the surface
during their perilous trek back to the Roman zone sat up
and looked him in the eye at Burrium: Ygerna was a
Silure princess and the governor's hostage, and no man
had any right laying a hand on her. Ygerna was fifteen.
Correus could find precious little excuse for himself.

With Ygerna beside him, they explained themselves
to the garrison commander at Burrium, who whistled ad-

275

miringly and sent a courier off to Isca with a message to send on to the governor and orders to bring Ygerna back some suitable clothes. In the meantime he gave her a military tunic to wear, called her a "brave little thing," and gave her his own quarters to sleep in. When she asked for a bath, he chased the lounging auxiliarymen out of it and posted a guard around the bathhouse for her privacy. Correus was given a spare tunic and razor, a cot in the patrol decurion's tent, and a lot of time to think.

Two days later they were on the road for Isca; Ygerna in her own gown and boots, bright with such of her hoard of jewelry as they hadn't given Nighthawk to buy them food or pay some farmer to look the other way; Correus, blessing the courier, on Antaeus, in his own uniform again. He looked sideways at Ygerna. She smiled up at him, a little sadly, he thought, and he cursed himself all over again. There was no way to talk to her with the patrol riding ahead and behind them, and there had been no way since before they reached Burrium. She was wearing the arm ring with the flower clasp, and Correus remembered her grim little prophecy when she had given him her own gift a year ago, a little amber drop on a ragged thong: *"Its luck comes somewhat sideways, I find, but I think it will keep you alive."* Yes, indeed. Ten miles now to Isca, ten miles to the governor, whom the courier had found in residence there, ten miles back to the army again, to Rome again, and no chance to say "I'm sorry."

Ygerna's hair was loose down her back now, and there was a gold fillet in it again, but she had left the silver moon diadem behind her in Dinas Tomen. That belonged to the Goddess, and she had left it for the next priestess when she had gone back to Rome with Correus.

Behind her, Llew and his seven warriors now rode with their feet lashed together under their ponies' bellies.

Correus stood at parade attention in front of the commander's desk at Isca and listened to the governor dock him three weeks' pay for three weeks' Unlawful Absence.

"I warned you, you know," Julius Frontinus said, glaring at Centurion Julianus's impassive military stare. There was a scar just over the centurion's lip, which someone said the fool had given himself. "I generally find it a mistake to go back on a warning."

"Yes, sir." Correus was wearing full dress kit to receive the governor's dressing down, and his helmet with its transverse parade crest was tucked under one arm at the regulation angle. He didn't look particularly humble, merely expressionless.

"It may interest you to know," Julius Frontinus went on, "that you have been proved right. Right enough to be an embarrassment to me, Julianus."

"I beg your pardon, sir?"

"I've read the scouts' reports of the hunt the Silures got up for you and that child," Frontinus said, "and they make the situation crystal clear, even to a man as aged and stubborn as myself. I can't think of any use the king would have for his niece alive that would warrant his pulling his fighting men off *our* trails to get her."

"Yes, sir."

"You were right, Centurion," Frontinus said again. "He would have killed her."

"Yes, sir."

The governor slammed a hand down on the desk, making his ink pot bounce. "Aren't you going to ask why I'm having your pay docked, then?"

"I assume, sir, because you *said* you would," Correus said.

Frontinus laughed. "Did I tell you, Centurion, that I served under your father once, when I was young? You put me forcibly in mind of him."

Something of the governor's amusement broke through Correus's unhappiness, and his mouth twiched into a half smile. "I'm not sure that's a compliment, sir."

"It isn't."

Correus was beginning to feel slightly foolish. He had discovered that Julius Frontinus could generally have that effect on him when he chose. "I apologize for being an ass, sir. I didn't kick about having my pay docked because . . ." Because he didn't care, but that wasn't the right thing to say. He tried to think of the right thing, but his imagination seemed to have deserted him. He ended up looking unhappily at the governor with the feeling that all his sins were written plainly on his face. Even Julius had given him an odd, thoughtful look when they had ridden in from Burrium, and Correus had swung around and glared at him, daring him to say one word.

Frontinus narrowed his eyes. "Sit down, Centurion, and suppose you tell me what's on your mind that's more important than money."

Correus sat. "Ygerna, sir. We've made her into something that's not Roman nor Briton, and now she doesn't belong anywhere, and I feel responsible." *And I made it worse;* but he couldn't say that, either.

"Ygerna must make herself useful, as we all must," Frontinus said. "It is the scheme of things." He sighed. "And like you, Centurion, there are times when I would like to go build a nice bridge somewhere and let the scheme go fall in the Styx, but there are difficulties with that, beginning with the Senate and ending with the emperor and my pension. But you are right about one thing —Ygerna needs to learn to be a Roman, with everything that involves that can't be learned in an army camp. And I want her where her uncle can't try again, now that he has made his intentions so clear. So. It may relieve your mind to know that I am going to send her into the civil zone where she can't be got at by her tribe and where she can learn what she'll need of our laws and history if she's going to govern her people someday."

"Where will you send her?"

"To Aquae, I think. It is very Roman at Aquae. And I have a female relative living there—one of those aunts in the third degree who always has more gentility than money. She will be very fond of Ygerna and spoil her dreadfully and make her thoroughly Roman in no time at all."

And the next time he saw her she would be queen of the Silures, Correus thought dismally. And then they would marry her to some man who had the right ties to Rome, and who wouldn't give a damn about her. *And just how did that make himself any better,* a voice at the back of Correus's mind asked acidly.

"May I be the one to tell her, sir?"

"If you wish."

"Thank you."

"By the way, Centurion, it seems that you have done Rome a service. So you may hang these on your harness—" Frontinus hefted a red leather bag—"with Rome's compliments."

He pushed the bag across the desk, and Correus un-

tied the thong at the neck. But he knew what was in it
before he spilled them out across the commander's desk
—eight silver gilt medals with the likenesses of the emperor and the principal gods of Rome. Military *phalerae,*
for services rendered to Rome.

"You look like a chariot pony." Ygerna poked at the
phalerae, hung on a leather harness across his parade
lorica. They had been presented again, publicly, on the
parade ground that morning.

"I feel like one, but it's an honor all the same." He
was trying to speak lightly, to recapture their old mood of
friend to friend. The Dobunni woman was in the next
room, and in any case, they had said "until Isca" and
had known that they had to mean it. Neither one would
go back on that now, but just for a moment, when
Ygerna turned her face up to his, he could see through
her gown to the flower petals on her breasts and the
whiteness of her skin, and remembrance came back like
a wave.

"So I am to go to Aquae Sulis and be a lady," Ygerna
said. She sounded stoic about it, but she turned her face
away from him. After a minute she said, "Don't be sorry
for me, Correus. I had what I wanted, and I knew it
wasn't going to be forever. But see if you can make your
governor let Llew go, for Owen Harper's sake. I used to
love his music so. It won't make any difference in the end,
you know. Tell the governor that's the price for my
queenship."

"I'll try."

"Thank you." She turned and looked at him across the
room. "The Shining One and the Mother go with you."

"You must be mad." Publia Livilla sat in the atrium
of her small house in Aquae Sulis and gave Julius Frontinus a look of bemusement. The atrium was shabby but
immaculately swept, and as she spoke, a serving girl came
in with a silver tray. "Do have some wine," Publia
Livilla added.

"Thank you." Governor Frontinus regarded the wine
dubiously and drank. "I fail to see the difficulty. You've
undertaken this sort of task before, and you could plainly
use the income."

Publia Livilla didn't bother to take offense. There wasn't much point. "Country farmers' daughters needing a little town polish, yes. But a native priestess who's been raised in the back hills all her life? . . . Julius, I do not think it's possible."

"She's lived at Isca—"

Publia Livilla raised her eyebrows in expressive comment on Isca.

"She's lived at Isca, or in my camp, for two years," Frontinus went on. "She speaks Latin reasonably well and has very little love left for her own kind. She is extremely intelligent. And I am willing to provide a suitable house and see that it is properly staffed." He sat back in his chair and looked expressively around the room. "When Ygerna has left, you may keep the house," he added.

Publia Livilla sighed. The discomforts of genteel poverty were an accustomed nuisance, but not one to which she had ever grown resigned. But if the child were bright and adaptable, *something* might be done with her. "Very well, Julius, I will take your little princess. But I don't promise you anything more than passable results."

"I'm not trying to turn her into a social belle," Governor Frontinus said. "I merely want her to think like a Roman."

Publia Livilla snorted. "That may be harder than anything."

Ygerna looked up dubiously at the blind outer face of the house in the Street of Lilies and turned to the cavalry decurion beside her. "What would happen if I just ran?" she whispered.

"You'd get hungry," the cavalryman said. "If I was you, I'd see what I got here before I turned tail. All right, here we are."

The door swung open, and a slave in a blue tunic bowed respectfully. "You're expected, miss." Another slave bustled past to collect her baggage.

"Well, I'll push off then," the cavalryman said cheerfully. He patted Ygerna on the shoulder. "You'll do all right." He inspected the house through the open doorway. "Better than an army camp. Wouldn't mind it myself."

The slave gave him a look of disapproval down his nose and bowed Ygerna in, closing the door firmly behind him. She followed him through a wide room with a little pool at the center, down a corridor to another, smaller room comfortably furnished with couches and cushioned wicker chairs. There was a picture on the floor of a man rolling a rock uphill, and an old lady with a tower of gray curls and paint on her face sat on one of the elaborate couches. The walls were painted to look like windows or archways opening onto strange landscapes or rooms full of statuary. Ygerna looked around her with mouth open, and the gray-haired lady held out a hand and said in Latin, "Welcome, child. Come and let me have a look at you."

Ygerna gave her a wary eye. "How do you do?" she said carefully.

The old lady nodded. "Well, your accent is good." Her own voice sounded like Correus's, or the governor's, Ygerna noted, not like Julius's, or Correus's soldiers.

"I learned it from Centurion Julianus," she said. She thought maybe it wouldn't be right to call him Correus to this imposing-looking lady.

"He seems to have been a good teacher," Publia Livilla said. She looked at Ygerna thoughtfully, closing her eyes briefly at the red and green checked gown. "Clothes," she said after a moment. "Clothes and a hair-dresser."

Ygerna looked rebellious, and the old lady smiled at her, an unexpectedly pleasant smile that softened the wrinkled face. "If you're going to be a Roman, you might as well dive in with both feet," she said. "My name is Publia Livilla, and you will call me 'Aunt Publia,' and I do not bite."

Ygerna nodded. "That is what Correus said. Centurion Julianus," she amended. "That I should learn to be a Roman."

"Yes, I have heard of what happened to you," Publia Livilla said. "My nephew Frontinus must have rocks where his brains should be to leave you in an army camp with no one but men to look after you."

"I had Correus," Ygerna said. "And it wasn't his fault what happened."

Publia Livilla looked thoughtful again, and an idea that she doubted had crossed her kinsman's mind worked its way into hers. Someone should be ashamed of himself, and she wasn't sure whether it was the governor or

Centurion Julianus. She laid a soft, manicured hand on Ygerna's. "I think that it is high time they sent you to me."

Back to the army again. Back to duty again. Back to the routine of wake up call and march and pilum practice, and the Eighth Cohort to whip into shape and remind them that they had a commander after all. A man could drown a lot of memories in that, Correus thought. He had spent too much time on his own in the last few years—he needed the legion to come home to, for a haven from his own thoughts.

And if Ygerna's white legs and dark hair came to him by night, by day they were only the stuff of dreams, the forbidden desires that all men long for in their sleep.

He rode out of Isca in a dawn mist, with a cavalry patrol and Llew. Llew's warriors had gone to the mines, but the governor had agreed to send Llew back to the king with one last ultimatum. Ygerna and Owen Harper would have to be content with that. The hovels that were the Isca *vicus* had grown to a village now, marked by the number of gray tombstones that lifted their heads through the mist along the road. Roman law forbade burial within inhabited land, and every city was ringed by its own graveyards. Correus watched them slide by through the mist. He had gone across Isca Bridge the night before to lay a handful of cornflowers on Freita's grave and had found a certain sad comfort there. Better not to be able to have Ygerna maybe, than to lose her. Better not to give her what he had given Freita.

They turned Llew loose outside the new outpost that the Second Legion was beginning to dig into the turf at Pen-y-Gaer. It was no more than five miles from Dinas Tomen, for a curlew. For a man on two feet, of course, it would take longer, but he would get there eventually. Especially if he went behind a shield and pilum with five thousand of his messmates.

"They will come," Llew said. He sat leaning on Owen's shoulder against the main beam of the warriors' house at Dinas Tomen. There was a peat fire burning in the hearth, and Llamrei sat cross-legged in front of it, polishing a dagger, her dark face expressionless. The first snow of winter was coming down lightly outside; still fair enough weather to go raiding in, for a man who knew the country, but there was no place left to raid. "They will come," Llew said again. "It will be famine winter this year, and then they will come with their siege machines and open Dinas Tomen like an egg."

"Shut up," Owen said.

"That is what the governor told me," Llew went on, ignoring him, staring at the fire. "And what Rhys, or whoever he really is, said to me when they let me go at Pen-y-Gaer. It was meant to frighten, but I believe it now. Now I have seen the Roman zone from the inside, and it was like looking into Annwn."

"*Shut up!*" Owen hissed again violently. "You sound like a Druid seeing visions in his soup! You are a fighting man!" He stood up and looked coldly at Llew. "Or is that gone, too?"

Llew shifted his shoulder against the beam, now that Owen had moved. "That's all that's left," he said thoughtfully. "If there'd been anything else to run to, I'd have gone the other way at Pen-y-Gaer."

"Damn you!" Owen turned on his heel and walked out, and after a minute Llamrei followed him.

Owen was standing by the well, watching the snow fall into it.

"Don't fight with him, Owen. There're not enough of us left to fight."

"He's not the same," Owen said. "He said *she'd* made the Romans send him back. She's a witch, maybe."

"And stolen his soul?" Llamrei looked disgusted. "Llew has always seen things a little clearer than most and made everyone uncomfortable by saying them. He's only seen something worse this time."

"Well, he needn't be talking of it. It's like listening to the Morrigan's ravens."

"Llew can't help talking," Llamrei said. "It takes some of the fear out of it, I think."

"Llew has never been afraid!" Owen said indignantly.

"Not of a spear point, no. But he sees too much. Sometimes I think he has the Sight. Hywel always said he did."

"Hywel gave up. And Hywel had his own reasons." Hywel hadn't come back from the last raid, and his men said he had ridden onto a Roman pilum. "He's been asking the ravens to come back for him since they took his wife and boys."

Llamrei sighed. "Another of us gone." The captains' ranks were growing thin.

"Rhodri was looking for you earlier," Owen said. "I think he's gone to the ponies." It was only a change of subject. Llamrei knew that Rhodri had been hunting her; she would have gone by now if she'd a mind to. "You should have married him," Owen said.

Llamrei shook her head. "I don't love him enough." She looked at Owen. "That's another reason for you not to quarrel with Llew. He came back for you."

"What do you mean by that?"

"He came back so you wouldn't have to fight without him. He meant it when he said he could have gone the other way at Pen-y-Gaer."

Owen made a strangled noise in his throat and stumbled back into the house, leaving Llamrei to watch the snow fall into the well. *One more winter,* she thought. *That's all we're going to have. No one should be alone this winter.* Through the inner gate she could see the roof of the pony shed in the lower court, and she went to find Rhodri.

"Why did you come?" Rhodri said. "You never came if I asked you before."

"I was never this lonely before."

They were lying together on their cloaks in an empty pony stall. Rhodri shifted his weight to take the strain off an old wound that ached when it was cold, and he grinned at her. "It is a bad winter that doesn't bring someone some good. I should count it lucky, maybe."

"Maybe you should." Llamrei had never gone to any man for the asking, save one, and he would never ask her again, she thought, not now, and no one should be *that* alone. She reached out and ran her hands down Rhodri's back and pressed her face against his throat, to blot the king out of her mind.

"And what will the king of the Silures do now?" Teyrnon Chief-Druid looked at him across the snow-covered lintel of Ty Isaf. They had come here to talk because it was a holy place and no one would disturb them in its shadow. Also, neither of them would lie.

"I came here to think about that," Bendigeid snapped. "And to ask the Chief Druid in his wisdom." He looked across the white bulk of the mound. The snow had begun to bank up among the trees that covered it, obscuring its shape. "They will make her queen," he said finally.

"Yes."

"And outlaw you. And what will the Chief Druid do then?" He mocked Teyrnon's tone.

"I will go," Teyrnon said.

"So simple as that?"

The old man nodded. *"My* life is not bound to one tribe." He gave Bendigeid a long look. "And no tribe's life is bound to mine."

"Then go away," Bendigeid said. He watched the old man trudge away through the snow, then sat down on the curbstone of Ty Isaf. It didn't feel threatening anymore, only dark and somehow safe, and certain things were very clear, sitting there.

I am the threat, he thought now. *I am the spear at their throats.* It was such a simple thought, to come so sharply into his mind. Maybe it had always been that simple—there was a price on life, a price on power, and always a price on kingship.

Bendigeid of the Silures had been a thorn in the Roman hide for more than ten years. While he ruled, Rome would make the harshest possible settlement of his people that she could. He would be taken hostage and used against them. Or Rome would exterminate the tribe in trying to take him. But if his successor were made king now—a man the tribe and Rome could both accept—it might be that Rome would let well enough alone if the Silures offered peace. And the tribe would live.

He could hear his own words in his head, spoken arrogantly enough one season ago, one short spring ago: *I will sell away any one man or woman of my tribe if it buys life for the rest.* And the Old One's answer came back to him, night-haunted even in the fierce sunlight that was reflected from the snow-covered shape of Ty Isaf: *Let the king of the Silures be remembering he said that.*

Bendigeid leaned his head back and watched a curlew

sailing on the updraft above him. The sky was clear now, dazzling above the snow, and all his thoughts came clear as well, sharply defined as a sword blade against that brightness. Had he known what the Old One meant, with some unknown part of his mind, even last spring?

The old king who had ruled before his father would have known. He had died in a famine year, when all the fields were parched dry, and on Midsummer Day he had gone out to hunt, or so he said.

They had brought him back on a shield, with a hole in his heart where a cornered stag had turned on him. The horned beasts were all the gods' creatures, and king and stag had gone to the gods together.

Bendigeid had been no more than three, but he could still remember how the old man had ridden out through the parched land, bright with his best jewelry and his gray hair freshly washed and shining in the sunlight. They had buried him with his weapons in a barrow beside the cornfields, and that night and through the next days it had rained and rained. There were some things that could only be bought with one price. And it was the life and the blood of the kingship that when it was asked, it was to be paid.

He watched the curlew swooping above him for another minute, memorizing that joyous shape against the dazzle of the sun.

"I cannot." Aedden stood like a man with his back to the last wall. "I thought I could, but I cannot."

"Then you are no king," Rhodri said, "and he will do it for nothing."

"This has not been done since we became the Sun's people," Aedden said. His face was painted in red and ochre, and above his brows Teyrnon Chief-Druid had made the King's Mark with blue woad. Underneath it his skin was white, and the dark circles under his eyes were from nightmares, not paint.

"It is the king's choice," Rhodri said. "Without it, it would not be certain."

"It is the king's *right!*" Teyrnon said. "If you can't look that in the face, Aedden, then Rhodri is right, and you are not a king!"

Aedden shuddered, closed his eyes, and then opened

them again slowly. "I can look," he said. "Give me my cloak."

It had snowed in the morning, and the upper court of Dinas Tomen was powdered with it, but the sky was clear and cold now, black against the stars. A circle near the inner wall had been swept clean of snow and a dais raised above it. On it, cross-legged like a statue, sat Teyrnon Chief-Druid, looking very old and fragile in the torchlight, bundled against the cold in a bearskin mantle. There was a staff with the golden circle of the sun laid across his knees, and his hands rested lightly on it.

All around the circle the fires burned, the Nine Fires of a King-making, as brilliant orange as the sun against the blackness. Outside the ring of fires, the people of the tribe waited, their faces tiger-striped with torchlight and shadow, their bodies never quite still, moving uneasily to the sound of chanting and of pipes that began to drift upward from the lower courts, as if some old magic, half-remembered, came upwards on the sound.

The chanting swelled, and from somewhere in the distance there was a low throb of drums that kept pace with it. Owen Harper, standing just outside the fires with the other captains, felt the sound twist around him like a woman and tried to shut it out. He was of the family, and it was to his blood that wailing chant called out. And if he would never have to pay the price for it that Bendigeid and Aedden would, it was still too near to be comfortable. He looked at Llamrei standing next to him, but her face was immobile, head thrown back, and her dark eyes never leaving the space at the center of the fires. Rhodri was on her other side, and he put a hand on her shoulder, kindly, but she seemed not to feel it.

The music came closer, higher, wilder than before, until they could feel it on their skin, and then the crowd rolled apart to make two gates between the first fire and the second, and the first fire and the ninth, on either side of Teyrnon's dais. Through the first gate, five women came, white-robed, singing, with mistletoe in their hands, and behind them four warriors, weaponless as were all the tribesfolk, their faces hooded under their cloaks. In their midst walked Aedden, naked except for the paint and something which shone white in his right hand. He stood in the circle of the fires, his eyes glittering in their light, with his warriors behind him, while the women wove their singing dance among the flames. In the old days, the young king had gone to his King-making this way. But in the old days it had been the pattern for them all, the death and the rebirth of the land through its king every seventh year, and the old king had gone into the fires with a drug in him as often as not. Tonight Owen thought they might have given it to Aedden.

The pipe music whirled and shuddered, an unearthly sound, and the crowd drew in its breath in a gasp that was almost fear as Bendigeid stepped out between the other fires. He, too, was naked, but his face was bare of paint. But even in the firelight, the blue tattooed lines of the King's Mark on his forehead blazed out like a brand, and even Teyrnon looked on him with awe.

The black hair was loose down his back, and it caught the fire and flared around him as if it burned. Above it was a cap made from a red horse's crest, with the gold diadem of the sun between its pricked ears, and there were heavy bands of gold about his forearms. His feet were painted with red clay.

Except that it was Teyrnon and not the Goddess on Earth who sat on the piled deer hides on the dais, it might have been a King-making from the dim and half-forgotten times that were only racial memory now, when Earth Mother was the force that ruled them all, before Lugh Long-Spear had mated with her and mastered her and brought the power of the sun with him. That is, until Owen looked into the king's eyes. They blazed like the sun, and the bronze knife was in his hand and the red clay on his feet because it was his choice and his right. *He would burn your hand if you touched him,* Owen thought.

The women finished their circle of the fires, and at the last, before Teyrnon's dais, they threw their mistletoe, and it cracked and blackened in the flames, and Teyrnon raised his hand.

The women and the hooded warriors drew back, one in each gap between the Nine Fires, and the crowd shivered and strained forward, like something on a leash. *They will tell their children,* Owen thought, *that once they watched a King-slaying.*

Teyrnon raised his hand again, this time with the sun staff in it. His eyes were ancient and veiled, and the expression on his mouth was hidden under his beard. There had been no love between the king of the Silures and the chief of the Druids, but that did not matter now. He let the staff fall silently in his lap and the music stopped, suddenly, like something severed with a knife.

They faced each other within the fires, the old king and the young one, naked in the biting cold. Neither seemed to feel it now, as they came together to fight for the kingship of the tribe—and the terrible power that went with it.

Llamrei watched, nails biting into the palms of her hands at her side, knowing that Rhodri was watching her. Her dark eyes were bright, with a glitter like the fires.

It was only a moment; a brief circling like a dance, a parry and the white flash of a knife. Then Bendigeid seemed to speak to Aedden, and Aedden's knife came up again into the king's breast, just beneath the bone that hides the heart.

The king's knife slipped from his hand. He stood for just a moment, a burning figure outlined against the fire, before he fell.

He could still see the fires and they blended into golden mist and he thought he could see the curlew again, black against them, and behind that, fiercer, brighter than the fires, the face of the sun. He tried to lift a hand to it, but the strength was gone, and he threw back his head and fell and let the brightness come to him.

A cry that might have been grief or triumph, or something of the two oddly mixed, came from the tribe circled around the fires, and Aedden bent and laid his knife beside the body of the king. He straightened slowly, turning in the firelight to show himself to the people, so that they could see that he was still unmarked. The king became the land and a maimed king brought a ruined land. He turned slowly so that they could all see him, with the blue paint of the King's Mark dark on his forehead. Tomorrow the priests would prick it in with needles and blue dye, and then he would bear it forever, until he died. But already he was king, and a king made this way could only be unmade by death. It was for this that Bendigeid had walked into the fires with him.

Aedden finished turning and came to a stop with his face to Teyrnon, and the old Druid came down from his dais and lifted the horse's crest from the head of the dead king. He fidgeted with it for a moment, and Aedden realized that it had been bound to the king's hair so that it would not slip. When it was free, Teyrnon lifted the red horse cap above his head so that the sun disc between the ears showed clear, and then he set it on Aedden's head.

He turned him gently by the shoulders, outward to face the people who were his people now, and from far away below the mountain the drumming began again, as if the People of the Hills knew that a new king was crowned in Dinas Tomen.

King—the chosen of the Sun Lord, the Horse Lord. The red stallion cap felt hot, as if something of the old king lingered in it still—or the power of the thing itself. The music of the pipes had begun again, too, from somewhere he couldn't see, and the night was laced through with it, a wild. white sound that ran through blood and bone. It seemed to him that he could see, just above the fires, a bright, terrible shimmer that would have burned his eyes before. He was Aedden, lord of the Silures, now, and it would never leave him, not until he, too, went at the end into that terrible blinding light.

Someone came forward and put a cloak around him, and he walked from the circle between the first fire and the ninth, where the old king had come in. He turned back once to see the man who lay still at the center of the fires. Bendigeid's chest was dark with blood, but his face was calm and oddly untroubled, more at rest in this death than he had been in life. It was like seeing a fire burned out to cinders.

They buried him the next day in a grave mound at the foot of Dinas Tomen, in the shadow of Ty Isaf. Above the wailing grief-song of the women was the harsh, triumphant cry of curlews overhead.

"We've got company, Governor." The chief optio's face had a slightly startled look. A little fall of snow drifted from his cloak and melted on the tiled floor.

Governor Frontinus glanced up. He was building a miniature watercourse across a table with a set of marble blocks and a bowl of damp sand. It was the dead of winter and cold even in the Praetorium with the hypocaust fired up and three-legged iron braziers burning in all the rooms. Outside it was snowing like hell.

"How did he arrive?" he inquired mildly. "Wings?"

"Horse," the optio said succinctly. He had been the governor's chief of staff for a long time. "And 'he's' a woman."

The governor waited. Optios never interruped him without good reasons.

"Claims to hold rank in the Silure war band," the optio said, "and to come from the king. Got a piece of evergreen stuck in her belt."

The governor heaved himself up from the floor and dusted the sand off his hands. "Mithras! Bendigeid does pick a time."

There was a certain amount of sympathy on the optio's face. "I expect they're hungry, sir."

"I expect they are." He shouted for his cloak and helmet, and two slaves bustled forward with them at once. "Where is she?"

"In your office, sir."

The governor strode across the snowy courtyard to the Principia, with the optio and the chilly legionaries who were his personal guards that day scurrying after him like harbor boats in a quinquireme's wake.

The woman was warming her hands at a brazier, and he paused for a moment in the doorway, inspecting her from under his helmet rim. She raised her head and appeared to inspect him, also. He handed his cloak to his optio, brushed the snow from the eagle feathers on his helmet, handed it to one of his guard, and closed the door in their hopeful faces.

"I am Llamrei," the woman said. "I have given my weapons to your soldiers."

"I expect you have," Frontinus said gravely. She wouldn't have had a choice. and they would have searched her, too, which must have been unpleasant, but she showed no signs of indignation. He looked at her curiously. He had heard that occasionally a woman of the tribe chose to spend her life in this fashion (all were trained for it in their girlhood and could fight with the men if worse came to worst), but he had never met one.

She had a dark, grave face and a low, attractive voice, and her hair was cropped off at shoulder-length. She wore a man's shirt and breeches of good cloth and a gold torque on her neck. There was, as promised, a green branch stuck in her belt, but he thought briefly of the tribune who had come back across his horse, and said brusquely, "Stand still." He ran his fingers around the insides of her boot tops and found an empty scabbard.

"They looked there," Llamrei said dryly.

"So I perceive." Frontinus straightened up and bowed her gravely to a chair. "I am Sextus Julius Frontinus, military governor of the Province of Britannia, in the name of Vespasian Caesar. I have the authority to speak with his voice." His British was badly accented, but clear enough. He settled himself behind his desk and crossed his arms on it. "Do you speak for Bendigeid, Llamrei the envoy?"

For a moment the woman's face seemed to cloud over into a mask, fixed and painted as a stage player's, with only some dark life behind the eyes, and then she spoke and the impression was gone. "I speak for the king of the Silures, who is Aedden ap Culwych, who was made king between the Nine Fires on Midwinter Night."

"Bendigeid is dead?" The governor's eyes dug into hers. "Why?"

"He was king," Llamrei said. "It was his time. There needed to be peace between us. Between your kind and mine, Governor."

"Do you mean he killed himself?"

"He chose his time," Llamrei said evenly. "If you mean, whose hand held the knife, it was the young king's. Kings made in that way, Governor, are never unmade."

"And so he fought us to the end, even with his death?" Governor Frontinus slammed his fist down on his desk. "Damn him! Damn him for the waste of it all!"

Llamrei sat looking at him.

"No," the governor said finally, "not a waste, was it?"

"He kept faith with his kingship," Llamrei said. "The Druids say that is never wasted."

The governor had a snort of irritation for the Druids. But all the same, he thought, Bendigeid had fired his parting shot at some target, and gestures like that had a way of hitting home. *And what about you,* he thought, looking at Llamrei. *What are you really thinking behind your druidical platitudes?* "Midwinter Night," he said. "The young king was speedy enough in sending you to Isca. I don't expect the old king's body was cold."

"Everything is cold at Midwinter," Llamrei said. "Even dead kings. I am still cold." She moved closer to the brazier.

"I am surprised you got here at all," the governor said, "in this weather."

"We wished to talk peace," Llamrei said with a wry note in her voice, "*before* you put your Eagle soldiers on the war trail again—and maybe found it easier to go on than to stop."

"Tell your young king," Frontinus said, "that I am *always* willing to stop when there is the possibility of peace. I wish the old king had believed that."

"Your definition of peace and his differed somewhat, Governor," Llamrei said.

The governor sighed. "Very well. In the morning we will argue over the differences. I am sure that you have your instructions, but it is necessary that I consult with my staff. I will have my optio show you to your quarters and bring you some clean clothes." He looked at her checkered woolen trousers and wolf-skin riding boots and the heavy cloak wound around her shoulders. "Does the king's envoy prefer men's clothes or a woman's gown?"

"Whichever is handiest." Llamrei said. "I am the king's envoy, not his dancing girl. But there are clean clothes on my horse, if you will have someone fetch them."

"Of course. I shall expect you to dine with me tonight," the governor added.

"Of course," Llamrei replied. "I should think the novelty will give your staff something to keep them amused."

"Oh, I should think so," the governor said.

"They must be very bored in the winter."

"Indeed they are," the governor said, "but they won't be dining with me."

She wore a gown. He wasn't quite sure why. She wore it with a certain natural grace but with none of the airs of a woman. The neckline was cut like a tunic, loosely draped, and he could see part of some pattern of tattooing above it.

For his part, the governor wore a tunic, gold-bordered, with military leggings under it, his concession to the cold, and no armor. She could strangle him over the sweets and wine, he supposed, but he doubted it.

His hair was neatly brushed. Hers was pulled back into a soft braid at the nape of her neck. He had lost more men and time than he wanted to think about to the stubbornness of her war band. She had watched her people grow few and hungry before the relentless march of his army, and the only man who had ever touched her soul walk to his death. They eyed each other warily and stretched out on the couches to eat.

A slave filled the two-handled silver wine cups and the governor lifted his. "To peace," he said over it.

"To life," Llamrei said. She sat up. "I am sorry, but I cannot drink this way. I will spill it." She curled herself up with her feet under her.

"It takes some getting used to," the governor said. He stretched himself out comfortably and dipped his hand into a plate of pastries. "Eat. You will need your strength to quarrel with me in the morning."

"Are you so sure we will quarrel?"

"A peace treaty is always one long quarrel. Each side throws its conditions at the other like so many half bricks until one has more bruises than the other, and then they sort out the bricks and make peace."

"We have only one brick to throw, Governor. The others are all yours."

"And whose name is written on it?"

"Aedden ap Culwych. Our terms are simple enough. You may build your roads and we will pay your taxes, but you must leave the tribe to its own governance."

"You should never give your terms away before you come to the treaty table. Have some of this. It's very good."

"Thank you. It doesn't matter. The terms won't change."

"And if I don't agree?"

"We are still strong enough to make trouble. Not to win maybe, but to give you great trouble with our dying. If you don't agree, I will go back to Dinas Tomen and show you that."

"I could always send you back to Dinas Tomen the

way Bendigeid sent me my tribune," the governor said thoughtfully.

"You could," Llamrei agreed. "But will you?"

"No." The governor leaned across the table and poured some more wine in her cup, without calling the slave back. They watched each other across the four-legged silver lamp that lit the table. "Military governors are not kings," he said at last. "They don't last a lifetime. I am being recalled next season."

"Why?"

The governor shrugged. "It is thought best that a man not have that sort of power for more than four or five years. Any bargain made with me might hold with my successor." He looked at her gravely across the wine cup and the lamp. "It might not. I find your company makes me honest."

"What kind of bargain did you have in mind?"

"The treaty table kind. Nothing more."

She ate a pastry and sipped her wine.

"I have a wife in Rome," he said idly.

Llamrei looked him in the eye. "You are asking if I find you attractive. For yourself."

"I am."

"And telling me I would not be binding myself to more than I wanted."

"Yes."

"Give me some more wine, Governor, but the answer is no. You do attract me—I didn't think a man of your people could, but you do. But I let one man touch my life who had another faith to keep than one with me, and I watched him die. With the rest of his captains, I dressed him for death, and I watched the life go out of him to keep that faith. I do not want to care, Governor, when your ship sails for Rome."

Frontinus nodded. "Nor I. I think maybe you are right, Llamrei king's-messenger. Bring your brick to my office in the morning."

XVIII

A Kindness Done to Lovers

THERE WAS PEACE. OF A SORT, AND FOR A TIME. LLAM-rei took the governor's message back to Aedden, and Aedden met with the Romans at Isca after the first thaw. He looked older than he had before Midwinter, and the King's Mark on his forehead had faded so that it seemed always to have been part of him. The conditions of the treaty were read in Latin and British—rate of taxes, civil upkeep of roads, any defenses over a certain height to be pulled down; two cohorts of men drafted for the auxiliaries, and all others to be pardoned. Not such harsh terms, all in all. A ruined land was of very little use to Rome.

For his part, the governor decreed the Druids outlaw (a stipulation he could not have avoided had he wanted to—and he didn't) and left the tribe to its own governance in all other matters.

"Until the summer," he said. "I am going back to Rome in the summer, and you will have to fight that one over again with my successor."

Aedden nodded. They were speaking formally, with Centurion Julianus as an interpreter, his usefulness as a spy having been ended at Dinas Tomen. "Tell your governor that I am king of the Silures, and that that is a choice that the gods make, not men, not even Romans when they have won. Tell him that if he thinks to change that, he will undo more good than his little queen is worth."

The governor watched them sweep away across Isca Bridge toward Venta, where the new tribal capital had been—ostensibly—settled. The king would spend no more time in it than was needed to keep his side of the treaty. The Silures would never develop a liking for having Rome looking over their shoulders. And that was why, perhaps, they would need Ygerna in the end.

The governor sighed. He had done his best to warn them of that. He had no liking for making promises he would have to break. *I shall go home and build waterways,* he thought again. And enjoy this season's campaign against Cadal in the knowledge that the outcome would be something some other poor fool would have to deal with.

There was peace. Peace to take the ruined fields back under the plow, to reclaim the orchards and entice the honeybees back into their abandoned hives. In the east, the Ninth Hispana was minding its steps and drills so well that the governor had pulled the Second Adiutrix out of Lindum entirely and parked them on the northern edge of Ordovician lands where they were turning the site of the old frontier post at Deva into a legionary base. The Twentieth Valeria Victrix at Viroconium had already begun the campaign to give Cadal of the Ordovices cause to wish that he had listened more carefully to the king of the Silures. The governor was at Deva or in the marching camps of the Twentieth or somewhere in between. In the south of West Britain, the Second Augusta found itself on garrison duty, a pleasant summer task which consisted largely, as Silvius Vindex said, of looking martial in the right places and keeping their beady eye on the civil officials who were being appointed for the territory, to make sure they didn't cheat the natives blind.

Correus and Vindex had their hands full, coping with the natural exuberance of legionaries let loose in spring with nothing to do but peacock about in parade dress and chase the local women. With the peace had come a civil population of wine sellers, tarts, traveling scribes, potion peddlers, and third-rate actors who seemed to spring up in the army's footsteps like so many mushrooms after a rain. Most of these new towns were no more than the beginnings of a *vicus* outside some fortress gate, with no guards or patrols of its own, and the centurions found themselves knocking civilian heads together—unofficially —as often as military, until the frontier settled down somewhat.

It was fun. They sampled the wine merchants' wares, listened to traveling players on makeshift stages where the "god in the machine" was the lead actor on a rope that broke, prowled marketplaces suddenly full of goods, and chased women themselves. A middle-aged innkeeper's widow fell in love with Vindex, much to his chagrin.

Correus found that that now half-misty interlude with Ygerna had loosed some things that had been lying low, and he took up with a whore named Aifa in an inn at Venta. She had red hair the color of a copper pot and reminded him a little of Emer, who was his father's kitchen slave and had been his first woman. Except that Emer must be older now, he supposed. Aifa was twenty, as close as she could remember, with a plain outlook on life. She liked to make love and she liked men who were good at it and she liked money, and for all of these reasons she liked Correus. He gave her a fair amount over and above the inn's charge, which she squirreled away in some secret recess in her room, and a red silk gown, which clashed horribly with her hair and which she adored. He spent most of his off-duty time in her bed, and killed a lot of memories, for the time being at least.

At midsummer the governor's replacement was announced. The southern frontier pulled itself together, paid its tavern bill, and shook the vine leaves out of its hair. Gnaeus Julius Agricola had served twice in Britain, first as a military tribune and then as legate of the Twentieth, and he was already legendary.

In August he landed at Isca, inspected a now pious frontier, and officially exchanged batons with Sextus Julius Frontinus, who left his half-built foundations at Deva with mingled wistfulness and relief and went to build his waterways.

So now he will sail for Rome, and this new man will do as he pleases, Llamrei thought, watching the new governor and the old ride side by side into Venta with an honor guard of the four British legions. She wondered if it would have helped if she had slept with him. Probably not. He had said it wouldn't.

They watched him, all of them, from Aedden and the king's captains and the council lords of the Silures down to the peddlers and beggars of Venta. What Julius Agricola saw fit to do was law, and their lives would hang on it.

"He has a nice face," Ygerna whispered, and Publia

Livilla gave a snort as her best opinion of the governor's nice face.

"Don't think you'll wind *him* around your finger, child, any more than my nephew Frontinus. I must have been mad to let you come here, and the thought of going all the way back to Aquae Sulis in that chaise makes my bones congeal."

Ygerna chuckled and put an arm around the old lady. "I expect your bones will get a nice rest while we wait for the governor to see me."

"He may not see you at all," Publia said repressively. "And pull your scarf around you before your heathen kinfolk see you instead."

Ygerna obeyed. She could see Aedden in the reviewing stand with the civil officials of Venta, and his captains nearby him in the crowd, but she thought in truth that they wouldn't notice her unless they were deliberately looking for her. Which was possible, of course, and one of the reasons Aunt Publia hadn't wanted her to come here. Ygerna had heard from Governor Frontinus, with a shudder of grim admiration, how her uncle had died, but she wasn't foolish enough to think that a successor of Bendigeid's choosing would be less ruthless where she was concerned. Still, she didn't look much like the royal woman who had run away from Dinas Tomen, mostly thanks to Aunt Publia.

Her hair was pinned up on her head now, trimmed in front into a soft fringe of dark curls, and laced through at the back with gold ribbon. She wore a blue silk gown and mantle and blue kid sandals, and Aunt Publia had shown her how to paint her face the way the Roman ladies did. Just enough to be respectably fashionable—Aunt Publia didn't approve of overdressing.

The governor's escort swung by—a handful of mounted officers with their men on foot behind them in parade dress. Ygerna caught sight of a blue silk banner with the capricorn badge of the Second Augusta and sighed. She wished Correus could see her, and then wondered if he'd like her this way. Their summer idyll was still bright in her mind, but blurred around the edges, fading, as the faces of her tribe had faded after the Romans had taken her to Isca, until she couldn't tell if her memories were truth or dreams. She could feel him beside her sometimes in the night, feel the way his hands had been on her skin, but even that might be only wishful longing for pleasures once tasted and now gone. Would he want her if he saw her now? Would he love her? Had he ever loved her? She shook that thought from her mind and watched the new governor's face, smiling, hand raised to the crowd that jammed both sides of the street behind the soldiers stationed every ten paces along it. What Correus thought wasn't going to matter if Governor Agricola wouldn't listen to her.

"Centurion Julianus. Do come in." The great man waved a hand at a chair beside his desk in the Isca Principia, and Correus sat.

The new governor had a strong-boned face, wide at the forehead and narrow at the chin, under heavy dark brows and a thick thatch of brown hair. "I haven't seen you since before you joined," he said. "At your birthday, I believe it was, yours and your brother's. I remember drinking far too much wine and listening to that poetic nuisance Martial bore everyone into stupefaction with an endless paean to the family name."

Correus chuckled. He couldn't help liking Agricola, but it was a wary liking with a great deal of respect in it. The general was still in his thirties and had risen high and fast, like an arrow shooting off. Few people wanted to get in the way.

"I'm pleased to see you've done so well for yourself since," Agricola said briskly. "And your father sends his love. I saw him before I left Rome. Now tell me, Julianus, just how well do you know that Silure woman and her tribe?"

"Reasonably well, sir," Correus said. "We were . . . friends." As usual he felt as if his sins proclaimed themselves on a banner across his helmet crest.

"She was lying in wait for me at Venta," Agricola said thoughtfully, "and staged a one-woman delegation outside my chambers until I gave her an audience. She does not wish to go back to her tribe and suggested that I apply to you for confirmation of her reasons."

"What was your decision, sir?"

"I didn't give her one." Agricola gave him a long, thoughtful look that made Correus want to twitch. "I've served here before, and I have a fair knowledge of the natives, but I would like *your* opinion on this, Julianus, if you feel you can make it sufficiently unbiased."

Correus took a deep breath. Cohort commanders were not generally invited to give advice to governors, and he had not gone entirely unscathed the last time he had done it. He felt he might as well be struck by lightning now as later. "I think it would be a mistake if you make her queen."

"Your reasons, please."

"She's grown up with us. She's *too* Roman now, and they won't ever accept her. I don't think she will live a month, curse or no curse, if you depose Aedden. And then I think we will have a war again. Either they will start it with what fighting men they have left, or *you* will have to start it when they kill her."

Agricola raised an eyebrow. "Practical, Centurion, and possibly correct. And your personal concern?"

"My personal concern is that we have diverted the normal course of her life," Correus said stiffly. "We have made her something that is neither a Roman nor a Briton. No one has ever had the slightest concern for Ygerna except for what use she could be to them, and we have been as bad as her uncle. Now she has no place in life except with a tribe she's afraid of or with an old lady in Aquae Sulis who's not even kin to her. I think we have been wrong."

Agricola watched him. *More there than meets the eye, and trying to stuff it away somewhere. Poor Ygerna— neither fish nor fowl, but a good deal like Centurion Julianus, poor man.* An ill-matched pair, one would have thought, but something was there.

"Very well," the general said aloud. "You are dismissed, Centurion. I will take your concerns under consideration."

Correus fled and went into Isca Town to get drunk, for some reasons of which he wasn't entirely sure, and Agricola put his feet up on his desk and thought about Ygerna.

A black-haired Silure witch with a grandmother out of a sidhe. Or a Roman lady with her lips tinted coral and her hair curled into a fringe with hot tongs.

"I don't know which I am, either, Governor," Ygerna had said, draping her mantle over a chair with the carelessly fashionable gesture Aunt Publia had taught her and helping herself to a seat. "But I do know that I'm going to be more trouble than I'm worth to you if you send me back there."

Agricola raised an eyebrow. "Are you threatening an imperial governor?"

"I don't have to," Ygerna said. "I won't need to make trouble. The tribe will do it. I was not overly fond of my uncle, Governor. But he was the king, and what he did was a great enough magic that even the Dark Goddess will pay heed to it. There is no place for me among the Silures. Not while Aedden wears the King's Mark. They will kill me. I have thought about it, and I do not think she will curse them for it."

"Then may I inquire," Agricola asked politely, "what the princess thinks I should do with her?"

"I don't know," Ygerna said frankly, "but if the governor wants the leisure to attend to Cadal of the Ordovices, he had best not send me to take Aedden's place."

He had ended by sending her back to Aquae and assuring her courtesy-aunt that his predecessor's stipend to their household would be continued for the time being. But what in Hades *was* he going to do with her? He couldn't leave her to kick her heels in Aquae indefinitely. The thought slid unbidden into his mind that her dark hair would look like a pool of ink spread out over a pillow. Unlike Correus, Governor Agricola had no blind spot about Ygerna's age. But like his predecessor, Governor Frontinus, the general had a reasonably proud wife in Rome. He wanted no mistress he would mind forgetting when he sailed. And he had the feeling that any man who had once had Ygerna in his bed would not forget.

A small grin crossed the governor's face. He would bet young Julianus was getting drunk right now.

Agricola swung his feet down from his desk and called to a slave for papyrus. Why not? He felt pleased with himself. He didn't get many chances to be kind; there was generally a military consideration in the way. But at the moment he had on his hands one extra woman, whose usefulness to the state was nil, and one cohort commander who was the son of an old friend and who had already, he had heard, lost one woman under tragic circumstances.

Item, he thought cheerfully, beginning to write: *one pension as a ward of Rome. Item: one Roman citizenship, subject to confirmation by the emperor. And item: one suitable dowry upon the marriage of said woman to a Roman citizen.* And that ought to sweeten old Appius.

He sealed the papyrus sheet and whistled up an optio. A kindness done to lovers was good luck, or so they said, and Julius Agricola wanted luck. This was his season, these next few years—his chance to prove himself the greatest general ever to come to Britain, or only another in a list of governors who had pushed the frontier ahead a few more miles only to have it come sliding back down on them. He would deal with the Ordovices first, and the druidical troublemakers who had flocked back to Mona—and then he would take the frontier of Britain to the edge of the world. And when, as inevitably happened, the necessity of it all was questioned back in Rome, the voice of Appius Julianus would be heard on the side of Julius Agricola.

Correus stood outside the house in the Street of Lilies in Aquae Sulis and braced himself to put hand to the door. Like most houses in the Roman style, it turned a blind face to the street. All its windows would open inward onto the garden, a private world secluded from the one outside. He wasn't sure what he was going to find in it.

The door was opened finally by an elderly slave in a blue tunic who presented him to another, more important, slave, who presented him to the household steward who led him finally to a lady with a patrician nose and an imposing headdress of gray waves anchored in ascending tiers and stuck through at the top with an ebony comb.

"I am Publia Livilla," she said firmly, as if to set matters straight at the outset. "I expect you have come from Julius Agricola."

"Yes, ma'am." Correus had his helmet and vine staff tucked under one arm, and the governor's letter in the other hand, but he felt as if he were somehow expected to kiss her hand. He settled awkwardly for a sort of half bow. "I have a letter from him for Ygerna." He still didn't know whether the governor had sent him with that as reward or punishment, for too-frank advice.

Publia Livilla gave him a look. "Are you Centurion Julianus?"

"Yes, ma'am." Was she going to throw him out on those grounds? He thought she looked as if she might.

The old lady seemed to come to some decision and rose from her chair. "Very well, Centurion. You may wait here." She departed through another doorway, leaving Correus to fidget and count tiles in the mosaic of Sisyphus pushing his rock uphill that gave an air of Plutonian gloom to the floor.

He was beginning to feel a certain kinship with the doomed king when a voice, near and heartbreakingly familiar, said his name.

She was older somehow, but the same somehow, in a gown of rose pink silk with a pattern of young ivy twining diagonally across the breast. There were roses in her hair and pale green sandals on her feet, and her face was painted—Ygerna's cheeks had never been anything but white, white like the rest of her, white as the white horse cut into the chalk downs by Calleva.

Correus got a grip on himself. *Don't think like that. Think that you are a Roman officer. Give her the letter.* "Here," he said gently. "It's from Julius Agricola. I hope it's what you wanted. I tried, too."

She looked up at him. She still didn't come above his collarbone. "You don't know what's in it?"

He shook his head. "No."

"You looked so solemn, I thought it must be bad."

Rome never let go of anything that might be useful, he thought, watching the hope in her face. They would keep a string on her somehow, but he thought Agricola had decided against making her queen. "It depends on your definition of bad, I suppose," he said.

She took a deep breath and lifted the purple seal with her fingernail. "As well now as later. Better yesterday than today. The Druids say that—they always give you answers like that when you ask them hard questions." She had started to read. "Mother-of-All! Correus! What did you say to him?" She sat down in a chair and looked up at him with her mouth open.

"Just what you did. What's he done?"

"Listen to this! A pension as a ward of Rome—a *dowry* if I marry—and he's even going to set it about in Venta that I've died—listen, he says, 'in case any of your loving family should decide to take precautions.' And Roman citizenship, too, though I don't know what good that'll do me."

"You don't know enough, my girl. That's the most useful of the lot," Correus said. "And the hardest to get." He was stunned. It was unthinkable. Why had Agricola done it? But he had, and Ygerna was free to go where she pleased. The unattainable had come suddenly into his hand, and here she sat in a chair smiling up at him, her dark eyes shining, and her heart written plainly on her face.

And then the fear hit him, like a wet, cold wind with rain in it, and he thought for a moment that he was actually looking at Freita's grave. It faded away again into the Sisyphus tiles under his feet, but he knew that Ygerna was waiting, waiting for him to say the words that any man in his right mind would say—and he couldn't. *No more!* Freita had been the other half of his soul and had left a hole as deep as Erebus when she died. To love Ygerna, to marry her, to let *her* into his soul under the old scars, and then to lose her, too—his whole body went cold with the fear of that. And that bone-deep fear outweighed everything, even love or lust or pity. Never again would another woman follow the army with him and die in a mud hut on the frontier.

"That's wonderful," he heard himself saying, like someone else's voice, some silly fool with a Rome accent in his educated Latin. "You'll be able to set up housekeeping for yourself anywhere you like. You could even go to Londinium—you'd like it there. Or travel—" He broke off because the look on her face bit through his platitudes like a knife.

Ygerna let the letter slide out of her hands onto Sisyphus's rock. Something was the matter. Something terrible that she didn't understand. *I will not cry. I am a Silure,* she thought desperately, repeating the childhood formula. *I am a royal woman.* But she wasn't, not even that, not now.

"Ygerna, forgive me." The words were whispered, twisted harshly out of his throat. He put a hand to her hair, and then turned and ran as if the Furies had flown past his head.

Outside the great bath of Sulis Minerva, he stopped and pressed his hand against the cool stone of the facade. *Isis Mother, what have I done?* And something in the back of his mind said with a sad certainty, *Don't go back. Let her go now, and she'll forget you. There isn't another way.* The stone was cool against his face, like a gravestone. He was a soldier, and there was a new campaign coming, a grand adventure to be the capstone of Julius Agricola's famous career. Nothing had changed, really. For a moment, he could have had Ygerna for the asking, and then he had found that he couldn't. But there was the army that had always been the core of his life since before he had ever seen Freita. He lifted his head from the gray stone. *And if I begin to think otherwise,* he thought, *I will go and look at Freita's grave again.*

Appius Julianus lounged in the chair behind his desk in his private study, his face as uninformative as the plain, buff plaster walls. He had successfully resisted the urgings of both his wife and mistress to have the walls painted with something fashionable, and the only adornments in the room were in the objects scattered on the scroll shelves—curios of old campaigns mostly, odd barbarian weapons and small pieces of artwork.

Appius's hands lay loosely on the chair arms and his iron gray head dropped as if asleep; but his dark eyes were awake, and Helva was not deceived.

"You've had a letter from Correus," she said briskly, settling herself into the chair opposite with her usual flutter of draperies.

Appius lifted his head slightly. "So have you. I sent it to you straightaway."

Helva smiled. She rested her elbow on the desk and put her chin in her hand. "But he never tells *me* the interesting things." She was still pretty. Pretty enough to be a menace, he thought, smiling back at her.

"That's because you're the least discreet woman I've ever known. If you're looking for something to crow about to my wife, forget it."

Helva looked offended, and then giggled. "No, I promise. But he doesn't tell me what he's *doing*. He just sends his love and says he's well, and he doesn't sound like him-

self." She looked honestly worried now, her blue eyes
thoughtful, and Appius relented.

"No, he doesn't sound like himself to me, either, my
dear. I'm afraid he's still grieving for that German
woman."

Helva made a rude noise in her throat, and Appius
nodded.

"You didn't think she was good enough for him, and
neither did I, but I think the bond was deeper than either
of us realized. You'll just have to give him time."

Helva narrowed her eyes. "That isn't all, Appius."

Helva had always been shrewd, too shrewd for comfort. Appius looked at her blankly, carefully. "That's all *I*
can discover. As for what he's doing, he's marching with
Julius Agricola, which is the best thing he *could* be doing
in terms of his career, Agricola is going to be remembered, and so are the men who go with him." Agricola
had also taken an unwarranted amount of trouble for an
obscure British princess, but Appius wasn't going to tell
Helva *that*, not until he had figured out why.

Helva had known Appius long enough to know when
there was no more information to be had. She came lightly
around the desk and kissed him with the familiarity of
long privilege and disappeared in a cloud of blonde hair
and primrose draperies, leaving a faint smell of oil of
roses in the air.

Appius leaned forward on his desk and stared out at
the falling leaves in the garden. Helva had left the door
open deliberately, he suspected, so he could see what a
charming exit she made, with the light breeze blowing
the primrose silk around her. It wasn't particularly cold, so
he left the door open and thought about Julius Agricola
and Correus. He had begun to have suspicions when it
dawned on him that the "kid" his son had referred to in
other letters was sixteen now and that the two of them
had apparently spent one entire spring living in each other's pockets in the British hills.

He passed the letter on the next day to Flavius, who
was in Rome with the praetorian prefect for the emperor's
birthday games, and Flavius raised an eyebrow and came
to much the same conclusion.

"He's ignoring it," Flavius said. "I think he's scared."

Appius began to say that Correus had never been

afraid of **anything**, and then dropped it **in** mid-sentence. Any man with any sense was afraid—Correus just didn't show it.

"Well, he's afraid of this," Flavius said. "I'd wager my best horse and half my wife's jewelry." He looked his father in the eye. "And if he comes round and you don't let him marry this one, I'll go over your head to the emperor, so help me Juno."

"Don't be an ass," Appius said irritably. "It's not what I'd hoped for him, but I wouldn't forbid it. This one has citizenship and some money of her own and rank in her own country."

Flavius grinned at him. "And Helva will hate her."

"Helva is my concern."

"No offense meant. Anyone who's managed that she-cat all these years has my utmost respect."

"Then see that you show a little more of it. And I forbid you to *mention* this British girl to Helva. I have enough problems at the moment with Helva brangling with your mother, without you starting something else. I'll make suitable arrangements if anything comes of it, so let that inspire you to tact."

"It inspires me to be faithful to my wife," Flavius said unrepentantly, and went off whistling, while Appius glared after him.

"Don't let Flavius tease you." Julia dropped a kiss on her father's forehead and sat down beside him on the bench by the atrium pool. "He's just set up because Aemelia thinks she's pregnant, but she won't let him tell anyone yet, so don't say anything. You'll be surrounded by grandchildren in no time at all." Her own small daughter beamed up at Appius and made a beeline for the pool with three-year-old Felix behind her.

"No," he said firmly, tugging her back from the edge. "Wet. You sit with me."

"Correus should come home," Julia said. "That child thinks Lucius is his father."

Appius sighed. "My dear, I don't know what he could do if he did come home. My boys thought old Alan was their father, for all they ever saw of me. He could hardly take the child with him."

"He could if he got married," Julia said.

Her father gave her a look. "If you turn into a matchmaker, you'll be a menace, my girl. Are you thinking of that British girl none of us has ever seen?"

"Correus wrote me about her," Julia said. "She doesn't sound much like Freita, but I expect I'd like her. She wasn't afraid of the governor. Besides," she added, "I'm very happy with Lucius, and Flavius and Aemelia are getting on now. I haven't anyone left to meddle with except Correus."

Appius gave a shout of laughter, and small Paulilla smiled up at him and toddled over and sat down on his foot. Felix followed her and began with great concentration to unlace the thongs of his grandfather's other sandal.

"You aren't so tough," Julia said affectionately.

"I'm getting old," Appius said. "Where's their nurse?"

"I expect she's run away," Julia said. "Felix put ink in the bathwater this morning."

Appius looked down at his grandson. "Why?"

"Pretty," Felix said succinctly.

"Pitty," Paulilla said experimentally, and her mother blinked at her.

"She doesn't even say 'mama' yet," Julia said indignantly.

"*Your* first word was 'gimme,'" her father informed her. "I was here."

"Pitty," Paulilla said. "Pitty pitty pitty pitty pitty pitty—"

"That will do, darling." Her mother scooped her up.

"Julia—"

She turned, the baby balanced on one hip. Felix detached himself reluctantly from his grandfather.

"Do you think this British woman can be . . . Roman enough? It will matter whom he's married to, later on."

"When he's a great man," Julia agreed solemnly. "I expect she can. Aemelia says she probably wears trousers and paints herself blue, but I think that's just spite. Aemelia still sees Correus as something just short of Alexander, but that's only when he's not around. When he *is* there, he scares her to death. She got cured of that infatuation in Aquae Sulis, I think, but she doesn't like admitting it. She and Flavius do very well together, and she had the praetorian prefect and all his generals eating out of her hand. Even the emperor told her she was an ornament to the staff and gave her a pearl necklace."

Appius groaned. "He's not——?"

"Oh, no. Aemelia fairly exudes virtue. He just thinks she's cute."

"I'm relieved to hear it. It's hard to turn down an emperor gracefully. But a wife who's a social asset is good to have, and Correus will need one, too, eventually. We've got off the subject. What about the British girl?"

Julia looked thoughtful. The question was important enough. An unacceptable wife was one thing for a junior officer in the field. For a senior official it was quite another, and few junior officers with unacceptable wives were promoted to *be* senior officials. Except for the Praetorian Prefect Titus, of course, and his difficulty was only a mistress, not a wife, a Jewess of a princely house, and even so, questions were always being asked in the Senate. If he ever got to be emperor, he was going to have to leave her. It wouldn't be so important for Correus, who was never going to be emperor, where his wife came from in the first place, as long as she was adaptable. But if she wasn't, Correus wouldn't divorce her. Julia was pretty sure of that.

"I don't know," Julia said dubiously. "I suppose I hadn't really thought it through. Not that way."

Appius handed her the letter from Agricola, and she sat back down, giving the baby the sash of her gown to play with. Paulilla stuck the tassel in her mouth.

"Well! Julius Agricola certainly thinks she'll do," Julia said when she had finished. "Do I read between the lines correctly?"

"I had the same impression," Appius said. "He's obviously hoping *I'll* be pleased, so she can't be out of the question, I suppose. It's not what I wanted for him."

"If he wants her, you let him have her," Julia said firmly. "You didn't see him in Aquae Sulis. He can't spend the rest of his life grieving for a dead woman."

"My children have grown up to conspire against me," Appius said. "By the way, yours is getting your girdle wet. Very well, if Correus wants her, he shall have her."

"That's what worries me," Julia said. "If he wants her."

The garden was empty, a little dreary in the fall air, deserted. Julia had gone home with her brood and their nurse and her personal maid in her opulent traveling coach. It was only a few miles, but Julia believed in taking advantage of such comforts while she could. Now that the baby was a year-and-a-half, Julia would probably accompany her husband on the next of his foreign jaunts. Flavius would go, too, as soon as Titus did, and there was no telling when Correus was coming home.

One of the cook's small daughters trotted through the gate into the kitchen garden with a pair of herb snips in one hand and a basket in the other. She made a hasty obeisance to the master when she spotted him and zipped through the gate. A red chicken feather drifted from somewhere past Appius's nose, which pretty well predicted dinner: chicken in an herb sauce, with the inevitable olives, wine, cream cake—Antonia's weakness—and hot bread and honey—his. The master and mistress found themselves dining alone tonight and were old-fashioned enough to believe that such dishes as peacocks and cold larks were best kept for company. A plain table, with little inspiration to set a more elaborate one. Appius looked around the empty garden. *I miss them,* he thought. More than he had thought he would.

When he had first retired, Appius Julianus had thought that his army days would never fade from him entirely, that his beloved legion, and later the military governorship that had been its reward, would hold a place in his heart that no family could quite match. But lately he had found the old days slipping away, and his pleasures here, bounded by the stables and garden and the wide acres he had always loved but had never really known. And his children. His sons, and the daughter who had somehow undergone a transformation of her own, from her mother's replica into a force to be reckoned with.

Flavius had always known the joys of other pleasures than the army, Appius thought suddenly. Maybe Flavius had been right. And Correus? Correus was his father over again, in love with his legion; but Correus, too, needed something more—Correus had seen too vividly the other side of life. *It's being slave-born,* Appius thought. *It still turns him inside out. It makes everything matter so much to him. Maybe it would have to me.* The gods knew there was something in a man's birth that drove him. With Appius Julianus, it had been equestrian rank, a proud heri-

tage of seven generations' service in the Eagles, but still
not enough to take a man to the top. Not enough for the
political offices that led to the top of the army commands.
Appius had reached the top of his own anyway and found
himself a famous man for it, with the pleasant privilege
(and good sense, he thought now) of refusing senatorial
rank when it had been ultimately offered. But he had
paved the roadway, for Flavius, at least. Flavius could
have a senator's rank as soon as his career required it.
Correus would have to do it his father's way or not at all.

The low murmur of voices outside the garden walls
drew him back from his thoughts—the field slaves coming
in from their work. Appius looked at the sundial and did
a quick mental calculation as to how much it would be off
at this time of year. He had an appointment with Forst
before dinner.

"It's early yet, lord, but I think we'll see results with
the two-year-olds this spring." Forst spread a fan of thin
wooden tablets on an iron ring out on the master's desk
—the breeding records of foals born two seasons ago.
"There's one in particular—that black colt out of Windy
Day, that looks to me like what we're after."

"I've seen him," Appius said. "There's a strong strain
of his sire in him, all right. What does Alan say?" Alan
had retired a year ago, but he still came down to the pas-
tures, as Forst put it, "to meddle about a bit."

Forst grinned. "That batch is all Alan's match-ups, so
he's pleased enough. It's when the fillies out of it are old
enough to breed back in that we may not see quite eye
to eye. There are three or four I'm pretty sure I want already."

"Keep any you want to, but we'll have to sell off the
rest pretty ruthlessly, or we'll have more horses than the
farm will carry. Diulius has been after me for a new barn
for the chariot stock, but there's no place to put it without running over our own pasture."

"To the east, sir? That meadow's not much good for
grass. Something in the soil, I think."

"I gave that tract to Flavius. I can't put a horse barn
under his balcony."

Forst laughed. "No, I suppose not. Let me talk to
Diulius, sir. He's got his old nose twisted by the attention

the new stock is getting, I expect. Maybe I can sweeten
him some."

"I should like to see that," Appius murmured. Forst
made an unlikely diplomat, with his strange, pale hair
coiled up in a knot on one side of his head, and the old
sword scars showing on his arms and under his tunic hem.
But he had proved undeniably valuable. It made this interview a gamble. Appius cocked an eye up at Forst,
standing above him, looking cheerful and unruffled.
"You're free."

"I beg your pardon, sir?"

"You're free. I have signed your manumission papers.
Your hide is your own now."

"Why?" Forst looked suspicious.

"Because you have earned it," Appius said. It was a
fairly silly reason, since Forst would undoubtedly be gone
over the Alps to Germany as soon as he could buy a
horse to carry him, leaving Appius to whistle for his time
and training and his breeding program. The real reason
had something to do with Correus. Appius was willing to
acknowledge that, but not to go into the particulars, not
even in his own mind. "I will pay you a suitable wage if
you stay on," he said. "If not, I will understand."

Forst looked thoughtful. "I can't say I know what
you've done it for, sir."

"Neither do I," Appius said, suddenly honest.

"It's been a long time since I was home," Forst said.
"I don't suppose I'd find much now." His eye rested on
a spearhead with a white collar of heron's feathers, lying
among the curios on Appius's shelves. "Best to bide and
mind my horses than go and look for ghosts, I'm thinking."

"I expect so," Appius said. "If I may presume to offer
advice, nothing is ever the way you left it. A lot of people
have broken their hearts on that fact." *And what am I
doing now, but trying to go back and meddle with the past,
freeing Forst because I feel at fault that my son is still
grieving for a German woman? Correus will hardly see
Forst as a substitute.* There wasn't much to be gained from
that line of thought, and it wasn't explainable to Forst.
"It is a custom in my house"—Appius turned his mind to
practicalities—"that when a slave is freed, he may ask
one further reward, within reason. You have certainly

earned that as well, and I'm inclined to stretch the limits
of reason fairly far, since *you* are inclined to stay with us.
Do you want land, Forst? Horses of your own?"

Forst shook his head. "You are generous, sir. But I
can buy a horse with my wages, if I should run out of ones
to ride here."

Appius chuckled. "All right, man, what *do* you want?"

"I want Emer, out of your kitchen, lord."

"The red-haired one?" As far as Appius could tell, all
she did with Forst was quarrel with him. He had come
upon them one day in the orchard, arguing in fierce, low
voices, and Emer had stamped her sandal down hard on
Forst's bare foot and run off, before she had seen the
master coming. Forst had glared after her, nursing a lac-
erated toe, and Appius had tactfully pretended not to notice. Every man deserved his dignity. But there were better rewards than a kitchen maid with a temper who was
no longer young. He said so bluntly, but Forst just shook
his head. Appius thought he looked amused and wondered
if he would repeat the master's description to Emer in his
wooing.

But he got her, with manumission papers signed and wit-
nessed, and Appius went in to dinner in a philosophic
mood. Love—between himself and a woman—had never
seemed particularly important. Lust and affection for
Helva, respect and affection for the wife who reclined in
her familiar place across the table from him—those were
familiar emotions, the stuff on which a solid way of life
was built. But his children had found otherwise—Julia
with Lucius Paulinus, Correus with his impossible German,
even Flavius in what had begun as an arranged marriage
with Aemelia. And now Forst, politely, but with a pighead-
edness that would grace a lover out of a legend, turned
away the chance of a real reward to ask for a red-
haired kitchen maid who was no longer young and certainly not a virgin. What was it that pulled at them in that
fashion, and what did it feel like? Appius wondered wistfully, over the bread and olives, if he had missed something that he was far too old to go looking for now.

Niarchos the majordomo came in with a trio of young
slaves while the olives and the salad and the herbed
chicken were cleared away and the beautiful silver wine
cups refilled and watered to the exact degree the master

and mistress preferred. It was warm for November, and one of the boys stood beside the table to wave a palm frond fan over their heads. A plate of cream cake appeared while Appius sipped his wine, and another of bread hot from the oven, with a glass pitcher of honey that bore three glass bees on the bowl. Antonia took a piece of cake while Appius poured honey on his bread, and they stretched out comfortably under the palm fan.

"Aemelia is pregnant, did you know?" Antonia said over her cake and wine.

"I thought it was a dark secret," Appius said.

"Oh, it is," Antonia agreed. "But she's just embarrassed. She'll get over it. I did."

She still looked young, he thought, even with the streaks of gray in the dark waves of hair about her face. Too young to have grandchildren. But she had married young, of course. He wondered if she wished she hadn't. No one had asked her opinion at the time, he supposed. "What, my dear?"

"Are you falling asleep?" She smiled at him. "It was nothing particularly important. We are going to have to rebuild the north wing in the slave quarters—it's beginning to be a disgrace to us. And Cook wants a new kind of stove that Julia's cook has told him about. I'm afraid I see a temperament coming on, but I can deal with him if you don't think we should get it."

"By all means, my dear, let Cook have his stove," Appius said good humoredly. It was pleasant to have no greater dilemma to resolve.

"We really should put in an appearance at the emperor's birthday games, don't you think?" Antonia went on. "Flavius and Aemelia and her parents will be dining with us afterward. I told Cook a family party. Nothing *too* elaborate. Oh, and the kitchen cat has had her kittens—in our bed, I'm afraid."

Appius began to laugh, his dark eyes crinkled shut. Antonia always saved these small domestic crises for a time when she thought they would amuse him. It came with years, that instinctive knowledge of how the other one thought. "Nothing particularly important," she had said. Only the things that made a marriage familiar and comfortable thirty years down the road. He didn't love her, not with that dreadful ache and longing that his sons seemed to feel, but he licked the honey from his fingers and laughed again and thought that he hadn't missed so much after all.

XIX

". . . And Roll in Me Arms"

CORREUS SAT WITH HIS FEET IN A POT OF HOT WATER in the privacy of Silvius Vindex's tent. The first week out of winter quarters was always murder, no matter how much drilling they'd done over the cold months, but it didn't do to let his equally footsore troops know it.

Centurion Vindex gave a grunt of pleasure as Julius knelt and poured a hot kettle over his feet, as well. A pot of wine was warming on the little iron brazier in the corner of the tent, and Vindex gave Julius a smile of thanks. His own body servant had been left behind with a broken arm in the hospital tent at Deva, the souvenir of a day's hunting in the wilds of Ordovician country, and Julius, whose devotion to his master generally extended to the master's friends, had adopted Centurion Vindex for the interim. He poured two measures of wine from the spouted pot on the brazier, and Correus and Vindex accepted them gratefully.

"When we get back to civilization, Julius, I'll buy you something," Vindex said. He leaned back on his elbows on the camp bed and wiggled his toes in the pot of water. His sleek cap of dark hair was powdered with dirt and bits of grass from the turf they'd cut that afternoon. "I want a bath," he said thoughtfully, weighing his dislike of being dirty against the fast-running waters of the snow-fed stream below the camp. It had looked depressingly cold.

"Bathe in this," Correus said, splashing his feet in the warm water. "You'll freeze solid like a Gorgon's stone in that river."

"Maybe I'll just get used to being dirty," Vindex said.

They were griping as usual over the discomforts of a campaign trail, but there was a gleam in their eyes all the same. They had spent the end of last summer detached from their legions under Agricola's direct command, chasing the Ordovices. Cadal, whom Correus rather liked, had made one desperate stand near Bryn Epona and lost the better part of his war band to Agricola's mixed force of legionary detachments and auxiliaries. It had been a short, fierce battle, a matter of tactics and a good general and the old, familiar discipline that was the army's pride.

Cadal recognized a certainty when it stuck its helmet crest in his face. He had shown his practical side and consequently got the best possible terms from Rome. Cadal might lack that bright fierce flame that had lit Bendigeid—and then consumed him—but Cadal made peace and Cadal would survive.

After that, Agricola turned his eye to Mona, which had grown into a druidic stronghold again in the years since Suetonius Paulinus had burned it and where Cadal's malcontents had gone rather than face the inevitable. The island attack had been decided upon at the last moment on the advice of the frontier scouts, who had said bluntly that *they* wouldn't turn their backs on Mona just now. There had been no fleet handy, and Agricola mulled it over for a day, then picked out the strongest swimmers from his auxiliaries, and launched a surprise attack.

Cadal's malcontents and the outlawed Druids had quarreled with each other over everything that could be quarreled over. The Ordovician warriors had waved their spears and shouted for one last fine charge for honor's sake, and the Druids had looked solemn and made great magics and tried to stave off Rome with a handful of mistletoe. And in the end, with each faction ordering the other to do it their way, they had squabbled and put curses on each other until, seeing Agricola's auxiliaries emerge like so many water-demons from the surf, they lost their heads completely and surrendered.

It was the sort of mopping-up operation of which Correus had never been particularly fond, although the aftermath had been reasonable—by Roman standards. The warriors might as well have stayed with Cadal in Bryn Epona and swallowed their pride, Correus thought grimly, watching a transport ship settle in the water as her hold was loaded

with chained figures. The Druids they could catch had
been executed, but it was thought that most of them had
sailed for Hibernia and found sanctuary there. Agricola
had looked wistfully across the Hibernian Channel at the
island in the west and told his second-in-command that
one legion with the right commander could take it. But
not this season. There were other horizons that beckoned
still more strongly.

They wintered around the new fortress at Deva, and
Correus breathed a sigh of relief because the holy women
on Mona had been left pretty well alone, and he had
made sure that the woman who had once been a princess
of the Silures was still among them. He didn't see her, but
he sent a letter to Ygerna by courier to tell her that her
mother was still alive. He tried to sound like an elderly
uncle when he wrote it, but he wondered if Ygerna would
be deceived.

But it didn't matter now. Nothing mattered now but the
new campaign and the fiery little general who led it. They
were on the march with the first thaw, north through Brigante country in two columns, one from Deva in the
west, the other from Eburacum in the east, laying down
a string of forts that would keep the Brigantes quiet while
Agricola took his legions northward. They would reach
the unknown wilds of Caledonia before they stopped,
where the Picts, the Painted People, lived in their mysterious mountain fastnesses.

It was high adventure, a campaign to make a reputation on, and Correus and Vindex would have traded years
of sore feet and no baths to be part of it. This was what
they had signed on for, what they had endured the miser-
ies of their cadet days for, to go where no Roman feet had
marched before and see what no civilized eyes had ever
seen. Lucius Paulinus would be gnashing his teeth with
envy, Correus thought, mildly surprised that his brother-
in-law hadn't shown up on the frontier before now to get
in on the fun. This was the campaign that every officer
waited for. They looked at each other over their wine
cups and grinned.

By late July they reached Brocavum on the edge of
the Lake Country, only a bit more than a day's march
from the Ituna Estuary that marked the boundary of Brigante lands from their wild kinsmen the Selgovae to the

north. It was wild land, gray blue and open, with wild water everywhere, and an edge-of-the-unknown feel to it that
made them just stand staring northward when their legion
halted its march at midafternoon. Even the news that the
emperor was dead hardly touched them here on the edge
of the wild.

Vespasian had died on 23 June of undulant fever and
a stomach chill caught in Campania, and now there was a
new emperor in Rome—the Praetorian Prefect Titus Caesar.

"Tchah!" Vindex made an irritated noise through his
teeth. "They'll be sorry they did that." For the first time
a son had actually succeeded his father to the purple of
the Principate, and opinion that no good would come of
it had run high in Rome since Vespasian had made his
intentions known. It was a peaceable way to settle the
succession, but Titus had led a rackety life and the Senate
gloomily prophesied the emergence of another Nero.

"I don't know," Correus said. "Flavius likes him, and
I've a better opinion of Flavius's notions than I used to."

Vindex chuckled. He had watched the brothers snarl
at each other all through the days of their cadet training
and thought that it was a wonder that one of them hadn't
strangled the other before they had got things sorted out.
"Well, unless he recalls everyone wholesale, it won't af-
fect us much out here." They were eating what passed for
dinner in a camp cook's vocabulary behind the newly dug
ditch and wall of Brocavum. "Still, I'd like to be comfortable about matters at home. What does your father
think?"

"He seemed to think well enough of him when Flavius
got his posting," Correus said. "Of course, that was before
Vespasian died. I hope there's no doubt it was natural
causes. We're so far behind with the news out here,
Rome could be overrun with little men from the bottom of
the sea, and we wouldn't know it for weeks. Father said he
was the sort of man to make—gestures. When Britannicus
died—Flavius and I were babies then, but Father told
us later—Titus was supposed to have finished off the wine
that Nero gave Britannicus and been sick for days. They
were the same age, about fourteen, and very close, and
of course there was talk about Britannicus's death for
years, especially after it got to be so plain that everyone

would have done better if someone had poisoned *Nero* right off and made Britannicus emperor. The story about Titus may be just palace rumor, but Father said it sounded like him."

Vindex looked dubious. "In the guards' camp they said it was as good as a death mark to look cross-eyed at him. And I don't much like his habits."

"Boys?" Correus shrugged. "Not in my line, but plenty of men do. I never heard they got any political favors. And if you mean his women and his wild parties, we're hardly in a position to fault a taste for those."

"He has a bad reputation," Vindex said. "It makes Rome look bad. That Jewess of his—"

" 'That Jewess' is Herod Agrippa's daughter."

"And *her* reputation is worse than *his*. Damn it, man, she lived with her brother!"

"Well, she's not living with him now," Correus said tolerantly. "And I don't care if he goes to bed with billy goats if he keeps the Senate and the army in order. He's not a Nero, Vindex, you wait and see. Besides, he won't have a prayer of keeping his Jewess now, poor woman. The Senate will be as obnoxious about her as you are."

"I am *not* being obnoxious about her. I know what you're thinking. But you can't equate your Freita with a middle-aged tart who married her uncle and committed incest with her brother. The Senate had every right to squawk."

"The Senate squawked because she's a Jewess," Correus said. "They didn't give a damn about her sex life. They were just afraid he'd marry her."

"Well, it would raise a hell of a stink, and that wouldn't keep things stable."

"No, I suppose not. But he has my sympathy, and I'll reserve judgment on his fitness for the purple until he's had a few months to dig in."

"Oh, I, too," Vindex said magnanimously. "Being as I don't expect I'll be asked for my views anyway."

They laughed and finished the disgusting remains of their dinner. The supply train hadn't caught up with them yet, and the camp cooks were improvising. They didn't cook very well even under optimum circumstances. They strolled off arm in arm to check their sentries and watch the moon finally come up over the heathered hills. A fox called somewhere in the distance, and the steady hum of insects swelled all around them as night fell.

"We'll be off again in the morning," Vindex said, and took a deep breath of the sharp, clean air.

Correus nodded, his eyes bright with the same spark. It was like standing at the edge of the world. He could bury a lot of doubts in the excitement of that.

The thin wooden leaves of the tablet sat staring up at him from his lap, weathered gray against the red leather fringe of his harness tunic. Orders, sealed with a lump of scarlet wax along the edge, inscribed unmistakably, indelibly, with his name and rank. Orders. The supply train had come in, with messages from the northernmost post station stuffed into the lead wagon among the grain sacks and onions.

The tablet looked up at him blankly, and he flicked a fingernail against the wax seal. He had taken it back to his tent because he didn't want to open it; and it was easier to not open it here, where he could sit and stare toward the blue green land in the north instead, than by the supply wagons, where his friends could give him the curious eye.

He slit the wax with his thumbnail and swore when it split the nail down to the quick. Like the rest of Agricola's army, his hands and nails were calloused and ragged from a summer of digging roads and ditches out of new land. He stuck the broken nail in his mouth for a second and then spread the wooden tablet open on his lap.

A naval posting at Misenum, Italy. A fat promotion for a career centurion. Correus made a face and read it through again. A shadow fell across the neat writing on the tablet. "Thinking of refusing a gift from Caesar?" Julius Agricola inquired. "Unwise."

Correus stood up and saluted, and Agricola dragged another camp stool into the tent doorway and sat on it. He motioned Correus back to his own stool. "What's the posting?"

"Marines," Correus said sourly. "Out of Misenum."

Agricola whistled.

"I don't want it," Correus said flatly. "Did my brother do this?" The tablet carried the emperor's cypher—all military orders did—but he suspected that in this case

Caesar's gift was literal as well as figurative. It came too close on the heels of Titus's accession.

"I expect he may have," Agricola said. "But you're overdue for promotion, you know. You'd have been recommended before now if you hadn't been so damned useful here, and I don't know why you didn't put in for it yourself. I was going to hunt you out a more senior post in Britain, but someone else's good intentions seem to have got in first."

"Flavius. I don't want it," Correus said again.

"What makes you think you have a choice?"

"Isn't there any way?" His eyes drifted to the north again.

"Well, you could refuse it," Agricola said. "If you've a fancy to command the Eighth Cohort of the Second Augusta for the rest of your life."

Correus grimaced. An officer with an eye to his future didn't turn down a promotion. Not if he ever wanted to see another one. "Couldn't you—?"

"No. I intend to walk very carefully with the new emperor. If you think this campaign is important to you, Julianus, mull over what it means to me." The general's jaw was shadowed with a stubble of beard, and his hands were as worn as Correus's. When Agricola said, "Dig a ditch," he, too, got down in the ditch and dug. He would take the north of Britain, Correus thought, if only because wanting to would burn him up if he didn't. And every step he took would be with that in his mind.

"Don't grieve over it, my friend," Agricola said now. His eyes, too, were on the blue green north, but they were ruefully honest under the dark brows. "You might get more glory in the fleet, where you can keep it to yourself. And you need this posting, you need the experience, if you're going to go beyond cohort centurion. Your father would tell you that. And someone thinks you're going somewhere, or you wouldn't have got the job."

Correus knew that, and he knew he should be grateful. The Misenum post was a way to give him naval experience, considered necessary to a well-rounded career —for a man who was going to the top. With most centurions, the army didn't bother.

Agricola's strong-boned face swung around and laughed at him. The general had taken his helmet off, and the twilight breeze lifted the thick brown hair. His neck scarf was powdered with dust from the dried edges of the turf blocks with which they had built their camp. "You'll get other chances to go exploring, lad. Take your medicine at Misenum and you might grow up to be a general. Maybe I'll leave Hibernia for you."

Correus smiled. "Not if you get bored, sir, you won't."

"No," Agricola admitted. "I doubt I would. But there'll always be some place no one else has looked at before. You'll find one. And for now, you'll say your good-byes and get on your horse for Misenum."

He stood up and put his helmet back on his head, and Correus stood, too, and saluted, trying not to make it too plain how much taller he was than the general. It didn't seem to bother Agricola. Agricola knew perfectly well that he could take on any two of his troopers, probably including Centurion Julianus, and tie them into sailor's knots with each other. He nodded briskly at Correus and set off to see what else needed straightening.

Correus put the wooden tablet into his marching kit and started packing. He could say his farewells to Vindex and the rest tonight, and maybe they'd get drunk together. Vindex was due for promotion, too, but the chances of them landing in the same spot were a million to one. Too many good-byes in the army, he thought, knowing that there was another good-bye he was going to have to say, and no pious self-delusion was going to get him out of it.

They got drunk that night. Or at least Vindex and his cronies did, while Correus sat like an Eastern god on the floor and drank enough wine for three men but somehow stayed sober. They put a wreath of heather in his hair and sang to him:

Farewell for I must leave thee, I'm off to the army,
And I might not be back when it's over,
So come and hold me hand and watch the moon
    arisin'
And roll in me arms in the clover!

They ended it with a long-drawn howl of appreciation, and someone brought in a woman they had found with the baggage train who looked as if she'd do most things for a price. They put a wreath of heather in her hair, too, and presented her with a flourish to Correus, but he just smiled and shook his head and gave her a coin anyway. She took it and the cup of wine someone gave her, and after a while he saw that she had gone away again with Centurion Aquila. They sang some more, old marching songs and "The Tribune's Horse," and a rude one that Vindex knew called "The Tax Man of Upper Aquitania." Correus laughed and started them on "The Quaestor from Paestum," which had verses that they made up as they went along, but his heart wasn't in it. He sat on the floor with his legs crossed under him and his hands on his knees, looking more and more like an Eastern idol with the heather wreath on his head and his face blank as a stone. Vindex sighed and shook his head and finally called for Julius to come and take his master back to his tent before he froze solid that way.

Correus drained his wine cup—they had been refilling it all evening whenever he set it down—and thanked them gravely. He stood up carefully and followed Julius to his tent, looking wistfully at the moonlight shining on the orderly tent rows along the way, set out carefully cohort by cohort, each century with its commander's tent at the end. His helmet and lorica sat waiting for the morning by the door flap of his own tent. He put the leather wreath around his helmet crest and lay down on the camp bed in the tent. Someone else would have the tent tomorrow, he thought tiredly, and the fun of following Julius Agricola north. But he knew, watching the moonlight slide through the tent flap and silver the heather wreath on his helmet, that that wasn't what was on his mind.

In the morning he had a bad taste in his mouth and the father of all headaches. The sun was like the bright flare of an open furnace door. He hadn't felt drunk. It was painfully clear that he must have been, anyway. He hurt all over, like sunburn. A fitting state in which to go say good-bye to Ygerna.

She would be seventeen now. He gathered Antaeus's reins into his hand. Another year gone by while he had buried his head in the army. She would have found a man by now, with luck. And he could take her a nice present and pat her head like an old uncle and run for Misenum. A magistrate's son, British born like herself, who

would understand her. Or a tribune, lolling out his army
hitch in Aquae, on the lookout for a presentable mistress.
Correus's mouth tightened. No, Ygerna would know better
than that. Ygerna should be married. Have babies, a
home, some place to settle in, finally. He kicked Antaeus
into line beside the empty supply wagons making the southward trek back to Deva, the jumping-off point for the
western column. They had a cavalry escort, Vettone tribesmen from Spain, bright in blue and scarlet trappings and
singing cheerfully in the morning sun. A lark danced above
them, amusing herself in the air currents.

Julius reined his pony in behind Correus, looking sourly
at the lark. Silly bird. It wasn't going to be any fun at
Misenum, he thought. It was closer to Rome, of course,
but Julius didn't like anything that went on water. He'd
have the choice of being seasick with the master or twid-
dling his thumbs for weeks on end in the fleet barracks.
And they'd be leaving the lady, he thought, thinking of
the grave by Isca River. That didn't seem right somehow.
And the other one—Julius shied away from contempla-
tion of Ygerna. He had never quite dared ask the centurion what had happened that summer in the hills, but
somehow he'd given up any thought of looking sideways
at her himself after that. They were going to Aquae Sulis
on the way to Portus Adurni, and if Julius knew anything
of the centurion, he'd be in Typhon's temper from there
to Misenum. Maybe he'd join up himself, Julius thought,
watching the troop horses and their jaunty riders trotting
beside the wagons, singing and looking pleased with themselves. The centurion had offered often enough, but somehow Julius had never seen much use in it. He'd seen as
much of the army as he wanted to in Correus's service,
and without having spears stuck in him for the view. Well,
he thought, resigned to Fate, he'd see what turned up at
Misenum first.

The sun drew full up above the Brigantian Hills, and
the cavalry started singing something that had the fast *clip-
clop* of a pony's hooves on the open road, and the lark
dived down out of her dance and swooped ahead of them,
flittering her wings.

Ygerna was older. No taller, but with the child entirely gone from her face. She had on a salmon-colored

gown and carnelian eardrops that made her white face and dark hair look like something drawn with ink. She looked at Correus consideringly and dismissed the slave who had admitted him with a little shooing motion of her hand.

He stood awkwardly, with his helmet under one arm, while the slave departed. The slave cast him a dark look from the doorway.

"He thinks it isn't respectable," Ygerna said wryly. "Aunt Publia's gone to the baths for the afternoon." She gave Correus a half smile and sat down.

"Ygerna, I—" he looked at the floor, feeling like a fool. Sisyphus was still struggling uphill with his rock.

"It's all right," she said, her voice prim. He realized she was speaking Latin to him. "We never made any promises. We didn't think there would be much use in it, did we—back then?"

"No. May I sit down?"

"Of course," she said gravely, and patted the couch beside her.

He sat carefully, so that his greaves wouldn't scratch the pale satin upholstery. "Are you . . . all right here?"

"Well enough." She shrugged and flicked a hand at the pale painted walls and the good furniture.

"Good. I hoped . . ." His voice trailed off. He felt as if he were running around in one of his own nightmares, and all words were the wrong ones.

"Correus, what are you doing here?" She asked it in British, and there was a bite in her words and her eyes snapped at him. She was Ygerna at thirteen again, threatening to make a magic and curse him.

"I've been transferred," he said baldly. "To Misenum. I came to say good-bye."

"Why?"

"Because I am leaving," he said again.

"No, why say good-bye?"

"Because . . ." She was watching him now, her face intent. "Because of the trail from Dinas Tomen," he said, goaded. "Because we were a part of each other once. Because I care what happens to you!"

"Why don't you marry me off?" she snapped. "That would make it tidy! The Mother knows Aunt Publia's been trying!"

"Ygerna—"

"Some nice boy from the farms around here—then you wouldn't have to worry! You and whoever it is that you think would make you a better woman than me!"

"I did hope you'd get married," he said. "Stop spitting at me. You should get married. You deserve more than I gave you." He ran a hand through his hair, feeling exasperated and cornered. "And there isn't any other woman."

She stood up and glared at him. "Come here. I want to show you something." She went through the far door with a swish of silk skirts, her mantle trailing its salmon stripes and pale fringe unnoticed on the tile behind her. She didn't look back, and Correus picked up his helmet and followed her.

She swept through an open doorway at the end of the corridor and looked at the maid who was dusting perfume bottles on a carved shale table. The table's legs had wild eyes and open mouths and tails that writhed up to support a marble top. The maid hovered, blinking curiously at Correus, who stood uncertainly in the doorway.

"Get out," Ygerna said. The maid fled, clutching her feather duster, and Ygerna shut the door behind her and dropped the bolt across it.

"Sit down."

"Yes, Princess," Correus said gravely, and she grinned at him but only for a moment.

"I wanted to talk somewhere where I could yell at you if I felt like it," she said, and dropped down onto the bed with one foot tucked up under her. There was a chair nearby, a flimsy, feminine wicker affair, and Correus sat in it gingerly.

"Misenum," Ygerna said thoughtfully. "That is in Italy."

"The coast. On the bay of Neapolis."

"What gives you the right to stick your nose in my life again, if you are going to Misenum?"

"Maybe I don't have any right."

"The trail from Dinas Tomen? Is that your right?"

"That was a long time ago," he said firmly.

She didn't say anything to that, just sat there on the bed, with her foot curled under her like a cat, and looked at him, and the Roman gown and the crimped Roman curls disappeared, and he saw her again by firelight, with her hair like a dark curtain down her back, and the five-petaled flower of a priestess tattooed between her breasts. White breasts, turned upward to his hand, and white legs pale against his spread cloak. . . .

He felt it reach out for him like an old familiar magic, a sidhe-magic out of the hills, and he put out a hand to push it back.

Ygerna stood up and began to pull the pins from her hair, letting it fall around her in a tangle of dark waves. It was like watching her undress, and he thought that she knew it. He could see the line of hip and breast beneath her gown. He thought that she knew that, too.

"Ygerna, stop it!"

She shook her head, and the hair swung behind her lazily. "I would rather that you remember me like this, and so remember that I am *not* a Roman."

"That has always been plain enough," he said, trying to make a joke of it. "Witch."

"Maybe." She reached for the carnelian pin at her shoulder.

"Ygerna!"

"I still have the mark. See." She let the gown slide free from her shoulder so that the five-petaled flower, paler now, showed against the skin. "They say that if you want something badly enough, the Mother will give it to you. You may be sorry she did, but she will give it all the same. I asked her for you."

"Stop it!" He was on his feet now.

"When I was thirteen." She took a step toward him and took his hand. She put it against her breast and held it there, feeling his fingers clench into her skin. "You know, you could leave now, Correus," she said thoughtfully. "If you wanted to."

"Damn you!"

She tilted her head back until her eyes met his. "Take off your lorica," she whispered.

They vanished, all his pious intentions blown away in the smoky cloud of her hair. He unbuckled the straps of his lorica and set it aside and was lost. Lost in the old magic of the Silure hills, in the twilight sidhe-dream that making love to Ygerna always seemed to him, lost in a tangle of salmon-colored silk and white legs on her bed. She pulled him down beside her and after that there was

very little need to coax him. Forgetting servants and Aunt
Publia, he slipped Ygerna's gown free and pulled his own
tunic over his head. She touched the drop of amber that
hung around his throat with a gleam of triumph in her
eyes.

He pulled her close, watching that little light in the
black depths of her eyes, under the winged brows. She
had laid a trap for him, but he didn't care, not now, not
with the feel of her breast under his hand, and the sharp
bones of her hips against him. Later, he thought, he would
care. . . . Enough to break him, maybe.

I was right! The knowledge of it sang in her blood
as she wrapped her arms around his back. *I will have
that to remember, anyway.* And maybe . . . just maybe, it
would shake loose whatever it was that made him make
love to her with such a hunger and then slam closed the
door between them. But probably it wouldn't. It would be
enough, she told herself, to have that precious piece of
knowledge. She cried out as she felt him go into her and
buried her face in his collarbone. Knowledge dearly bought.
All her life long, what man would ever be able to live up
to Correus?

Afterward she lay beside him and watched the pattern
that the honeysuckle vine outside the window made on
walls and ceiling. "I am not thinking that this will change
your going to Misenum," she said finally.

"No."

"It is only that I wanted to know something."

"Well, now you know," he said sadly. "What good does
it do either of us?" He sounded drained, his voice gray,
defeated.

"That now you will tell me why," Ygerna said.

He didn't bother to ask "Why what?" He said, "Fear,"
dully, and stared at the ceiling.

She sat up cross-legged in the bed and stared at him.
"What?"

"Fear," he said. "Freita. My wife. I saw her die. I
loved her as much as I love you."

She didn't stop to gloat over that. "I don't understand."
Her voice was questioning, prodding gently.

"I have nightmares." He watched the ceiling, and the
visions came parading out for him. A man with a knife,

and Freita with a cold, still face and a gown soaked with blood. "She died because she was with me."

"She died because she was in the governor's bed," Ygerna said.

"She died because she followed the army," Correus said flatly. "I won't take another woman to live in a hut on the frontier and die with a knife in her."

"Misenum is not the frontier."

"Misenum won't be forever. There will be another war, and a frontier."

"Shouldn't you ask what *I* want?"

"It doesn't matter," Correus said. "I can't. And how happy would you be if I took away and left you in Rome to be safe? With my family?"

"Not very," Ygerna said frankly. "I survived my uncle and your governor, Correus, and I survived this war. I will survive your frontier."

He shook his head and watched the horrors that walked on the ceiling. "I can't."

She swung her legs off the bed and stood up, snatching up her gown. Her hands and her voice were shaking as she jammed the pins into the shoulders. "There are some things that are worth being afraid of, Correus. This isn't one of them!"

She turned on her heel and threw the door open and then slammed it closed behind her, leaving him alone to fumble for his tunic and armor, before the servants blundered in or Aunt Publia finished her afternoon gossip in the baths.

She was gone when he crossed the atrium, but the gray and white cat—Freita's cat—stuck one foot up over her ear and looked at him under it. He found his way to the door and closed it behind him.

The evening sun splashed across the paving stones in the street outside, and up the next street two auxiliary-men turned arm in arm into a wineshop, singing:

> . . . So come and take me hand and watch
> the moon arisin'
> And roll in me arms in the clover.

XX

Pompeii

FLAVIUS LOUNGED IN THE ROSE-COLORED COURTYARD OF the best inn in Pompeii, his long legs stretched out in front of him on the rose red tile, and his helmet pulled a little over his eyes. The old fig and pomegranate trees made a cool splash of shade across his corner of the court, and the herb garden at the center was thick with bees. There was a plate of fruit and sweetcake and a cup of wine and honey on the stone table beside him, and the inn's serving girl had left a cloth over it to keep the countless insects that zoomed and buzzed in the August air from falling in. He wore his parade tunic and military sandals, but his cuirass and greaves were in his rooms on the inn's second story. The helmet was more to keep the sun out of his eyes than a concession to military regulations.

For the next week or two, he thought with relief, he wouldn't be required to appear plated like a tortoise at every waking moment. For a man who hated armor so much, the army was a highly impractical career, he thought lazily, watching the bees droning in the peppermint. He was going to enjoy the next few days. The emperor's business at Misenum was concluded, and no one wanted him anywhere in particular until the end of the month. And Correus was due into Misenum, probably foaming at the mouth at being dragged away from his British campaign. Flavius had left a message with the commander at Misenum and a promise of dinner as amends.

The square shadow of the innkeeper fell across the tiles. "There is a commander of marines waiting to see you, sir, but I felt perhaps I should ascertain—?"

Flavius pushed his helmet back on his head and looked up. "What did he say?"

"I'm afraid he was rather . . . uncomplimentary, sir." The innkeeper had been the majordomo in a gentleman's house before he bought his freedom, and his dignity was

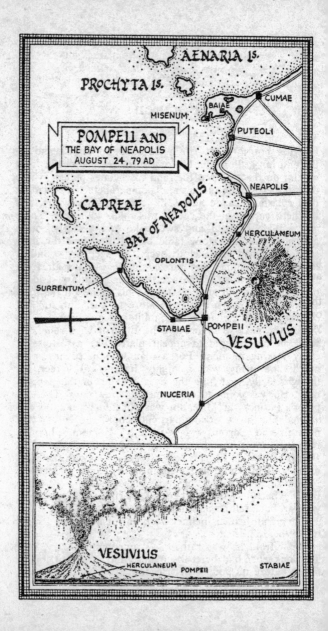

AENARIA IS.

PROCHYTA IS.

MISENUM   BAIAE   CUMAE

PUTEOLI

POMPEII AND
THE BAY OF NEAPOLIS
AUGUST 24, 79 AD

NEAPOLIS

CAPREAE

BAY OF NEAPOLIS

HERCULANEUM

OPLONTIS

SURRENTUM

STABIAE   POMPEII

VESUVIUS

NUCERIA

VESUVIUS

VESUVIUS
HERCULANEUM   POMPEII   STABIAE

mighty. "He, uh, declined to give his name, but he has quite a look of you, sir. Would he be a relative, perhaps?"

Flavius grinned. "He would. I expect he would also be in a temper. Well, bring him in. And I want your best dinner. Was he alone?"

"Quite, sir."

"Then we'll want some entertainment, too, I think. Those twins—the ones who dance."

"Uh, to dance only, sir?" The innkeeper coughed discreetly.

Flavius thought about the British girl, who might or might not account for his brother's temper, and about Aemelia, patiently awaiting his return in Rome, but out of reach for the moment. "To do whatever seems to suggest itself," he said. "I'm not quite sure at the moment."

The innkeeper nodded sagely, hands crossed across his stomach. "Certainly, sir. One never knows quite how an evening will go."

"No," Flavius said. "Indeed one doesn't. You may send the commander to me here. Perhaps I can take the kinks out of him before dinner. It would be a pity to waste your lobsters." He pulled his helmet down over his eyes again and appeared to sink into thought.

Pompeii was a luxurious town. In the height of the summer season, the twenty thousand residents jostled elbows with almost as many holiday-goers who had come to soak up the sun and the sea breezes and the famous fruit and Pompeiian cabbages that flourished in the fertile volcanic soil around Mount Vesuvius. In the off-season, Pompeii was a town of farmers and fishermen and good, solid businessmen who took their profits seriously. There was a thriving wool trade and factories for Pompeii's two famous exports—perfume of roses, and *garum*, the concentrated fish sauce that was a Roman dining staple all over the empire. It was all very important, Pompeiian business— *Salve lucrum* was a not uncommon inscription for the entrance to a businessman's home—but the citizens of Pompeii happily put the fortunes which such work afforded them into the pleasures of their leisure hours. The city supported more than forty bakeries, twenty wineshops, and well over a hundred small eating places. Architects and artists did a thriving business year-round, and the rebuilding that had been done since the great earthquake of Nero's reign was accounted some of the finest town design in Italy.

It was impossible to be gloomy in Pompeii in August. While the more inland towns sweltered in the summer sun, the cool salt breeze from the bay took the edge off the heat in Pompeii. The streets were thronged with holiday crowds—nurses with droves of small children out for their daily airing, mothers shopping for essence of roses in the perfume stalls, and fathers earnestly talking politics with cronies under awnings in front of the bread-and-soup bars. Officers on leave from Misenum mingled with parties of theatergoers and processions of the hopeful going to sacrifice at the flower-garlanded Temple of Fortune. There was a smell of fresh fruit and wine in the air, mingled with the salt scent of ocean and the heady odor of the perfume factories. And everyone in Pompeii was turned out in his best: light summer gowns and tunics like a pastel flower garden against the white togas and bright splashes of army scarlet and naval green.

Flavius seemed to have sunk into the summer indolence like a cat, Correus thought, coming into the rose-tiled court. He looked like he was asleep, his chin on his chest and his helmet pulled over his eyes. There was a green beetle walking up his sandal laces. Correus prodded Flavius with his foot, and the beetle fell off.

"You couldn't be asleep. The innkeeper was just talking to you."

Flavius opened his eyes and grinned at him. "Ah, I see you got my message. I was just thinking," he added with dignity, "whether we should have oysters with dinner."

"It's not the season for them. You'll poison yourself. Yes, I got your message. From old Plinius at Misenum when I reported in. He told me you were over here lolling about on a mound of lobster shells and cherry pits, drinking yourself into a stupor."

"No, he didn't. He told you, quite politely, to come and have dinner with me."

"I drew my own conclusions. Are you responsible for my being here?"

Flavius sat up straight. "I might have happened to mention to the emperor that I had a brother who was obviously destined for great things and was unfortunately wasting away in Britain."

"I had a good posting in the best campaign that's come along in years!" Correus snapped. He glowered at Flavius and sat down.

"You had a posting in a campaign that isn't going to reap any glory for anyone but Julius Agricola," Flavius said. "You wouldn't have got so much as a bronze torque out of it. Tell me I lie."

"Agricola halfway said the same," Correus said grudgingly. "Damn it, Flavius, I was happy where I was. Take care of your own career."

"You were hiding where you were," Flavius said. "You can't go on mourning that woman for the rest of your life. And don't tell me I didn't like her, because I did . . . sort of. And if you won't listen to me, ask Lucius Paulinus. He's the one who suggested I put in my oar in the first place. Thought of it myself, too, though."

"I'm surprised Lucius didn't do it himself," Correus said. "A man can have too much well-intentioned family."

"I was in a better spot," Flavius said. "Titus is still deciding if Lucius is going to be useful to him, or if he was too much Vespasian's man. He's had him cooling his heels in Rome since Vespasian died."

"What does Lucius think? About Titus, not me."

"He thinks we have a good man," Flavius said. "So do I. So I expect they'll get on well enough. Titus has settled down considerably. It's a bit wearing being the heir apparent. He used to take a lot of it out in wine and dancing girls, but he sobered up overnight when his father died."

"What's he doing with Lucius?"

"He called him back to see if he knew anything Vespasian hadn't been telling," Flavius said. "I expect he did, but I don't think Titus will hold it against him." Vespasian had trusted no one completely. Even his spies didn't know what his other spies were doing. It was more than likely that there would be a few gaps in his heir's knowledge, as well.

"We've got off the subject," Correus said, but it was hard to stay irritated when Flavius was plying him with wine and figs and was so patently glad to see him.

"Have a fig," Flavius said. "Are you going home?"

"Yes, in a couple of days. I've got some leave, but it feels odd."

"I don't doubt it," Flavius said, biting into a fig and flicking the stem into the pomegranates. "You've got a son who thinks Lucius is his father, and you don't know how he's going to take to you."

"Probably scream and dive under the bed," Correus said, "but I don't know what to do about it. And he knows who his father is."

"I spoke figuratively. Has he ever seen you? Since he was old enough to notice?"

"How often did we see our father?"

"He came home on leave," Flavius pointed out. "Where have you been spending yours?"

Correus was silent. There was a lot in that. "I'm afraid to go back now, I think."

"In case Felix runs under the bed? Well, if you wait much longer, you won't need to bother. But you're lucky you can catch up with them at all, this trip. Julia trails those babies around after Lucius every place he goes, unless she's pregnant. Come to think of it, I think Aemelia said Julia was, last letter, so maybe she'll stay put for a bit."

Correus looked at his reflection in his wine cup. There didn't seem to be much to see there but a centurion's helmet. "You have a baby yourself now, don't you?"

"Three months old now," Flavius said proudly. "Looks like a monkey, but I'm told that wears off. Aemelia assures me I'll find her vastly improved when I get home. We call her Appia. For Father, of course."

"Of course." Flavius wouldn't have dared not, even with a daughter, and they both knew it.

"You should get married," Flavius said. "Have another fig. You aren't cut out to be a bachelor any more than I am."

"I tried once, if you will recall," Correus said shortly.

"If you still had Freita, I wouldn't be telling you that," Flavius said. "But you don't, and you wouldn't have Freita now, even if you'd married her. It wasn't lack of a marriage that got her killed."

"I know that," Correus said. "Flavius . . . don't."

Flavius gave him a long look and closed his mouth. He wished he had closed it a sentence sooner. "Come and have dinner," he said cheerfully. "I've got just the girl lined up for you. She swears like a Tiber bargeman and dances like a snake. You'll love her."

The dancing twins proved to be Syrians, bronze-skinned with long black braids knotted with beads, and both wore diaphanous gold trousers that would have made Venus blush. One played the cithara while the other writhed her way around the floor, shaking the hip belt of coins and lapis lazuli that appeared to be all that kept her trousers from imminent descent. She fluttered her dark lashes at Correus, and an overpowering smell of oil of jasmine drifted past.

Flavius grinned and watched him, but if he was hoping for his brother's discomfiture, he was disappointed. Correus followed her progress appreciatively, and when her swaying hips moved close enough, he tucked a silver coin into her belt. It slipped down the inside of her trouser leg to where the gauzy folds were drawn tight at the ankle and jingled there with Flavius's offering. After a while she changed places with her sister, her long nails picking the music from the cithara while the other girl wove her way about the room, inviting similar largesse.

The food was extraordinarily good: lobsters in their shells cooked with *garum* and spices, a basket of pears, stuffed hare in white sauce, spiced raw lamb, wild lettuces, and bowls of the sweet fresh fruit for which Pompeiian farms were famous, four courses of wine, and, at intervals, baskets of small hot rolls with which to wipe their plates.

"I begin to see the attractions of Pompeii," Correus said sleepily over his fourth cup of wine, and Flavius laughed and they toasted each other and then toasted the dancing girls for good measure. By the time the last course had been cleared away, Correus somehow found that one of the dancing twins was sharing his couch, feeding him cherries. He laughed and put an arm around her waist and saw that Flavius had progressed somewhat further with the other twin. The thought of Aemelia dutifully awaiting him in Rome would probably be irrelevant, Correus thought. Flavius kept his life neatly compartmentalized. And in any case, it was easier to lie here on the couch while the dancing Syrian rubbed his neck and shoulders than to tell this nice girl he didn't want her.

Somehow they progressed to the bedchambers upstairs —it was all very hazy in his mind—and the experience was so pleasant that he and Flavius kept the girls as sort of pets for the next few days, exploring the amusements of Pompeii by daylight and the dancers' talents by night. They were running up an awful bill, Correus thought, but Flavius said grandly that it was a welcome-home present, and he could do his penance by behaving himself in Rome. As a sop to his conscience, Correus sent Julius on to Rome with most of the baggage, so Flavius wouldn't find himself entertaining him as well.

Neither one of them, they admitted, watching the famous actor Paris at a performance in the Large Theater, much wanted to go home. It was easier to be friends in Pompeii than in the house of Appius, where the old rivalry lingered in the shadows and almost certainly, in the persons of their respective mothers. And each admitted the lurking suspicion that maturity somehow vanished at the gates of their father's house. Here in Pompeii they were up-and-coming officers, equals and gentlemen. At home they were Appius Julianus's boys. It made it very pleasant to be in Pompeii.

"All the same," Flavius said finally, as Paris in a gold wig declaimed the tragic ending of *The Medea*, "we are going to have to go home. You'll use up all your leave if you don't, and the emperor's going to start wondering what I'm doing."

"And conclude that it's not much," Correus said. Paris, in the white tragic mask of Medea, was making his last bow, while boys in the sponsor's house colors ran up and down the tiers with programs of the musical and pantomime to follow. It was getting hot, especially in the front rows where the bowl of the theater blocked the sea breeze, and the theater crew began to run out the red and white canvas awning over the audience. The rigging rumbled as the awning unfurled, and the audience was clapping and stamping and calling compliments to Paris, and it took a moment before anyone felt the other tremor that underlay the rest.

Correus and Flavius jerked upright in their seats and looked nervously first at each other and then at the heavy scaffolding of the awning over their heads. They could feel it through the stone seats of the theater, a vibration in the ground and then the sudden sickening sensation of having the earth lurch out from under them. The rest of the audience was noticing it now, too, but they seemed calm enough. Tremors were a part of life in Campania. The inhabitants were used to them and simply got out from under anything heavy and waited for it all to settle down again. Paris had made his bow and had gone with care for his dignity slowly out the stage exit, and his audience was preparing to follow. Correus noted that the holiday visitors among them didn't seem quite so unconcerned, but the audience made an orderly progress through the theater's main doors into the courtyard of the Gladiators' School beyond. The ground lurched again, and those still inside began to push. Above the rumbling in the earth, the shrill voice of panic had crept in.

Correus and Flavius stumbled out into the courtyard and stopped to catch their breath. Being buried alive was not a fate either of them looked for eagerly, and theaters had been known to fall inward during an earthquake. The ground shivered again and then was still. The silence was uncanny. There were no bird notes, no sound of human voices, nothing but the shrill, hysterical barking of a dog in the distance, barking frantically on and on at some unknown terror it could feel but not see. Then the silence broke in a spate of question and exclamation, a counting up of bruised ribs and sprained ankles from the mass exit, a sigh of relief and nervous laughter as the normal noise of the city came back with no greater damage to show for the tremor than a few toppled statues in the Colonnade.

Pompeii went back about its business, but Flavius looked dubious. "Maybe it's because I don't live here," he said, pacing and fidgeting about their room at the inn. "Nobody else seems to be worrying, but I didn't like the feel of that."

"Neither did I," Correus said fervently, and they both laughed. "Do you think there'll be more?" he added seriously.

Flavius shrugged. "There was a bad one in Nero's reign that wrecked half the city. It can always happen again. I'm wondering now if I *ought* to leave. If we're going to have a civil disaster on our hands, the emperor will just send me back again to help mop up. It might make more sense if I stayed put."

"And got squashed in the wreckage, I suppose," Correus said.

"Don't worry, I'll watch my step. Panic and crowded buildings kill more people than the earthquake, usually." He rummaged around in his traveling kit and fished out a message tablet of thin wooden leaves, a pen, and dry ink. He poured the ink in a wine cup and added water from the jug on the table.

"Whom are you writing?"

"The emperor," Flavius said. "Don't distract me. This is my only tablet, and I don't want to have to buy another one."

Correus stretched himself out on his bed and kept quiet. Flavius's handwriting was better than anyone's in the family (being left-handed always made Correus's scrawl a little sideways) but for reasons unknown to anyone, he hated to write. Letters could only be pried out of him in times of dire emergency and then were achieved after much agonizing and revision. Flavius bent a look of great concentration on his tablet and finally sat back with a sigh of relief. "There. Bericus can take that. I can live without him a few days, I suppose. I've told the emperor we're getting tremors, and I'm going to stay until I'm sure they aren't getting worse. Subject to his orders, of course."

"I'll stay, too," Correus said.

"Oh, no. *You* have business at home. And no business nursemaiding me. Remember?"

"All right." Correus really didn't see what he could do, except follow Flavius around to pull him out from under falling rocks, which was a little silly when he thought about it. And it was clear that Flavius didn't want him to. "I'll take a few days to settle in at Misenum, and then head home. Don't stand under any statues, will you?"

In the morning he rode around the curving edge of the bay, through the cities of Oplontis, Herculaneum, and Neapolis, to the naval base that perched on the northern tip of the crescent that formed the bay of Neapolis. It was a full day's ride and would have been shorter by ship, but he was shortly going to be spending more time than he wanted to on ships, and it was a pleasant ride by land—cool with the salt breeze and enlivened by the coastal traffic of farm wagons loaded with their market wares and by vacationers out for a day's airing. The ground shivered under them once or twice and Antaeus pricked up his gold ears and snorted, but the sky was bright and the sun warm on the rolling farmland to their right and calm on the sea to the left. No omens there.

In Misenum no one had noticed the tremors at all. Correus stabled Antaeus and made his respects to Gaius Plinius, the elderly fleet commander, and was promptly invited to dine with the commander and his nephew and sister, who appeared to be semipermanent residents of the Praetorium. The tremors reached Misenum with the second course, and the commander smiled wryly at Correus's expression and told him genially that he would get used to them.

"Does this go on all the time, sir?"

"No, not as to say all the time. But Campanian earthquakes are like Pompeiian cabbages. A specialty of the district. You get so you sleep right through anything less than a real shocker."

"*I* don't," the sister said firmly, "and furthermore I am sure I never shall. But one does get accustomed."

Two days later Correus had decided that the human body was, after all, remarkably adaptive. He would never get entirely used to having the ground wiggle under his feet, but he had got so that he didn't look wildly around him and jump like a startled cat every time it happened. It would all die down in a day or two, everyone said, going about his business. In the face of all this aplomb, Correus went about his own, acquainting himself with the men who would be under his command and the ships' captains with whom they would sail. Misenum was a mixed base of sailors and marines, and the niceties of etiquette between the ships' captains and the marine commanders could get a bit tricky. At sea, the captain was the ultimate master. It was his business to take the marine commander where he wanted to go, unless the captain deemed it dangerous or downright impossible. When the ship was beached, authority shifted to the commander of marines. While the men under them might regard each other with something less than love, it behooved their officers to get along. Correus spent some time laying the groundwork, drinking and swapping lies with the marine and naval officers and getting himself invited to dine with Caritius—captain of the *Merope*, flagship of the Misenum Fleet—and his pretty Neapolitan wife. She proved to be the sister of an old comrade from the Rhenus days, and Correus enjoyed himself hugely while Caritius gave him a rundown on life at Misenum.

"We're mostly chasing pirates these days," the captain said. "Not very glamorous work, but it keeps us all busy."

"They are really a menace," his wife said. "The minute we slacken up on patrols, they're out again like sharks, and some of them aren't above raiding the coastal towns if they think they can get away with it."

"We're due to make another sweep in a couple of days," Caritius said. "That is, if the whole damned base doesn't fall in the sea," he added as the floor began to shake again. "Oh, Typhon!"

The whole room lurched suddenly and the lamp, suspended from three silver chains above the table, swung and tilted as one chain snapped, pouring burning oil onto the table.

Cursing, they pulled the tablecloth up and rolled it in on itself, singeing their hands, and Correus grabbed the first thing handy, which was a pillow off his couch and smothered the flames with it. The floor was a mess of spilled wine and broken dishes, and Caritius's wife stood looking at it with her hand over her mouth, while slaves came running from all directions.

"Are you sure this is normal?" Correus said looking from Caritius to his wife to the dangling lamp.

"No," Caritius said grimly, "it's not. Something's cooking. We may be in for a bad one. If you don't want to get stuck helping clean up, you'd best get out in the morning and take that leave you're due. One pair of hands more or less won't make any difference, but you're likely to get detailed for it anyway, if there's any damage."

"I was going to anyway," Correus said. "If the gods don't bury me in my bed tonight," he added, making it a joke.

But in the morning he somehow found a thing or two to do, and then something else, and then it seemed that one of Antaeus's shoes was loose and should be looked at. The trouble was, he acknowledged, sitting outside the blacksmith's barn, he couldn't get over the feeling that he was dodging something. Flavius had told him to go, Caritius had told him to go, even the commander, Plinius, had taken it for granted that Centurion Julianus would take the leave due him before he reported officially for duty. None of them seemed to feel that Correus's presence would avert disaster or be of much use in the aftermath, with a whole naval station of able bodies at Misenum to help pick up. And they were all perfectly right, but he still felt silly galloping out of town under the threat of earthquake. Too much care for his own dignity, he thought wryly, and if he didn't go and see his father, he'd never hear the end of it. And there was Felix. And there was also Flavius, out of whose business he had solemnly promised to keep his meddling self. He shrugged. When Antaeus's shoe was fixed, he would leave.

"Here you are, sir." The blacksmith emerged with Antaeus, who seemed to have worked his usual charm on strangers. "Good as a baby," the blacksmith proclaimed. "Good thing you brought him in. Be a shame to lame a nice beast like him with a thrown shoe. He'll see you home now, sir." The blacksmith rubbed the gold nose, and Antaeus slobbered happily down his apron. "Holy Isis, what's that?"

"What?" Correus looked up. The blacksmith, oblivious to Antaeus now, was pointing a sooty hand to the southeast. As they looked, the commander's sister came running past, her trailing gown clutched around her plump figure. Above the rooftops, a mottled mass of cloud rose, blotched and threatening, from across the bay.

"Centurion Julianus!" The commander's sister swerved as she saw him. "Have you seen it? We must tell my brother immediately!"

"Of course," Correus said, rising gallantly to the occasion. "Do let me escort you." She looked thoroughly unnerved. "Put him in stables for me, will you?" He gave Antaeus's reins back to the smith.

"Thank you, Centurion." The commander's sister tucked an arm through Correus's. "I feel quite faint. What could it be? We must find my brother!"

"Dunno what she thinks *he* can do about it," the blacksmith said, watching her tow the centurion off in the direction of the Praetorium. But there was a growing feeling of unease in the air and as the cloud rose above the mountains across the bay, someone said the terrifying word "Volcano."

The Praetorium was a pleasant house just above the sea, and they found Misenum's scholarly commander hard at work on his books, oblivious to natural disaster.

"Good heavens!" he said mildly when his sister informed him of events, and he called for his shoes.

They climbed up on the outer wall, and from this vantage point it was clear that the cloud was rising above the mountains beyond Pompeii. It leapt upward in a single column and then billowed outward in great blotches that shaded from white to black. Gaius Plinius peered at it and then patted his sister on the shoulder. "This bears looking into, I should think, but I wouldn't worry about it this far away. I shall want a boat." He smiled at his sister's son, who was peering dubiously at the cloud from his side. "Would you like to go with me?"

"I think I should finish my studies, sir," the nephew said firmly. "You set me some extracts to write, you remember." He edged back from the wall before his uncle could think to relieve him of this duty, and collided with a slave coming from the house on the run.

"This just came off a fisher boat for you, sir." The slave handed the commander a hastily written message scrawled on wax.

"Dear me." Plinius frowned as he deciphered it. "This changes things, I'm afraid. Centurion Julianus, would you be good enough to order the launching of every warship we have as soon as possible? I will take the flagship. It appears that Mount Vesuvius has exploded." His eyes strayed back to the letter. "Silly woman," he said sadly. "She should have come herself and *left* her damned silver-ware."

A sheet of fire blazed like the mouth of Erebus half-way down the mountain. In the bay the air was thick with falling ash and hot as a furnace. Pumice and blackened stones, charred and cracked in the flames, rained down on the *Merope*'s deck. Correus stood in the bow with the commander and Caritius, and watched death fall out of the sky.

The fleet was strung out behind them, pitifully few to take away the refugees of five cities.

"We'll never make shore here, sir!" Caritius shouted above the roaring in the air and the beat of the *hortator's* mallets, trying to hold the ship steady in the heaving sea. Before them lay the shallow waters of Oplontis harbor, broken into angry reefs by the black, piled debris. The sea swelled with the shaking earth, and the spray lifted angrily over the cinders and wreckage. "Best we turn back, sir!" Caritius shouted. "We'll break up in there sure!"

Plinius sighed, the hot wind lifting his gray hair into little tufts around his ears, but he shook his head. "I fear we're too badly needed. Fortune keeps an eye on the courageous, Captain; let us give her the chance. Can we make Stabiae?"

"Wind's right," Caritius said. "Blow us clean to hell if you want." But he signaled the *hortator*, and the *Merope* slipped slowly down the coast to Stabiae with the fleet behind her.

"We must hope for a change, Captain," Plinius said. "To blow us back out again. Us and the poor souls on shore."

Caritius looked grim, but he didn't say anything. There wasn't anything to say, Correus thought, that wasn't plain to them all—if the wind didn't shift, the Misenum Fleet would never take anyone back from Stabiae. The *Merope* came in on the mouth of a storm. There would be no going back through it.

In Stabiae harbor, there was full-fledged panic. Most of the populace with any access to a boat had loaded their goods on board already in the hope of a favorable wind. The rest mobbed the *Merope* as she came in, fighting each other hysterically as they plunged through the shallow water to her. Stabiae lay on the far side of a smaller bay within the great one, and so far the danger was only a black and burning threat to the north, but the air was hot and darkening, and the Misenum sailors found themselves fighting the people they had come to save to prevent them from capsizing the ship in their terror.

Plinius came upon a friend praying hysterically on the dock beside his laden ship and commandeered his house for a headquarters. "You will feel much better with something to do, my friend. Captain, I wish to be notified the moment there is the slightest chance of putting out from here. In the meantime, signal the fleet to stay well back, and we'll move what folk we can south by road."

The signal flags ran up on the *Merope*'s mast, and in a few minutes they could see the fleet begin to tack back out into the bay. Correus shook himself out of a trance. It was like watching monsters come up out of the earth, looking at that black and fiery cloud for too long.

"I have a brother in Pompeii, sir." No going back to Rome now, not in the face of the hell-wind, whatever Flavius said. "Permission to go and help there. They'll be worse off than Stabiae."

Plinius sighed. "Permission granted, Centurion, but I'm afraid you'll find no good there. If you can, though—remember, the important thing is, don't let them panic. They'll trample themselves to death in a panic," he said tiredly. "Just like sheep, you know."

The road was choked with the terrified, running to anywhere from the horror at their backs. A riderless horse careened by, foam-flecked, with its reins dangling. Correus grabbed them and pulled himself up, forcing the animal back the way it had come. The sky was turning black around him. He would never get to Pompeii on foot. If he didn't kill the horse doing it, he might have a chance that way. He forced his way against the tide, fighting the horse as much as the terrified stream of people who poured out along the road on mules or wagons or were pushing their household goods in carts. A pig ran squealing under the horse's feet, and a woman on a mule sat in the saddle and screamed endlessly while another woman walked beside it and held the bridle. She looked at Correus blankly as he rode by, whipping the horse into the darkness that had been Pompeii. He had to fight his way through the town gates in pitch blackness. It was mid-afternoon, but the dark had come down around them like night, lit only by the fires of burning buildings and the distant wall of flame that blanketed Vesuvius.

Correus pushed his way past the theaters and the Gladiators' School more by instinct than by sight. He couldn't tell if the inn was standing or not—half the buildings around him lay in rubble, and the hot ash and pumice had already begun to drift up against the doorways.

Suddenly the inn's walls loomed up in front of him, the sign momentarily illuminated by a torch in someone's hand. A woman ran past, clutching a silver pitcher to her breast, and another dragged two terrified children behind her.

"No! Get out, you fools, you'll die in there!" the man with the torch shouted, and dragged the innkeeper and his dancing twins bodily into the street. "Make for the gate! Get *out!*"

The innkeeper said something that was lost in the chaos, and the twins each grabbed a hand and ran, with their master stumbling between them.

The man with the torch turned round and his light fell on Correus, tying his terrified horse to a ring in the wall. "Get out of here, damn you!" he screamed. It was Flavius, his hair and clothes gray with ash and his face furious.

"Flavius!"

"Correus?" Flavius squinted at him, coughing from the choking ash in the air.

"Come on, you can't stay here!"

"I know! But they keep going back to *get* things!" They were still shouting to make themselves heard over the rumble of the mountain and the terrorized screaming of the refugees. "Get out to the gate and try to keep them from turning back and jamming up. Keep them moving."

"*You* get moving!"

"I will, but don't wait for me! We need you more at the gate!"

"All right!" Correus shouted. "But you take the horse —you may have to get out fast!" He turned and plunged back toward the gate on foot, collecting stragglers as he went, pushing, shoving, shouting at them to keep moving. Behind him he heard Flavius, one small voice of authority in the darkness, ordering people from their houses.

XXI

A Mountain of Fire

IT WAS A SCENE STRAIGHT FROM EREBUS, THE BLACK-
ness lit only by forked tongues of flame from the burning
mountain, the air thick as if they stood not in the open
but in a sealed tomb from which all light had been withdrawn. The ground heaved beneath them so that carriages
rolled wildly this way and that, dragging their terrified
horses with them, smashing carriage and occupants against
the slowly falling city walls.

Correus stood well back from the Stabian Gate, fighting to see with streaming eyes through the black air,
shouting, "Move! Move, damn you!" as the miserable
townspeople milled in the gateway, all sense of purpose
vanished in the panic fear that drives out reason. They
responded somewhat to orders, relieved that some voice
told them what to do, and they pressed out through the
gate toward Stabiae, screaming in the dark for their lost
children and kin. A howling child ran by Correus and he
caught it by the arm and grabbed a woman from the flood
at random.

"Here! Hold onto this!"

They seemed to accept this chance mating and stumbled on.

The air was choking with the smell of sulfur and the
falling ash, and Correus pulled his scarf up over his face,
wondering as he did so if anything could filter that deadly
air for long. He had no idea what time it was. In Pompeii, it was night, as if the thing that shook the ground
now reached up to pull down the sky. The flood of refugees was increasing, pushing against those ahead of them,
but somewhere on the road they were hopelessly jammed
up, too frightened to move, ready only to sit down in the
road and die. Correus began to work his way down the
side of the road, his feet braced against the heaving

ground and his back turned firmly away from the fire behind. If it came for him, he thought, there would be little use in seeing it.

"All right, then, keep moving. We're going to make for Stabiae. And take your baggage with you," he added, a voice of authority from the darkness, which miraculously they heeded. If they began to abandon the baggage, which they had dragged this far, they would block the road beyond clearing.

Somehow the mass began to move again, inching its way toward Stabiae, carrying Correus with it. To go back was impossible, and he knew that even if he could, without some force to drive them on, they would stop and mill like sheep or sit screaming and praying by the roadside, waiting to be buried in the endlessly falling ash.

"It's the gods' vengeance for our sins!" an old man screamed as Correus pushed him along.

"If you want to give yourself to the gods, don't do it in the road!" Correus shouted back, and a woman came up beside them and pulled the old man along with her.

Slowly they fought their way from Pompeii to Stabiae, through a sulfurous world of fire and blackness where demons stalked abroad, and Correus found himself praying, also.

"Mithras, give us back the light. Lord of Light, put out your hand to us." And let Flavius be among the refugees that swelled the road behind them.

It was no more than a few miles to Stabiae, but it was an eternity on the way, a walk along the heaving banks of the Styx, where nameless things reached out their hands, and for each man the terror in his soul was greater than the fire behind him. The sky lightened a little to a murky haze as they neared Stabiae, through which pale faces, gray as corpses with the falling ash, floated like the ghosts in Erebus.

He found Caritius of the *Merope* on the shore with Plinius, dismally watching the heaving sea.

"The fleet's got to move out, sir," Caritius was saying. "We've got to back them off while we've got light enough to signal!" Night was falling fast, and the ominous dark shroud that had hidden Pompeii all afternoon was beginning to flow over Stabiae. "A sorcerer couldn't bring 'em in through this! D'you want to lose them where they sit?"

Plinius sighed and peered through the murk as Correus' face appeared beside the captain's. "Julianus! I was afraid we'd lost you."

"You nearly did, sir," Correus said, trying to catch his breath. Even here the air was too thick with ash and fumes to breathe comfortably. Plinius and the captain had their cloaks pulled around their faces. The ground lurched again, and they stumbled. In the bay, the waves sucked out as if swept by a giant hand and crashed back again, smashing on the wharves with a splinter of pilings.

"Pompeii?" Plinius asked.

"Gone, sir. Or it will be. Ahriman's loose on that mountain."

"The fleet, sir!" Caritius said again urgently.

Plinius nodded. "Very well, Captain. You may signal." He sighed again. "I had hoped to take some of these poor souls off by sea."

"It's impossible, sir," Caritius said. The sailor beside him began swinging his lantern above their heads. Then he steadied it and began to open and close the lantern face toward the bay. He counted to twenty, swung the lantern aloft, and signaled again. "Hope they see us, sir," he murmured, "but I wouldn't be betting on it."

"Keep signaling," Caritius said.

"Oh, aye, sir, we'll signal."

The sea swept out again, leaving a phantasmagoric scene of ocean floor abruptly bared and exposing strange sea things stranded in the sand before it rushed back again against the shore. With the beginning of the storm they had hauled the boats of Stabiae farther up the shore, and Caritius had ordered the *Merope* dragged up with them. Now the smaller craft were sucked back seaward with the deadly tide, and as they watched, the *Merope* heeled over in the sand with the crack of a snapping mast. The spray broke around them and drenched them to the skin, and the sailor yelped as the *Merope* slipped seaward with the next wave.

"Poseidon Father!" Then, "Sir, they've seen us!"

Far out in the raging bay a faint prick of light showed and went out.

"Sea Father grant we signaled in time," Caritius said. He gave the commander a black look.

"We needed them," Plinius said, "while there was still

a chance." His voice wheezed under the folds of his cloak. "The refugees will have to go by road, I fear—the ones who can."

"We'll try to keep them moving, sir," Correus said. He peered at the commander's gray face in the gloom. "You should go too, sir."

Plinius took a wheezing breath and coughed. "No, there will be less panic, perhaps, if it's known that I haven't bolted yet. I fear it is all I can do of any use. My lungs are not what they were." He coughed again. "I shall go and rest, I think." He turned toward Stabiae, a stout, dignified figure with his cloak over his head.

People were beginning to stream through the gates of Stabiae, too, to join with the flood of homeless that poured south from Pompeii. Those who would not abandon all they owned to the looters, who were roving the streets, barricaded themselves within their houses until the falling rubble blocked the doorways and they were forced to break them open or be buried. Slowly Stabiae darkened to black under that dark rolling cloud that seemed to press down the sky, and its people milled in the streets, afraid of the rocking, swaying walls inside and the falling pumice stone without.

Correus again found himself pushing, shoving, and kicking, trying to herd the panic-stricken, to get them moving anywhere except here in the street, where a wall was likely to fall in on them. Caritius, cursing his lost ship and all his gods, worked with him, and once they saw the commander with a pillow tied on his head watching calmly from the steps of his friend's house, with the household gathered around him.

By morning every town along the curving, lovely seacoast that had been the bay of Neapolis was crowded with a terror-stricken mob, looting, fighting, trampling each other while they waited for someone, anyone, who would tell them what to do and where to run.

In the morning, Pompeii was dead. Dead and buried almost to the rooftops in cinders and rubble, choked into silence by the poisonous air. Soon even the rooftops would be gone, blotted out by the still-falling ash.

Flavius had waited until the last minute, until the horse that Correus had left him had torn its reins from the ring and bolted, until the streets were knee-high with fallen rock, so that he found himself clambering over it, his head above the door tops. There would be no pulling anyone from those doomed and shuttered houses now.

The fumes had grown steadily worse, and a scorching rain had begun to fall. It burned his hands and face and combined with the ash caked in his hair, turning it to glue. And with it, the tumult in the streets died to an ominous quiet, with only the burning rain for a background, and the voice of an occasional straggler clambering over the rubble to the gates.

Time to be going, Flavius thought. Or stay and sink beneath the earth with the city. The rain had put out his torch, and he fought his way over the rubble by instinct, hoping that instinct held true. He could still see the fire on the mountain behind him and tried to judge the direction of the gate from that. There were bodies in the road now, the old or weak of lung, and he fell over them as he went. Not everyone had made it that far. Those who had decided to wait out the holocaust indoors would never come out again, suffocated by the poisoned air, walled up behind the rising tide of stone and ash. He could feel his own chest tighten with every breath.

He thought that the gate was not far now. He might even make it, if the walls didn't fall in on him first. Had Correus made it? Or had Flavius unknowingly fallen over his brother's body? He prayed briefly, ugently to the god whose word was Light, for one breath of clean air, one sight of the sun, and one sign that the world had not been tipped wailing into the pit. Logically, he knew that Mount Vesuvius, long thought dormant, had wrenched itself open at last, and that beyond its range there would be sunlight and trees and the world as it had been. But here at the foot of the fire, it was hard to believe in anything but black chaos and death—Ragnarok, Forst would have called it, the final battle of the gods.

A flicker of flame glowed to his left, and there was the sound of furious, desperate sobbing. Flavius lurched toward it and fell over another body. A woman was kneeling by a fall of rubble, trying frantically to dig the stones away with her hands. They were under the sloping overhang of a half-fallen building, and the torch was sheltered from the rain by its eaves. Another stone rumbled and slid.

"Get out of there!" Flavius said. "The whole thing's going to come down!"

"I can't!" the woman shrieked. "She's caught!" She was well over the edge of hysteria, oblivious to everything but the other woman who lay with her leg pinned by a tangle of stone and roof tile. The first woman turned a frantic face to Flavius, and he recognized one of the Syrian dancers in the nightmarish light of the torch.

"Help me!" She dragged at the stone, her fingers bleeding.

Flavius knelt beside her. "You won't get anywhere like that. Clear off the stuff on top, one at a time." The woman under the stones never moved, and he wondered if they were digging for a corpse.

They shifted the stones on top while more rock rained down around them, and Flavius saw why her sister had been unable to pull her free—one leg lay under a fallen column of marble a good three feet in diameter.

The dancer began to tug at it, screaming.

"We might—roll it," he said. "It will hurt." He looked at the woman's still face and thought perhaps not, but it was plain that her sister wouldn't leave her. "Here, help me."

The woman lay on a sloping bed of broken stone, and they stood one on each side of her and pushed at the marble column. It turned slightly, and the woman opened her eyes and moaned. She was alive, at any rate, Flavius thought. For now. He shoved at the column again, trying to gain momentum, and it rolled. The woman screamed as the whole weight of the column rolled over her foot and down the slope. It thundered to a crashing stop against the building opposite, and the wall behind them shivered. Flavius picked up the woman and screamed too as the whole wall began to slide.

"Get out!"

They half ran, half slid down the rubble slope into the street as the wall crashed in behind them, blotting out the torch's small light.

Somehow they made it through the gate, one woman a dead weight in his arms, the other stumbling beside him, calling urgently to her sister in a childhood language

Flavius didn't know. *I'll never make it*, he thought as they stumbled over the half-buried roadway, the woman like an iron weight on his arms and his lungs tightening with each breath. A few stragglers stumbled with them, the last ebbing tide of the human flood that had fled Pompeii.

Somehow they made it, a few desperate miles toward Stabiae, and sat to rest by the roadside with their backs to a fallen tombstone until the air grew too thick to breathe. Then they got up, shook off a shower of ash and cinders that had fallen on and around them, and went on.

They reached Stabiae at dawn, if the rising sun could have been seen through the blackness, and staggered on southward along the coast with the refugees out of Stabiae, until it was plain to Flavius that he could go no farther even if he died here by the road.

He put the unconscious woman down and sat, pulling the other sister down with him. She half fell against him, and they sat, too tired to speak and too afraid to sleep for fear of choking to death as they lay there, and waited for whatever it was that would come—death or the fire or daylight. Every so often they stood up to shake away the ashes and cinders—Flavius thought they might otherwise have been buried as they sat there—and tried not to think of water. His mouth was dry, and he could hear himself and the two girls wheezing like old men, and the air was foul with the smell of sulfur. Behind them the mountain still burned, and the drifting ash came down to bury the ravaged cities at its foot.

After a while they began to talk, to blot out the other sounds that came horribly from the darkness around them: the prayers and entreaties, and the low, hopeless sobbing of the living as they tried to shake their dead back to life.

They had been among the first to leave. The woman cradled her twin's head in her lap as she spoke and held her mantle over her face to shield her from the falling ash. The column came down as they neared the gate.

"What happened to your master?"

"He was going to leave her," the woman said. Even under the exhaustion her voice was venomous. "He tried to make me come with him, and a roof tile came down and hit him on the head."

And so the innkeeper was dead in Pompeii, Flavius thought. Dead not more than a mile from the inn with its beautiful rose-tiled court where he had wanted to stay in the beginning. *I should have let him,* Flavius thought. *It wouldn't have mattered.*

"You should have gone with him," he said softly, watching the injured woman. The sky had lightened a little, and he thought she was sleeping. He knew from carrying her that the leg was crushed beyond repair. It would be gangrenous in another day. She had lain in his bed, the injured one. He didn't want to watch her die.

The sister didn't speak, but crooned some soft nursery tune as the injured woman stirred. There was a bond with the twin-born, he had heard, that was stronger than other ties. Oddly, he thought of Correus, who was only half-blood to him, but born on the same day. Would he know if Correus were dead? He had somehow always thought that he would. Their bond had chafed him almost beyond bearing. It had done small good to Correus, either. Now—now, since Britain, it had become a tie to be protected. *Maybe we have grown up. Mithras, let him live. Let me find him alive in Stabiae.* If there would ever be any going back to Stabiae.

The sky went black again with a fresh fall of ashes, but this time there was no new outcry. They sat by the roadside with the rest of the homeless, numb and afraid, and waited—for daylight or the end of the world.

It was light. The sun came slowly through the smoke, dark yellow like an eclipse, and the living rose and looked around on a buried world. The mountain in the distance was pale as a snow peak under the last sullen drift of smoke. Beneath it, everything was white, sunk under a blanket of ash like an Alpine field after a fall of snow. Pompeii was entirely gone beneath it, and Herculaneum on the coast to the north was gone also, obliterated in a flood of boiling mud born of Vesuvius's ashes and the burning rain.

Everywhere the living shook away the white ash as the sun rose, and looked around them in numb exhaustion. Slowly they gathered their packs and bags, their salvaged treasures, and began to move, some of them homeward, others without direction, knowing that there would be no home to find there now.

Correus climbed up out of a roadside ditch into which he had fallen and decided that he might as well stay, and he looked in awe at the landscape.

Beside him a white mound heaved and floundered, and Caritius stood up, shaking the ash from him like a dog. "Mother-Of-Us-All, did we come through *that?*" he asked softly.

The road was lined with the uprooted stones of tombs and buckled in places with its paving stones angling crazily to the sky. Here and there a tomb itself had been heaved up and opened in a grotesque display of white bones and rotting grave-cloths. The sky above was sullen yellow, and the foul taste of sulfur was in their mouths.

"Are we alive?" Caritius said.

"I think so." Correus found that his hand was still on the amber bead that hung around his neck, where it had been all night. *Its luck comes somewhat sideways, I find, but I think it will keep you alive.* The words rang like old ghosts in his ears, out of another lifetime. "Alive." He hadn't thought he would have cared so greatly about that, one way or the other.

They turned with no further word—there was none to say—back toward Stabiae. Caritius shaded his eyes with his hand and tried to peer, futilely, through the haze to Misenum across the bay.

"I think they will have been all right, that far out," Correus said gently, remembering the captain's pretty wife and the small, cheerful girl-child who had pattered in after dinner to say her good nights.

Caritius shook his head. When he got to Misenum and saw them, then he could be certain. And she could be certain of him. "She'll be half-frantic, too," he said.

Flavius, Correus thought, his heart sinking. He couldn't have made it. Not through this. They trudged on, the soft ash rising in clouds around their feet, making thirst almost unbearable. Somewhere there must be one undamaged well in Stabiae, Correus thought. If there wasn't, they would lose more than those already dead. So many dead. All dead. For a moment he wanted to sit down and howl like a wolf by the road. But he went on, between Caritius and a gaunt old woman with a sack over her shoulder whose survival was in itself a miracle. Back to Stabiae and the choked, obliterated road from Pompeii.

At Stabiae, Caritius turned down to the wreckage on the shore, wallowing through ashes and fallen roof beams to the beach. The *Merope* was a heap of gray-shrouded spars, smashed as if by an angry child, and lesser craft lay around her. Stabiae's wharves were no more than broken pilings now, with the sea running noisily in and out between them, and all along the beach were the carcasses of fish and shore birds, thrown up by the sea or battered down by the deadly weight of the air.

The beach was almost deserted, the Stabians turning first to what remained of their homes, and a few scattered officials trying vainly to organize the rest into some sort of order. He should go and help them, Correus thought, and knew that he didn't want to because that was where Flavius would be, and if he didn't find him there with the other officials, then he would know for sure. A sudden wail that made his skin crawl rose in the air, and he turned toward it, half expecting to see the ban-sidhes behind him, the Britons' witch-women whose cry is death.

Instead it was only a serving girl with her shawl over her head, who knelt beside a stout, familiar figure on the beach.

"Stop that row!" A gentleman in a mired and ragged tunic aimed a cuff at her head, and she subsided into hiccups.

Correus knelt also and looked at the still, pale face of Gaius Plinius, commander of Misenum, with his pillow still tied bravely to his head.

"Poor old gentleman," the girl sobbed. "He wouldn't leave, not for anything he wouldn't. He wanted to be an example, and he promised me a whole silver denarius, just for bringing him his wine!" She began to wail again, and the man gave her an exasperated look.

"Are you crying for him or your denarius?" he asked gruffly. "Now go away." He looked at Correus and Caritius, and they recognized him as the commander's old friend. "His lungs just wouldn't stand it. We tried to make him leave with us, but he was stubborn as a mule. And then he just choked and collapsed. Someone's going to

have to tell his family," he added. "I—I can't leave here
now."

Correus bit back a retort. If he did leave, the looters
would leave nothing of his house by the time he got back.
He looked at Caritius. "You go."

To take the commander's body to Misenum—that was
a priority errand that could commandeer whatever trans-
portation Caritius could find. He could be in Misenum
by nightfall. He nodded. "Thank you."

"You go back to your house," Correus said to the commander's host. "The girl can stay with him."

The man nodded and shambled away gratefully, and
Caritius ran up the slope to find something, anything to
carry the body.

Correus watched him go and hoped that he found what
he was looking for at Misenum. The ash there wouldn't
have been as bad, but the ground was rocking even now,
and earthquake and panic were death-bringers enough.
Mithras grant that *someone* found his kinfolk still alive.
He turned back to the girl. "Will you stay with him till
the captain comes back?"

She nodded, the tears leaving wet streaks in the ashes
on her face. "He was such a *nice* old gentleman," she said
loudly. Her voice shook. "It *wasn't* the denarius!"

"No," Correus said gently. "No, I know it wasn't." He
went slowly back up the beach through the fallen columns
of a seaside villa to make himself useful.

Like most resort cities, Stabiae boasted a high population of physicians, and someone had rounded up those
who could be found and by some force unknown had set
them to work in the great square in front of the town
basilica. The basilica itself was leaning dangerously into
the columns of its portico, and a rope had been stretched
in front of it with the red rags of someone's military cloak
tied on as warning flags.

The sick and hurt were laid out in rows in the courtyard where miraculously the marble conch shell of the
fountain still streamed water into the pool below. Some
were untouched, only poisoned by the ash and sulfurous
air. Others lay with arms and legs at unreal angles, broken
by falling stone or trampled by their fellow citizens in
flight.

Correus touched a physician on the shoulder, and the

man turned and glared at him. He was blond, with a peeved, boyish face.

"How can I help?"

The physician's expression relented a little. He peered at the scarlet rags that had been Correus's uniform tunic. "Army? Know anything about wounds?"

"Some."

"Some is better than nothing," the man said shortly. "Go down that line and tie a rag or something—whatever you can find—around the feet of the worst ones."

Correus nodded and began tearing his red neck scarf into strips. That would last for a while, and then he would find someone's cloak. If they didn't mark the worst wounded, most of them would die waiting for their turn. The basilica square was almost shoulder-to-shoulder with them.

A woman with a horribly mangled leg, her face gray-green with the pain, lay at the head of the second row with another woman crouched over her. Correus bent down to tie the last strip of his scarf around her other foot and recognized in the contorted features one of the little dancers from Pompeii. He put his hand on the other woman's shoulder and shook it urgently.

"My brother—have you seen my brother?"

She looked at him with vacant eyes and shook her head. He sat back on his heels, tying the red rag mechanically around the dancer's foot, fighting the panic that jumped under his breastbone like an animal. There were thousands in Stabiae. One woman who hadn't seen Flavius meant nothing. Ygerna's amber bead seemed to crawl against his skin under his tunic. *Its luck comes somewhat sideways, I find. . . .* No! Not again, not this time, not again to find himself alive and the other dead. Not again, not with Flavius . . . He felt his stomach wrench, and he turned away gagging in the still drifting ashes.

"A physician is coming," a quiet voice behind him said, "but the leg is going to have to come off. You are to come to me afterward, do you understand?"

There was no reply, only a little crooning song from the crouching woman, and Correus gagged again, choking on the ashes and thirst and the hopelessness that let voices unbidden into his head.

There was a sharp intake of breath behind him, and Flavius's voice said tentatively, "Correus?"

Correus spun around. Flavius stood behind him, his dark curls gray with ash, but his sharp-angled face and queer, long-fingered hands unmistakable in the smoky yellow light.

Correus shook his head to chase the cobwebs out. He felt odd . . . drunk. He pointed to the crooning woman. "I asked . . ."

"She didn't understand you," Flavius said. "She's been like that since last night." He looked sharply at Correus. "Here, you don't look so good yourself—"

"I'm all right . . . now," Correus said.

Flavius nodded, understanding in his dark eyes. "I was afraid you were dead, too. Someone said that Plinius was dead—I was afraid you'd been with him."

"No," Correus said. "I was . . . down the road. In a ditch." He managed a smile. "Is this your doing?" He waved a hand at the scene in the basilica square. "I should have known I'd find you in the middle of all this . . . organization."

Flavius grinned, the reckless, flyaway grin he wore when he was pleased with himself. "I grabbed all the soldiers I could find, and they grabbed the physicians and dragged 'em back here to me. I put the soldiers to guarding the physicians' houses for them, but they were none too happy all the same. I waved the emperor's name around like a club."

"Are you in charge?" Correus asked.

"I think so," Flavius said. "No one else seemed to want to be. I went to commandeer some opium for the girl," he added. "There isn't much. We ransacked every place we could think of, but it's all in a shambles. Half the town's fallen in, and the rest of it's unsafe." He looked at the girl sadly. "She's going to lose that leg, and I only hope her sister hasn't permanently lost her wits. She started singing like that last night. I think it's only fright—she spent a whole day trying to dig her sister out from under a piece of marble until I came along. I don't think she even recognizes me now. I've told the physician to make sure they're sent to me when—" He broke off suddenly and glared at Correus, sitting in the ashes looking up at him with the color beginning to flow slowly back into his face. "I know how she feels! Damn you, why didn't you get out of here to Rome five days ago when I told you to!"

Correus glared back at him. "Why didn't you?" He stood up and suddenly they were both laughing like fiends, ash-white mirror images in the dark yellow light, while the wounded stared at them curiously. Correus put out both his hands and Flavius wrapped his own four-fingered ones around them, and then they were in each other's arms, somewhere between laughter and tears, with their feet in the ashes and their heads bent to each other's shoulders.

XXII

The Samhain Wind

VESUVIUS IN ITS REAWAKENING HAD WRECKED A WORLD in a day, but even worse, Correus thought, sweating in the ash-laden streets of Stabiae, was the aftermath.

Of the twenty thousand inhabitants of Pompeii alone, some two thousand had died, but the rest were homeless and they were the emperor's responsibility now.

Pompeii and Herculaneum were gone; Oplontis and Stabiae lay in ruins. Survivors and looters were already burrowing through the cooling ash or sifting earthquake-toppled wreckage in search of treasure. These, the thieves and the dispossessed, had been handed to Flavius to manage.

"Take a look at this." With a weary smile Flavius passed Correus an official tablet, much begrimed about the edges. His message to Titus must have reached the emperor just as the first eruptions began, and now Flavius had his reply, brought by a courier who had finally got up his nerve to ride into what was left of the bay of Neapolis.

Correus opened the tablet and tried to focus on the words. Everyone's eyes had been red and streaming for days from the ash in the air. *Remain in Pompeii as the representative of the emperor. Report further, and take whatever measures you deem appropriate in the event of a natural disaster.* He gave his brother a tired grin, twin to Flavius's. "Bit of an understatement."

"I'm trying to compose a reply that doesn't sound aggrieved," Flavius said. They had been "taking measures" for two days now, sorting out the flood of refugees in Stabiae. "It isn't Titus's fault."

"No, but people will blame him for it anyway, I expect," Correus said. A natural disaster was generally thought to carry a message with it.

"I'm sure they will. A priest never wastes anything useful," Flavius said, with his mouth compressed into a tight, irritable line, and Correus wished he had kept quiet. Flavius was still steaming because he had found a devotee of some obscure sect working his way through the streets of Stabiae to proclaim that doom had come upon them through sin and loose ways and "women such as this"—here he had paused to shake his fist in the face of the Syrian girl whose leg had been amputated at the hip two days before, and Flavius had lost his temper completely and ordered the man out of Stabiae under guard.

"What are you going to do about those girls?" Correus couldn't see Aemelia finding them work in the kitchens, and he had offered before to take that responsibility off his brother's hands, but Flavius had just shaken his head and said, "No, they're my problem." His face was stubborn, and his expression said plainly that he had found them and they were his. It seemed he was not the only one with an inclination to collect strays, Correus thought, sadly amused. The women were free now—their master was dead and buried with the city of Pompeii, and no one would ask for an accounting—but one girl had had her leg cut off, and the other had a vague and clouded look in her eyes that made Correus's skin cold every time he looked at her. Of the bright creatures who had danced in their diaphanous trousers in Pompeii, there was very little left to find.

"I don't know yet," Flavius said now. It was what he had said before. "Something will dawn on me, I expect." He looked too tired to think about it. "I've given them enough money to come to me in Rome when Naamah can travel."

If she ever did, Correus thought, remembering the infections in Flavius's mutilated hands. There were plenty of ways to die of an amputated leg, and medical supplies had been hard to come by in Stabiae. A few were beginning to come in now from Neapolis and Misenum and the inland towns, but they had wounded of their own to deal with. The earthquake had split and cracked the cities it hadn't buried. It was worse than a war. Correus choked as an oxcart piled high with a family's salvaged goods rumbled past, raising a cloud of dust and ash. A small, grimy child sat on top of the bundles, clutching a dolly with only one arm. You couldn't fight a volcano; you could only accept it, dig out, and start over. Correus watched the oxcart disappear. There was something important about that thought that had been hanging in the back of his mind ever since he had awakened on the Stabiae road to find himself still among the living, but whatever it was, it came no further forward when he chased it.

He gave it up after a minute and turned his mind instead to the immediate—the necessity to keep the homeless and the roving opportunists who followed inevitably upon the heels of upheaval firmly in the grip of authority and back from the edge of anarchy.

Flavius sent a status report and what he referred to frankly as a "yell for help" to the emperor and continued to "take measures" with Correus as a self-appointed aide. Correus discovered to his inner amusement that under a light coat of ash, very few people could tell them apart. After that, the emperor's representative managed to be in a number of places at once.

They prodded the town's civil officials into action and bullied those with houses still intact into hospitality. What food they could salvage was ruthlessly rationed, and the refugees who had some place to go besides Stabiae were encouraged on their way. A danger zone was marked off in the worst damaged sections, and buildings that looked likely to come down were made off-limits even to former tenants.

"We have enough bodies to bury," Correus said flatly to a protesting merchant barred from the leaning remains of his seaside villa. "Are your damned account books worth getting flattened for?"

The merchant looked as if they might be, and Correus gave him a look that sent him on his way regardless, and made a mental note to get that building pulled down as quickly as possible before the old fool tried to sneak back in. At least he had gone quietly enough for the moment. Correus chuckled. People didn't waste his time demanding to see the man in charge when they thought they were talking to him. And some of these old boys had enough clout to have been pests otherwise. It occurred to him that he was almost enjoying himself. There was a certain exhilaration in simply wading in to cope with adversity. It must be Flavius's influence. Flavius was in his element.

For the next week they sifted through ash and rubble, settled disputes over recovered property, and negotiated with inland cities willing to absorb a quota of the homeless. Flavius sent a reassuring message to Aemelia and received a completely hysterical one from her in return, which must have crossed on the road with his.

Caritius appeared, the panic-stricken look gone from his face, and Correus knew without asking that he had found his wife and child alive. Miraculously, he was leading Antaeus. His normally sleek gold hide was rough and scarred with a healing cut on one flank, and he had apparently been fending for himself for several days, but he butted his head against Correus's tunic and slobbered down the front of it affectionately, and seemed to have taken no permanent injury.

"I found him eating daisies in a garden," Caritius said. "I thought I recognized him, so I dragged him back to the stables and one of the grooms there remembered him. I gave him a good feed this morning."

"Thank you." Correus rubbed the gold ears gratefully. "He seemed remarkably sleepy about the whole thing."

"Antaeus is the calmest horse ever foaled," Flavius said. "A mere earthquake wouldn't trouble him. How is it at Misenum?"

"In mourning for the commander," Caritius said. "And some dead in the quake. But mostly what we'd heard was rumors. One old farmer on the way back there assured me solemnly that the ground had opened up and a giant worm had swallowed the whole naval base. But everything is pretty much standing. You've had the worst of it out here."

The worst of it . . . Correus watched a leaning column being lowered carefully in the noon sun the next day and thought that Caritius was wrong. And *he* had been wrong. The worst of it was in Pompeii. And Herculaneum. This was easy. The column came down, and the work crew looked at the sky and decided it was mealtime. Correus, knowing that nothing kept a Campanian from his lunch, went off in search of Flavius. He stopped and dipped his hands and face in the fountain in the basilica square on the way, just enjoying the feel of the water. He felt good suddenly, and a little guilty about it.

And then abruptly it was like waking up after an illness to find that everything was healthy again. And it was Flavius who had done it—Flavius, whose worth had always been measured by a father's or a general's standards and found lacking.

Flavius was standing on a pile of rubble in the street, hands on hips, laying down the law to a stout, exasperated magistrate who wanted to dig into his caved-in wine cellar. To Correus, he came sharply into focus in the dusty sunlight, clearly defined as the lines of a painting. His voice was firm and with a touch of sympathy for the lost wine at the back of it, and he explained it all to the magistrate one more time. Never had Flavius looked closer kin to Correus. If Freita had been the other half of him in one way, Flavius was his twin in another. And Flavius was still alive. Correus had run like a frightened hare from Ygerna. But he had allowed himself to love his brother, with no pious debating, Correus thought wryly. Flavius would have lived no matter what Correus thought of him or died in spite of it, if that was his Fate. The only thing that might have been lost would have been their friendship—neither would have that, only a small empty spot instead. Flavius could have told him that, he supposed—had been trying to, if it came to it.

Flavius, oblivious to having been the subject of this lesson, climbed down off his rubble heap and gave Correus a quick grin. "Poor man, I can't say I blame him. There are four crates of Falernian under all that mess. But I can't spare the men to excavate it, and if he does it himself, he'll end up down there with his wine and he won't come out. The whole thing is still sliding. Let's go see if we can find a drink that's above ground. I've had ash in my mouth all morning."

Correus nodded, and they made their way across a cleared space to where a tavern keeper had set up his salvaged stock in a motley structure of boards and broken columns, roofed with a torn canvas that might have been a ship's sail. His prices were exorbitant, but he had a corner on the market and business was brisk. Flavius ordered whatever was available, and it appeared in two mismatched cups. They sat down under the awning to drink it, while beside them a disgruntled customer carefully chalked his criticism of the wine and its prices on the side of the shed.

"Will they rebuild, do you think?" Correus asked, watching the bustle around them. Stabiae in disaster was almost as busy as it had been in prosperity.

Flavius shook his head. "I doubt it. There's enough left to go on with maybe, but there's the ash—just too much of it to clear. It'll be years before a good soil builds up and they can farm the area again. With no farms, the city won't be worth having. They'll have a little business this season and then move on, I should think."

Correus sat silently, idly watching the scene. Everything faded and moved on. Life progressed. But man hung on while he could, the way the Stabians were hanging on. *He* hadn't wanted to die, Correus thought; and since Freita had died, he had imagined that he didn't much care about that. But when the mountain had begun to burn, he had known that he wanted to hang on, too. And now he knew why.

He thought it was Flavius who had triggered that knowledge. But it could have been the wineshop keeper with his ragtag stall; or Naamah, the Syrian girl now with only one leg, calmly preparing to take her sad, blank-eyed sister back to Syria, in spite of Flavius's offer. Or maybe it was the mountain itself, the unknown, That Which Is and cannot be fought. But somehow, as the Demetae had been Flavius's salvation, so Vesuvius was his, and its message had burned clear—nothing is safe, there is no certainty. Death is a knife in the dark or a volcano or a runaway carriage in the street. Either he chose to accept that, or to go lonely the rest of his life out of fear.

"There are reinforcements coming," Flavius said, and Correus shook himself out of the fog and looked at his brother.

"I thought you'd gone into a trance, like the Sibyl," Flavius said.

"Close," Correus said.

"Well, wake up. You're about to get out of here. The emperor is sending a staff to cope with this, and medical supplies, and we get to go home. Or at least you do. I expect I'll have to stick around a while yet, but you're overdue in Rome."

"So you've said. When does this relief column arrive?"

"A day or two," Flavius said. "You'll get some extra leave, by the way, for heroic services rendered. If you want to buy me a drink in thanks for my glowing descriptions to the emperor, I won't object."

"You must have lied like a fiend," Correus said. "But I'll buy you the drink."

Flavius laughed and lifted his cup. "To home," he said. "Finally."

Correus grinned back at him and drank, but he wasn't going home. Not yet.

"This is not particularly informative." Appius Julianus tapped the small, neatly rolled scroll and gave his son the eye of suspicion across it.

"I don't expect it was meant to be," Flavius said blandly.

"He was with you in Pompeii, Flavius. I have not yet attained the degree of senility with which you and your brother apparently credit me. Where has Correus gone?"

"He didn't tell me, sir, and that's the truth." Flavius bowed gravely to the statue of Athena beside them by way of emphasis.

"But you know." Appius gave him the look before which countless subordinates had been made to quail, and Flavius found himself cursing Correus for unnecessary mysteriousness.

"I think I do, sir." He resisted the urge to fidget with his clothes. "But nothing may come of it, and I think he'd rather not think we were putting bets on the results. It may not come off, you know."

"You mean she may throw a vase at him," Appius said. "I think I get your drift. I don't know what hap-

pened when he left Britain, but Helva tried to pump
young Julius in her inimitable way, and he shied like a
nervous horse."

"That may have been just Helva, sir." Flavius grinned
at him. "She's a bit . . . overpowering."

"She's a disgrace," Appius said, "and she gets worse
as she gets older. It comes of keeping her looks so well."

"Well, if Correus marries, she can go live with him,"
Flavius said cheerfully. "And you can, uh . . . visit."

Since he was well aware that his father still slept in
Helva's bed occasionally, even these days, this bordered
on the inexcusable. Feeling that he might have gone a bit
far, Flavius bowed hastily and beat a retreat to the center
of the rose garden, where Aemelia was proudly displaying
her daughter to her mother-in-law. He had only been home
a day, and already Correus's absence was proving something of a trial. Aemelia had seemed more relieved than
not, but after Bericus had assured himself that there were
no holes in Flavius's own hide, he had brought Julius to
him to be assured that the same could be said of Correus.
When he discovered that Correus had gone off without
him to parts unknown, Julius had declared loudly that
he *knew* no good would come of leaving the centurion on
his own in Pompeii like that. He appeared to hold himself personally responsible for both the volcano and
whatever the centurion was doing now.

Flavius had no sooner ordered Bericus, with his most
awful glare, to remove his brother's body servant from
his presence, than Helva had fluttered in with much the
same performance, although with more tears and effusions.
No wonder Correus hadn't wanted to come home first,
Flavius thought, finally left in peace. If he were Correus,
he would have given a second thought to coming home at
all, especially if he had fulfilled his family's worst suspicions in the meantime. So far as he knew, no one had
ever mentioned Ygerna to Helva, but Helva had her
methods of gathering information. He sank down gratefully on the marble bench between his wife and his own
mother and put out a finger for his daughter to play with.

"You look very pretty and restful," he said admiring
the view, and they smiled at him affectionately. They
were dressed in light summer silks, and they were reflected in the clear waters of the fish pond behind them.

A cat had appeared from somewhere and was regarding the water thoughtfully. It stuck out a paw and ripples spread around it, and all the fish hurled themselves to the far end.

"Thank you, dear," Antonia said placidly. "It's very restful to have you at home. We were quite worried."

"We had hysterics," Aemelia said firmly. "At least I did. I've never been so frightened."

Flavius took a deep breath of roses and warm air, and the faint lemony scent his wife was wearing. "I wasn't exactly calm about it myself," he said, and they smiled at him proudly, admiring such understatement. He felt like a cat, basking in so much patent admiration. He knew he shouldn't do it, it would only give him a swelled head, but it was too pleasant to resist.

"I'll need to go and see Forst about a horse," he said. "I lost Nestor in Pompeii." He grimaced, embarrassed at mourning a horse so much, but he'd ridden Nestor for seven years, since his cadet days. Even Bericus had cried when he'd heard that the big bay was gone. "I want one of that gray's colts if Forst has one to spare," he said, trying to bring the light mood back. "There must be some of the first crop ready to sell off."

"You must ask him yourself, dear," Antonia said. "I'm afraid I don't understand Forst's Latin very well."

Antonia understood his accent well enough, Flavius thought. It was Forst himself she couldn't fathom. The German had his mysterious moments for Flavius, too—he doubted that anyone in the family really knew what Forst was thinking, not even Correus—but he liked the German. "I understand he's starting a family, too," he said, jumping a bit as his daughter tested her gum power on one finger.

Antonia clicked her tongue. "Yes, with that red-haired girl from the kitchens that he made your father give him. I have never thought she was suitable."

You knew she was sleeping with my brother and wondered if she was sleeping with me, Flavius thought, but there was no point in starting something. "Well, she only has to be suitable to Forst," he said, extracting his finger from his daughter's mouth and putting his arm around Aemelia. "If he's happy, who are we to quarrel with him?" Personally, he thought Emer had too much red hair in her character to make a comfortable wife, but not everyone had the same notions. Correus, for instance. Flavius would as soon have had a she-cat to wife as Freita, and no one had a notion what this British girl was like. A barbarian in plaid trousers, Helva had said, weeping on his tunic front. Helva and Aemelia had seemed to see eye to eye on that. Flavius chuckled to himself and tightened his arm around Aemelia, and she snuggled comfortably into his shoulder. Forst and Correus could look out for themselves. As for himself, he had an overdue leave to enjoy.

Julia sat comfortably embedded in green silk pillows in a hooded wicker chair that kept the sun out of her eyes and watched Felix and Paulilla playing in the mint that grew in a damp tangle by the stone fountain. It looked very cool and wet, and she wondered if it was worth the effort of having her chair moved over there. It was a baking September afternoon, and she was pregnant again and disinclined to move anywhere if she could help it. The pale yellow silk of her gown stuck unpleasantly to her skin, and she had kicked her sandals off to wiggle her toes in the breeze. The breeze was provided by a page with a large silk fan on a stick, but since Felix and Paulilla were playing with a big-footed black and gray hound puppy, the page was inclined to let his attention wander to them, and the cooling breeze would go off in another direction entirely.

Their nurse was enjoying a well-earned rest (her afternoon breakdown, as Paulinus put it), and for the next two hours they were all hers, she thought with satisfaction. It wasn't considered fashionable to spend too much time looking after one's own children, but Julia had always looked forward to it. Maybe that was because she didn't do it all the time, Paulinus had said the last time he came to keep company with them and had sat on an unnoticed, half-eaten sweet in the cushions of his chair.

Today she watched Felix wistfully. He was four years old, and he had always seemed like her firstborn. Maybe she should have pressured Correus to let them adopt him when Freita had just died and he didn't really care. That wouldn't have been fair, but she thought maybe she didn't care about that.

There was a footstep on the polished stone behind her.

"You look very pretty," Paulinus said. "Like a pear in a fruit basket."

She made a face at him.

"Brooding?" Paulinus asked, watching her eyes turn back to the children.

"We're going to lose him, aren't we?"

"You knew you were going to eventually," Paulinus said. He pulled another chair over and put his hand on hers. "You said yourself that Felix should be with his father."

"I'd just . . . got used to things. But he's going to come back with a wife, isn't he?"

A year ago she had said Correus should marry this British girl, but now, watching Felix, she found that she didn't like the idea so well as she had.

"I hope so," Paulinus said. "Your brother's been sitting damned close to the edge since Freita died. If this one won't have him, I don't know what he'll do."

"Oh, dear. And I've been hoping she wouldn't."

"Well, don't."

"But we don't know anything about her!"

"That's what Helva said, I understand. She had hysterics all over Flavius when it dawned on her why Correus hadn't come home."

Julia made an irritated noise, and her face took on an expression strongly reminiscent of her mother. "I don't know what Papa *sees* in that woman."

"I do," Paulinus said bluntly. "Don't be girlish. And you can hardly blame Helva. She had something better in mind for Correus than some obscure niece of a British clan chieftain, with nothing to recommend her but a citizenship and a bit of a dowry that Julius Agricola pried out of the Senate."

"Oh—" Julia waved both hands in the air, trying to pinpoint her objections. "What if she doesn't *want* Felix?" Felix's head snapped up at the mention of his name, his green eyes curious, and she lowered her voice. "You know how difficult he can be."

"He's a terror," Paulinus agreed solemnly.

"He has an inquisitive mind," Julia defended.

"That's what I meant. But there's nothing you can do about it. If Correus wants him, you're going to have to let him go, Ju."

"Correus can't give him what we can."

"Do you mean money? And are you going to be rude enough to say so? Besides, I'm not so sure. If we adopted Felix, he'd have to come second to our sons, and that's not much of a start."

Julia was silent, watching Felix and the puppy falling on each other in the mint.

"Would it comfort you any to know that I've made my peace with Titus? After this baby comes, we can go some-where—wherever *you* like this time. Would that help?"

Julia kept her eyes on the children. "It doesn't help to-night," she said sadly. "I expect it will tomorrow, though." She put out her hand, and he took it in his again.

The channel was gray, the water the color of ashes, and the air above was heavy with the feel of something com-ing. The boom of the *hortator*'s mallets made a hollow note from under the decking, and the oars swung at dou-ble time. The *Arethusa* was trying to outrun the storm.

Correus leaned on the bow rail waiting for the low, green shape of Vectis to lift itself out of the water, oblivious to the weather and the rhythmic creak of the oar locks. He didn't much care if he got rained on, but he cared violently if a storm made them tack their way labori-ously into Vectis water or, worse yet, blew them miles off course down shore.

"First posting to Britain?" the captain asked him geni-ally. "Most folk aren't so eager to make shore. Damned heathen outpost," he added emphatically. "Steal the san-dals off your feet while you're watching your cloak."

"No," Correus said. "This is . . . a visit."

"Can't say I admire your choice," the captain said, "but each man to his own. Me now, I'm going to retire to a little place on Sicilia someday where a man can get some sun. Hang onto your bags, Centurion, we'll make Portus Adurni by nightfall if Sea Father doesn't blow up any trouble."

Poseidon obligingly restrained himself, and the *Arethusa* slipped past Vectis into Portus Adurni as the harbor torches began to glow. They made gold patterns in the wa-ter with the *Arethusa*'s bow lights, and the dock crew ran out to tie her up as the captain wiggled her into port, without a bump, between a transport and a grain ship.

Correus slung his kit over his shoulder and gave the *Arethusa* a last glance. She would sail again in a week with a cargo of tin from Dumnonia, and he had booked two return passages on her. But there was something he had to do first.

Antaeus came lumbering up out of the hold, snorting at the salt air in his nose, and Correus wondered for the thousandth time why he had bothered to bring him instead of just hiring a horse. He thought maybe it was because he wanted the company . . . someone who had known them all those years back.

The road into Isca was properly surfaced now with well-cut stone, built to last longer than the sweating legionaries who had made it. Correus sat leaning on the saddle horns with the bunch of blue cornflowers beginning to droop in his hands. There were more graves than before, he thought. But he could have found Freita's in the dark. He swung himself down from the saddle and walked to it, a plain gray stone among the wild grasses. In the spring, someone had once told him, there were anemones here.

DIS MANIBUS . . .
TO THE GODS OF THE SHADES

He knelt and put the little handful of cornflowers by the stone.

FREITA, LOVED WIFE
OF CORREUS APPIUS JULIANUS,
CENTURION OF THE NINTH COHORT,
LEGIO II AUGUSTA

It was all such a long time ago, he thought. He wondered if he had kept such a grip on her memory that he might have held her earthbound here, and kept her from Elysium, or whatever paradise her soul had chosen. *I should have let her go.*

"Forgive me, my dear," he whispered, and put a hand lightly on the grass. Then he swung back into the saddle and pointed Antaeus's nose for Aquae.

Somehow, without their noticing, summer had faded to fall in a flurry of dry leaves that rustled down the streets between the tidy houses. Ygerna, sewing a fine stitch by lamplight with Aunt Publia, heard them and wondered if there was anything blowing with them in the wind tonight.

It was Samhain, the ancient Night of the Dead, that was older than the houses and graceful temples of Aquae Sulis, although maybe not older than the sacred spring itself. Samhain, when the gates of the sidhe and the Underworld swung open, and those within were free to roam the land above. Every British hall would be shuttered tight tonight against whatever might walk the Samhain wind, and every feast table would have its empty place and turned-down cup in case the dead should come and dine.

Ygerna set another stitch and shut the whisper of the wind out of her mind. Samhain was a British festival, and she was Roman now, and in any case there were no ghosts to come and haunt Aunt Publia. And if there were, Aunt Publia would meet them at the door with a broom and beat them back. Magics didn't work on people who didn't believe in them, Ygerna had decided. It was why she made no more of her own now; she had lost the belief and the sense of power that she used to feel run through her when the Goddess was with her. The Goddess would have gone to another woman by now.

She had tried only once that summer, stifling by the fireside to make a singing magic. But it was only Ygerna, combing her hair by the hearth for the cat to play with, and not a magic at all; so she had put away the bone comb and the dried rowanberries and put her gown back on before Aunt Publia should come in and be shocked.

The wind came up a little stronger and rattled through the shutters, and Aunt Publia said, "*Tchah!*" as one of the lamps went out. She clapped her hands for a slave to relight it, and the girl came in looking jumpily at the vibrating shutter.

Aunt Publia watched in exasperation as the girl lit the lamp and scuttled out again. "That one gets flightier all the time."

"It's Samhain, Aunt," Ygerna said.

Aunt Publia made a noise with her teeth and put her needle down. "Well, I don't know what she thinks is going to get her here. This house was only built three years ago. Hardly long enough to acquire a past."

"My uncle Bendigeid, maybe," Ygerna said, and then

wished she hadn't. That was not a joke, and for a moment she almost saw the king's dark face in the lamp smoke.

"Don't be morbid, child," Aunt Publia said and gathered up her sewing. "I am going to have Simplicia take my hair down. I find that this way of dressing it gives me a headache." She stooped and kissed Ygerna on the forehead. "Don't sit up too late, mind. Tribune Albinius particularly asked for our company tomorrow, and I think we should oblige him, don't you?"

Ygerna smiled at her. "Yes, dear, I expect we should." If Aunt Publia was hoping for a more flattering reaction to Tribune Albinius's desire for their company, she was doomed to disappointment. She sailed away down the corridor, her gray coiffure bobbing regally in the lamplight and the doors opening in her wake as her maids scurried out to attend her.

Ygerna put her own work down and stared at the wall. Samhain made her sad. There was something pathetic about old ghosts coming back to sit invisibly where once they had lived, like herself trying to call a lost magic out of the fire. And in any case, the only face she wanted to see wasn't dead, but only gone away. Gone far enough that even a Samhain wind couldn't blow him back. And that left Aunt Publia or Tribune Albinius, and how could anyone spend her life with him, who'd had Correus?

The tribune was a good enough young man, earnest and honest, and he wanted to marry her, which was more than she could have hoped for, Aunt Publia had told her bluntly. He had taken them on a picnic and sat and held her hand and told her carefully how he would have a government career someday. And that no one would ever know, to look at her or talk to her, that she wasn't a Roman. Except himself, he had said huskily and tried to kiss her. It was the wildness in her that set *him* wild and made him love her. She had pushed him away and had run off to feed the swans that sailed majestically on the pond in the public garden, but she had known then that she couldn't marry him. If he ever did see the wild side, really, he would never understand it.

The leaves rustled in the street, tugging at her hearing. *I'm not so Roman after all,* she thought. *If I opened the window now, would something come and get me?*

She stood on a couch, gently slipping the shutters back and peered out, braced a little against what might be there —the nameless things that rode a Samhain wind, or only the dead leaves. The courtyard was empty. There was a moon caught in the branches of a tree among the thinning leaves. Somewhere in the distance she could hear the click-click of the mailed sandals of the town's guards as they made their rounds.

A solitary figure turned the corner into the courtyard, and a face, angular and infinitely familiar, turned upward to the face in the window. She closed her eyes tightly until white flashes raced across the blackness and opened them again carefully.

"Ygerna?" He halted, more uncertain now than ever of his welcome. She was gone from the window in a flash, and he stood waiting in the wind while someone inside scrabbled with the bolt on the door. The door opened and she was running across the courtyard, but she stopped three paces from him, her face white as the moonlight.

"What are you?" she asked, as she had once asked him all those years ago.

"Not a ghost," he said softly, and her eyes found his, but she didn't move.

"Did you come back for me?" she whispered. "Tell me the truth, Correus."

He nodded and started to say something more, some apology, but she was in his arms, and his face was buried in her hair. "Why didn't you write?" she whispered.

"I was afraid you'd tell me not to come," he said.

"If you leave me again, I will put a curse on you," Ygerna said distinctly. "All your hair will fall out, and nothing will work, and no woman will have you."

She tilted her head back and grinned at him, and suddenly he grinned back and lifted her off the ground in his arms. The Samhain ghosts blew by them like dry leaves, gone for good now, leaving only the two of them under the rising moon.

Glossary

Achilles	Legendary Greek warrior-hero
Aesculapius	God of healing
Ahriman	Persian personification of evil
Annwn	Celtic land of the dead (pronounced "Annoon")
Arianrhod	Celtic goddess
Athena	Goddess of wisdom
ban-sidhe	Celtic supernatural being whose wailing foretells death (pronounced "ban-she")
basilica	Public building housing law courts and exchange
Blodeuwedd	Faithless maiden created from flowers as wife of the Celtic hero Llew
century	A unit of eighty men; six centuries comprise a cohort
Cerberus	Three-headed watchdog of Hades
Charon	Boatman who ferried the dead across the River Styx
Cohort	Six centuries; ten cohorts made up a legion
corona aurea	Roman army decoration for extraordinary bravery
corona civica	Roman army decoration awarded to a soldier who has saved the life of a fellow citizen
cuirass	Close-fitting body armor covering the torso
Druid	Celtic priest
Elysium	Paradise
Epona	Celtic goddess of horses
Erebus	The darkness through which souls of the dead travel to Hades

Furies	Avenging goddesses
the Goddess	Earth Mother in her many forms
Gorgons	Three frightful sisters whose look turns the beholder to stone
greaves	Lower leg armor
Gwydion	Legendary Celtic bard and wizard
Hades	Lord of the Underworld; also the name of the Underworld itself
hurley	Celtic ball game, somewhat similar to hockey
Isis	Earth Mother in her Egyptian form
Juno	Wife of Jupiter, goddess of marriage and childbirth
legate	Commander of a legion
lorica	Body armor of several types; at this time the legions were beginning to change from mail to segmented plates
Lugh	Celtic sun god
Lughnasadh	Festival of Lugh, August 1
Mithras	Persian god of light and truth, mediator between man and the supreme god; his worship was popular in the Roman army
the Morrigan	Celtic goddess of battle; Earth Mother in her warlike aspect
Ogham	Celtic runic alphabet
Olympus	Mythical home of the Roman gods or the summit of Mount Olympus in Thessaly
phalerae	Roman military decorations in the form of medallions worn on a leather harness across the chest
Pluto	Roman name of Hades, lord of the Underworld
Poseidon	Sea god and creator of the horse
Priapus	God of gardens and fertility
Primus pilus	Commander of the First Cohort; in the field, second-in-command of a legion

Ragnarok	"Twilight of the Gods." In German mythology, a doomsday battle between gods and giants, and the destruction of the world
Rhiannon	In Celtic mythology, a woman of the faery folk who married a mortal; singing of her three birds could cause death or restore life
Salve Lucrum	Latin for "Hail Profit"
Samhain	Celtic Feast of the Dead; November 1
sibyl	A female prophet or seer; she often spoke her predictions while in a mystical trance
sidhe	In Celtic legend, the hollow hills of the faery folk; here used to mean a dwelling of an older race, the Dark People (pronounced "she")
Sign of Horns	Invoking the Horned God (similar to Pan) to ward off evil
Sisyphus	A King of Corinth who, having incurred the wrath of the gods, was condemned in Tartarus to forever roll uphill a boulder which always rolled back down again
Styx	River which flowed around the Underworld, over which the souls of the dead were ferried to Hades
Sulis Minerva	British goddess of the warm springs at Aquae Sulis (modern-day Bath, England), identified by the Romans with Minerva (Latin name of the goddess Athena)
Tir-na-nOg	Land of the Young, Celtic happy otherworld in legendary islands in the west
tribune	Officer of a legion, generally a young man serving a short term before beginning a political career
Typhon	Fire-breathing monster and creator of hurricanes, said to have a hundred heads and terrible voices

Vercingetorix Gaulish warrior-hero who fought against Julius Caesar

vicus Civil settlement outside a Roman fort

vine staff A centurion's staff of office; literally a cane cut from vine wood

Wisdom A Celtic board game resembling chess

Zeus Supreme god of the Greek pantheon, equivalent of Roman Jupiter

THE CENTURIONS
BOOK III

A TRAITOR FROM THE ROMAN SHIPPING OFFICE IS FEED-
ing vital information to a band of desperate pirates. Correus Appius Julianus, disguised as a pompous Roman, is
sent by the emperor into the brigands' lair to shatter the
conspiracy. All signs point to the traitor as being Senator
Aurelius Vettius, a master of political intrigue. This accu-
sation, veiled in a coded ransom plea, is sent to Flavius
Appius Julianus, Correus's half brother and aide to the
emperor. But the emperor refuses to act against the senator without evidence. Correus and Flavius have none.

The brothers meet their most vicious enemy in Vettius,
a patrician with limitless influence, ambition, money, and
capacity for evil. Vettius learns about their charges, and
his thirst for revenge is insatiable; he sets out to destroy
the Julianus family.

His first target is Aemelius, Flavius's father-in-law.
While his family stands helpless, Aemelius is stripped of
his lands and wealth through a conspiracy of forgers,
usurers, and bribed judges. Setting his sights next on
Correus and Flavius's sister, Julia, and her husband,
Lucius Paulinus, Vettius threatens their lives and the
lives of their children by trapping Paulinus in a plot to
assassinate the emperor.

Even Correus's life and military career are jeopardized
when Vettius contrives to have himself named as Correus's
direct superior. Vettius leaves him to face a war band of
fierce German barbarians, and Correus's only protection is
a demoralized and poorly trained legion at his back.

Set against the background of Emperor Domitian's final
assault on the Free Lands of the Agri Decumates, Cor-

reus and Flavius must save the lives of their family before Aurelius Vettius can destroy them. CENTURIONS III carries on the legacy of the half brothers whose lives and loves are inextricably intertwined. THE CENTURIONS is the latest successful series produced by Book Creations, Inc., producers of the KENT FAMILY CHRONICLES, WAGONS WEST, THE AUSTRALIANS, and the AMERICAN PATRIOT Series.